TW,

w

CH00939345

Child of Earth

Child of Earth

MAUREEN PETERS

ROBERT HALE · LONDON

© Maureen Peters 1999
First published in Great Britain 1999

ISBN 0 7090 6374 1

Robert Hale Limited
Clerkenwell House
Clerkenwell Green
London EC1R 0HT

2 4 6 8 10 9 7 5 3 1

Typeset in North Wales by
Derek Doyle & Associates, Mold, Flintshire.
Printed in Great Britain by
St Edmundsbury Press Ltd, Bury St Edmunds, Suffolk.
Bound by WBC Book Manufacturers Limited, Bridgend.

What have these lonely mountains worth revealing?
More glory and more grief than I can tell.
The earth that wakes one human heart to feeling
Can centre both the worlds of heaven and hell.

Emily Brontë 1818–1848

Afterwards

There was an east wind that day, cutting a swathe through the graveyard and whirling up the dying leaves with their crinkled edges of brown and gold. Martha had lit the fire earlier and the wood crackled and sizzled as the wind blew down the wide chimney, bringing with it little specks of soot, like blots on a life.

Papa had retired to bed, tapping on the door as was his invariable custom, before putting his head round to intone,

'I am going to bed now. Good night, Charlotte.'

'Good night, Papa.'

'Don't sit up too late!'

'No, Papa.'

Nine o'clock. The end of his activities for the day. For herself and the others the beginning of the enchanted time. Walking, walking, walking. Round and round the table with their footsteps muffled by the pile of the carpet and their skirts whispering softly, rhythmically. One behind the other with herself as eldest in the lead. Behind her the taller Emily, her shadow elongated, pencil-thin; Anne bringing up the rear, her fingers often grasping the ends of Emily's shawl.

Talking, talking, talking. Sometimes one reading aloud from the sheaf of papers she carried, sometimes earnest discussions, sudden bursts of laughter hastily stifled – 'Hush, Papa will hear!'

Tabby had limped her way to bed, mumbling as she went. Her hearing was rapidly diminishing, her remaining teeth rotting, but her mind was still sharp even though her eyesight was beginning to fail. She was woven into their lives like the thread that made a banknote legal tender, giving them a shape, an identity. If anyone knew the truth of it all it was Tabby but she had never spoken, never would speak.

Martha had slipped down the lane to spend the night at her parents' house. She was eighteen was Martha, small and plain but with soft brown hair and an eager winsome way. The east wind gave her neuralgia and she had wrapped her shawl closely round her face, holding a corner of it across her mouth to protect her aching teeth as she quietly closed the door.

Keeper lay on the hearthrug, black muzzle propped on his paws, his ears pricked for the sound of other footsteps. Flossy lay in state on the black horsehair sofa with no Aunt Branwell to scold her down. There had been other, earlier pets – Grasper, the rough haired terrier whom Aunt had allowed in the house only at stated hours, little black Tom over whose death Emily had shed a few rare public tears, the tame pheasant Jasper and the geese, Adelaide and Victoria, confined to the peat store in the back yard, and Nero, the injured hawk that Emily had tamed.

Nero had clung to Emily's shoulder when they all went out on the moors, making short, uncertain flights but always returning, chained to his perch indoors with his bright black eyes fixed thoughtfully, hungrily on Anne's little yellow canary, Dick, hopping safely in his cage.

Only Keeper and Flossy were left now. Charlotte pretended to herself that they were company for her but the truth was that they regarded her with only polite affection, patiently waiting for the others to return.

Was that a footstep behind her? A single, soft footstep to tell her she was no longer alone? For a moment her heart beat rapidly under the child's camisole her flat chest required. Turning slowly – would they be altered beyond recognition? – she saw the gleam of white paper that had only been blown to the floor by a sudden draught that sighed through the keyhole. And hers was the only shadow that moved about the walls, in and out of the flickering firelight and the steadier glow of the oil lamp on the table.

She had gone up earlier in the day to the tiny room where six of them had once huddled together and where in the end Emily had slept alone and, kneeling, prised up the floorboards beneath which they had hidden the toys that had survived childhood: a couple of battered wooden soldiers, a tiny smoothing iron, a doll with a straw hat on its head, a riding whip that had never touched the flank of a horse, two tin boxes like others which had been thrown down the well years ago. These lay now on the table next to Emily's little writing desk which she had perched on her knee, seated on a three-legged stool by the blackcurrant bushes.

She had written constantly, feverishly during that final spring and summer hardly pausing or raising her head, showing what she wrote to nobody.

'It is my duty to go through my sisters' papers,' she had told John Nussey, Ellen's brother. 'They may have left much that will add to their reputations.'

Their local reputations were hardly shining. She had heard the odd remark hastily stifled when they realized she was in the vicinity. 'Slinky'. 'More like a lad than a lass'. 'Sour-faced spinsters'.

What, she wondered, did the villagers think of her? Of Papa? He had never troubled about what other people thought of him. Neither, she told herself firmly, had she, but the truthfulness that lay at her core told her that she had been hurt by some remarks. 'Little Miss Brontë' sounded kindly enough but not when it was said with a smile that was half pitying, half sneering. The villagers had been offended by Emily's depiction of them as savage and brutish. Her book wasn't eagerly sought by borrowers from the Mechanics' Institute. Few had ever spoken to her and of those who had few had received more than a curt, monosyllabic answer.

What was here, written during her last year, might restore her reputation, might teach the local people to think of her more kindly, to recognize the true nobility of her nature.

Stooping, she picked up the piece of paper. On it in Emily's version of the minute handwriting they all, save Anne, had employed were words, long sentences with punctuation indicated by long dashes. She put it neatly on the table and stood, her tiny hands gripping the edge of the table, her hazel eyes magnified behind her spectacles, staring down. In order to read it and the rest of the unpublished, undiscussed material she would need a magnifying glass as well, and her own wasn't powerful enough.

She opened the door and crossed the narrow hallway into the parlour where her father had spent so many of his waking hours. He still sat there much of the time, had his meals carried to him there, conducted morning and evening prayers though now only Tabby, Martha and herself comprised the congregation. Hanging shelves at each side of the fireplace flanked a print taken from one of John Martin's apocalyptic studies and held her father's treasured and meagre stock of books, much thumbed and annotated. On the table lay the big, round magnifying glass with its short handle. The lamp with the etched glass had been snuffed but she knew the way about every room in the house blindfold. Unerringly she stretched out her hand and lifted the glass. Before she retired to bed she must take care to replace it in precisely the same spot as before.

She and her father had always been alike in their habits of neatness. So had Aunt Branwell and Anne. Emily had been untidy, defiantly slapdash in her ways, both in the arrangement of her possessions and in her person.

She had stridden through patches of mud and streams with scant regard for her boots or the hems of her narrow skirts; her luxuriant hair had escaped from its Spanish combs to hang in thick, curling locks about her face; her long fingers had been stained with pollen. Charlotte stood in the emptiness of the parlour, her eyes closed, summoning up the image of her sister. It wasn't possible. She could picture her only in those last weeks, skin stretched so tightly over the bones of her face that one could discern the shape of the skull beneath, lips bloodless, nose filling her face, eyes glazing and only the long curling hair retaining its shine.

Mr George Smith, her publisher, had agreed that she ought to go through her sisters' unpublished writings and edit them. He had an eye to the main chance did the charming Mr Smith but he knew how desperately she wished to present her siblings in their true selves to the wider world.

Anne's relics had been sad but not painful to examine. Dear Anne with her mild blue eyes and fair ringlets and delicate, porcelain skin had been the more yielding of the two. Her first novel, *Agnes Grey*, had been a charming little tale, displaying a sly sense of humour , making a good case for the emancipation of governesses. Yet she hadn't been entirely amenable to suggestion.

'My love, writing about such matters will make you ill. It will affect your health!'

'It is my duty to try to instruct my readers, Charlotte. If I can save just one young man from going down the path that Branny has taken then I will be content.'

The Tenant of Wildfell Hall had shocked Charlotte with its unsparing description of a marriage in crisis, an alcoholic husband and runaway wife, but Anne had quietly and determinedly gone on writing the book. It had been better received than Emily's novel though there were always the critics to complain of coarseness, but it had gone into a second edition for which Anne had written a rousing preface asserting her right to speak the truth.

She hadn't written another book though she had made several false starts but she had written a lot of verse – Charlotte hardly liked to call it poetry which had been so despairing in tone, so empty of hope, that Charlotte had retained only a small portion of it. The verses, she felt, were not Anne as she had really been, quiet and gentle and accepting, but revealed a creature terrified by the prospect of death, cowering from the world. Anne, in full health, would never have permitted such misery to be displayed. Dear Anne!

Going back into the dining-room, drawing the lamp nearer and adjusting the flame, Charlotte sat down at the table and drew one of the tin boxes towards her. She had already been through the contents of Emily's desk, with the published reviews of *Wuthering Heights* carefully cut out and folded away.

Poor Emily! The critics had in the main savaged her novel, fulminating against the raw brutality of the characters, the lack of moral preaching, the atmosphere of – yes, of sexuality! that brooded over and coloured every sentence of the tale. Yet it had power and even beauty. Charlotte could appreciate that. The tale, she felt, had been culled from some deeply private place in the spaces of her sister's heart. Not many would appreciate that! If there was something in the unpublished, later material that would display a smoother, more fluent Emily at the height of her powers, then she would be happy to lay it before the public.

There were poems in the box, some corrected and polished, others mere scraps of images and feelings, vivid but nothing unless some discipline of form and syntax was imposed upon them. One, longer than the rest, seemed to tell a narrative tale.

It had a trenchant beginning: 'Ask not to know the date, the clime.' That was Emily all right! Obstinate and unyielding where her own ideas were concerned. Daring ideas some of them had been. Revolutionary concepts that few women had held before.

It was a bad poem, abrupt, highly coloured, reeking of old ballad styles, with a violence that would repel people. One day perhaps? Charlotte put the poems back and reached for the second box.

This looked more promising. This surely was what Emily had been writing out in the front garden during the spring and the summer. She had liked to write prose during the day and wait for dark for the poetic muse to descend.

Setting her spectacles more firmly on her nose Charlotte held the large magnifying glass carefully and began to decipher the tiny, cramped handwriting in the mellow light of the lamp.

She read slowly, concentrating on each word, each phrase, heaving a sigh of relief when the second page proved like the ones following to be penned in the larger script which Emily had used when she copied something for publication. She read more speedily now, moving her head from side to side like a small seeking bird. This was a fruitful branch – no, an entire tree. Written at white heat, words spilling out into phrases that tore at her heart. This was no Gothic fantasy. Every sentence bore the stamp of truth. This was Emily unadorned, turned inside out for the world to see.

It was a slender manuscript, yet so rich and complete in itself that Mr Smith would be able to publish it almost as it stood, perhaps with a short selection of poems to make a thicker volume.

Wuthering Heights had been the promise. This had the fulfilment of a giant talent in every syllable. It was greater than *Jane Eyre* or *Villette*. Once it was printed Emily would be seen in her full glory. Once it was printed all the secrets would be laid bare.

Charlotte laid down the pages. She would read more during the daylight hours. As it was she would find it almost impossible to sleep tonight.

The clock that stood – had always stood – on the turn of the stairs, struck eleven. She stood up, took the magnifying glass back to the parlour, siting it exactly where it had been before, returned to the dining room, turned down the lamp and snuffed the final tiny flame, checked that the leaping flames in the hearth had dwindled into ashes, and picking up the two tin boxes carried them upstairs, holding them slightly away from herself as if they contained scorpions.

One

Will the day be bright or cloudy?
Sweetly has its dawn begun
But the heaven may shake with thunder
Ere the setting of the sun.

Emily Jane Brontë

'This is a bad business! Can you be sure it's certain?'

'I can be sure of nothing, brother, but the symptoms match what I have read about the disease. You did not expect this when you came. I look on your being here at this time as an answer to prayer.'

'Do you so? Had I known what awaited me I'd've stayed in Ireland so I would!'

The elderly man who had just finished speaking rose from his chair and went over to the window that looked out across the weed-encrusted garden to the flat slabs and obelisks of the tomb-stones that separated the parsonage from St Michael's Church. He was a tall, well-built man, six feet four in his stockinged feet, traces of red still in his curly grey hair, his hands calloused after years of road mending and road building.

'You came to pay your respects after the death of my dear son,' the other said. 'For that I already thank you. This further favour—'

'Favour! You speak as if it was a little thing.'

'It is a most serious thing.'

'A hanging offence – or do they do things differently in Yorkshire?'

'No, but I have searched my conscience and feel that in mercy—'

Hugh Brontë turned to survey his eldest brother with affec-tionate exasperation. At seventy-one Patrick was still examining

13

his most convenient conscience, his pale blue eyes full of earnest sincerity, his crest of snow-white hair vying with the huge cravat that enveloped half his head as if he were in training for the wearing of a halo.

'You have suffered greatly through the loss of three of your children,' Hugh said in an altered tone. 'Since I never married then your pain is not a pain I can feel truly. But what you ask – Pat, how can I?'

'It may not be necessary. The dog may not have infected—'

'You spoke of symptoms,' Hugh said sharply.

'Violent headaches, swings of mood that terrify and confuse her sisters, lapses of memory – she eats scarcely anything!'

'I must consider this carefully.' Hugh Brontë moved to the fireplace again and sat down in the high-backed chair, stretching his long legs to the heat. He had visited his brother before and nothing had changed in the bleak stone house that stood at the top of the small village and was hidden from the steep main street by the bulk of the church and the graveyard that spread itself in a rash of grey stone and black marble round three sides of the building.

The parlour, as Patrick liked to call it, had the same shutters folded back from the uncurtained windows, the same faded carpet, the same books in the hanging shelves. Opposite the parlour was the dining-room, really the living-room, where the remaining members of the family ate their meals with Patrick joining them only at breakfast and occasionally for tea.

Behind the dining-room a small room held stores, sacks of flour and cakes of sugar and potatoes carefully wrapped against decay. Behind the parlour was the kitchen where the two servants, Tabitha Aykroyd and Martha Brown, generally sat. Tabby, as the family called her, had been sent to stay with her sister in the village during Hugh's visit, and Martha was only a slip of a girl, plain and timid.

Hugh would have felt more at his ease in the kitchen where his rough black suit and heavy boots would not have seemed out of place. Instead he sat with his clergyman brother and tried to find in the hard, seamed countenance the handsome lineaments of the lively young man with whom he had grown up.

Curiously, reverting to the Gaelic which had been their first tongue, he asked,

'Do you ever think of Drumballyroney? Of the old days?'

'Not often. I live in the present,' Patrick said in English.

It wasn't strictly accurate. As age gripped him more tightly the old days became clearer. He had been the eldest of ten, five sons followed by five daughters, his mother a beauty from the south whose brother had objected strongly to her marriage with Hugh Prunty. The McClorys were Catholics, in name at least; the Pruntys nominally Protestant. There was a rumour that they had gypsy blood, a wild streak. It had come out in William who had fought for the United Irishmen during the rebellion of 1798 and had kept a shebeen. It had been a relief all round when he'd upped and emigrated to Australia with his wife and children.

James, like Hugh, had spent his life unmarried as a labourer, though James was the practical joker in the family, inciting the others to terrify the neighbours with ghost stories and japes. In contrast Welsh, the youngest of the boys, had always been more gentlemanly than the other boys, fond of wearing smart clothes and endeavouring to lose his Ulster brogue. He had also married and farmed his small patch of land as proudly as if it had been a great estate.

'There's the future to think about now,' Hugh said. 'Why did you send for me? Why not one of the others?'

'Because you will keep silent,' Patrick said. 'The others . . . Welsh would not agree, James would babble in his cups, William is not here and I'd not trust his silence either. I have always regarded you as the prudent and steady brother.'

Hugh repressed a smile. Patrick had chosen to forget the pranks they had played in the old days, the craich that had kept them in roars of laughter, the way in which the five brothers had marched in step across the fields, leaping the low hedges in perfect time with one another, the sound of the buffalo horn blown by one of the sisters to call them home for cornmeal bread and colcannon with a slice of bacon if times were good.

'You were the ambitious one,' he said aloud. 'Even when you worked for the blacksmith or sat at your weaving a book was never far from your hand. Not many lads in our position start a school of their own and then go on to Cambridge.'

'I believe I was the first,' Patrick said, quietly proud.

'D'ye ever wonder what might've happened if you'd stayed in Ireland and married that girl – Helen, wasn't it?'

'A youthful indiscretion.'

'Very youthful! She was fifteen, wasn't she, and your pupil?'

'We were a hot-blooded family,' Patrick said excusingly.

Hugh nodded, his thoughts running on.

There'd been rumours of another affair after Pat had obtained his degree and been ordained as minister. Some girl called Mary Burder, only seventeen and pretty as a picture. There'd been some trouble with her family and Pat had been transferred to another living. Hugh didn't know whether she had jilted his brother or if it had been the other way round. At any rate the affair had come to nothing and Pat had come north into Yorkshire and married a Cornish lady who was visiting her cousin in the district.

'When I met Maria,' Patrick said as if he had followed Hugh's train of thought, 'all other women faded from my mind. She came from a very good family, you know. Her father was a most respected merchant and one of her nephews became Mayor of Penzance. A lady beyond compare.'

She had been thirty to his thirty-six, both approaching their middle years, both a little lonely. Maria had been tiny with a long nose and blue eyes and a lively manner. He had been auburn-haired then and handsome, highly strung and passionate. He could remember snatched moments when they had visited in the grounds of Fountains Abbey. . . .

'You married her pretty quickly,' Hugh said with a mischievous glance. 'Met her in August, wed her in December, eh?'

And sired six children on her in seven years, he thought. All tiny and delicate save for Emily who had inherited the Prunty height. He'd never met his sister-in-law, since nobody from his side of the family had been invited and it seemed nobody from the Branwell side had come.

'Our minds were alike,' Patrick said with dignity.

'You ought to have come home more often, Pat,' Hugh said abruptly. 'Our mammy missed you sorely.'

'I sent money,' Patrick said stiffly. 'I came to pay my respects.'

'Two years after the wake?' Hugh raised an eyebrow.

'I had other duties – first my curacy in Hartshead-cum-Clifton, then a better post in Thornton, and then Haworth – cradle of the Revival Movement! I was proud to take up the burdens laid down by William Grimshaw.'

'Sure you were!' said Hugh, never having heard of him.

'A great man! Whipped his parishioners into church, preached for two or three hours at a time. In that, my own health being frail, I've never been able to emulate him.'

And thank God for that, Hugh reflected piously. As it was he'd have to endure an hour of his brother's preachifying come Sunday morning. Pat did relish the blood and thunder aspects of religion.

'So, have you decided?' Behind the spectacles Patrick's pale blue eyes were piercing.

'I must talk to Emily first,' Hugh said.

'She will talk to nobody,' her father said.

'I can try. Have I your leave?'

'She'll be in her room.'

Hugh nodded, put his hand briefly on his brother's shoulder and went out, climbing the bare stone steps to the upper floor where, sandwiched between the four bedrooms, was the tiny slip of a chamber which Emily had appropriated as her own.

He tapped on the door, heard a murmur which he chose to regard as an invitation and went in.

The little room looked exactly as he recalled it from his previous visit. Its uncurtained window looked out over the sodden graveyard to the church tower, its walls were whitewashed, its bare floor partly covered by a circular home-made rug in a variety of faded colours. A narrow bed was set against the window wall, its white coverlet rumpled by a small spaniel dog; on the left a low chest of drawers held basin and ewer; on the right a cloak and a dressing-gown hung on hooks. The young woman seated on a stool had a portable writing-desk on her knee but she wasn't writing. At her side Keeper, the fierce bull-mastiff who tolerated visitors after considerable persuasion, crouched with his hindquarters firmly entrenched on his mistress's trailing black skirt.

'Niece!' Hugh greeted her with a light touch on her shoulder from which she flinched. 'I'm told you are not well?'

'It's nothing. Merely a cold,' she answered indifferently. 'Charlotte fusses.'

'You're wise not to venture out of doors.'

'Papa's curate, Mr Nicholls, has offered to walk the dogs. I shall be out and about as soon as the rain ceases.'

She could be no worse off than in this icy little space, he thought.

'I believe there was a thunderstorm the day Branwell was buried. That would've pleased him, I think.'

'Aye, it would,' she said.

'And another on the night you were born. Your father wrote and told us about it. There'd been a month of hot sultry weather and then you arrived with thunder and lightning!'

'I bought a dress once of purple with white flashes of lightning all over it,' she said suddenly. 'Miss Nussey was very shocked.'

'Miss Nussey?'

'Ellen Nussey. She is Charlotte's friend.'

'But you like her?'

'I think well of her. What did you want, Uncle?'

She had moved her head to look up at him and he was startled by the pallor of the thick, pasty skin, the blackness under the blue eyes.

'Your father has told me about the dog bite. I wanted your opinion.'

'It was a stray dog,' she said. 'I saw it in the lane, panting with its tongue hanging out so I took out a bowl of water for it. The poor creature snapped at me and drew blood. It ran off and a couple of farm lads came by and told me it had run mad and they'd orders to kill it.'

'What did you do?'

'Came into the kitchen, heated the iron in the fire and cauterized it with the red-hot tip. I felt faint and sick for a moment but that passed. Nobody would've known but Charlotte noticed the mark on my wrist and wormed out the tale.'

Charlotte would, Hugh thought. His surviving eldest niece was like a small sharp needle, bright eyed, bustling.

'Knee-high!' James had commented after one of his own visits. 'Fit for nothing except ornamenting a mantelpiece.'

'Rabies takes time – up to six months to develop,' he said carefully.

'I have read everything written about it.' She twisted her full, mobile mouth into a wry grin. 'Papa, you must know, has a medical directory in which he has studied for many years.'

'And you have the symptoms?'

'I have a cold.'

She gave a slight cough as if to prove the point and doubled over in a paroxysm, holding a cloth to her face. When she took it away he saw blood on it.

'Headaches? Fever? Swings of mood?'

'Are you a doctor, Uncle?' She shot him a mocking little smile. 'You should have come earlier when Branwell was coughing his lungs out and the family prayed for him to stop drinking. I've no need of you.'

'You have no fear of having contracted the disease?'

'None,' she said indifferently.

'Then you're either a fool or a liar,' Hugh said bluntly. 'Rabies victims die raving mad in agony. Do you know what is generally done?'

'They are suffocated between two feather mattresses. Fortunately there are none in the house. We were reared to be hardy.'

'Sometimes a strong dose of laudanum given by a sympathetic hand—?'

'So that's why you have stayed on here!' She swung around on the stool, the writing desk tilting sharply. 'Does Papa wish it?'

'He doesn't wish you to suffer.'

'Nonsense,' she said lightly. 'Suffering cleanses the soul!'

'Is there laudanum in the house?' Hugh asked.

'Of course there's laudanum in the house! Branwell kept himself very well supplied. Laudanum and opium too! We are very well prepared I promise you.'

'And you yourself—?'

'Then Papa will not be able to bury me with a clear conscience. No, I shall wait for events to unfold.'

'If it becomes necessary – if you are no longer able to make a rational decision then – I am offering my services,' he said.

'I see.' She was silent for a moment. Then a smile lit her face. 'If it becomes necessary,' she said quietly, 'make it a good strong dose, won't you? If I should decide to go more quickly, then . . . I shall tell them that I'm ready for the doctor. You may take it from there, Uncle, if you've the will. My own thoughts are optimistic.'

So were the thoughts of many with consumption, he thought. They believed right up to the last breath that they were on the mend.

'They say you don't eat and you don't speak,' Hugh ventured.

'I speak when I've something to say and I eat when I'm hungry. Don't fuss!'

She turned her head away to cough and he heard the rasping of her breath.

'I'll leave you in peace,' he said. His hand was on the door as she raised her head again, pushing back her heavy dark hair.

'I wrote a book once,' she said, 'but don't tell anyone you know.'

'A printed book? That's clever!'

'Nobody read it. It wasn't important anyway.'

He went slowly down the stairs, feeling the weight of his years. How old was she? Thirty. It struck him as impossibly young.

In the hallway Charlotte, a tiny black moth, drew him into the dining-room.

'Would Emily talk?' she asked in a fluttering whisper.

'Yes.'

'She will not admit that she's ill,' Charlotte said. 'I have begged her to let me send for a doctor but she refuses. When Dr Wheelhouse called she locked herself in her room. I wrote to a specialist in London, without her knowledge, giving as minute a description of her symptoms as I could – the hacking cough, the expectoration, the fever, the rapid pulse – she has begun now to suffer from diarrhoea but she considers it will cleanse her. The specialist sent back an obscurely worded note that didn't help at all. Mr Williams who is . . . an acquaintance of mine in London suggested homoeopathy and sent a book about it. Emily read the book and said it was well-meant quackery.'

The words were tumbling out of her, her eyes huge in the strained little face.

'Your sister told me about the dog bite,' Hugh said.

'That was such a brave thing for her to do,' Charlotte whispered. 'To cauterize the wound herself and say nothing about it. Now she can hardly bear to have the event alluded to. Papa is so anxious about her. He tells me that I must bear up for he will sink if I fail him! I am wondering if it might help to send for Miss Nussey, my great friend. She has offered her services.'

'Perhaps it would be best not to involve anyone outside the family?'

Her eyes flew to his face again, her small fingers twisting together. She said in a terrified whisper, 'Because of infection but—'

'Your brother took laudanum.'

'Took it! Branwell practically bathed in the stuff! Why do you—?'

'I think it as well to have a good supply to hand in case it becomes necessary. I've spoken to Emily about it.'

She was so white that he feared for a moment she was going to faint. A shudder convulsed her tiny frame. Then she put her hand on the arm of the sofa and said very quietly, 'I have feared of late that her mind is becoming affected, though I believe that consumption, when it mounts to the brain, can . . . laudanum would be kinder then. Papa would be obliged to you.'

It was an odd phrase under the circumstances.

'I'll do what's necessary,' he said again.

'Anne must be told.' Her voice was a thread. 'She and Emily were – are very close you know. And Martha also – you may trust that child. She is utterly and completely loyal. But perhaps – perhaps it will not be—?'

'Perhaps not,' Hugh said.

'I will write to Ellen Nussey and tell her not to come. Emily cannot endure visitors just now. Thank you, Uncle.'

She gave him a desperate little smile, drew herself up to her height – about four feet eight inches he reckoned – and went quietly away.

James had been wrong, Hugh thought. Charlotte was good for more than being an ornament on a mantelshelf.

Charlotte, Patrick thought, would cope with whatever befell. She had always had a core of steel in her small, still childish body. She would cope with the loss of Emily too. They would all endure.

It would be Christmas soon. He had never objected to decorations of holly and ivy, to mince pies and plum puddings though strictly speaking they were relics of pagan belief. Once a year it did no harm to unwind a little, to let in the local carol singers for a glass of hot punch. This year . . . would Emily survive that long in her right mind if not in health of body? Hugh's coming was providential. Of all his brothers he had always favoured Hugh the most. 'Giant' they'd nicknamed him in youth as he strode about flourishing his shillelagh. Yet for all his vigour Hugh had never taken a wife, never begot child after child on a slender white body.

Maria, Elizabeth, Charlotte, then the blessing of a son, Patrick Branwell, who had grown up to be Pat in the village and Branny to his adoring sisters.

He had called himself Little King and straddled their world.

The thirtieth day of July in 1818. The date was imprinted on his memory. Maria, born so quickly after her parents' marriage that he had taken good care the exact date would be nowhere recorded, had been a miniature edition of her mother with a long nose and light hair and blue eyes alight with intelligence. He had known from the beginning that Maria would be a spiritual being, a soul to be guided along the path of self-sacrifice and self discipline. Elizabeth had been a rough copy of her elder sister with duller hair and eyes that were set too wide apart in her narrow face. Slow to walk or talk, slow to ask questions, more clumsy than her sister, she had invited pity. Charlotte . . . her sex had disappointed him. After two daughters he had hoped for a boy. And Charlotte had been a quaint plain little girl – but with a quick intelligence. She had had a habit of saying odd unexpected things. Once she had set off to walk to Paradise after hearing him read from *The Pilgrim's Progress*. The local carter had spotted her trudging along the Bradford road and had the sense to deliver one would-be pilgrim safely back in Thornton.

Patrick's hands clenched on the arms of his chair when he thought of the modest parsonage that stood in the main street of that bustling village.

After the cramped house at Hartshead where the two eldest girls had been born Thornton had been a lively little metropolis. He and Maria had enjoyed an active social life there, he perhaps more than she since she had borne four more children during the five years he had been curate there. But she had entertained the local ladies to tea, had invited her sister to stay for two extended vacations – rather too extended he'd felt at the time.

And Miss Elizabeth Firth, only daughter of the local squire, she of the impertinent nose and slender waist, had taken up the Brontës with unremitting enthusiasm. Just seventeen, with something about her that reminded him of his former sweetheart Mary Burder and of that long-ago girl in Drumballyroney

Child of Earth

too. They had played cards and drunk tea at her father's handsome house, had entertained her in their more modest dwelling. He had been writing at that time, two short novels and a book of poems which had gone into a second edition and gained him a reputation as a man of letters. Dear Maria had been frequently weary during her pregnancies and Miss Firth had provided a welcome alternative ear as they strolled in the lanes around the village or sat in her father's drawing-room.

Once or twice he had taken her to Bradford to buy books or to attend a lecture. Once he had taken her to the theatre. Maria had been in the seventh month of her fourth pregnancy and had begged off, bidding him escort Miss Firth instead.

'For there can be no impropriety in your going to see a Shakespearian production, my dear. Clergymen should associate themselves with cultural events. You will tell me all about it when you return!'

He still remembered vividly that performance of *Othello*, with the Irish actress, Dora Jordan, playing the role of Emilia. A very lively and fetching Emilia too! Not until the end of the play had he recalled that the actress in real life was the long-time mistress of the Duke of Clarence, had indeed borne him several children. Patrick had admired rather than condemned her courage in continuing to earn her own living. And the name Emilia, anglicized into Emily, had a pretty ring about it. If the new baby should be a girl he would name her Emily.

It had been the longed-for son, as red-haired as his father, and a little king from the beginning. Gazing at the baby Patrick had allowed himself to wonder which path in life his son would tread. A clergyman perhaps, whose fiery sermons would inspire his parish? A great writer? Patrick's happiest hours had been spent in the composition of poetry. A soldier? At Cambridge he had drilled with the militia and been praised for his marksmanship. A physician? Patrick was keenly interested in all the recent advances in medical science. The name Emily would be saved for the next child.

That there would be a next child he never doubted. Dear Maria was proving exceedingly fertile. There were times when the chatter of the toddlers, the fretful wailing of whoever was cutting another tooth, the smell of wet napkins irritated him into an attack of indigestion. He had employed two servant girls,

23

sisters, who were hardworking and willing, but Nancy Garrs was only fifteen, her sister Sarah thirteen, and they did their work with a great deal of joking and talking and clattering of pots and pans. It was no wonder that occasionally, very occasionally, his Irish temper got the better of him and he expended his rage on furniture or cut the billowing sleeves out of one of Maria's favourite gowns. Dear Maria had taken it as a joke and he'd bought her a more expensive gown the very next day but the incident made him feel secretly ashamed.

On 30 July, 1818 he had paced his little study in the time-honoured manner, hearing the boiling of kettles of water in the kitchen, the half-stifled cries of dear Maria as the light faded, and lightning catclawed the livid sky though the sultry heat wasn't relieved.

The baby had been small and had a feeble cry. As a precaution he had arranged to have her baptized within a month. Emily Jane. Jane for his favourite sister who had died back in Ireland earlier in the year. Emily because it was a new name in the family, having the meaning of 'industrious'. Pushed beneath conscious level was the memory of that pretty Mistress Jordan declaiming her lines on the Bradford stage while he sat rapt next to Miss Firth of the impertinent nose and the slender waist.

Hugh, coming into the parlour, coughed gently.

'Emily spoke to you?' Patrick's pale, fierce gaze was fixed on him.

'She has agreed that if necessary the laudanum should be administered,' Hugh said, 'but she herself remains hopeful.'

A flicker momentarily disturbed Patrick's granite features and then was gone.

'We must wait and see if rabies or consumption defeats her in the end,' he said dryly. 'Will you have a pipe with me before Martha brings the tea?'

Hugh, nodding, taking his seat, wondered if he would ever begin to fathom his older brother.

Two

There are two trees in a lonely field,
They breathe a spell to me;
A dreary thought their dark boughs yield,
All waving solemnly.

Emily Jane Brontë

She was eighteen months old when she began to be aware of herself as a person separate from the figures moving about her. There was Mama who lay in bed propped up with pillows and held a small creature.

'This is your new baby sister, Emily. God has sent her to us. Her name is Anne.'

God kept Mama in bed while Nancy and Sarah bustled round the little house. Nancy did the cooking and the washing and Sarah dressed them and bathed them in the tin bath that hung on a hook in the yard and was taken down and filled with hot water once a week for the bath. First Branny, who was the boy and important, then Maria and Elizabeth – Emily found her name impossible to say so compromised on Ellis – then Charlotte and finally her small self by which time the water was quite dirty. Sarah took them for walks along the street and down the lanes beyond and to the cold grey building where Papa, very tall and slim in his black cassock and high white stock, talked in a loud sonorous voice about sin and God who was somewhere around watching. In the house Papa spent most of the time in his study, often with Maria, and afterwards Maria would come out and tell them stories and explain what the government was doing. Emily, snuggled on Sarah's knee, generally drifted off to sleep.

After Anne came she began to hear a particular word often spoken.

'My dear, the moorland air of Haworth will soon invigorate you again.'

'Is it true we'm going to up sticks and move to Haworth, Missus?'

'The Reverend William Grimstead was curate of Haworth and left a most godly example for Papa to follow.'

'Not Grimstead, my dearest Maria, but Grimshaw. And he was indeed a very great man. If the trustees of Haworth accept me this time then we shall move to Haworth in the spring.'

Emily liked the word, liked breathing out the H in a big gulp. H was for Heaven where people went when they died. Not all people, said Papa.

Sinners went to Hell which was a lake full of fire. Papa was afraid of fire. He wouldn't allow curtains on the windows or carpets on the floors, and he never let Nancy dry anything on the brass rails of the fireguards.

Hell must be a terrible place.

Spring came and the furniture was loaded on to carts, their garments packed away in brassbound trunks and several ladies came to kiss Mama who was being lifted on to a mattress inside one of the covered carts and to shake hands with Papa. Miss Firth, Miss Outhwaite and Miss Atkinson chittered like mice, ribbons fluttering on their bonnets and their high-waisted frocks.

'My dear Miss Firth, we shall only be five miles off. There will be many occasions for visiting,' Papa was saying.

'I want to sit with the driver!' Branny was demanding.

Branny was nearly three and nearly always had his way. Papa picked him up and put him on the high seat with a warning to hold tight and the rest of them piled in behind round Mama who was holding Anne in her arms.

Afterwards the journey, taken at walking pace with Papa striding along at the head of the line of carts, blurred in her memory. She couldn't remember either her first sight of the steep village street or the grey parsonage behind the church or the moors that enclosed them and reached to the far horizon. She grew up regarding them as an extension of herself in a way the people in her world could never be. She did vaguely recall being lifted down from the cart by a rough-looking man who exclaimed,

'Eeh, lass, tha's little enough to fit in a laundry basket wi' thy brother and sisters!'

The house with the patch of garden in front of it, the yard behind and the tombstones encircling them was like a shell encasing her from harm. Each room of the house had its own particular function. The dining-room on the left was where they ate their dinner and their supper and where Papa some-times came, stepping from his study which was officially the parlour just across the hall to hear them say their lessons. Behind the dining-room was a smaller room where provisions were stored. Behind the parlour was the kitchen which was always the warmest room in the whole house, with a scrubbed table where they sat to eat their breakfast and where Nancy sliced vegetables and kneaded bread in a big earthenware bowl. A flagged passage led out of the kitchen into a back kitchen with a loft above where Nancy and Sarah sometimes played hide and seek.

The stairs went up past the grandfather clock that Papa wound every night to a landing with four bedrooms opening off it. Papa slept in the one over the parlour and Branny had a room of his own behind.

'The only son must have his own space,' Papa said.

Emily yearned for her own space but it was seldom available. Mama, who was still not very well, slept in the bedroom over the dining-room with Anne in the cradle at her side and Nancy and Sarah slept in the small chamber behind it.

A fifth door on the landing led into a very small room, squeezed in over the front porch. There were camp beds here, one for Maria and Ellis, and one for Charlotte and herself. In the morning the beds were taken down and the room used as a study for them when it was too wet to go out for a walk with Sarah.

Downstairs at the side of the staircase a door led down twist-ing stone steps into echoing cellars with ceilings supported on arches and at the far end a stone wall with an old door in it which had been sealed up years before.

'On the other side of the wall is the crypt where the dead are buried. It stretches to the church and beneath it,' Papa told them. 'We must remember to say a little prayer when we come down here in memory of those who have gone before us.'

Emily thought of the dead and wondered if heaven or hell lay beyond the wall. Perhaps they were both the same place. Or

27

perhaps the dead were only asleep after all and one day would wake up and try to open the door.

It was better to be out with Sarah, trotting along and holding her skirt as they went down the lane that ran along the side of the parsonage and climbed the stile into the fields that lay like a green patchwork below the wilder land where great swathes of gorse and heather swept down to the black peat.

Mama didn't get better. Now and then Emily glimpsed her coming very slowly down the stairs and holding on to the rail, and once she and Charlotte had peeped into the dining-room and seen Mama half lying on the black horsehair sofa with Branny on a little footstool at her feet. The room had danced with firelight and Mam's hand had played with Branny's shock of red curls.

After that Mama lay in bed all day and other, unfamiliar footsteps were heard on the stairs and strange adult voices murmured together.

Sarah took them out twice a day to walk on the moors and never minded if they yelled and skipped and pushed one another. In the house they must be very quiet and creep about so as not to disturb poor Mama.

'She is very ill,' Maria said gravely. 'God is calling her home to heaven.'

At night Emily lay wakeful long after the other children had fallen asleep, listening to the soft padding of footsteps and the lowered tones of Papa and the two gentlemen with black bags who came and went in the watches of the night. Once she heard, or thought she heard, someone say, 'It could not have lived to full term. Too frequent pregnancies have hastened the growth of the tumours.'

Once, coming upstairs after a long walk on the moors, having dashed ahead of the others, she saw one of the doctor gentlemen coming out of Mama's room with a bloodstained apron tied round his waist and heard him say, 'We must hope it does not recur in another organ.'

Not a baby, it seemed, but cancer. Nancy and Sarah whispered together and a woman from the village came to sit with Mama during the day.

Then came the time when Nancy and Sarah sat crying together in the kitchen and the doctor gentlemen stayed nearly all night with Mama. Emily could hear a moaning sound coming from the bedroom over the dining-room and hear Papa's voice raised in prayer. He was begging the Devil to withdraw from his dearest wife and leave her in peace to accept the will of the Lord. Not all the words were clear or even made much sense, because if Mama was so good why was the Devil there?

What stayed in her mind ever afterwards was when in the cold light of a September morning she was bundled into her clothes and led with the others to stand at the foot of Mama's bed. What was propped up in the bed didn't really look like Mama at all. It was a thin white thing with lank hair and lips drawing back from the gums in a kind of grimace, but the voice was the one the three-year-old remembered.

'Oh God! My poor children – what will become of my poor children?'

And of the rest of the day she recalled nothing save that Charlotte had cried herself sick and Miss Outhwaite had come to take her back to her own home in Thornton for a few days.

Life wasn't very different after Mama's death. She had been ill for such a long time that having Nancy and Sarah to take care of them had become quite natural. Yet the habit of creeping about in the house without raising one's voice persisted.

'They're that spiritless, poor mites,' Nancy said, shaking her head as she sat with Sarah enjoying a pint of ale drawn from the barrel in the cellar.

'Missing their mam,' Sarah said. 'Happen they'll get a new one soon.'

'I am going over to Thornton for a day or two, children,' Papa said, coming in with his overcoat on and his boots gleaming. 'Mr Firth and his daughter have kindly invited me to stay with them. Don't give Nancy or Sarah any trouble while I'm away.'

So the new mama was going to be Miss Elizabeth Firth with whose name Emily was familiar though she couldn't remember what she looked like. But when Papa returned just before Christmas he came alone and said nothing about Miss Firth or a new mama. Emily didn't mind much because she had Sarah who was always ready to give her a cuddle or sing her a song.

The next thing Emily retained in her child's mind was Papa coming into the tiny study with a letter in his hand and a sad look on his face.

'I have received a letter from my brother Hugh in Ireland,' he said. 'My beloved mother, Eilis, has passed away peacefully.'

'Like Mama?' Branny asked.

'Not from the same cause,' Papa said. 'Your own dear mama died from the scourge of cancer. My own mother has died from consumption at a more advanced age. My father passed away shortly after I took my degree – you will recall that I have a Cambridge degree, children – so now I am the head of the family.'

He meant of the Irish Pruntys, Emily knew. She wondered how it would have felt to be called Emily Jane Prunty which would have happened if Papa had not changed his name on coming into England. Some of his brothers and sisters had changed to Brontë too, which sounded, Papa said, as if they were all ambitious to rise in the world.

'What was she like – your mother?' Charlotte, who always asked the question everybody else would've liked to ask, piped up shrilly.

'She was tall and slender,' Papa said. 'Her eyes were blue and her hair which curled to her waist was golden. Pure golden.'

Eilis was the Gaelic for Alice and sounded like Ellis. Emily, who loved playing with words in her head, gave the small, closed-mouth smile that momentarily lit her solemn face.

After that Aunt Branwell came. Maria and Elizabeth remembered her from before when she had spent time in Thornton but to the younger ones she was unfamiliar, yet curiously familiar too because she was tiny with a long nose like Mama and the same soft accent, so that in a peculiar way it was like having Mama come back again, but older and changed.

'It was my duty to come so I came, Mr Brontë,' she announced. 'I cannot pretend that I find Yorkshire particularly congenial but I will naturally remain until you find someone to replace poor dear Maria. You may rest assured that I will supervise the household and make it my business to instruct the girls in the rudiments of reading, writing and sewing.'

'They all can read and write a little already but my parish duties—' Papa murmured.

'They naturally occupy a great deal of your time – and you have your own writing too,' Aunt Branwell said briskly. 'You may leave the education of the girls to me. I would not of course presume to instruct Branwell. His education must be in your more capable hands. The girls however will not suffer from any neglect on my part – Anne surely cannot read!'

'Of course not but I believe she will be intelligent,' Papa said.

'And will not lack for care,' Aunt Branwell said, her expression softening as her eyes rested on the cradle in which Anne was taking a nap. 'You may leave all in my hands, Mr Brontë.'

Before she had been in the parsonage a month it felt as if she had been there for ever. She moved into Mama's room where Anne also slept, bringing with her all her possessions from Helston and Penzance: a large rug at which Papa looked askance, muttering about the dangers of fire, a whatnot filled with ribbons and bits of jewellery, and trunks of dresses with high waists and bunchy skirts in the style, said Nancy who took an interest in such matters, of twenty years before. She brought her two sewing boxes and a beautiful ivory and silk fan which fascinated Emily, and a pile of magazines on which the older children's eyes fastened hungrily.

'These,' said Aunt Branwell, stacking them carefully, 'are magazines which are distributed by the Methodist Society. I am a Methodist as was your dear departed mama, and we took great pleasure in our reading. While your sewing lessons go on I will read you some of the stories from them.'

She had all the girls except Anne seated up in her bedroom on hard little stools sewing and mending before the first month was out. They all hated it because only Charlotte could make neat small stitches and she had to bend right over her work in order to see it.

Happily the stories in the Methodist magazines proved more exciting than they had dared to hope. They were full of shipwrecks and lunatics locked up in cellars and unhappy wives who ran away in the dead of night and fell through the ice or were kidnapped by bandits or swept away in a flash flood.

When the sewing was done Aunt Branwell taught them reading and writing, though Maria could already do both, and set them spelling-bees which were not quite as successful because Aunt Branwell herself often wasn't certain what order the letters went in a particular word.

She taught them in the mornings and after dinner they were released into the custody of Nancy and Sarah who bundled them up in their cloaks and took them off across the moors. The children apart from Anne ran on ahead, chasing one another, stumbling in the heather while the Garrs sisters walked together, arms wrapped in their shawls and complained about Aunt Branwell of whose regime they thoroughly disapproved.

'Half a pint of ale atween us and she draws it hersen because she doesna trust us! Eeh, she's a mean one.'

'A bit of a tyke,' Sarah agreed.

'Let's pray Maister teks Miss Dury as a wife and then Miss Branwell can trot back to Cornwall,' Nancy said.

Charlotte whose ears were sharper than her eyes asked,

'Who is Miss Dury? Are we to have a new mama?'

'Nought to do wi'ye, Miss Charlotte,' Nancy scolded. 'Miss Isabella Dury is sister to t'Rector of Keighley and a very pretty young lady. Happen your papa's courting her but you'll not repeat that!'

Isabella. Isabella. The name sang in Emily's mind. It was a pretty name and she could see a fair-haired young lady with roses on her dress who might have such a name.

'Isabella,' said Maria who hadn't appeared to be listening, 'is the Spanish form of Elizabeth.'

'I said it's not to be repeated, Miss Maria!' Nancy said sharply. 'The things that child knaws about! I never saw anyone so clever!'

Papa thought his children might be clever too. Not Elizabeth, of course, though he admitted she had plenty of good sound sense, but the others were in his opinion very bright.

The next day after supper when Aunt Branwell had retired to her room and the servants were seated in the kitchen Papa called the children into the parlour.

'We are going to play the Great Game,' he said, having ranged them in a row before him.

Emily had heard the Great Game mentioned before but had been too small to play it. Now she watched eagerly as Papa turned and put something over his head. When he turned round again his face was the face of a skull, white bones shining on black, pale eyes glinting through the eyeslits.

'This,' said the sepulchral voice from behind the mask, 'is the Day of Judgement. Answer each question truthfully.'

Emily felt herself vibrating with excitement. Papa was usually too busy to play games with them though he had told Maria that during his Irish boyhood he and his brothers had played pranks on the neighbours.

'Each of you,' pronounced the sepulchral voice, 'will don the mask in turn and answer the question put to him or to her. I shall begin with Maria.'

He removed the skull head and became Papa again, handing the mask to Maria who obediently donned it.

'What,' Papa enquired, 'is the best way of spending one's time? Answer quickly and without fear.'

'By laying it out in preparation for a happy eternity,' Maria said. Elizabeth took the mask.

'What education best befits a woman?' Papa asked.

'That which teaches her to rule her home well,' Elizabeth said.

Emily felt a twinge of disappointment. They all knew the right answers to the questions already because Papa was always telling them these things when they sat in the pew below the high pulpit from which he preached every Sunday.

'Charlotte, name your favourite books!'

'First the Bible and then the Book of Nature.'

And that, thought Emily, was a lie. Charlotte buried her big nose in Aunt Branwell's Methodist magazines whenever she got half a chance!

Branwell was fidgeting, hopping up and down, his face all impatience.

'It isn't fair,' he said sulkily. 'As the boy I should have been asked the questions first!'

'It isn't for you to set the rules,' his father said mildly.

'But Papa—'

'For that Emily shall wear the mask next. Give it to her!'

Scowling, Branwell obeyed. Emily pulled the mask over her head and felt safe and powerful in a way she'd never felt before.

Papa was still looking uneasily at Branwell. He said, not averting his gaze, 'What should I do with Branwell when he's naughty?'

That was a new question. He'd never talked about that in the pulpit before. Emily said loudly, savouring her power,

'First reason with him, then if he won't listen to reason whip him!'

'Give your brother the mask.'

Emily, queen of her five-year-old world, pulled it off and handed it to Branwell who made a hideous face at her before he put it on.

'Branwell, is there any difference between the minds of men and women?' Papa asked.

'In order to answer that we must first consider the difference in their bodies!' Branwell flashed triumphantly.

Boys, Emily thought, had something extra, to be displayed only at bath-time. It didn't follow their brains were stronger or bigger. She opened her mouth to point out the fact but Anne, a minute thing in a white pinafore with a skeleton head, was obediently lisping the answer to her question,

'What does a child of your age need most?'

'Age and ex-experience,' Anne said.

Emily wondered if that was true and if Anne really believed it. Papa was looking gratified.

'You have shown me your true selves,' he said. 'Maria carries the palm for her answer. A spiritual, God-centred answer will always triumph over the physical and mundane. I require your company, my dear Maria. The rest of you may go.'

It was always Maria's company he sought when he had time to spare. They spent hours together closeted in the study, sometimes descending into the cellars. Did they listen there for poor Mama knocking on the other side of the wall? Emily had never dared to ask. She loved Maria dearly of course because Maria was so good and told them stories out of the newspapers and made up little plays for them to act when they were on the moors, but she felt more comfortable with Elizabeth who was slow and placid and found all lessons hard.

In the autumn they lost both the elder girls when they were sent away to boarding-school in Wakefield. It was, said Papa, an expensive school where the children were happy but so expensive that some of his Thornton friends were footing the bill. If he could hear of a cheaper school then they would all eventually go except for Branwell of course. Papa would instruct Branwell himself until the time came for him to win a scholarship to one of the great public schools.

Either the fees proved too high for everybody or Maria and Elizabeth became sick at the school because they were both home within a couple of months and soon after that the whole lot of them went down with measles and whooping cough and were confined to their beds while Aunt Branwell and Nancy and Sarah rushed about with bowls of gruel and hot possets and the doctor came and went.

Emily had the illness more lightly than the others but she still felt dreadful and cried fretfully along with everybody else. When the doctor came with a long face and announced they had scarlet fever too, though not very badly, Papa became extremely alarmed and Emily, wishing her throat would stop hurting, wondered if they were all going to die.

'Nonsense!' Sarah said roundly. ''Course tha's not going to die! Tha's too young and too wicked!'

After that Emily felt better and was soon out of bed making a nuisance of herself as she went round the bedrooms 'sick visiting' and making her sisters and brother laugh as she bounced on the brass posts of the beds pretending she was on a horse.

When they were all up again Papa announced that they were to go to school.

'Back to Wakefield, Papa?' Maria asked, looking pleased. She and Elizabeth had liked the quiet routine of the school and the company of the other girls there.

'To a new establishment founded recently by a famous clergyman called Carus Wilson,' Papa said. 'It is named the Clergy Daughters' School and the school itself is at Cowan Bridge, Casterton, nearly forty miles off. It is on the borders of Lancashire and situated according to the prospectus that I have received in a very pretty part of the country. The fees are so moderate that in time I hope to send all you girls there. Maria and Elizabeth will go late in July. By then they will be stronger and able to join in all the activities there.'

Before they went Maria and Elizabeth, who were now out of bed, had to help sew the two sets of new underwear, the brown holland frocks and pinafores, the purple cloaks and black stockings which were required.

'It's not fair,' Emily heard Sarah grumble to Nancy. 'Those bairns need good fresh air and play, not hours set in a stuffy bedroom darning and hemming. They look as if a wind'd blaw 'em away!'

'Hold your tongue,' Nancy advised. 'She'll tak' no heed if you say owt!'

'It's not reet,' Sarah muttered.

But on 29 May which was a Saturday, Aunt Branwell announced her intention of going into the village to catch the gig over to Keighley where she intended to do some shopping. Since she never left the parsonage except to attend church this was regarded by the children as a red-letter day, and they saw their aunt off with almost parental solicitude.

'Aunt won't be home until suppertime and Papa's gone to Bradford,' Branwell exulted. 'What games shall we play?'

'We still have our sewing to do,' Maria said.

'It's Oak Apple Day!' Branwell cried. 'The anniversary of the day when King Charles the Second hid in a tree – an oak tree – while the Roundheads searched for him.'

'He wasn't yet king when that happened,' Maria said.

'Well, Prince Charles then! Shall we act it out? I shall be the prince.'

'You'd better not, Branny,' Elizabeth warned. 'You know you get dizzy just looking out of a high window.'

'I can climb!' Emily pushed forward. 'I've got the longest legs too, so I could get from branch to branch. We could use Papa's tree.'

The others looked at her doubtfully. The tree in question was not an oak but a fruit tree of some sort which bore magnificent blossom but never any fruit. It grew closely against the walls of the parsonage, its topmost branches easily gained from their father's bedroom window.

'Wouldn't it be very wicked?' Maria said.

'Papa says that before we can enter heaven we must repent,' Charlotte said. 'If we are never naughty we can never repent.'

'We'd better ask Sarah,' Maria compromised.

Sarah when appealed to proved enthusiastic. 'I see no great harm in't, provided tha doesna hurt the tree,' she opined 'but tha cannot climb in a frock, Miss Emily. Theer's an old pair of trews that Master Branwell never wears. I'll get 'em!'

They were all of them, even Maria, suddenly imbued with the spirit of holiday. Nancy might have put forward objections but she had slipped away on some business of her own and it was an excited group of children who hid themselves around the garden while Emily, attired in her brother's pants which ended just below the knees of her longer legs, opened the window and carefully stepped out into the topmost branches of the tree.

'Now we must all look for the fugitive prince,' Branwell ordered.

'I am a Royalist,' Charlotte argued. 'I don't want to be a Roundhead!'

'You and I and Maria shall be Royalists waiting to rescue the prince and Elizabeth and Anne can be the Roundheads,' Branwell decided. 'We shall hide and you two must run about looking for the prince.'

'He's up the tree,' Elizabeth said helpfully.

'You both have to pretend you can't find him,' Charlotte said.

Four-year-old Anne trotted after her older sister. Pretend games confused her because they weren't true.

'Do we find the prince?' Elizabeth asked.

'No, of course not! Look for him and then run away into the yard. Do get on with it!' Branwell shrilled.

The sound of the young voices reached Sarah who was tidying the dining-room. She paused to listen, thinking it was seldom enough they broke out and had a bit of fun.

There was suddenly a rending crash accompanied by loud shrieks. Sarah rushed out in time to see Emily, bits of broken blossom caught in her hair, rise somewhat dizzily from a mass of splintered wood and twigs.

'The branch broke when Emily put her foot on it,' Maria said, her blue eyes dilated in her pale face. 'Papa will be very angry.'

'Are you hurt, Emily?' Elizabeth was asking in concern.

'Not a bit! It's one of the lowest branches,' Emily said.

'We can't possibly hide it.' Branwell was surveying the damage. 'The place shows where the branch broke off.'

'I'll run to Mr Brown and get some dark paint,' Sarah said, thinking rapidly. 'No, soot! Soot'll serve better. There'll be some in't grate. Branwell, you get busy now! Tek that branch to th'woodshed and Miss Emily, change tha clothes!'

Emily, long legs dragging, went back indoors. She was praying inwardly that Papa wouldn't notice the missing branch. He didn't approve of children climbing and Sarah would certainly get into trouble for allowing Emily to do so. If only she'd been a boy then he might not mind so much.

By evening the bark left visible after the fall of the branch had been thoroughly rubbed with soot and the branch itself carefully concealed at the back of the woodshed. The children, scrubbed and shining, sat at the table waiting for the sound of their father's footsteps along the gravel path. Aunt Branwell had come home shortly before, declaring she was exhausted and had no intention of stirring from her room until the next day. Sarah might carry up a tray with bread and butter, anchovy paste, and the wherewithal for brewing a pot of tea.

The footsteps came. They paused. Then they resumed and the gleam of the lantern with which their father illumined his long tramp home across the moors was seen through the unshuttered window.

'The tree has one branch fewer,' Papa said, coming in and setting the lamp on its hook. 'Someone has attempted to conceal the wound to the bark with soot. I deduce therefore that someone from this house broke the branch, probably by swinging from it or jumping on it. Stand up, children.'

Six small figures rose up silently. Sarah, hovering in the doorway, twisted her fingers together.

'If the person responsible owns up there will be no punishment.' His pale gaze swept the semicircle. 'Answer truthfully as I ask you. Maria, did you damage my tree?'

'Not I, Papa,' Maria whispered.

'Elizabeth?'

Elizabeth shook her head.

'Charlotte? Was it you?'

'No, Papa.' Charlotte's face was contorted.

'Branwell, was it you?'

'No, Papa.'

'Em. . . ?'

'It were me, master!' Sarah blurted. 'I were just playing a bit of a game wi' th' childer and I climbed down the tree. I trod on it too hard and th'branch snapped clean off.'

'What on earth,' he enquired faintly, 'were you doing up a tree?'

'It's Oak Apple Day, master. I were Prince Charles. It were just a game.'

'Sarah, you are nearly twenty years old! What in the world got into you? Well, I have promised no punishment but I am disappointed in you. I had hoped that you had acquired some sense of responsibility since coming to be part of our little family. I shall take supper in the parlour and we'll not mention this again.'

'Thank you, sir,' Sarah said meekly.

Patrick allowed the door to close behind him before his mouth twitched into a smile.

'Get on wi' tha vittles,' Sarah said, hurrying back to the kitchen.

'You miserable little coward, Emily Jane!' Branwell, his face as flaming as his hair, turned with fury in his face. 'How could you stand there and let Sarah take the blame! You're evil!'

'Branwell, we are all sinners,' Maria said gently.

'Emily's a big sinner!' Charlotte said fiercely. 'You let Sarah take the blame.'

'I'll go now and tell Papa,' Emily began.

'You can't!' Maria put out a restraining hand. 'If you do then Papa will know that Sarah lied and the one thing he will not endure is a servant who lies. Sarah will be dismissed without a character!'

'Aunt says liars go right to hell,' Anne piped.

'Then Sarah will go to hell.' Maria looked distressed. 'She cannot confess her sin and so cannot repent. What are we to do?'

'Emily should've stood up and said right out it was her fault,' Branwell said. 'She's a miserable coward and I'm not going to play with her again for years and years.'

'Much I care!' Emily sat down and shrugged her thin shoulders.

'We'd best leave Emily to contemplate her sin in silence,' Maria said.

'I won't speak to her for a week,' Charlotte said virtuously.

'I don't care if you never speak to me again!' Emily said. 'I don't care about any of you. I like being a sinner.'

Her remark was greeted by a shocked and disbelieving silence.

'We had better eat our supper,' Maria said tremblingly.

Emily ate with the rest or rather pushed food into her mouth and swallowed it. She kept her eyes lowered and pretended not to notice the slight scraping as the others shifted their chairs a few inches away from her.

After supper which was later than usual tonight there was family prayers. Patrick, for reasons best known to himself, gave a short and, to one small girl, searing homily, about the thief crucified next to Christ and sent them upstairs, Anne docilely following Aunt Branwell who had overcome her exhaustion and descended to prayers.

Branwell went up to his own room which he still occupied in solitary state, leaving his four remaining sisters to put up the trestle beds in the slip room and scramble into their night-dresses.

Maria was praying softly for divine grace, her joined hands digging into Elizabeth's back; Charlotte had pointedly wrapped herself in a shawl and lay on the extreme edge of the narrow bed as far from Emily as she could get.

'Because of me,' Emily thought, 'Sarah will go to hell. She will burn for ever. And I will burn too because I'm a miserable sinner!'

Perhaps if she did some repentance then God would let Sarah off. She lay stiffly, waiting for the breathing of the others to slow and deepen.

Then she slipped noiselessly out of bed, her bare feet making no sound on the bare floor and went softly downstairs. A light gleamed from under the parlour door where Papa still sat. She stole to the cellar door at the back of the stairs, opened it and felt her way down the stone steps, her fingers brushing the rough-cast walls.

If she sat in the cellar all night perhaps God would notice and forgive her and Sarah. It was the only thing she could think of to do!

The whitewashed arches gleamed faintly. Emily waited until her eyes had become accustomed to the dark. It wasn't completely dark because a window set high in the wall at ground level in the back yard provided a faint illumination.

She made her way to the far wall past the barrel of ale from which Aunt drew a half pint of liquor to be shared between Nancy and Sarah. Sarah. She had lied for Emily's sake. She would go to hell because she had lied. Emily couldn't tell the real story because then Papa would dismiss Sarah for being a liar. People who were dismissed for lying would be unable to find another situation and they would go to the workhouse or end up as a bundle of rags on the street.

She sank down on to the floor, knuckling her closed eyes.

Sarah would never love her again. Sarah would think of her always as the one who left her to tell a lie. And the others would remember. They might not say a word but they would remember. Even when they were all quite grown up they would look at her and remember she was a coward and because of that Sarah would go to hell.

She wished Mama hadn't died and gone to heaven. At least Papa had told them all that Mama was in heaven. At least her soul was. Her body was under the church floor at the other side of the wall. If she knew that Emily wanted her she would push up the lid of her coffin and drift over to the wall and begin to tap, tap, tap.

A scarlet radiance shone across the wall. Emily stared at it, her heart thudding. She was not quite six years old and she wanted her mother. She didn't want her dead mother but the living one she could scarcely recall. Mama was dead and Sarah was going to hell and . . . 'Please God,' she babbled under her breath, 'I want to be dead. Please, God, make me be dead!'

High above her head through the cracked window a high sweet note shivered like a bell.

Sarah, fetching wood from the woodshed, was singing an old ballad her own mother had sung long ago. The episode of the tree had almost faded from her mind for the moment. With Miss Branwell safely in her room and the children tucked in bed she'd risk asking the master if she and Nancy could have a drop of ale before they too went to bed.

She came through the flagged passage, set down the wood, ignored by Nancy who sat dreaming of other things, went through into the hallway and frowned at the partly open cellar door. Someone could fall down those steps in the dark. Curious, she pulled the door wider and went carefully down the steps, holding the lantern high and letting its red light play about the walls.

An angel was coming to take her to heaven, Emily thought. She struggled to her feet, feeling the cramp strike and cripple her bare toes, feeling all the guilt mounting up into her head. Her shriek echoed and re-echoed through the cellar.

'Miss Emily! What in God's Name art tha doing down here?' Sarah cried, rushing forward.

Emily's blue eyes were raised to show the whites beneath, a

line of spittle drooled from the corner of her mouth.

'Master! Master, come quick! Miss Emily's had a fit,' Sarah began.

The blue eyes lowered and Emily stood up, wiping her mouth on her long cambric sleeve. She looked deadly white but otherwise herself again.

Sarah was too young and inexperienced to realize that the child she picked up, exclaiming, 'Eeh, lass, tha's been sleep-walking!' – that that child was in some hidden part of her self changed.

'I'm perfectly all right,' Emily said, sliding neatly on to her feet again. 'I shall go to bed now. Good night, Sarah.'

Part of what remained of the Emily who had come down into the cellar longed for Sarah to pick her up and make a fuss of her again.

'Are tha sure, Miss Emily?' Sarah picked up her lamp. 'Best get to bed now, theer's a bonny lass.'

'Good night, Sarah.' Emily walked stiffly across the stone floor and up the steps.

She was a funny lass, Sarah pondered. The prettiest of the girls and the strongest but with something about her that was . . . funny somehow. She watched the white figure mount the steps without turning and then followed. She'd not mention this to the master, but she'd ask for the drop of ale.

Three

'Reads very prettily and works a little'
Cowan Bridge Register

It had been a very long journey, exciting at first because she had been riding in a public coach which bounced up and down at the rough bits in the road. It was warm inside the vehicle but when they stopped to water the horses and Emily was lifted down she felt the freezing December wind on her face.

Maria and Elizabeth had been taken to Cowan Bridge School by Papa five months before, looking important in their brown holland frocks and purple cloaks. Everybody had waved them off as the gig which would take them to the coaching station rattled down the steep main street.

Papa had stayed overnight and returned looking satisfied.

'The building is low-lying but very prettily situated near to the river,' he informed the other children. 'The Reverend Carus Wilson is a handsome, well-spoken man in his mid thirties – old enough to have a responsible head on his shoulders but young enough to recognize the importance of giving females a decent education. I am paying extra to provide dear Maria with instruction in French and drawing. I believe they will quickly see the excellence of her intellect.'

'Will Ellis have French too?' Emily wanted to know.

'Elizabeth has not Maria's gifts,' Papa said. 'One of you will be needed to act as housekeeper here when your aunt wishes to return to Cornwall. Elizabeth will succeed her.'

So there wasn't going to be a new mama after all despite all the whispers about Isabella Dury. It seemed that nobody was willing to marry Papa.

A month later Papa had returned to Cowan Bridge taking Charlotte with him.

'Maria and Elizabeth were waiting to greet her,' he said on his return. 'Now we must wait a little before your turn comes.'

It had seemed odd with half of them vanished, but it at least meant, that, with Branwell spending an increasing amount of time with Papa, she and Anne had Sarah's undivided attention and spent long hours playing on the moors, each day walking further until they could climb up past the Heaton reservoir towards Crow Bog which was wild and lonely and just below the great rock of Ponden Kirk.

They had set out one day though the air was close and still and Sarah, looking up apprehensively, had prophesied rain. 'With a bit of thunder too,' she added.

Timid Anne clung more tightly to the servant's hand but Emily laughed and ran on ahead. She loved storms and regretted it when Aunt insisted on closing the shutters and covering up the mirrors and putting the cutlery away in the drawers. Now as she skipped ahead she glanced up the long slope of the land towards Crow Bog and hoped they could reach the brow of the hill in time to see the white fire flash above the fading heather.

Instead of the expected rumble of thunder there was a silence. Sarah had paused nervously, instinctively drawing Anne closer. Emily, poised on a flat stone ahead of them, stopped too, scarcely breathing. In that moment she felt as if everything both inside and outside her had ceased to be. And then the rending crash tore up trees and boulders which hurtled down the slope, gouging great gobs of earth out as they thundered down.

Rain, torrents of it, poured down making a quagmire for their feet and the wind, having lain in weighty silence along the clouds, swooped down, bending bushes to the ground, turning a nearby stream into a bubbling cauldron.

Sarah had managed to grab Emily and, bent double with the force of the wind, was trying to shelter both her and Anne under her cloak.

Overhead forked lightning struck white fingers into the horizon. Sarah was sobbing aloud though only her face betrayed the fact for the elements stole the sound she was making and shared it out among the crashing of rocks and trees.

Emily tried to twist out of Sarah's restraining grasp, to run back up the hill, clawing at the gouged earth to reach the top and stand there defying the whole world, becoming one with the storm.

Other figures had appeared, blurred by the driving rain. Someone seized Emily and threw her across his shoulder and ran with her. Others were helping Sarah and Anne along. Then the crashing was over and thunder was growling along the inch-cape grasses.

They huddled in the porch of a stone farmhouse, obviously unoccupied since its windows were boarded up, and planks were nailed across the inner door.

The man who had seized Emily set her down and said breathlessly, 'Lucky for thee we were out on't moors doing a bit of shooting! Ye'll be t'parson's childer.'

'Yes, sir, Mr Heaton,' Sarah was stammering.

'Aye weel, t'worst's ower now. A landslide I'd call it. Happen tha were frightened, sweetheart?'

She vaguely recognized him now. Mr Robert Heaton of Ponden House was one of the most important gentlemen in the district, not wealthy according to rich peoples' standards since he'd made some foolish investments and trusted the wrong folk, Papa said, but still a landowner and a millowner who spoke, Papa said, fluent French and Italian but spoke the local dialect to remind himself not to be proud.

'No, I wasn't frightened,' Emily said truthfully.

'Reckon tha's got t'speerit of a lad,' Mr Heaton said.

The rain and the thunder and the lightning were retreating as unexpectedly as they had arrived, leaving a devastated landscape.

Sarah was cuddling Anne who was hiccoughing, her fair hair plastered to her head. Emily stood very straight, excited colour still in her cheeks, her dark hair curling wildly about her face and gravely offered her hand.

'Thank you. We shall be quite safe now,' she said with dignity.

'Happen tha will!' His teeth were white and sharp in his brown face. 'Get along now. Tell Mr Brontë I'll be at Trustees Meeting on Sunday! Little un'll catch her death.'

He meant Anne who was shivering violently with her teeth chattering. To Emily he gave a pat on the shoulder and an approving nod as if she really was a lad. Glowing she hurried home to be met by an agitated father who sounded more Irish than usual as he assured them he'd been convinced so he had that they'd all been killed and he would preach a sermon on the earth tremor the very next Sunday so he would.

She was remembering that now as the coach rolled on through the twilight of a bitter December day.

'I shall take you to Leeds to catch the coach from there and continue my own journey,' he had told Emily. 'You will be safe in the charge of the guard. Be a good child at school and work hard.'

Papa was going to Ireland to settle his mother's affairs though it was fully two years since she had died. When Emily thought of the grandmother none of them had ever seen she saw not an old lady but a tall slender golden haired girl, Eilis McClory, who had married Hugh Prunty against the wishes of her family.

The coach had stopped and Emily was lifted out past a lady with a big shopping basket at her feet and a man who reeked of cigar smoke, her trunk lifted down after her. The coachman rang the bell at a door in a high wall and the door opened.

'The little girl from Haworth, ma'am.'

'Ah yes. Thank you, coachman. Emily Jane, is it not? Come along in, child. I will help you carry your luggage.'

The door was closed behind them. At the other side of the wall she heard the retreating wheels of the carriage.

'I am Miss Evans, the Superintendant of the Clergy Daughters' School,' the lady said, taking her hand as they started up a flagged path to a range of low buildings. 'First you shall have a cup of coffee and a slice of cake and then we will test you on your reading and your sewing. Your sisters will be eager to see you after that. They are at lessons now.'

Emily felt a start of surprise. It was already evening. They had lessons very late here, she thought.

'Come along, child! We don't dawdle here!' said another sharper voice belonging to a shorter lady with her hair in spiky corkscrew ringlets. 'Miss Andrews is my Deputy with direct responsibility for the girls here,' Miss Evans said. 'Perhaps you would see to Emily's trunk, Miss Andrews?'

'Certainly, Miss Evans.'

The tones were refined and polite but Emily sensed the two

ladies didn't like each other. Her trunk was whisked away and she trotted in the taller lady's wake up stone stairs into a small carpeted parlour with a fire in the grate and two lamps burning.

'The coffee is almost brewed.' Miss Evans was untying her bonnet strings and her purple cloak. 'Sit by the fire and eat this slice of cake.'

The cake was full of raisins. Emily wished she wasn't so tired then she could enjoy it more but she chewed her way through it manfully, drank the half cup of weak milky coffee bestowed upon her and felt more lively.

'Now we must take some details for the register.' Miss Evans drew a large ledger towards her and sat down at the other end of a long table. She gestured with a long pale hand and Emily went obediently to stand at the other end of the table. 'I have some details already.' Miss Evans read aloud. ' "Emily Jane Brontë aged five and three quarters." '

That wasn't true, Emily thought. She was almost six and a half. Someone had made a mistake. She opened her mouth but Miss Evans was continuing.

'I see you have been vaccinated against smallpox and have had measles, scarlet fever and whooping cough. Now sit down, my dear, and see if you can hem this square of cambric.'

She moved the lamp nearer. Emily, perched on the chair, made a few small stitches and was overtaken by a yawn.

'Let me see. Yes, well, we shall record that you can work a little,' Miss Evans said kindly, taking the cambric away. 'Now take a moment or two to look at the book on the table before you and then read the first page aloud to me.'

The book had a picture of a little girl in bed on its cover. It looked rather dull, Emily considered, and the first page of the story was duller still, all about a child named Jane who ate and ate and finally died of it and went straight to Hell. The only way to get through it without yawning again was to act it out. Emily proceeded to do so, puffing out her cheeks and giving the greedy heroine a voice that sounded like someone speaking with her mouth stuffed full.

'Very pretty,' Miss Evans said in a curiously shaky voice when the reading was done. 'You will wish to see your sisters now. Come with me.'

Emily followed her down the stairs and along a passage set at right angles to the hall which ended in a long room with trestle tables set down one side and what seemed to Emily like a great many girls seated on benches down both sides. Three of them stood up.

For a moment she stared at them uncertainly in the dim light and then they left their places and rushed to greet her, Charlotte doing most of the talking as usual.

'Did you have a good journey? How is Papa? And Sarah and Nancy and Anne and Aunt?'

The one called Miss Andrews rapped with a wooden spoon.

'That is sufficient. We must endeavour to suppress our natural instincts that they be rendered subordinate to the service of the Lord,' she said in her sharp clear voice. 'Emily Jane, come with me. You are to share a bed with your sister Charlotte. You will be tired after your journey and may retire early this evening.'

There was no sign of nice Miss Evans. Emily followed Miss Andrews up more stairs and along a dingy corridor to a long raftered chamber with beds ranged sedately along one long wall and a row of washstands along the other.

'Your hair is too long. Stand still!'

The teacher unclipped a pair of scissors from her belt and proceeded to clip off Emily's mass of curls as close to the roots as possible. All the other children, Emily realized, had had their hair clipped close, even her sisters. It made their noses look bigger.

'Undress – no, not like that!' Miss Andrews yanked at her impatiently. 'You must put on your nightgown and slip off your garments underneath. In that way we avoid looking at our sinful bodies which will be in due course carrion for the worms.'

Bewildered, Emily struggled to obey.

'Your prayers! Surely you kneel and pray before you lie down,' Emily was suddenly being shouted at so loudly that she jumped.

'We have prayers all together with Papa,' she said shiveringly.

'Your papa is not here. Kneel and pray – silently if you please. It is good practice to imitate the virtue of silence. Then get into bed. Good night, Emily Jane.'

Miss Andrews went out. Emily, kneeling on the hard boards, put her hands together and prayed silently that the worms would come and eat up Miss Andrews while she was still alive, and then scrambled on to the lumpy mattress, trying to snuggle down under the thin, darned, inadequate blankets.

She was still awake when the others came to bed. In the flickering light from the two candles in their sconces against the wall they looked like grey ghosts, undressing under their nightgowns, kneeling to pray silently. When Charlotte finally got in beside her her sister's feet were so icy that Emily gave a yelp.

'Hush!' Charlotte whispered. 'We are forbidden to speak. What is it?'

'I need to go,' Emily whispered back.

'There's a pot in the cupboard at the end of the room.'

'One pot for everybody?' Emily said, horrified.

'Six for all the pupils. Hurry and use it!'

By the time she had used it and crept back into bed Charlotte was asleep. From another bed came the sound of a hacking cough, quickly stifled.

A loyal affection kept her silent when Charlotte, waking in the first hour before dawn, prodded her awake, whispering, 'Emily, do we look peculiar with our hair cut off?'

Emily shook her own cropped head as a bell clanged and in unison the pupils pushed back the bedclothes and went to the washbasins.

'The water's frozen again!' someone exclaimed.

'I'll break it for you!' A big, rough looking girl was coming along the line with a wooden mallet.

Emily dabbed her face and hands and wished her teeth would stop chattering.

She pulled on her clothes and looked round for Maria and Elizabeth. Elizabeth was putting on her shoes but Maria was still lying on the bed with a small group of girls hovering anxiously.

'I feel so bad,' she said, giving the hacking cough that Emily recognized from the previous night.

She looked bad too, Emily thought with a little clutch of fear as she drew nearer. Her face looked like Mama's on the day she had died and her eyes were sunken.

'Maria has begun to bleed,' Charlotte whispered. 'All girls bleed every month when they begin to grow up.'

But Maria was not yet twelve. She wasn't grown up yet. Emily began dimly to understand certain mysterious remarks exchanged between Nancy and Sarah, a bucket of bloody cloths she had once noticed in the shed before Nancy whisked it out of sight.

'You stay there,' the big, rough girl said. 'I'll get Miss Evans and tell her you're not fit!'

'No, you must go first to Miss Andrews,' another girl said.

'I shall get up,' Maria said, stifling another cough. She reached for her stockings and began slowly to draw them on.

Miss Andrews came in – whirled in would have described it better as apparently taking in the situation at a glance she swept to the bed, the girls scattering before her, and seizing Maria by her arm threw her bodily off the bed on to the floor.

'Idle slattern! Lazy, good for nothing miserable little wretch! Displaying your legs for the world to see! Get dressed. Girls, form lines! Now!!'

The girls shuffled into place and went two by two down the stairs and along another passage into what was clearly a large classroom, with stools set round a series of small tables and two blackboards on the walls.

Miss Evans stood on a rostrum, a book in her hand.

Miss Andrews muttered a word and received a frown in return.

'You are certain? She has not looked well for some time,' said Miss Evans.

'I am quite certain,' Miss Andrews answered.

'Very well. Let us begin.' Miss Evans sounded weary.

Emily, squashed between Charlotte and another girl in the front row, shifted her eyes to the door. Maria was coming in, grey as the light that filtered through the high windows, her head drooping.

'Maria Brontë, you are late for prayers!' Miss Andrews took advantage of a pause in the reading to address the latecomer. 'Fetch the birch and undo your pinafore.'

One of the bigger girls hissed. Miss Evans compressed her lips and said nothing. Maria took down a bundle of twigs from the wall, undid the neck of her pinafore and bent her head.

'For laziness, for untidiness, for daydreaming!' Each fault was accompanied by a stinging blow. Emily watched, a curious kind of excitement mingling with her terror. She felt angry and pitying and queerly stirred all at the same time.

Maria, a thin trickle of blood showing at her neckline, went meekly and silently to a vacant space.

So this was school. Emily pushed away the small helping of burnt porridge in her bowl only to see one of the other pupils snatch it and devour it.

Prayers and readings had lasted for two hours, breakfast had taken less than ten minutes. Lessons followed, the girls divided out among the tables, with the bigger ones sewing sheets and pillowcases and the little ones chanting their tables.

Emily was relieved to find herself with Charlotte in the group taught by Miss Evans while Maria and Elizabeth sat under Miss Andrews's eye.

At midday a bell rang again and they marched into the long dining-room where bowls of stew were being ladled out.

'Don't eat it,' Charlotte whispered. 'The meat is left over from two days ago.'

It smelt like it, Emily thought, wrinkling her nose up while her small stomach heaved.

The milk pudding was marginally better though the milk had been mixed with water and there were bits floating in it. After the meal, as before it, there was a long grace and then they put on their cloaks and went out into the enclosed garden where a covered walk provided some shelter from the wind that blew flurries of snow over the regimented vegetable plots.

'I shall tell Papa,' Emily said to Charlotte as they tramped up and down. 'He can't know how bad it is!'

'They read our letters before they are posted,' Charlotte whispered back.

'Then we shall tell him when we go home for Christmas.'

'We are not going home until next summer,' Charlotte said. 'Papa cannot afford the long journeys by coach.'

'Stop talking, girls!' The hated, metallic voice cut into their whispers. 'You do not speak here unless you are spoken to and then you answer very quietly with your eyes upon the ground. Custody of the eyes and tongue, girls, remember and reflect!'

If she wasn't allowed to talk or look around her, Emily pondered, then she could live inside herself until it was summertime and they could tell Papa what a dreadful place this was. He wouldn't send them back here, she was sure of that.

The days melted into a succession of endless hours, distin-

51

guished only by the clanging of the bell. Maria drooped and sickened and coughed night after night, leaving a dull reddish stain on the blanket she pulled up to stifle the sounds that kept her fellow boarders awake. Elizabeth went docilely in the wake of the others with a blank unseeing look in her too wide eyes, Charlotte pushed away the uneatable food and cried silently at night from the hunger pains in her stomach.

Emily survived, locked up in her silent self, forcing down the food her sisters couldn't eat. Within herself, now and then, she sensed another self, strong and bold and fierce. For the moment she kept this inner self concealed, masked by a face that was still pretty despite the cropped hair. Miss Evans often took her up into her own sitting room to give her a piece of cake or an apple. Even Miss Andrews sent her an occasional smile frosty with disuse.

The Reverend Carus Wilson came to harangue the pupils and staff about the evils of greed and pride and vanity, his handsome features and smart greatcoat a kind of mockery as he surveyed the rows of cowed children ranged before him. When he came Miss Andrews cut Emily's hair even shorter and placed her in the back row. For some reason she and Miss Evans were agreed on that.

The ice was dripping from the eaves and Maria was being bundled up in shawls and carried down the path to the door in the wall. Papa had been advised that his eldest daughter was ill, too ill for the school authorities to take responsibility for her any longer.

'Papa will come in and see us and we can tell him about the food and the cold,' Charlotte whispered to Emily.

They stood at the window and Maria waved to them as she was carried out of sight but Papa never came in or asked to see them. His mind was set on his beloved Maria.

'She will tell him how it is here and he will come and get us,' Charlotte comforted.

But the weeks went by and evidently Maria said nothing because Papa never came. The spring came and with it a low fever that struck most of the girls who sat about with their heads lolling and scratched at rashes that disfigured their skin, moaning that their heads were burning while Miss Andrews went round wielding her birch twigs to no effect. Miss Evans decreed that lessons be suspended for a time and the girls be allowed to play in the woods that ran along the river. Emily liked the woods where she could hide herself among the long grasses that grew up around the leafy trunks. Charlotte liked the river and often stood for an hour at a time on a large flat stone near the burn where the current divided into two broad ribbons of water. Elizabeth was not with them. She had been hurt.

'An unfortunate accident,' said Miss Andrews.

'Quite a severe wound to her head. I shall allow her to sleep in my room,' said Miss Evans with a look that dared her deputy to argue.

A doctor had been called and went round poking into the cupboards and using words like 'disgraceful'. Perhaps he would tell all the fathers, Emily thought hopefully, and they would all turn up in a body and take their daughters away.

Then the three of them were summoned to the office where the Reverend Carus Wilson came to inspect the accounts. He was there, with Miss Evans and Miss Andrews flanking him.

'Children, it is my solemn duty to inform you that your beloved sister, Maria, has been taken into a higher sphere,' Mr Wilson said. 'On earth she had faults – a tendency to daydream, untidiness, lack of serious application to her tasks, but I am assured by your papa that after three months suffering during which she exhibited traces of a heart beneath Divine influence she passed away peacefully. Strive to follow her example, my dear children, that when the Grim Reaper calls you may not be found wanting.'

Charlotte had begun to cry softly; Elizabeth stared dully as she did these days for most of the time, the wound on her head still plastered.

'I won't cry,' Emily thought. 'I won't cry. I won't cry.'

The truth was there were no tears inside her, only an aching hole. She had loved Maria but there had been many times when she had wished that her sister wasn't quite so good and patient. It was almost as if Maria had enjoyed being ill and unhappy. Even to think that was wicked. Maria was dead and lying now with Mama under the floor of the church behind the cellar wall; two sets of fingers tapping.

Then a few days later, or maybe it was the next day, Elizabeth began to cough weakly, gobbets of blood spurting out of her mouth on to her pinafore. Some of the bigger girls ran to find Miss Evans and within an hour one of the school servants who was a big, brawny woman was carrying Elizabeth down the path and through the door in the wall to the waiting coach.

'Do wave!' Emily pleaded under her breath.

But Elizabeth, her dear kind Ellis, didn't wave. Charlotte turned away from the window, her face ugly and swollen with tears as the door opened and Mr Wilson came in.

'Your sister has been taken home,' he said. 'I have decided that you and your sister would benefit from a few days quiet in my own house at Silverside near the sea. Come with me now.'

He addressed his remarks to Charlotte but his eyes slid to where Emily stood, the curl springing into her hair again.

Another coach ride. A big white house with carpets and curtains and sparkling chandeliers. Like a palace, Emily thought. A lady gave them toast and stewed fruit for their supper and then Mr Wilson came in, very tall and broad.

'Charlotte may go to bed,' he pronounced in his grandest manner. 'Emily may come with me. I have advice to impart to her.'

It was like going down into the cellar again though she couldn't have told why. She trailed after him along the corridor and up the carpeted stairs to the big bedroom revealed when he opened a door, with the huge curtained bed and the lamps glowing all round.

'Shut the door, my dear,' Mr Wilson said. 'I have a secret to share.'

Slowly the child Emily Jane closed the door and hid in a far corner of her own mind as Mr Wilson beckoned.

The next morning Papa came, having driven all night after seeing the state Elizabeth was in. He and Mr Wilson were briefly closeted together, and then Papa came out, shaking hands, and Charlotte and Emily were hustled into the waiting coach.

Papa was talking of Maria, of her patience under affliction, her clever mind. Emily yearned towards Elizabeth who would surely get better when she saw her sisters. Nancy and Sarah would see that she got better.

The horses strained up the steep main street, turned into the narrow lane. There was still blossom on the tree that grew below Papa's window. Emily was out of the stage and running round to the back of the house. The back kitchen door stood open and she darted through it, down the flagged passage into the warm, familiar kitchen.

An elderly woman was stirring something over the fire. Emily stopped dead, staring at her.

'Where's Sarah?' she demanded. 'Where's Nancy?'

'Nancy left to get wed and Sarah went wi' her,' the woman said.

'Are they dead?'

'Nay, child. They'm not dead! What iver put that in thy heed?' the woman said.

Emily stared at her, speechless. This was her fault. She'd made Sarah tell a lie and now Sarah had been sent away.

'You'm Emily Jane I'll be bound.' The woman wiped her hands on her apron, looked at her. 'My name's Tabitha Aykroyd. I'm come to keep house for thy feyther. Tha may call me Tabby.'

She didn't want to call her anything. Backing slowly, Emily turned and ran up the stairs past Aunt Branwell who was opening the front door for Papa and Charlotte.

In the tiny study room Branwell, who hadn't grown an inch though his hair was redder than ever, was drawing on the wall with a thick pencil and a tiny creature in a black frock was perched on a stool.

'Annie? Branny? Where's Sarah? Where's Nancy? Where's Ellis?' Emily wanted to know.

'In Aunt's room,' Branwell said. 'Is Charlotte come?'

'She's downstairs with Papa,' Emily began.

Branwell threw down the pencil and dashed past her.

Emily went across the landing and pushed open the door. The room smelt funny, sickly sweet. Elizabeth was propped up in the big bed with a camp bed at the side where presumably Aunt Branwell spent her nights. Ellis looked as if she was wearing the mask again save that the blackness was now only about the eyes and her mouth was a thin, bloodless slash in the midst of protruding bones. She turned her head slightly, showing the half-healed gash on her head and made a terrible grimace that was supposed to be a smile.

Ellis was only ten. She was too young to die and not yet as good as Maria. She'd had a habit of sulking when anything displeased her, pushing out her underlip, her eyes downcast.

'Come away, child!' Aunt Branwell had pattered up the stairs in her wooden-soled shoes that kept the damp from her feet. 'Elizabeth is very weak. We must all pray.'

But praying wasn't any good. Within the fortnight Emily stood at the foot of the big bed and watched the creature of bones and sunken flesh breathe more and more slowly and leave silence behind.

'Her passing was less painful than Maria's,' Papa said, leaning to close the vacant blue eyes. 'Maria would have made a great name for herself had she been spared but Elizabeth would have become a useful member of society I believe. Children, you may go to your beds.'

They went without a word. Only when they were snuggled together did Charlotte whisper,

'We cannot tell Papa how dreadful it was at Cowan Bridge. He would never forgive himself. Promise you'll not tell.'

'I promise,' Emily said.

Her feet were cold and her hands were icy. At that moment she felt as if everyone was vanishing around her. Soon only she would remain.

Standing in the church, watching the narrow coffin being lowered below the church floor, Emily felt as if the clock had run backwards and she was a tiny thing watching them lower Mama into the crypt. There were three of them down there now, waiting beyond the wall. She felt herself begin to tremble violently and in the same instant felt her icy hand taken in a comforting clasp. The woman called Tabby neither looked at her nor spoke but her hand was like a rock in a drowning sea.

'The school reopens next week,' Papa said. 'I'm assured that the cook who provided such badly cooked and inadequate meals has been dismissed and since I paid in advance we cannot waste the money laid out for your continued education. You will feel more cheerful when you are with your schoolfellows again, eh?'

Charlotte made some indeterminate noise which he took for assent. Emily stood motionless, her eyes downcast. If she spoke she would break her promise – not only to Charlotte either.

'This is our secret,' he had said. 'Part of your education, pretty Emily. Our secret.'

Had Maria or Elizabeth had secrets too? Other secrets?

Emily stood stiffly, retreating to a far corner of her mind. Inside her a bewildered child was sobbing but it made no sound upon the air.

Four

O God of heaven! the dream of horror
The frightful dream is over now.
The sickened heart the blasting sorrow
The ghastly night the ghastlier morrow
The aching sense of utter woe.

Emily Jane Brontë

The school experiment had been a failure. Patrick Brontë, seated in his parlour, acknowledged that with regret. He couldn't blame the Reverend Carus Wilson whose motives had been of the highest, but the establishment had been poorly funded and badly run, and a clergyman with so many calls on his time could hardly be expected to poke about in the kitchens and check the bed linen. Other pupils had sickened and died at the school and others been removed by parents or guardians. Out of seventy pupils fifteen had died, most of typhus fever. His own dear daughters would, he consoled himself, probably have died young anyway. Both had inherited the delicate Branwell constitution. But neither Charlotte nor Emily had fared well at all after their return to Cowan Bridge. They had grown thinner and paler and within a month, after a brief visit and a consultation with an anxious Aunt Branwell, he had removed them. By the end of July, just before Emily's seventh birthday, she and Charlotte were at home again.

Now he considered his four remaining children. Branwell came first into his mind. The boy was almost nine now, short and wiry with a mop of curly auburn hair and a bright, handsome face. Friends had suggested that he might profit from a few years at school but the standards at the local grammar school were not high and it was out of the question to send him to boarding-school. Branwell's occasional spells of what appeared

59

to be almost unbearable excitement which culminated in either hysterical tears or a kind of fainting fit were not subjects for public discussion. He would almost certainly grow out of them but meanwhile it was wiser to keep him at home. And besides, instructing his son was a pleasure rather than a burden. The boy had taken to Latin and Greek like a duck to water. He was passionately interested in literature and history and politics; he constantly sketched and painted and he had a leaning towards music, already playing quite creditably upon the flute. The problem was not to find something that might be developed into a career but to decide which talent would lead to one.

Charlotte was ten but still very tiny, with a head that seemed too large for her body. And distressingly plain, with her big nose and crooked mouth. Her eyes were large and beautiful but they were shortsighted like his own and though she had a sweet voice her deportment, despite Aunt Branwell's efforts, was clumsy. Charlotte, he thought, was unlikely to marry. So since his own modest income and their tenancy of the parsonage would cease upon his death he expected that she must eventually go out as a governess. Anne too would very likely take the same path though she was prettier with eyes of so dark a blue they looked violet in certain lights, and long dark blonde ringlets. Perhaps Anne would marry. He frowned, not much liking the notion of entrusting her to the governance of another. In any case since the deaths of her older sisters she had developed very worrying attacks of asthma which left her weak and breathless and she had a slight stutter which he trusted would vanish as she grew older.

He had avoided considering Emily until the end. She had grown taller than her siblings since her return from school and she was healthy, though there were occasional nights when, blank-eyed, she would open her mouth and give out a strange howling sound and struggle frantically against some horror she never remembered when awake. Highly strung, he decided. And not as clever as her sisters, alas! She could read well enough but her writing was appalling with letters formed backwards and spelling mistakes littering the page. Her aunt declared that her sewing left much to be desired. She was happiest, he suspected, when she was released from needlework to go out and play on the moors.

Emily could possibly replace poor Elizabeth as housekeeper when Aunt Branwell finally returned to Cornwall. He had hoped to marry again, but ladies were becoming fussy these days, unwilling to take on a widower with a ready-made family and a low income. He had even tried to renew his old romance with his former sweetheart, Mary Burder, but she had rejected him in such stinging terms that it had quite put him off trying a spot of courtship in any other direction.

He rose and went over to the table to look again at the presents he had bought during a two day trip to Leeds to attend a clerical conference.

He had intended to buy a gift for Branwell's birthday and had fixed his choice on a box of brightly painted wooden soldiers. Branwell was keenly interested in military matters and playing with soldiers might lead to a military career, provided he shot up in height during his teens. Boys often did. The toyshop had yielded other temptations. Before he knew it he had splashed out his money on a set of ninepins for Charlotte, a toy village with little animals and people to be fitted into slots for Emily, and a doll with a red frock and a straw hat on for Anne.

Emily, roused in the morning by Branwell's bursting in, sat up blinking.

'Papa has bought me a whole box of soldiers!' her brother was crying. 'Twelve of them and all different! You may have one each for your own.'

Charlotte was already out of bed, seizing one of the figures as she declaimed in her irritatingly important way, 'This is the tallest and the most perfect in every part. This is mine and he shall be the Duke of Wellington!'

'Then my chief soldier shall be Bonaparte and I shall call him Boney!' Branwell had snatched up another.

'You choose, Emily!' Charlotte urged.

Emily got out of bed and chose one with a long face and large tricorne hat painted on the top of his head.

'He's a gloomy looking fellow!' Branwell said. 'Best call him Gravey!'

'Only when he's on duty,' Emily said. 'At home his name is Clown!'

Anne, released from her night's incarceration with Aunt

Branwell, came in, and chose a small soldier which was promptly christened Waiting Boy.

Later on they would be renamed according to the whim of the moment and the other eight also given names. Gravey alias Clown would end up as Parry whose explorations in the Arctic regions were being eagerly followed by all of them.

The other gifts were downstairs, Anne's doll being named as Heroine to be kidnapped and rescued over and over, the ninepins which were shiny and black being pressed into service as Ashantee warriors to be conquered by the Twelve, and the toy village providing both a city to be invaded and an army camp.

Emily already had a toy of her own, a humming top and whip. It was one of her most treasured possessions, to be lent only seldom. On the rare occasions she was alone she took out the top and whipped it so severely that it spun round madly and fell dead, satisfying something inside herself which was raw and angry though she didn't know why.

Life had become a pleasant routine, a safe and orderly sequence of events. They rose at seven, breakfasted in the dining-room with Papa who was fond of telling them ghost stories during the meal. They were all intensely interested in ghosts and ghouls and macabre hauntings and Papa told the stories so well that the events he described seemed almost to be taking place before their eyes. He told them about his old home in Ireland and the pranks his brothers had played, creeping about the village to wail and moan with lighted turnip heads held on sticks to peer through the windows and terrify the neighbours. But too soon he called Branwell into the parlour for his lessons and the girls went reluctantly to their aunt's bedroom for the long morning of sewing and reading aloud and set questions on history and geography. Emily was making a sampler as all little girls must do in order to demonstrate the variety of stitches they knew. Maria and Elizabeth had made samplers too and much good it had done them!

By midday Papa was off on his parish rounds and Aunt Branwell, having received her own meal nicely set on a tray, closed her door with relief, leaving the children free to eat their dinner in the dining-room and give Tabby a hand with the washing up and general tidying. Branwell being male was, of course, excused household tasks but the others must learn how to keep a house neat and clean. Anne was too little to do much and poor Charlotte so shortsighted that she constantly dropped and broke things, but Emily enjoyed the rhythms of sweeping and dusting.

Then they were free! When it wasn't raining or snowing they went out for a walk with Tabby. Walk didn't really describe it because Tabby was the only one who actually walked while her charges ran, jumped, skipped and rolled down the grassy slopes, acting out the stories their father had told them and the exciting events in history that they read about in their books. When the play got too noisy Tabby would call them to order sometimes but usually she was far behind, giving her legs a bit of a rest, because they were near sixty years old and needed it while Anne, who found it hard to keep up with the others sat by her making daisy-chains.

Then it was home for tea with Aunt still in her room and Papa eating his in his parlour.

'Chattering upsets my digestion, my dear,' he had warned his dearest Maria years before. 'I must eat at least one meal a day in peace and quiet. It is not too much to ask, I hope?'

After tea Aunt came down and read the newspaper to him since his eyes were becoming uncomfortably strained and then the children were called upon to recite what they had learned that day – in Emily's and Anne's case little enough, but it didn't matter because Charlotte and Branwell were the ones who competed fiercely.

After that there was an hour before bed when they could either huddle round a candle in the little study before the bunk bed was put up for Charlotte and Emily, or they could sit by the fire with Tabby who had lived in the district all her life and knew every skeleton in all the cupboards.

'Tek t'Heatons now! Long since a man named Casson wed a Heaton widow and cheated t'heir out of his reetful inheritance. Then one day Casson went missing and were niver seen again. They do say his ghost stalks t'moor on winter nights.'

'Papa's own father, Hugh, was kidnapped by a wicked uncle and his land taken away,' Branwell said excitedly.

'An adopted uncle, taken into the family by my grandfather out of the kindness of his heart,' Papa had told them. 'He proved a cuckoo in the nest, my dears, for he treated my father like a farmhand until he ran away from him and wed my mother.'

'What happened to the bad uncle?' Emily had asked.

'Welsh? I daresay he came to a bad end. My father never regained his farm.'

So everywhere there were strangers waiting to steal land and kidnap people. Emily thought that the evil Casson and the wicked Welsh sounded exciting.

The wooden soldiers had all acquired names and personalities by this time. *En masse* they were the Young Men who had many adventures as they journeyed to the coasts of Africa, braving storms and mutinies and shipwrecks along the way, only to be forced to conquer the savage black tribes before they could found their colony which, at first called Glasstown would later be known more grandly as Verdopolis.

Moving the little figures about over the floor, inventing for them a high-flown way of speaking in which Charlotte and Branwell excelled in using the longest words, killing them off and then making them alive again with a magnificent incantation, kept them happily occupied for hours. When they grew bored with one game another was speedily invented.

One such was the Islanders, invented on a cold December evening when they sat round the fire with Tabby, who sat as she always did at the end of the day knitting the stockings they seemed to grow out of so quickly.

'I'm bored, Tabby!' Branwell said restlessly, fidgeting on his stool.

'Then go to bed,' was Tabby's uncompromising answer as she neatly turned a heel.

'It's so dark!' Charlotte, who generally echoed Branwell, grimaced. 'Can we light a candle?'

'Nowt wrong wi'firelight,' Tabby said firmly.

'I wish we were very rich and owned an island each,' Branwell said.

His remark lit the spark, all that was needed to set them to arguing fiercely as they chose their islands and peopled them.

'The Isle of Arran,' Emily said dreamily.

Arran was wild and lonely, she knew, and part of Scotland. Aunt Branwell, who always gave the children a book at Christmas-time, had given them *Tales of a Grandfather* the previous Christmas. Emily, who had never met a grandfather of her own, thought that it would be delightful to have one like Sir

Walter Scott who wove exciting stories much as Papa did, and promptly stuck him on her imagined island possession, giving him his son-in-law and grandson for company! No other women, since she herself intended to be the only female around.

That Christmas Aunt Branwell presented them with the *Arabian Nights*, and within a few days of reading it the children had elected themselves as Genii, with Branwell latinizing their names.

Chief Genius Emmii sounded rather splendid, Emily thought, picking up her soldier Parry and staring at him. The game of the Young Men and even the Islanders were beginning to lose their appeal since they were all rather weary of constantly fighting native tribes, not to mention the fact that the ninepins were getting a bit knocked about with the black paint peeling off, and a game called Our Fellows which had replaced it was losing its novelty value. But to have the power of life and death and of bringing to life again was a heady prospect.

'We shall divide the kingdom of Verdopolis between the four Genii!' Thus Branwell, taking up more space than his small frame warranted as he lay on the floor, kicking his legs wildly in the air, his red hair tousled. 'We shall be the four rulers of the firmament! We shall be ten miles high.'

'Not even genii are ten miles high,' Emily objected.

'They can be any height they choose to be since they are omnipotent,' Charlotte said loftily, siding as usual with Branwell. 'You want to be ten miles high, don't you, Annie?'

'Yeth,' Anne lisped obligingly.

'I shall be four miles high,' Emily declared.

'You're that already,' mocked Branwell, eyeing her long legs.

Emily, having no answer, punched him and received a shove that sent her flying.

'I am still four miles high,' she said loftily, picking herself up.

From the landing Aunt Branwell, on her way down to the kitchen, coughed warningly. 'Not so noisy, children! Your father is writing his sermon,' she said.

In the parsonage quiet play was the rule since Aunt liked to rest when she had spent the morning trying to get a sufficient amount of sewing out of the girls and a sufficient amount of information into their heads, and Papa, who walked miles across the moors to visit the sick and was constantly chairing meetings of the Church Trustees, and writing long letters to the newspapers on a variety of subjects, needed quiet in order that his delicate digestion should not be upset.

On the moors, with Tabby and Anne lagging behind, it was permissible to be noisy because the wind caught the sounds and carried them away. And on the moors everything changed as the seasons flowed, unlike the small, grey-washed rooms at home where nothing much changed at all. Emily thought with fierce longing of the stunted thorntrees that grew near the old farms of Top and Middle and Lower Withins, of the whinberries that could be gathered in the early autumn and the purple heather that lay in great sweeps and curves across the land for such a short time before it became dry and brown and the first snows came.

Yet there was a charm of its own in being indoors too, with Aunt pitter-pattering about on the uncarpeted floors in her wooden pattens and Tabby rolling out the dough in the kitchen and Papa in the parlour, spectacles on the end of his high-bridged nose as he composed a sermon or made notes in the margins of his medical directory about various cures for the diseases that might attack them all in the parsonage.

'But not me!' Chief Genius Emmii thought.

Genii were immortal. Nobody would ever put them under the church floor, to lie in a narrow box that would crumble and moulder until the gnawing of the worms disturbed their slumber and they rose to tap on the wall that kept them out of the cellar.

'Why don't you go to sleep?' Charlotte whispered the words as Emily stayed sitting up, looking into the darkness.

'I'm not tired.'

She couldn't describe to her sister the horror that came when she slept because she couldn't remember it when she woke up. She only knew that it had to do with the cellars, with a red light shining on a wall, with a bedroom door closing in some large house within sound of the sea.

'I have a new game.' Charlotte tugged Emily down. 'We shall make Maria and Ellis alive again. I shall be Maria and you shall be Ellis. We are now in our teens and will soon be presented at court because Papa has inherited a large amount of money. What kind of dress will you wear, Elizabeth?'

'White and silver,' Emily whispered promptly. 'With very big sleeves.'

'You can borrow Aunt's fan. I shall wear white and gold.'

'And never have to go down into the cellar,' Emily murmured.

In the darkness Charlotte's plain little face creased in bewilderment but she answered soothingly, 'You have the keys to the cellars so you can go into them or not as you choose.'

There were cellars in Verdopolis too, deep under the sparkling palace with its four golden thrones on which the Genii sat. Down in the cellars naughty children were tortured but now that she possessed the key Emily could let them out whenever she chose. She could let out the children and lock up the dark nameless thing that came when she slept.

Charlotte and Branwell were spending a lot of time in writing down the adventures of the Twelve and the other characters that had crept into the ongoing saga. They used tiny print, so minute that no grown up would ever take the trouble to decipher it, and so neat that it looked almost like print, with pieces of paper cut into four inch squares containing as many as five hundred words on one page, the whole stitched neatly together by Charlotte between covers made from the bags in which the loaves of sugar came from the village grocer.

Emily and Anne weren't invited to join in but their elders read aloud the articles and stories and reviews of imagined art exhibitions and books contained in the magazines so dramatically that the younger children felt as if they had actually experienced all the exciting social activities themselves.

'Children, you are invited to a party,' Aunt Branwell told them one day.

'Where?' Charlotte wanted to know.

'To Ponden House.' Aunt spoke with a certain quiet satisfaction, it having long been her wish to see the children mingle more with the 'nice' children in the district.

'To the Heatons?' Branwell spoke eagerly, having a brief acquaintance with the small Heaton boys which consisted mainly of pulling faces at one another when they locked glances in church or Sunday school.

'Their cousins are visiting them from Royd House,' Aunt explained. 'It will be a tea-party with games and a romp. I must make sure that your handkerchiefs are ironed.'

They had often passed Ponden House in their longer walks, and admired its long, low façade parallel with the road and separated from it by a low wall. Papa occasionally visited Mr Robert Heaton who was a Church Trustee and a landowner of some importance.

'Used to be very warm in't pocket but they trusted t'wrong soart!' Tabby told them as they sat round the kitchen fire. 'It were a crying shame what went on t'year afore tha came t'Haworth!'

'Mama died and went to heaven,' Branwell said.

'Aye, poor soul! But I were telling of t'Heatons. Maister Robert Heaton had a sister, Elizabeth. She run off and wed John Bates who come from Bradford and were a bad lot accordingly. He did treat the puir lass that cruel that she upped and ran home and gave birth to a lad. There's them as say t'bairn were made atween 'em afore they wed but I niver tek heed of slanders!'

'Elizabeth is Spanish for Isabella—' Charlotte began.

'No, it's not! It's the other way round,' Branwell said impatiently. 'Elizabeth is the English for Isabella, Charlotte.'

'Well, Maister Heaton's sister were Elizabeth,' Tabby said. 'A good Yorkshire name. But she were that thin – starved and white when she ran back to Ponden House that she didn't last more'n a twelvemonth. She died and her mither took the fever and died too.'

'What happened to the little lad?' Emily asked.

'He's still about the place. Be about nine year old by now. Maister Heaton'd not tuirn off his sister's son. They do say that after dark Mrs Heaton and her daughter walk in t'orchard, weeping and clad in white. They've been seen by church folk.'

Elizabeth was Isabella was Ellis, Emily thought dreamily. Isabella Dury had never become the new mama and Elizabeth Heaton and Elizabeth Brontë had died, the one to walk in an orchard with her mother, the other to tap on the cellar wall with Mama and Maria.

'Look at time!' Tabby was exclaiming. 'Near half past and the lot of thee still chattering! Off to bed!'

Mama might be dead but Maria and Ellis came alive every night as she and Charlotte huddled in the camp bed.

On the day itself Papa, as if to emphasize the importance of the visit, hired the gig to take them the two miles to Ponden House. It was a fine sunny day and they would have preferred to walk but since the gig was expensive to hire and Papa thought to please them with the drive they kept quiet and sat, pretending to be quite grown up and at ease, as the gig bowled over the high moorland path and came down to Ponden House where the tall dark Mr Heaton and his wife waited to invite them in.

The big house might not be much like the sparkling palace inhabited by the Genii but it suited Emily's tastes better. She looked round at the wainscoted hall with the high carved mantelshelf beneath which, despite the heat, a fire blazed and crackled, at the huge dresser which towered against one wall, its open shelves glinting with copper and brass.

Then the magic was spoiled as a crowd of other children streamed in, all laughing and chattering, the girls in pastel frocks with bright ribbons in their curled hair and dainty shoes, the boys in breeches and velvet jackets. The Brontës huddled together, conscious of their dun-coloured, home-made garments and sturdy boots, of Branwell's unfrilled shirt and nankeen trousers.

'We shall play musical chairs. My husband shall provide the music on his flute after which we shall have tea,' Mrs Heaton was announcing.

There was a row of chairs in the middle of the long room and the children were being marshalled into line. Emily looked for guidance from Charlotte but her sister stood stiffly against the wall and Branwell was staring at the floor as the flute shivered its notes into the air and the children began to dance round the chairs, scrambling for them when Mr Heaton took his fingers from the instrument. Every child had a chair except one small girl who was promptly removed from the rest and given a small cake. Then one of the chairs was taken away and the music started again.

'Come along, come along! We can place more chairs,' Mrs Heaton cried genially when the music ceased again and another child was removed with a sugar cake as compensation.

'We ... prefer to watch,' Charlotte said politely, taking the lead.

So they stood watching, longing to march round and scramble for the remaining chairs but too nervous to move.

All the games were like that – not difficult to pick up but noisy with lots of shoving and giggling. They were not in the least like the games of pretend they played when they huddled in the tiny study and moved the wooden figures about. Running and laughing loudly were only for the moors, not for inside where other people might see and hear.

When they were called to the table the number and variety of the dishes bewildered them. At home they ate porridge or bread and butter with a cup of tea for breakfast. Dinner was always potatoes with carrots or turnips and meat when they could afford it with a fruit pie or a milk pudding to follow and at supper they had sandwiches and tiny barm cakes if Tabby had made any and sometimes sardines. They stared suspiciously at the bright jellies, the mounds of cream tarts and hot scones piled with raspberry jam, the ham and tongue and salted beef that were being dispensed with a liberal hand. The other children were eating heartily, drinking the orange and lemon cordial, not minding when they spilt crumbs on the floor. At home Papa told ghost stories at breakfast time but took his other meals in the privacy of his parlour and Aunt Branwell had all her meals carried up to her bedroom except for the rare occasions when she joined them for a cup of tea.

After tea there were more games, none of them intelligible, and then some of the children took turns to stand up and recite a poem or sing a song. One child in a frilled frock with blue ribbons in her hair actually danced, kicking up her legs and showing the edges of her pantalettes without being scolded!

Emily began to slide herself along the wall until she reached a side door and could slip out into the garden that extended right round the house. Here was a seat overhung by an arching tree with tiny, ripening fruits glowing pale yellow among the green leaves.

'Art tha not feeling weel, child?' Mr Heaton had come out and stood looking down at her from dark brows.

'I am quite well, sir,' Emily said.

'But tired of silly games, eh?' He looked down at her with a quizzical little smile curving the corners of his mouth. She was a pretty lass, he was thinking, with dark curly hair glinted with chestnut and beautiful eyes that seemed to move and shift in a pale, high-nosed face. Blue eyes that changed their shade from pale to violet as they shifted rapidly from one spot to another.

'They're giving out the presents now,' he said coaxingly. 'Will tha not go in and take one?'

Emily shook her head.

'Tha's one of Maister Brontë's little lot. Emily, in't it?'

'Emily Jane, sir.'

'Aye, tha was out on't moor when Crow Bog burst. So, what would tha like for a gift?'

'A little tree,' Emily said, her eyes flicking to the unripe fruit.

'A pear-tree? A little pear-tree for thine own?'

She could climb up and hide among the leaves and eat the juicy fruit and it wouldn't matter if she damaged one of the branches because it would be her own tree.

'Fust thing in morning I'll be ower wi'one for thee,' Mr Heaton said.

Her smile lifted the prettiness of her face into beauty.

'Thank you, sir,' she said breathlessly.

He had the impression that she would have flung her arms about him and hugged him but that something stronger than shyness held her back.

'How old art thee, Emily Jane?' he enquired.

'Nearly ten, sir. My birthday is at the end of July.'

'Thy feyther is fortunate to have three daughters. I have only boys.'

Emily looked at him in surprise. In her experience girls were not regarded as highly as boys. Branwell was Little King in the parsonage.

'Dost tha like horses?' he asked.

'Oh, yes!' Her face glowed again. 'I like all animals but I don't know any horses personally.'

'I've a new foal in't stables. Come!'

He headed for the stables, with Emily trotting behind. The doors were wide and the whinnying of the animals as they scented their master rose up as they went into the straw-scented gloom.

'Here they are! Mither and son.'

She stood on the wooden rail and peered over, her eyes glued to the long-legged creature.

'They're beautiful! If I had a horse I'd saddle him in silver so I would!'

She had forgotten her shyness and the Irish intonation in her voice made Mr Heaton smile. Patrick Brontë might play down his Ulster origins but his daughter had picked up his accent. She had inherited his long legs and high-bridged nose too. The other Brontë children were small and colourless.

'Dost tha have no pets?' he asked.

'Aunt Branwell is scared of animals,' Emily told him. 'She thinks they make a mess. Papa speaks of getting a guard dog but so far. . . .' She gave a curiously adult little shrug.

'I've a dog you might like to see.' He had dropped his dialect and spoke to her unconsciously as if she were the same social class as himself 'He's house-trained and good-tempered. Wait! you shall take a look at him.'

He had turned, leaving her to scramble down and follow him out into the stableyard again. A small boy in jerkin and breeches was coming under the archway and hesitated there.

'Heaton, tha's not at t'party!' Mr Heaton beckoned him over. 'Tha's reet welcome there wi'thy cousins and their friends.'

The boy was about ten, olive-skinned and black-haired with a sullen set to his mouth. He said, 'Don't like parties!'

'Aye, and tha doesna like washing thysen neither. Bring me the brindle terrier and then get thysen summat nice from t'kitchen. Off now!' He heaved an audible sigh as the boy went off.

Emily, watching, thought, 'That's the lad whose mama died and walks in the orchard, His father treated her so cruelly that she ran away from home. He is the Bates boy and his uncle has given him the name Heaton but he is not really part of the family.'

Then she forgot about the boy as he came back with a square-muzzled terrier straining on its leash.

'He's not yet named but he has a good temper and is clean,' Mr Heaton said. 'I'll bring him over tomorrow with the sapling tree if you think Mr Brontë would like him.'

'Oh, Papa will!' Emily was already crouching to stroke the dog. 'I would like to call him Grasper!'

'As you please. We'd best get back indoors or the other guests will think we've run off! Heaton!' His tone had roughened as he reverted to the vernacular. 'Get t'hound back in't kennels and pick up thy share o'th'dainties in't kitchen! Come, Emily Jane!'

They had scarcely returned to the great hall where Mrs Heaton was trying in vain to coax Charlotte, Branwell and Anne away from the wall against which they stood as if awaiting a firing squad when the sound of wheels in the road heralded the arrival of various sets of parents.

Mr Heaton had vanished, presumably to his library, and when Papa came in it was Mrs Heaton who greeted him with ill concealed relief and assured him that his little family had been perfectly behaved which was true as far as it went.

Driving home in state in the hired gig the others regained their self-confidence and chattered excitedly, describing the games in which they had not joined and the delicious food they had barely tasted. Emily stayed silent, hugging to herself the promise of the next morning.

That night her dreams were not of a nameless horror but of a rough-haired puppy with a square muzzle and a sullen-faced boy with black hair hanging in elflocks about his face.

They had just finished breakfast when the clip-clop of hoofs sounded in the lane and a moment later a somewhat flustered Tabby was opening the front door to Mr Heaton who contrary to his custom wore breeches and a seaman's jersey and had abandoned his top hat in favour of a cap.

'Good morning to thee, Maister Brontë! Nay, I'll not come in. My boots are mucky! I've a dog wi' me that I've nae use for on't farm, and it seemed to me tha may hae use for a guard dog. Name's Grasper. He's of good temperament, safe wi' childer.'

'Good morning, Mr Heaton. I have indeed thought of obtaining a guard dog. In these troubled times one cannot be too careful. It is extremely kind of you to think of me!'

Aunt Branwell, hovering in the rear of the hall, said sharply, 'A dog in the house will make a great deal of work!'

'Good morning, Miss Branwell! I trust you are well!' Mr Heaton was suddenly the squire again. 'Of course Grasper is house-trained and very loyal but he's accustomed to sleeping in a kennel. I have—'

'There's that big old kennel in the yard, Papa!' Branwell tugged at his father's coat. 'He could sleep there and just come into the house at certain times.'

'Well, I've no objections then.' Patrick Brontë ruffled his son's hair. 'We're vastly obliged to you, sir. Will you step in?'

Aunt, suddenly conscious that she was still wearing an apron, uttered a smothered protest and vanished heavenwards.

'Not with these boots on, Mr Brontë. Besides I'm here to do a small task,' Mr Heaton said easily. 'Your daughter Emily had the goodness to admire my orchard yesterday so I've brought a sapling pear for her to have as her own tree, and with your leave will plant it for her. It will fruit next year, we may hope, for the parent stock is sound and pest-free. Now where would suit it best?'

He had even brought a spade! Papa, unused to a personality strong as his own, deferred graciously. The hole was duly dug and the sapling, held upright between two stakes, duly planted. Then the kennel must be inspected and pronounced dry and roomy and Grasper given a bowl of water and some hard biscuits under Tabby's supervision.

Even Aunt Branwell, a lace fichu replacing the homespun apron, descended and brought out small glasses of sherry for the adults and agreed the addition of the pear-tree would increase the beauty of the garden.

'Though only Emily takes much interest in the plants here,' her brother-in-law admitted. 'The others are more intellectually inclined.'

'You have plans for them all, I'm sure,' Mr Heaton said, preparing to take his leave.

'Not fully formulated yet, sir. Branwell has many talents and my chief occupation must be to explore with him all the possibilities for his future career. My dear Charlotte and little Anne will likely find their niche in governessing, for they too must eventually earn their living. And my Emily will, we hope, take her aunt's place as housekeeper when she's of an age to shoulder domestic responsibilities.'

'I have a large library over at the house.' Mr Heaton handed back the glass and gathered up the reins of his waiting horse. 'I hope they will all feel free to borrow books from it whenever they choose. Yourself too, of course! I can lock up those you may deem unsuitable for children.'

'My little family read what they please, sir. I do not subject them to censorship,' Mr Brontë said. 'A mind nourished on strong meat will reject the bad automatically. My thanks to you, sir.'

'About the Trustees' meeting next week. . . .'

They were off on parish business. The children straggled back into the house.

'I do think,' Aunt Branwell said thoughtfully, 'that an occasional social event may be productive of some benefit. Now I have it in mind to arrange a visit to your uncle Mr Fennel. You know dear Jane was his daughter and was married on the same day as your dear mama. Mr Brontë, I have been thinking that a visit to Stone Cross might afford pleasure to the children. What is your opinion?'

Mr Brontë, coming up the front steps, raised sandy eyebrows.

'One must not indulge children with too many pleasures, Miss Branwell,' he said.

'Next autumn perhaps?'

'Next year, if Providence spares us all, might be an ideal time. By then this current excitement will have evaporated somewhat and another treat might well be in order. We shall discuss it. Now, Branwell, the morning grows apace into afternoon and your Latin awaits. Miss Branwell.'

'Come along, girls. There are the pillowcases to finish.'

Aunt Branwell swept ahead of them up the stairs.

Emily, trailing behind dreamily, reflected that, with a pear tree and a dog to pet, sewing didn't seem so wearisome after all!

Five

Harp of wild and dreamlike strain
When I touch thy strings
Why dost thou repeat again
Long forgotten things?

Emily Jane Brontë

'Why cannot everything stay peaceful always, Tabby?' Emily, scraping potatoes at the kitchen table, looked across to where the servant was chopping up a large piece of beef.

'Because life goes up and down and up like t'roundabout at a fair,' Tabby said.

'Do you remember when Branwell went to Keighley Fair?' Emily put down the scraper and laughed. 'Papa said he might go with the Heaton lads and he became so excited when he rode on the swingboats that he stood up and clung to the ropes and screamed his head off!'

'And then had a fight wi'another lad on't road home and lost his eyeglasses. And then it all came out – the fuss and pother he'd made at t'fair! I said at time – "lads will be lads, maister!" '

'Branny is not just a lad, Tabby. He's a genius,' Emily reproved.

'Tha's all a sight cleverer than meself,' Tabby agreed. 'Miss Charlotte now reading all them books and wearing her eyes out wi' drawing, and Miss Annie tekking Latin wi' Maister Branwell in't parlour.'

'And I am very good at peeling potatoes,' Emily said. 'Well, as I'm to keep house here when I'm grown up it doesn't do for us all to be clever!'

'Tha's not peeled that potato very well!' Tabby said, picking up the offending vegetable and squinting critically at the

77

shreds of skin still adhering to it. 'Tha dreams too mich, Miss Emily.'

'I was thinking about the holiday we had at Stone Cross last autumn,' Emily said. 'We travelled there in the gig and I feared that I was going to be homesick but when we got there it was almost like being here. We could see the same moors from the windows and we copied drawings out of some books that Uncle Fennel had and heard him preach in the church and helped clear away the dishes.'

'Stone Cross is nae more than eight miles off! Tha might as well hae stayed at home,' Tabby said.

'The change quite set us up for the winter.' Emily imitated her aunt so neatly that Tabby stifled a chuckle.

'Thy feyther would hae done weel had he gone too,' Tabby said.

'I wish Papa was feeling quite well again.' Emily sighed and took up another potato. 'It seems so odd to have him confined to bed with that awful doctor coming every other day.'

'T'doctor does his best. Bronchitis is a nasty illness, Miss Emily!'

'If Papa had died of it,' Emily said, scooping two eyes and a mouth out of the potato, 'then we'd have had to leave here for the next curate to come. I wonder what would have become of us.'

'Happen the Branwells would've ta'en thee in.'

'Not all four of us at the same time. Anyway only Aunt has ever helped out of all the relatives we have in Cornwall and Ireland.'

'No sense in fretting!' Tabby removed the bowl of potatoes deftly. 'Thy feyther is on't mend and not like to die for years.'

'Papa is fifty-three years old,' Emily said gravely.

'And I'm sixty-three but don't go putting me in't grave yet! Have the carpets been done?'

Emily shook her head.

'Then tha's best get on wi'it! Brushing them's thy task, Miss Emily!'

'All right, all right! I'll get the broom!'

Usually Emily enjoyed sweeping the carpets in the parlour and the dining-room and helping Tabby with the vegetables but today she felt restless. Charlotte and Anne were sewing up in

Aunt Branwell's room, making something or other for the poor. Aunt believed firmly that making garments for the poor improved one's character. Emily thought that in her case it merely made her feel terribly irritable.

She opened the cupboard under the stairs and took out the broom. First damp tea-leaves had to be sprinkled over the carpet and then the stiff bristles cleared up dust and tea-leaves together. Emily put the broom back and shut the door again.

'Miss Emily, whativer art tha at?' Tabby demanded from the kitchen.

'Just going out for a moment or two,' Emily called back and was through the front door before the old woman could ask more questions.

October was come again and the summer was fading before she had fully enjoyed its glories. Papa had been extremely ill, so ill that his breathing could be heard all over the house and the doctor and Aunt Branwell, conferring together, had looked stern and solemn.

'If Papa dies we shall be forced to leave our home,' Charlotte had whispered at night. 'Branwell will likely be taken by Uncle Fennel and perhaps Aunt will find a place for Anne and herself. She has fifty pounds a year of her own. But you and I – we will have nowhere to go.'

She sounded almost excited about it as if she was making out a pretend.

'We have to go somewhere,' Emily said.

'To Cornwall? Mama's family has never taken any interest in us and as for Papa's relatives ... I imagine Ireland is a very barbarous place.'

'We could work.'

'Now you're being ridiculous!' Charlotte had snorted her contempt. 'We are too young and not trained for anything. We need more education than Papa or Aunt can provide.'

'I don't,' Emily said serenely. 'I'm going to keep house.'

'Not for years and years. Aunt may live to be terribly old and so may Tabby, so you'd not be needed. You might have to become a governess like Anne and me.'

'I don't like children,' Emily said flatly.

'I don't think one has to like children in order to teach them,' Charlotte whispered thoughtfully. 'But one must be literate,

Emily. You are twelve and you still spell the alphabet the wrong way round and your letters back to front.'

'It comes out of my head that way. I know how to do it properly.'

'And your sewing looks so dreadfully untidy,' Charlotte was continuing.

'So is Anne's.'

'Anne is only little yet but you ought to be able to hem and darn and embroider. It worries me that we know so little.'

'Be Maria,' Emily had coaxed. 'I'll be Ellis and you'll be Maria, both come alive again. Please, Charlotte?'

But Charlotte had turned her back saying in a cross whisper, 'People don't come alive again. That was just a silly childish game. Go to sleep, Emily.'

Was it so wrong, Emily thought now, climbing the stile that led to the patchwork of small fields that lay below the surrounding moors, to be childish? Being grown-up meant worrying about work and money and having to walk demurely and not run and jump. It meant other things too, terrible things that females had to endure, ugly words whispered in a bedroom with a red light casting its colour of blood across the walls. It meant bearing children and year after year growing weaker and paler until in the end they put you under the church floor.

She would stay young for ever, she decided. Branwell and Charlotte and Anne might choose to grow old and staid but she would remain a child. Being a child held at bay some ultimate horror that still overshadowed her sleep.

One of the local farm lads was driving some sheep across the grass, a black and white dog snapping at his heels. It was seldom they saw other children of their own age when they played on the moors. The gentry sent their boys to school and employed governesses for their daughters, while the working class youngsters had an hour or two of reading and writing before they went off down into the valley to work in the mill or serve in the shops or work in the carding sheds.

The boy was about twelve but tall for his age, his black hair hanging about his face. He crossed in front of her without turning his head but she recognized him from the party two years before. It was on the tip of her tongue to call 'Heaton', but she held back, watching him with her shifting blue eyes as he drove the sheep up on to the moor.

When he was out of sight she began to run, whirling round and then running as fast as she could over the crisp turf that was broken by a hundred streams, winding their course down the rugged slopes.

At last she reached Ponden Kirk and began the laborious climb up the steep path that rose and fell with the contours of the landscape until she stood on the high flat rock that hid beneath it a deep fissure through which, it was rumoured, a woman who was childless would quicken if she crawled through it without turning back.

'And that's nae true,' Tabby had informed them, 'for I've crawled through many a time wi'out looking back and though my late husband were a proper man and most loving there niver was a bairn made atween us.'

'You have us,' Emily said.

'Aye, that's true, and a passel o'bother yah be when truth's told,' Tabby agreed. 'Mind, there's other things on't moor. Things ye'd niver pray t'see on a winter neet.'

'Fairies?'

'Nay, t'last fairish were seen in my mither's day over at Top Withens. The mills came and drove 'em away. But there were a shepherd lad some twenty year ago who went out in't snaw t'seek his maister's sheep and were niver seen again.'

'There's a column to his memory towards Keighley,' Charlotte said.

'Aye, so theer is! But on winter neets when a storm rages they say if tha sets a candle in thy window the shepherd boy comes, crying to be let in. Greeting and crying fit to break thy heart! Aye, mills or no mills queer things go on.'

Emily stood on the high rock and looked down towards Ponden House. At this height and distance it looked like one of the houses from her toy village. She pictured Mr and Mrs Heaton, the latter having just had a fifth son, seated at their ease in the big hall with the moulded ceiling and the high dresser with its display of copper and brass and silver, and the little boys playing musical chairs round and round.

There was no sign of the boy called Heaton who was nephew and yet not really part of the family. Emily felt a dart of pity for him and then she scrambled down, to the great damage of her boots, and rolled the last few yards, picking herself up and starting back towards the village because her stomach told her it was near teatime.

She knew the moment she arrived in the yard that trouble was brewing more quickly than the tea.

'Thy aunt wants thee,' Tabby said.

Emily pulled her features into a grimace and loped through into the dining-room where she found her three siblings seated at the table and her aunt, hands clasped at her waist, her large mob cap bristling with indignation.

'Where,' said Aunt Branwell, 'have you been?'

'Nowhere, Aunt.' Emily shuffled her feet.

'You've been out on the moor, haven't you? Alone and without leave? Haven't you?'

'Yes.'

'With your poor father recovering from a most dangerous illness and your household task undone! Emily, you are twelve years old and must begin to develop some sense of responsibility. Surely you can see that?'

Emily looked at the floor. The mud from her boots was making jolly little patterns on the unswept carpet.

'Take off your boots!' Aunt Branwell had also noticed the patterns. 'Go into the back kitchen and clean them, then wash yourself. Then you will sweep the carpets.'

'It's teatime,' Emily said brightly.

'Bad girls don't get tea. Do as I bid you at once!'

Emily untied the boots, tugged them off, dislodging more mud in the process and under her aunt's affronted gaze carried them along the flagged passage into the back kitchen. She scrubbed the boots ferociously wishing she could scrub them away and wear silver shoes with red heels. Once, long ago when she was tiny, Papa had refused the gift of several pairs of brightly coloured boots for his children on the grounds that such finery would spoil his children. At least that was what Sarah had heard though Maria had said it wasn't true. Papa refused to allow them to have second-hand boots because it would hurt the shape of their feet. But Sarah might have been telling a lie. She was in Bradford now and had married and planned to move to America. They never came to see the children. They might be dead and not in Bradford or going to America at all. Everybody got dead sooner or later and tapped on the cellar wall or wandered over the moor crying to be let in at a candlelit window.

She put on her slippers and came through the kitchen, glancing at Tabby whose hunched shoulders and averted gaze spoke of disapproval, came into the hall and went up the stairs. In a moment she'd sweep the carpets but first she wanted to check that her chief soldier Parry was all right. Branwell, who was rough with his toys, sometimes borrowed those assigned to his sisters.

Charlotte was there, bent low over one of the tiny magazines that she and Branwell wrote constantly.

'You ought to mind Aunt Branwell,' she said, looking up and frowning. 'She makes a great sacrifice in staying here to help Papa. If you don't do what you're told how can you be trusted with the care of the household? Honestly, Emily!'

'Mind your own business, Talli!' Emily snatched up her soldier and inspected him for damage.

'It is my business!' Charlotte was in a lecturing mood. 'Emily, if Papa had died of his bronchial attack did you ever stop to think what might have happened to us? We would be destitute, and even if Papa lives until we are quite grown up we shall still find it very difficult to get a good position. Aunt means well but she can't teach us all the things that Anne and I will need to know before we can teach other people's children. I have made up my mind and decided that one of us at least must get a formal education. I have spoken to Papa and he agrees with me. I am going to school.'

'You can't!' Emily was gasping as if all the breath was being knocked out of her body. 'Charlotte, you can't! Have you forgotten what it was like? We were cold and hungry and afraid and the food was not fit to eat and there was ice in the water jugs and ... Maria and Ellis died, Charlotte. You can't have forgotten that!'

'Not one moment of it. One day I shall have my revenge,' Charlotte said softly. 'But I'll not go back to Cowan Bridge, though they say it's vastly improved these days. I shall go to a better school. Do you remember Miss Firth from Thornton?'

'A bit. Papa wanted to marry her.'

'Well, she married another gentleman called Mr Franks and they would help with the fees if I spent eighteen months at Roe Head School. It's a very well conducted establishment at Mirfield and I shall work hard and then come back and teach you and Anne what I've learned.'

'Teach Anne! I'm not going to be a governess.'

'Even a housekeeper must be able to read and write properly. Papa has approved my plan.'

'But what about the Twelve and the Genii and the magazines you and Branny write?' Emily said.

'We can't play pretend games all our lives, Em. We have to grow up and live in the real world,' Charlotte said.

'No we don't! And the Twelve and the Genii are real because they're us! You can't destroy the US!'

'It will be very hard but duty is important too.'

'And what about Maria and Ellis?' Emily's blue eyes blazed in her white face. 'We bring them alive in bed every night.'

'Maria and Elizabeth are dead,' Charlotte said. 'We can't really make them alive again.'

'We can! We can!'

Emily flew at her smaller older sister, pummelling her hard.

'Emily Jane!'

Papa, fully dressed, stood in the doorway, his voice rolling like thunder round the tiny room.

'You can't go to school! I won't let you!' Emily shouted.

She felt strong and powerful as if the dark boy who lived inside her had leapt into conscious life.

'Go down into the cellar and wait for me there!' Papa said. His voice was suddenly quiet, menacing. Emily scrambled up off the weeping Charlotte and dashed out of the room and down the stairs. Not until she was in the arched and echoing vaults with only the light filtering through the high narrow window did the dark boy begin to dwindle down.

She stood uncertainly near the big barrel of ale, looking towards the far wall as the light slowly died. They were going to leave her here. Papa didn't believe in corporal punishment for girls and had been very angry when he had heard about some of the practices at Cowan Bridge. He wouldn't slap her or whip her but he was capable of leaving her down here all night until her temper had cooled.

There was a pitcher near the barrel. She seized it and turned the key in the keg that brought a thin stream of ale frothing out. When she drank it the taste was cool and brown and faintly bitter. She gulped down another pitcherful, spilling some of it, and felt light and dizzy and very tall as if her head was touching the ceiling.

'Emily, come up here!'

Tabby's voice! Emily set down the pitcher with a clatter and weaved a path to the cellar steps. Odd but they were more difficult to climb than the slopes of Ponden Kirk!

'Thy feyther's in't parlour and thy aunt's consoling Miss Charlotte,' Tabby said, taking her by the arm and thrusting her across the hall into the kitchen. 'I doant knaw what got into thee, child! Drink some tay now and get on wi' peeling these apples for tomorrow. I promised tae look in on my brother. I'll be no moor than an hour. Sit quiet naw!'

She had on her shawl and bonnet and was evidently in too much of a hurry to notice the smell of the ale.

Once, years before, after Tabby first came and wasn't used to their ways, they'd taken advantage of the fact that Papa and Aunt had gone to Keighley and made such a racket as they chased one another and screamed all over the house that she'd rushed down to see her nephew, William Wood, begging him to return with her because the children were all run mad. How they had laughed and teased her when she panted back with the young carpenter in tow!

The tea tasted peculiar. She pushed the cup away, grimaced at the pains in her stomach which had troubled her over the last few days, picked up the sharp little knife and looked at it thoughtfully.

Everybody went away and left her or died. Mama and the baby who was never born, Eilis the Irish grandmother she had never seen, Maria and Ellis, Nancy and Sarah, and now Charlotte was going away soon. If she didn't die she would come back changed, alien. And the secret world where they were all powerful was dying too, killed by Charlotte. Perhaps it would be better if she went away too. She set the sharp blade of the knife against her throat.

'Emily, whatever are you doing?' Branwell's voice shrilled from the doorway.

'I'm going to cut my throat!' Emily suddenly shouted. 'This time I'm dying! This time I'm going away!'

'You're drunk!' Her brother stepped closer, sniffing the air.

'Or maybe yours! You want to send Charlotte to school too, don't you?'

She was on her feet, the apples rolling about on the table, the knife in her hand glinting. The pains in her stomach were so bad that she gritted her teeth against them.

'No, I don't, honestly!' Branwell was backing away.

'I don't want to be me!' Emily cried.

'Then be someone else,' Branwell said, looking alarmed. 'Be Parry or Chief Genius Emmii or. . . .'

The dark boy was growing inside her. She could release him and never be a feeble girl again who had to sew for the poor and clean the carpet and listen to sermons about hellfire. In a moment she would be invincible.

'There's blood running down your leg,' Branwell said. 'Did you cut . . . Emily?'

Maria had lain on the bed at school with blood on the sheet. Some of it had come from her mouth and some of it – no, this wasn't happening to her.

'Emily, I told you to remain in the cellar until your temper had cooled.' Papa was suddenly there, sounding more alarmed than Branwell. His face kept changing into Mr Wilson's face.

'She's drunk and she's going to cut her throat!' Branwell said loudly.

'Branwell, go upstairs and stay with Anne and Charlotte.' Papa sounded very calm. 'Emily, we will deal with the drinking later. I suspect that the headache you have tomorrow will be punishment enough.'

Aunt's voice sounded from the top of the stairs. Mr Brontë raised his own.

'Everything is all right, Miss Branwell. I am dealing with Emily, that is all.'

Branwell had gone. Papa was pulling her along the flagged passage into the back kitchen and holding her head under the pump. Cold water took her breath away and soaked her head and hair.

Sobered she twisted from his grasp, the knife falling with a clatter.

'Child, what ails you?' He had her by the shoulders, shaking her slightly.

'I am . . . am . . .' Her mouth twisted into a grimace.

His pale piercing gaze travelled downwards. 'You have the curse of Eve come upon you,' he said, quietly, sadly. 'It is the punishment visited upon all women, the sign that they are fit for marriage and childbearing. Not yet, of course. Not for many years. Your sister Maria – my dearest Maria – Charlotte has not yet – it is a natural process, my dear. Original sin hangs more heavily upon the female than the male. They are created to serve – certain duties to perform. There are men who will try to take advantage of you, try to lure you from the path of virtue. I have the duty to warn you against such men, such practices. Come!'

They were going down into the cellar again. She felt sick and her head had begun to ache. Behind her, over her, the nameless thing hovered. It had no real power over her if she crept into a corner of her mind and hid there, let the dark, sullen boy come down and take his place, passive behind his mask of indifference, secretly mocking.

Charlotte, already smugly in bed when a nightgowned Emily came into the tiny room, lifted her head from the pillow.

'Where on earth have you been?' she demanded. 'Branwell said you were drunk and bellowing like a bull and waving knives about, and Aunt said we must stay upstairs. What's going on?'

'Nothing,' Emily said. 'Nothing at all.'

'I'm sorry about the quarrel.' Charlotte's cheeks were flushed. 'You do see that it's for the best – my going away to school, don't you? We can play at Maria and Elizabeth until I've gone.'

'They're dead,' Emily said flatly, getting into the narrow bunk and turning her back on her sister. 'You can't really make people be alive again.'

'And the four Genii?'

'They're dead too,' Emily said calmly.

Somehow it was easier to keep them dead while the preparations for Charlotte's departure to Roe Head went on. There were new garments to be made, exercise books and pens and pencils to buy, letters of thanks to be written to Mrs Franks and Miss Atkinson who were helping with the fees.

She left in January when the snow had become sleeting rain.

Papa's recent illness had left them short of money and so instead of travelling in the gig with Papa she went alone in a covered farm-cart the fourteen miles to Mirfield. Aunt had made valiant efforts to curl her hair which frizzed out round her face and her green dress had a high waist and a bunchy skirt. She looked resolute, her crooked mouth firmly set, her square chin thrust out.

'I shall work hard, Papa, and not waste your money,' she said.

She would probably die, Emily thought bleakly. She would either die at school or be brought home like a little bag of bones.

She gave her sister a quick, cool nod and turned away, shiveringly.

As the cart rolled away down the lane a small hand stole into hers.

'I – I know about a new l-land,' Anne whispered.

'What?' Emily looked down at her.

'S-somewhere to go in our heads. You know.'

'Yes,' Emily said. 'Yes, I know.'

The dead couldn't be made alive but there was always new birth to lift the heart and push the shadow away.

Six

Love is like the wild rose briar,
Friendship like the holly tree
The holly is dark when the rose briar blooms
But which will bloom most constantly?

Emily Jane Brontë

They had been four and now were two pairs. On the surface the violent quarrel with Charlotte was forgotten. Emily, in calmer mood, had grown to understand that her sister had been anxious only to fit herself and her sisters for the real world outside the safety of the parsonage, and that she had suffered herself when she had decided to abandon their games and take herself off to Roe Head with a view to future independence.

'It is a splendid school!' she had enthused when she returned after the first half-year. 'A big house in a lovely garden, with warm beds and well-cooked food. When I told Miss Wooller that I disliked meat she offered to provide a substitute for me. She is very gracious in her ways, small and plump but most dignified. And the other girls are very friendly. They teased me when they realized that I couldn't see the ball well enough to play games but I prefer to stand aside and watch the sky anyway. And my particular friends have been so very kind.'

Her particular friends were Ellen Nussey and Mary and Martha Taylor. All three, according to Charlotte, came from good if slightly impoverished families, and vied with her for the first place in class. Ellen was gentle and very devout and Mary was so pretty that Miss Wooller declared her too pretty to live, but she had a blunt manner and no airs and graces, and her younger sister Martha, who was nicknamed Patty, was enchanting, always up to mischief but so amusing.

In the year since she had returned home for good Charlotte had spent a considerable time writing to Ellen and waiting anxiously for return post, and extolling their virtues to the rest of the family. There were times when Emily would have liked to hear less about Charlotte's friends.

'Mary Taylor says that we remind her of potatoes growing in a cellar,' she remarked one day.

'Why?' Anne wanted to know.

'Oh, our writing tiny magazines with stories and articles and—'

'You didn't tell her about the secret world!'

Emily had paled, her blue eyes glinting.

'No, of course not!' Charlotte had flushed slightly. 'Of course I didn't. I merely mentioned in passing that we sometimes wrote things down. I used to tell ghost stories in school after lights out and she thought I ought to write them down, that's all. I did think of showing her—'

'*No!!*'

'But I changed my mind,' Charlotte said hurriedly.

That she had even considered betraying their shared fantasy had horrified Emily. It showed how far Charlotte had moved away from their enchanted childhood. Neither did they play the Maria and Elizabeth game either any longer. Both were dead and could no longer be revived. Charlotte, in a sudden burst of confidence to Emily, had told her haltingly,

'If I dream about them now I see them as grown up, very fashionably dressed, and they walk round criticizing the furniture.'

Yet the secret worlds had endured after all, though now Emily and Anne played at Gondal and had begun to write stories about it and Charlotte and Branwell were writing feverishly about Angria which had begun as a province of Verdopolis and become a mighty nation in its own right. Though Charlotte and Branwell kept the younger girls up to date with doings in Angria and Emily and Anne told them something of Gondal the two worlds never impinged on each other.

Branwell was still writing interminable accounts of constant battles while Charlotte, from what she let drop, was bound up in the various love affairs of her milk-and-water heroines whose portraits she sketched in their gauzy draperies and soulful expressions.

Gondal was very different; it was a land of high crags and trackless forests and caves where outlaws skulked, and it was ruled by a woman.

'Shall we call her Victoria?' Anne had enquired, knowing that Emily was interested in the princess who would one day be queen.

'Her name is Augusta,' Emily said. 'When Princess Victoria was born her parents wished to name her Augusta but the king said the name was too grand for her and ordered them to name her Victoria instead. So my heroine shall be Augusta. Augusta Geraldine.'

'That's Irish.'

'It's a name I like,' Emily said in a tone that brooked no argument. 'Augusta Geraldine . . . Almeda. She is born into the royal house of Almeda.'

Anne refrained from pointing out that Almeda sounded Spanish. The names sounded splendid anyway. Neither did it matter that Gondal was officially a Pacific island since it had a landscape like the landscapes their favourite novelist Sir Walter Scott described and weather that was amazingly like the weather in Haworth.

What it lacked were magic beings who could bring people to life again.

'When anyone dies in Gondal they stay dead,' Emily said firmly.

Charlotte had come home with a silver medal for being the brightest pupil in Miss Wooller's little school, which meant that apart from the hated and obligatory sewing for the poor they were freed from Aunt's hit and miss methods of instruction. Not that Charlotte's were much better, Emily thought with a smile. Poor Tallii tried so hard to set a regular timetable and pass on the grammar and arithmetic and history she had been taught at Roe Head but often she would be so busy writing her Angrian romances that she would quite forget to mark their work, and when the weather was fine it was much more agreeable to wander on the moors, with Mr Brontë innocently unaware of the dramas of love, war and revenge acted out on the high hills since he was under the firm impression they were studying plant life and taking drawings from nature.

The main focus of the family was Branwell who had finally

decided that Art should be his chosen profession. Meanwhile he was studying drawing and painting with an art master from Leeds who came over twice a month at a fee of a guinea a time to coach the boy and to give an occasional lesson to the girls. They had also acquired a second-hand pianoforte and the church organist came to give them musical instruction. Branwell could already play both the flute and the pianoforte and frequently played the new organ in church, but Charlotte had dropped the music lessons because she couldn't see the keyboard clearly.

And now Ellen Nussey, whom Charlotte regarded as the pattern of perfection, was coming for a few days holiday, and Charlotte had been busy for days doing her best to beautify the drab interior of the parsonage with vases of wild flowers and red cushions on the black horsehair sofa.

'The Nusseys live in a much larger house, of course, and one of Ellen's brothers is surgeon general to the King! She has the most elegant manners and scarcely a trace of a Yorkshire accent. Of course she is the youngest of twelve and has an invalid sister so she will have only a small dowry but her character is so elevated that she will be greatly sought after when she has come out.'

'Come out where?' Emily was deliberately misunderstanding.

'In society of course! The Nusseys are very well connected.'

Emily, retreating to the kitchen where she could joke with Tabby, felt that if she heard one more word about the elegant Nusseys she would either throw up or break something!

The subject of Charlotte's rapturous descriptions was in due course delivered at the parsonage. Ellen, who had spent fifteen miles being jolted in a small carriage and had closed her eyes in terror as the horses came up the precipitous main street, alighted shakily and was seized upon by her friend who bore her triumphantly through a side gate, along a gravel path past a roughly trimmed and rather weedy lawn with a couple of straggling blackcurrant bushes near the wall and two rather spindly trees to soften the light grey façade of a neat building with a front porch and a fairly wide hallway beyond.

'Papa, may I present my friend, Miss Ellen Nussey? Miss Nussey, this is my father.'

Ellen curtsied and shook hands with a tall, well-built man in black broadcloth with a high white cravat and curling greying hair.

'Miss Nussey, we have been looking forward to this occasion with keen anticipation and look forward to your deriving equal benefit from this visit,' he said.

'Thank you, sir.' Ellen curtsied again, feeling slightly over-awed by his grand manner and its contrast with the bare, uncarpeted hall.

'Let me take your bags upstairs!' Charlotte was fluttering round like an anxious hen. 'Emily has agreed to sleep in Tabby's room while you're here so you and I will be in the tiny chamber I told you about. We shall be able to have private conversations.'

The said chamber was scarcely larger than a cupboard and as bare as the rest of the house, though Ellen politely hid her surprise and Charlotte evidently didn't notice that the most anyone could say for her home was that it was scrupulously clean.

'Tea is ready in the dining-room. You shall meet the rest of my family there! Papa has his meals apart from breakfast in his parlour. He has a very delicate digestion. May I present my brother, Branwell? Branwell, this is my friend, Miss Nussey.'

They were on their way down the narrow stairs as Branwell crossed the hall. He paused, bowed and promptly vanished again, leaving an impression of a small, neat figure and longish red hair curling almost to his shoulders at each side of a sharp-featured white face with a pair of pale blue eyes peering over gold rimmed spectacles.

'My brother is always in a great hurry,' Charlotte said affec-tionately. 'Come and meet the others.'

The dining-room was carpeted, with a couple of red cushions on the sofa and some wild flowers in a plain glass bowl on a low sideboard. At the head of the table a tiny woman, with ginger hair showing beneath the frills of a huge mob cap, was pouring tea from a large teapot on which something was engraved in gold. Ellen, whose eyesight was keen, deciphered the motto *Thou, God, seest me* before the lady put down the teapot and offered her hand with a ceremonious air.

'Welcome to Haworth, Miss Nussey. We've all looked forward to your coming and trust you'll have a pleasant visit. Please sit down. Charlotte has been looking forward so greatly to this event. We live rather quietly here but in Penzance many years ago I was used to quite a sociable way of living.'

'May I hazard the guess,' said tactful Ellen, 'that you were accounted quite a belle?'

'You are right, my dear!' Aunt Branwell smiled and nodded. 'Yorkshire is not my native setting but when my poor sister died I felt obliged to give up my home and take care of her children. I consider it a sacred duty.'

'You haven't met my little sisters yet,' Charlotte said brightly. 'This is Emily Jane who is just fifteen and this is Anne who will be fourteen next January.'

The younger girl was pretty, though her nose was too long, but her long dark blonde hair fell in graceful curls on her neck and her eyes were large and brilliantly blue, shaded by long lashes. She smiled and bowed her head without speaking. The older girl merely nodded brusquely, her eyes sliding away, her frizzy dark hair escaping from its combs. She too had long eyelashes and a high-bridged nose that reminded the visitor of Mr Brontë.

Tea was plentiful and conversation unexpectedly lively. Branwell flashed in to grab a couple of sandwiches and declare he was off to do some practising before dark; Aunt Branwell plied Ellen with cake and at the close of the meal offered her a pinch of snuff from a small ivory box. She gave a light laugh as she saw the expression on Ellen's face.

'Do excuse me, my dear Miss Nussey! In my youth in Penzance it was quite de rigueur to offer snuff to young ladies,' she said. 'It clears the nasal passages admirably.'

'Spitting works as well and is cheaper,' Emily said.

Her voice, Ellen noticed, was peculiarly sweet and for an instant eyes of greyish blue were raised and glinted with mischief.

'Emily! My dear girl, the word s-p-i-t-t-i-n-g,' said Aunt Branwell, spelling it carefully, 'is not a suitable word for young ladies to employ! Anne, you have your feet on the rungs of your chair again, dear. That also is highly improper. Charlotte, you will not forget to introduce Miss Nussey to Mrs Aykroyd, will you? She is most anxious to meet her. Now I must retire to my room. I lead a very regular and quiet life, Miss Nussey as the climate in Yorkshire does not agree with my constitution.'

She rose, picked up the teapot and sailed out, her wooden

pattens click-clacking on the floor. In her wake Emily and Anne, muttering some excuse or other, followed.

'Come and meet Tabby!' Charlotte was on her feet. 'She is regarded as one of the family. Tabby, Miss Ellen Nussey is come!'

She whisked Ellen into a small kitchen where a small spry-looking woman with a brown, gypsyish face sat knitting.

'Miss Nussey! I thought as how I heerd voices.' Tabby rose and offered a heavily calloused hand. 'Tha's reet welcome! Miss Charlotte's bin in a reet stew mekking ready for thee.'

'I'm very pleased to be here, Mrs Aykroyd,' Ellen said politely.

'Tha moost call me Tabby! All the family calls me Tabby.'

'Tabby then. I am pleased to be regarded as one of the family,' Ellen said.

It had been a good beginning. Charlotte was flushed and smiling, pleased her friend had made such a favourable impression. Up in the tiny chamber again she chattered eagerly about mutual schoolfriends.

'Mary Taylor will make her own way in the world for she has an independent spirit and Martha will be wed by the time she's seventeen for who could resist her charm? Tell me what you have been doing, Ellen, since that last day at school? Do you remember. . . ?'

By the time the bell rang for family prayers they had gossiped themselves into tiredness.

Morning began at seven with the loud crack of a pistol that shot Ellen out of bed.

'What on earth. . . ?'

'Papa always discharges the shot in his pistol across the graveyard first thing in the morning,' Charlotte said sleepily, sitting up. 'He was in this region during the Luddite Riots, and he has gone armed ever since. Don't fret! He only aims at the church tower.'

Tabby brought up hot water, apparently in compliment to the guest for she observed on leaving the room, 'When tha's used to our ways, Miss Ellen, tha can wash in't back kitchen same as t'others!'

They were scarcely dressed when a bell rang for morning prayers which were briskly conducted by Mr Brontë before they repaired to the dining-room where bowls of oatmeal gruel, a mound of bread and butter, and tea poured from a plain earthenware pot, awaited. A rough-haired terrier had been admitted and, stationed between Emily and Anne, slurped the leavings in their bowls.

'You'll likely not have heard much of our neighbours, Miss Nussey?' Mr Brontë turned his light piercing gaze upon her.

'Not very much, sir.'

'We do not mingle with them very much. Since leaving Thornton I have not encountered a mind commensurate in intelligence with my own. There are the Heatons, of course. They dwell at Ponden House which is of course haunted.'

'Tell Miss Nussey, Papa!' Emily said eagerly.

'First there was Casson in the sixteenth century – nearer the seventeenth to be accurate. A handsome gypsy fellow who came to labour on the estate, and, the owner being then a widow, had his way with her, seducing her and once he was sure she was with child then marrying her by force. Her first two children by her deceased husband were set to work in the stables while his own son begotten upon the widow was raised as the heir.'

'Go on, Papa!' Emily's eyes were fixed on her father. A quiet smile of satisfaction played round her full mouth.

'One day the child died – poisoned perhaps. And then Casson himself disappeared. Nobody could or would tell where he had gone. After seven years the widow applied for leave to presume him dead and the estate reverted to the rightful heirs. After that the hauntings began. Casson was seen, gnawing the flesh from his own bones. Perhaps he was shut up in the cellars of Ponden House and starved to death.'

Ellen had begun to tremble. The sepulchral voice, the horrid details, the blunt manner of the telling made her feel sick and faint. In the tiny pause before he resumed the grisly tale she glanced up and saw him looking at her with a gleam in the pale eyes behind the spectacles and a mocking little sneer on his mouth. Ellen looked down at her plate again, deciding that though she could never admit it to dear Charlotte she really didn't like Mr Brontë very much.

To her relief breakfast came to an end and he stalked into his parlour, pausing only to say, 'Charlotte, my dear, it would be best if you remained indoors today. You look as if you are coming down with a cold.'

'But Papa! Yes, Papa,' Charlotte said miserably.

'Aunt is waiting for me. Excuse me, Miss Nussey.' Anne unwound her feet from the rungs of her chair and went out.

'It's such a beautiful day,' Charlotte said mournfully. 'It isn't fair to confine you to the house merely because I have the sniffles!'

'I can accompany Miss Nussey for a walk if you wish,' Emily said unexpectedly.

'You! Well, if you don't mind . . .' Charlotte looked doubtfully at Ellen.

'Thank you. I'd love to come,' Ellen said firmly.

'I'll get my shawl!'

Emily went into the hall and was back in an instant, a plaid shawl draped round her.

'Don't take her too far,' Charlotte said anxiously. 'She is not used to long walks.'

'I'll take her as far as the inchcape grass. Grasper, here!' On the front step Emily stuck two fingers between her rather prominent front teeth and uttered a piercing whistle.

'Emily! Aunt will hear you!' Charlotte cried.

'Aunt is too busy piling mending on Anne in an effort to save her soul,' Emily said. 'Come along, Miss Nussey!'

They stepped out along the lane with the dog trotting at their heels.

'Aunt Branwell means well,' Emily said, 'but she's dreadfully missish in her ways! Give me your hand and I'll pull you over the stile! Now let us run across the near fields and get some fresh air in our lungs and then you shall see the moors in their glory!'

Before she knew quite what had happened the sedate Ellen found herself tearing across the field, the bonnet she had hastily donned bouncing on her head. Emily hadn't troubled to put on a bonnet and her long hair blew out round her face.

'Now look!' She had gained a grassy knoll where she stood with her long shawl trailing from her thin shoulders, her lips parted and her eyes fixed with peculiar intensity on the undulating landscape, golden now in the morning sunshine with darker patches of peat to add contrast and here and there a stunted tree twisted by the prevailing wind resembling some goblin species that dwelt in wild places.

'It is too beautiful for mere words,' Ellen said quietly.

'Yes. Yes it is!'

The face turned towards her glowed with delight; the long-lashed eyes were sparkling violet and a smile lit the plain features into a rare loveliness. Impulsively Ellen held out her hand.

'I don't like to be touched,' Emily said. 'Only Anne has that right. It is nothing personal, Miss Nussey. I will help you back over the stile.'

'May we not walk a little farther on?' Ellen said, dropping her hand.

'You are not tired? Charlotte will fuss if we are absent too long.'

'I am not in the least tired. I envy you having this on your doorstep,' Ellen said.

'Yes. We are very fortunate,' Emily said. 'Most of this is common land, which means that we both own it after a fashion.'

'But you,' said Ellen in a flash of insight, 'own it in a very special way.'

'It has been part of me since I was a small child,' Emily said quietly. 'Charlotte tells me you are sixteen. Have you no place that is entirely yours?'

'Not really.' Ellen thought of her own large house with its many chimneys and landscaped grounds. 'There are twelve of us, you see, though not all of us live at home of course. My father died and it's only through the kindness of other relatives that we are able to stay at Rydings at all. We have breeding but no brass as Mary Taylor says.'

'Mary Taylor had best keep her opinions to herself,' Emily said with a sudden snort. 'I've not met her yet but she strikes me as too free with her opinions!'

'She has a kind heart.'

'Then we'll forgive her. Come, I'll show you the place where the wild garlic grows. Tabby uses the herb in her cooking!'

They walked on, apart but talking and laughing as the dog ran ahead and then doubled back.

The first person they met as they returned to the parsonage was Charlotte whose worried face appeared at the window of the dining-room. As they went through the porch she bustled into the hall.

'Did you enjoy yourself, Ellen?' Her voice was anxious.

'Very much,' Ellen began.

98

'And Emily?' Charlotte had lowered her voice as her sister went through to the kitchen. 'How did Emily behave? She can be very difficult at times.'

Emily had her hand on the knob of her kitchen door as Charlotte's words reached her. The animation had died out of her face and her heart, so light a moment before, sank like a stone.

'I like your sister very much,' Ellen said tranquilly.

The stone became a heart again. Emily breathed deeply. Ellen Nussey could never be her special friend because Charlotte had first claim, but she had accepted her. She had not thought her odd or ungainly or made any comments about the way she shoved her hands deep into the pockets of her narrow skirt. One day soon she would make Ellen part of Gondal. A new female character was required to push the epic in a more unexpected direction. Ellen, of course, would never know.

She opened the kitchen door, went in and hugged Tabby, who replied to the rare caress with an irritable, 'If you've nowt better t'do wi'thy hands than squeeze the breath out of honest folk tha can start buttering the bread!'

By the next morning the cold threatening Charlotte had vanished and with Branwell bidden to accompany them they set off across the moors, Emily striding ahead with her brother and frequently exhorting the others to hurry up or the best part of the day would be gone. At times, as if impelled by some force within herself, she broke into a dance, whirling round with her dark hair flying, clapping her hands in a way that would have reminded her father of his sisters had he been there.

'We shall go to the waterfall today,' Charlotte said breathlessly. 'My sisters discovered it and named it the Meeting of the Waters after the poem Thomas Moore wrote. It's our special place.'

'Can you manage alone?' Branwell had turned. 'I have to see John Brown about something?'

'Much use you are anyway!' Emily teased. 'If I hadn't placed stepping-stones Miss Nussey would've drowned in the brook. We will see you later.'

'Branwell is very friendly with our sexton,' Charlotte said. 'He is older than our brother but a steady respectable fellow.'

'With a couple of illegitimate children and a great capacity for liquor!' Emily said, laughing.

'Emily!'

'Which is not to say I don't like him. He is, despite his faults, a good man. Race you, Annie!'

'They are such children,' Charlotte said indulgently, watching her sisters as they sprang ahead.

'I like them both,' Ellen said.

Emily had run on, outstripping the others as her feet raced up the high twisting path that dipped down below high crags to a shallow valley in which, surrounded by high rushes, a pool was formed by the cascade leaping down the rocks. In the pool tadpoles darted and arrowed tiny black bodies beneath the surface of the rippling water.

'Look at them!' Emily flung herself down at the side of the pool. 'Look how they wriggle and dart when I agitate the water with my hand! See how brave a few are, swimming up to investigate this strange five-branched thing in the water while the rest turn tail and swim for their lives.'

'Like people,' Anne said, perching carefully on a large flat stone.

'Anne is the philosopher,' Charlotte said.

'Up here we could all become philosophers I think,' Ellen said.

'The Four Philosophers! It sounds like a secret society,' Charlotte remarked.

'The Magnificent Four!' Emily rose in one graceful movement, shaking droplets of water from her hand. 'We are magnificent, are we not?'

'Aunt won't think so if we're late for dinner,' Anne reminded them.

'Race you down the hill!' Emily was already flying ahead.

'We shall take the path more cautiously.' Charlotte linked arms with her friend. 'This is my sister's world where we walk carefully.'

'Tomorrow we will all be walking carefully,' Anne reminded them. 'The Sunday school tea, remember?'

'Oh Lord! I had almost forgotten.' Charlotte groaned. 'Not the children but the older girls who come to Sunday school. They already earn their bread on weekdays by working in the mills and on the farms. Anne and I do our best to make them feel at home but it's uphill work.'

'Charlotte teaches in the Sunday school,' Anne said. 'She is very strict and precise. When I am older I will teach there too when I am at home.'

'Between governessing!' Charlotte sighed.

They came the next day, a dozen hefty young women in their 'teens, eyes bright, hair neatly combed back, tongues clacking in a dialect so thick that Ellen could barely understand it. They crowded into the dining-room where benches had been set and demolished the ham sandwiches, the scones and little cakes that Tabby and Emily had been making all morning. Aunt Branwell had retired to her room with a headache remedy; Mr Brontë had found a sick parishioner who lived at a distance and must be visited; Branwell was nowhere to be seen.

'Eh, tha sets a reet guid spread, Charlotty!' one of the girls exclaimed.

'Tastier than a funeral tay!' another agreed.

'Shall us play games now?' A girl with sandy hair was looking eagerly around.

'Games?' Charlotte cast a trapped glance towards Ellen. 'What kind of games had you in mind?'

'We'm women now but us still play hopscotch when mill's shut! Can't tha play hopscotch, Annie?' another appealed to Anne.

'I've heard of it.' Anne wrinkled her forehead.

'We can play in't back yard!' Another girl had jumped up. 'Hast tha a bit o'chalk?'

'Yes, but I really don't—' Charlotte yielded abruptly. 'If you like!'

Ellen, assuming the role of spectator, watched in amused disapproval as squares were marked out and the Sunday school scholars did their best to initiate the three Brontës into the mysteries of the game.

'Em's got th'hang of it!' shrilled the sandy-haired one. 'Aye, you'm tekking great hops, our Em! Charlotty's too short and Annie's skeered she'll show her drawers! Nay, tha mun goa this road now! See?'

'I don't understand the rules at all!' Emily said, breathless and laughing.

'Aye weel, tha might be powerful larned but tha's a bit back-ward in other things,' another said critically.

'Emily, ought they not to be taught to address you more

respectfully?' Ellen, her social sensibilities wounded, touched Emily's sleeve as she dropped out of the game.

'Vain hope!' Emily said with a mocking little grin. 'They call a spade a shovel in't Haworth, tha knows!'

By the time Mr Brontë came home the millgirls had departed, each with a bag of cakes for younger brothers and sisters, and Emily, her skirt tucked up, had washed out the chalk marks.

'Did it go well?' Mr Brontë put his head in at the dining-room door.

'Very well, Papa. They appreciated our efforts very much,' Charlotte assured him.

'They are good souls – a mite rough round the edges but goodhearted,' he agreed. 'It benefits them to enter a household which is genteel and cultured.'

'Yes, Papa.' Anne spoke gravely, eyes downcast.

'We shall have ghost stories tonight after supper since with the teas to prepare you were denied them this morning.'

His smile included Ellen.

The week drew to its close amiably. There was another visit to the Meeting of the Waters, a rainy morning when Charlotte brought down sketching materials and they drew one another and giggled over the results, an afternoon when they played at Truth and Consequences and a board-game with lettered counters at which Ellen won and Emily got nowhere.

'We must consider how we are to deliver Miss Nussey back to her family,' Mr Brontë remarked. 'Or have arrangements been made?'

'Ellen's brother will meet her at Bolton Abbey if we can escort her there, Papa. Would that be possible?' Charlotte looked anxious.

'My family would of course pay for the hire of transport,' Ellen said.

'My dear Miss Nussey, we are not so impoverished that we cannot afford to see our honoured guest off in style.' Mr Brontë had drawn himself up stiffly, his Celtic pride clearly touched. 'We can hire the gig, I think, and Branwell can drive you the seven or eight miles there.'

'Could we all go, Papa?' Charlotte asked eagerly.

'My dear Mr Brontë!' Aunt Branwell broke in. 'For a whole week the girls have enjoyed a positive vortex of dissipation and scarcely put a needle and thread into anything. A jaunt to Bolton Abbey strikes me as rather too much icing on the cake. They did have a holiday at Stone Cross.'

'Four years ago,' Charlotte muttered.

'I cannot agree with you, Miss Branwell. A little jaunt as you term it would make a fitting end to the present agreeable visit from a most charming young lady,' Mr Brontë said. 'No, ma'am, I must have my way in this! If I recall there is a pleasant inn near the abbey where one may obtain a meal at moderate cost. I would, of course, give Branwell sufficient money to defray all expenses. So, girls, you may go! Were I not so burdened with parish work and were the gig somewhat more roomy I would join you myself!'

'Mr Brontë, I am endeavouring to rear my nieces without spoiling them,' Aunt Branwell objected.

'And I believe that an occasional treat renders the normal course of life more palatable. We will say no more upon the subject.' He rose with some hauteur and stalked from the room.

'We had best find something decent to wear.' Charlotte was on her feet, towing Anne in her wake.

Emily, following, paused briefly by the teapot. 'Thank you, Aunt,' she said softly.

Aunt Branwell inclined her mob-capped head, her tight mouth curving in a tiny smile.

The gig having been hired and Branwell having agreed to show off his driving skills and Charlotte having fussed over whether to wear her green weekday dress or her grey silk which was for Sundays, Ellen's bags were packed and she went into the kitchen, armed with a lace-edged handkerchief she had slipped out to buy in the village.

'For you, Tabby, because you have looked after me so well.'

In Ellen's world servants were tipped when one left after a visit but Tabby was hardly the usual kind of servant.

'For me? Eeh, Miss Nussey, fancy tha remembering me! Just look at that! Look at that lace on't border! Tha's a good lass, Miss Ellen, tha is!'

Delighted, the elderly woman reached up and hugged her warmly.

'She won't use it you know,' Emily murmured as they went out to the gig. 'She will wave it about in church and wait for the compliments.'

'You will come again, I hope, my dear.' Aunt Branwell came to the side of the gig as they clambered up.

'I shall look forward to it,' Ellen said sincerely.

'My felicitations to your family, Miss Nussey. Your presence has graced our humble abode.' Mr Brontë was at his stateliest. 'Branwell, drive with care! You carry a precious cargo.'

Branwell, red hair tumbling about his face, leapt up into the driving-seat. His cravat was untied and his boots were already dusty but his high spirits affected them all and they bowled down the high street at a pace that sent bystanders scurrying into doorways and set Anne giggling.

'You have enjoyed yourself, haven't you? You'll come again?' Charlotte plucked at her friend's sleeve.

'I've had a wonderful time,' Ellen said, surprised to find that, despite the ghost stories and the narrow bunk-bed she had been forced to share, she felt more alive than she had felt for months.

The Brontës were an interesting family once one penetrated their shyness she decided. She looked forward to introducing them to Henry and George, her favourite brothers who would meet them at the abbey.

The ruins of the abbey, the surrounding green of the woodland, the long low inn with its thatched roof awaited them as they bowled along the track and drew to a halt.

'What a pretty place!' Emily exclaimed. 'You should've brought your sketching materials, Branny. You have Gothic romance aplenty to inspire you here!'

A smart coach was drawn up before the inn and as the Brontës alighted from the gig a group of young people headed by two smartly clad young gentlemen rushed across the green to engulf Ellen with a burst of greeting and chatter.

'Henry! George! Ann! Everybody! May I introduce my friends with whom I've been staying? Mr Branwell Brontë, who was kind enough to bring us safely here. Miss Charlotte Brontë, my great friend from school and her sisters, Miss Emily and Miss Anne.'

The four Brontës stood stiffly, all animation drained from them. Charlotte was mentally comparing their plain dresses and unadorned straw bonnets and thick boots with the frilled skirts and dainty parasols of the girls now being introduced. Emily stood as stiffly as a poker, her eyes downcast, her full mouth clamped shut while Anne, suddenly turning into a scared rabbit, had grabbed her tall sister's hand tightly and was holding on for dear life.

'Dinner is already ordered and about to be served,' Henry Nussey said. 'After the meal we can walk round the ruins for a spell. Mr Brontë, will you take a glass of wine with me before we eat? Ellen, would your friends like some lemonade? I fear it was a thirsty drive.'

'We shall have an entertaining meal.' One of the girls was smiling at Branwell. 'You must tell us about your artistic ambitions, sir. Nothing is more guaranteed to absorb the interests of a young lady!'

They were idiots, Emily thought, surveying them from beneath lowered lashes. Shallow, fashionable idiots! How could nice Ellen Nussey endure their chatter or Branwell regain his self-confidence and begin chattering and laughing with them? Even Charlotte, who was escorted by Henry Nussey into the inn, had a coy, missish expression on her face. She took a firmer grip of Anne's hand and followed them into the inn.

It was midafternoon before the ordeal was over. At least they had been left free to wander through the grounds and admire the scenery since she had remained obstinately silent, merely nodding and shaking her head when a remark was addressed to her, and Anne's one stumbling remark had been incoherent as her stammer overcame her. Charlotte had forced out a few sentences and Branwell had drunk two glasses of wine and talked entertainingly as if he had mingled in polite society all his life.

With infinite relief Emily climbed back into the gig and sat as the leavetakings were completed.

'How did you endure it for a whole week?' Ann Nussey, pressed against her younger sister in the coach, asked the question seriously.

'At home they are quite different,' Ellen said excusingly.

'The brother is amusing enough, fancies himself as a poet and an artist, but the sisters! Rub the three of them together and you'd not get one decent conversationalist!'

'Miss Charlotte struck me as a sensible young woman,' Henry said thoughtfully.

'But the other two. Are they quite right in the head?' someone else asked.

'I like them both very much,' Ellen said, disappointed but loyal.

'They are probably more at ease in their own home,' George suggested.

'In a glass case in a waxworks show!' Ann Nussey said and giggled into her handkerchief.

Seven

'Taby said just now. Come Anne pilloputate (i.e. pill a potato) Aunt has come into the kitchin just now and said Where are your feet Anne Anne answered On the floor Aunt. Papa opined the parlour door and gave Branwell a letter saying Here Branwell read this and show it to your Aunt and Charlotte. The Gondals are discovering the interior of Gaaldine. Sally Mosely is washing in the back kitchin.'

Emily Jane Brontë

'Charlotte is right,' Emily said soberly, reading over a light-hearted account of a day's events penned in the kitchen the previous November. 'My spelling is dreadful.'

'And your punctuation leaves something to be desired,' Anne said in a neat parody of her sister's manner.

'I don't see that it matters much when I am never likely to write a letter to anybody,' Emily said carelessly.

'You cannot spend your whole life in ignorance, not when you have such a brilliant mind,' Anne said in her own voice.

'You're the only person who thinks that, Annie!' Emily grinned and leaned back on the sofa. 'The truth is that I've always been slower than the rest of you.'

'The truth is that you can spell very well when you take the trouble!'

'Stop scolding me. You're not a governess yet,' Emily said lazily.

'I've never even been to school,' Anne said wistfully.

'You don't really want to go, do you?' Emily sat up and stared at her younger sister.

'It would be an experience.'

'Not all experiences are pleasant,' Emily said soberly.

'Cowan Bridge was a long time ago,' Anne said. 'Roe Head School is a well-regarded institution. And Miss Wooller has offered Charlotte a splendid opportunity. She is to teach and one of us is to have a free place there.'

'And Charlotte wants me to go. I don't want it!'

'But you will go, I think,' Anne said.

'Did you ever try to stand out against Charlotte once she got something fixed in her head?' Emily said impatiently.

'She wants us all to get on,' Anne said. 'Now that Branwell is going to the Royal Academy in London we may all three have to contribute eventually to our own livelihood until he is firmly established.'

'He is extremely talented. Surely he'll make a name for himself quite quickly?'

'He probably will but it's as well to be sure that we ourselves will be able to manage. You must see that, Emily.'

'I do and I wish that I didn't.' Emily rose and went over to the window. 'But to leave Haworth and settle in with a crowd of strange girls who probably never have an idea in their heads worth expressing – why must I do that? I'll be like a fish out of water! You crave learning so you ought to be the one.'

'You're the elder. It's only fair that you should have the chance. 'You can come back and teach me everything you've learned,' Anne said.

'Perhaps,' said Emily, cheering up slightly, 'I'll get another attack of erysipelas as I did after Miss Nussey's first visit.'

'When you were very feverish and the bad stuff had to be cut out of your arm? You hated having the doctor come.'

'All doctors are pretty useless. The flesh will heal itself. It seems there's no help for it then. I shall be a captive in the Palace of Instruction and pine away.'

'No you won't! You'll work hard and obtain top grades and in the holidays we will play at Gondal again. There will be free time at Roe Head for you to make things out and I shall have time in which to imagine events moving forward too while I'm sewing. And you'll be with Charlotte.'

'Yes,' Emily said, staring through the window. 'Yes, I'll be with Charlotte.'

She loved Charlotte but the old closeness had vanished years ago. She knew that Charlotte longed to share things with her again, especially now that Branwell was going to London, but Gondal was for herself and Anne. It was complete and unique and she didn't want her sister taking over, imposing her own ideas on the epic that ran constantly through Emily's mind, scenes unfolding that were more vivid than reality behind her open eyes.

She could see no way out. Charlotte was right to want the three of them to be literate, to acquire some social skills. Emily stifled a sigh. How much more peaceful it would be to stay safely at home, joking with Tabby in the warm, untidy kitchen, running up on the moors with Anne at her heels, playing with Grasper and the other animals she had managed to bring home – the tame geese, Adelaide and Victoria, originally meant to provide Christmas dinner but spared because nobody in the household could find the heart to slaughter them; the doves, Diamond, Rainbow and Snowflake who flew to her hand to be fed; the pheasant, Jasper, who followed her round like a dog. Aunt Branwell had protested in vain, complaining that the parsonage was turning into a zoo.

'Don't fret,' Anne said softly. 'I'll take good care of the animals.'

'I know you will, Annie!' Emily spoke warmly but her mind was racing ahead, looking for a way out.

They left in the gig on the morning of Emily's seventeeth birthday, Charlotte anxiously exhorting Branwell to write from London and tell them all about the Royal Academy and the great buildings he would see and the important people he would meet. Emily climbed silently up into her seat and thought of the fourteen miles that would stretch between her home and Roe Head. It seemed like an ocean dividing two continents.

Then she reminded herself that she carried Gondal in her head wherever she went and pleased the watching Anne by turning and giving a cheerful wave as the driver climbed to his seat.

Her heart sank as they left the high ground behind and the cobbled street and rough track became a civilized highway with other vehicles passing. There were more houses here with bits of garden enclosed in stone and the smoke from the surrounding mills blurred the clarity of the air.

'My salary will clothe both of us,' Charlotte was saying. 'And your having free tuition will be a great load off Papa's mind. You will like it, Emily. The conditions are so comfortable and the routine so placid.'

Augusta Geraldine Almeda was a hostage, straining her eyes through the bars of her dungeon in the southern wall, knowing that somewhere someone galloped to her rescue. Lord Alfred of Aspin? Fernando de Samara?

'I shall do my best,' Emily said quietly.

It was a large handsome house with lawns and flower borders around it and long curtains at the plate-glass windows. Emily followed Charlotte into a polished hall where a small, plump woman with her hair plaited in a coronet on top of her head and a long, white dress on that looked as if she were dressed up as a nun, was kissing Charlotte and giving her what was obviously an affectionate welcome.

'And this is Emily? Charlotte has spoken of you often, my dear.'

Miss Wooller's hand was outstretched. Emily put both hands behind her back and managed a stiff bow.

'We must test you on your present knowledge and then you may eat supper with the other pupils,' Miss Wooller said, giving the tall girl an uncertain smile. 'This way, my dear. Charlotte, you know the place assigned to you. I'll have the porter bring up your things.'

What had Charlotte been telling people about her? What did Charlotte know that she herself couldn't remember?

Emily followed another woman whose name she didn't catch into a long room furnished with long narrow tables and stools. They reminded her of Cowan Bridge, though the walls here had pine panels and lamps with cut-glass shades.

'We will begin with a piece of dictation,' the other said. There was paper and a pen and an ink-well. Emily took off her cloak and the black straw bonnet Charlotte had insisted on her wearing and picked up the pen.

'You are left-handed, dear?' The teacher was frowning slightly.

Emily nodded.

'That should have been corrected in your childhood. Never mind. Now let us begin.'

Emily wrote, her underlip thrust out. Nobody at home minded that she was left-handed. Even Aunt Branwell said it was normal for some people to write with that hand. Nobody had regarded it as a fault. She scrawled the words that seemed to be coming from a distance.

Once, long ago, she had pleased a nice lady with her reading and been given coffee and a cake with currants in it. Then later on, much later, there had been two small living skeletons, a door that opened into a red-shaded bedchamber within sound of the sea. Her mind shut down, her hand suddenly shaking and sending a fine spray of ink across the page.

'Let us try the reading, dear,' the teacher said.

She wasn't her dear. She wasn't anyone's dear. She was the dark boy trapped in the body of a girl who was trapped in a big house that was trapped in a garden that was imprisoned by walls.

'Thank you, my dear. Perhaps you are weary after your journey. Shall we go into supper?'

Another room with two long tables and girls seated at them. There were sandwiches and fruit tarts and raisin bread and mugs of coffee. The other girls were chatting freely and now and then came a burst of laughter. Charlotte was sitting at a smaller table at the other end of the room.

I am going to die here, Emily thought. *I am going to die.*

But in the morning, waking with nobody beside her – 'You are somewhat older than the other pupils, my dear, so you may sleep in a bed of your own,' Miss Wooller had said kindly – she felt cold and stiff. All night she had lain open-eyed, missing the warmth of another body next to her, waiting for the dark shadow to come.

At Cowan Bridge there had been hunger and cold and beatings and fear. At Roe Head there was unfailing kindness, plenty of food, regular lessons, walks in crocodile round the neighbourhood, ball games on the lawn, bells to separate one part of the day from another.

'Miss Brontë is such a great tall girl,' she heard one pupil whisper. 'Surely she's too old to go to school!'

At home Branwell had painted two portraits of them all. In

111

one he had impatiently obliterated his own image saying he would finish it later but his sisters were there; Charlotte with her square face and round eyes, Anne gazing limpidly into the middle distance, Emily looking bored and sulky. Posing for Branwell could get tedious. In the second portrait he had included himself, taller than he really was, with a bush of carroty hair, and some dead game-birds on the table. She was in profile in the second portrait, her hair curling on her neck, her features delicate.

Looking at it Anne had breathed, 'Branny has caught your soul, Emily.'

But here she had no soul. She was a great girl, five feet seven inches tall with a big nose and a pouting mouth and long legs and blank, veiled eyes. Only once had she known anything like pleasure; one afternoon her class had taken their sketch-pads into the fields and she had made some quick, lively drawings of some cows, and sneered silently at the other girls who had hastily decamped when one of the animals ambled over to take a look.

'You must make an effort, Emily,' Charlotte urged, seizing a chance for a private word. 'I know it's hard. It's hard for me too, but don't waste this opportunity.'

Charlotte had locked up Angria and thrown herself into teaching, a task she found difficult because she had little patience with the mistakes of others.

Gondal had fled of its own accord. Augusta Geraldine Almeda was silent and invisible, her lovers shadows without features. Emily couldn't bring them back. Only the dark boy struggled fiercely to break through the prison of flesh in which he was contained.

Emily stopped eating. Meal after meal her plate was pushed away with only a couple of mouthfuls taken, meal after meal she sat, taking a sip of tea or coffee now and then, lifting her fork and holding it suspended as she stared at the pine panels of the wall desperately trying to limn the beautiful features of her vanished Gondal queen on the polished wood. She felt light and airy, the voices of others echoing faint and far away.

'Miss Brontë, we must do something about your sister.' Miss Wooller had nerved herself to speak to the small determined young teacher who tried so hard to divert attention from her strange sister.

'She does not mean to be difficult, Miss Wooller.' Charlotte twisted her small hands together. 'She is homesick, that's all. She wishes to learn and to fit in, but when she wakes every morning the vision of the moors and of our home rushes upon her and darkens her horizons. She has tried so assiduously to conform but she cannot. She needs such tender understanding.'

Miss Wooller, being privately of the opinion that Emily might be the better for a good slap, said, 'I fear school life does not suit her temperament. You have a younger sister?'

'Anne, yes. She is not yet sixteen.'

'Would she benefit from the curriculum here?'

'I am sure that she would. I can write to Papa. About fees—'

'Her tuition and board here will be free as is Miss Emily's.'

'Thank you, Miss Wooller. I shall write to him today,' Charlotte said gratefully.

She had not expected raptures from Emily when she informed her that she would be going home and Anne coming to replace her but she had expected gratitude. Emily, however, merely looked at her dully and nodded.

Anne had wanted more formal education. Anne had her wish. She would be homesick here but she would lock Gondal away to be resumed when the holidays came and she would work hard and well. She herself had failed. She had meant to fit in but something within her had been stronger than her outward will. It had dulled her appetite, banished her sleep and made it impossible for her to articulate her feelings. Now she was going home and she didn't even know if Gondal could be recaptured.

When the gig came which would take her home for good and Charlotte for the weekend before she returned with Anne she nodded brusquely to Miss Wooller and climbed up into the seat, her long skirts emphasizing her loss of weight.

'I shall work very hard and fit myself for my future career,' Anne said when, after the initial greetings and exclamations of dismay from Aunt Branwell at Emily's wasted appearance, they were alone together.

'Career? A governess or a teacher is the least regarded of professions,' Emily said.

'It is at least a living,' Anne said placidly.

'Why is Branwell still at home? When does he go to London?'

'He did start for London but there was some muddle over funds.' Anne looked unhappy. 'Apparently he was robbed in the coach and had to return. Papa thinks that a period of further study will be of benefit. He is still only eighteen, and more practice at various painting techniques will be of benefit. He'll be glad of your company when Charlotte and I are gone.'

'And you will have Charlotte, though she is much occupied with teaching.'

'Perhaps I will make a friend at school as Charlotte did,' Anne said.

There was no time to seek Gondal that weekend since Anne's packing had to be speedily accomplished and Emily's appetite hadn't returned. Though Tabby scolded and sat her down before a mound of mashed turnips and potatoes peppered and buttered Emily managed only a few mouthfuls.

The gig bore her sisters away on a day that showed October at its best, with the leaves turning red and gold and the blue haze of autumn on the far hills.

Emily went indoors and took out the tin box in which she and Anne, in an imitation of their elders, had jotted down half-finished tales and scraps of poetry about Gondal. They struck her now as impossibly childish and suddenly impatient she shoved the papers back into the tin box and went out into the graveyard to throw it down the well. If Gondal wasn't going to return then she wanted no reminders.

'Why don't you put on your cloak and go for a short walk?' Aunt Branwell suggested. 'A little exercise and fresh air will benefit you.'

'I believe I will.' Emily took up a small pail. 'There may be some late whinberries up on the moor.'

At least she could make herself useful by providing fruit for a pie, she reflected, as she picked her way along the lane, eyes downcast. By now there'd be talk in the village about Branwell's abortive trip to London and her own swift return from Roe Head. The locals, according to Tabby, had nothing better to do than clack about their superiors.

'Miss Emily, I'm glad to see you a little better.' Mr Greenwood who kept the stationery shop in the High Street had paused to address her. He was a blustering little man, perhaps because he was scarcely bigger than Charlotte and limped in an ungainly fashion. Emily looked down at him and smiled, seeing the genuine kindness in the pouchy eyes.

'Thank you, Mr Greenwood.'

She walked on, feeling slightly more cheered. Mr Greenwood had always done his best to keep in stock the paper and pens the family needed.

She crossed the lower fields, crisped with the approach of winter, and struck out on to the higher ground. The heather and gorse had all faded now but the holly berries were ripening. When she raised her head she glimpsed a skein of wild geese flying south.

The landscape was empty of humankind apart from herself but teemed with the hidden life of animals. When she gained the high crags she sat down and let the edges of her mind probe into their hidden places, under the surface of the earth, hidden in the grass, glinting in the pools that made fairy mirrors in the hollows.

She was escaped from the Palace of Instruction. Augusta Geraldine Almeda had escaped. She saw her, dimly at first and then as clearly as if she stood in a shaft of mellow sunlight, long dark hair curling wildly about her slim shoulders, eyes blue and alert, head tilted proudly.

She had fled to the heathland and called her supporters now to join her, called them to help her regain her throne. The outlaw Douglas was striding towards her, black hair tumbling about a savagely handsome face, cloak swinging from broad shoulders. He stood before her, awaiting her command.

' 'Morning, Miss Brontë!'

Her pseudonym but not her essential self. In public places it was needful to wear a mask.

'Heaton.' She bowed her head graciously, acknowledging that he too wore a public mask.

He was Douglas, outlaw and Quashia, the mulatto borrowed from Angria whose origins were mysterious and sinister. He pretended to be Heaton, bastard cousin to the five sons of Mr Heaton who had carried her to safety during the Crow Bog burst and brought Grasper to the house and planted a pear-tree for her. They were both pretending.

'Grand morning, Miss Brontë!'

'Indeed it is!'

115

She watched him turn away, whistling to the sheepdog that padded after him. It was the longest conversation they had ever shared and her heart made an epic of it.

When she came into the kitchen, cheeks flushed from the wind, Tabby shot her a surprised stare as she put the pail, almost full of whinberries, on the table.

'What's gotten in't thee?' she demanded.

'Hunger,' Emily said. 'I could demolish a feast fit for the gods.'

'I made a tray of drop-scones. Help thysen.'

Emily took four, slathered them with butter and sat down to eat them.

'Happen tha's better,' Tabby said. 'I allus did say as tha'd not stand school. Not that anyone teks notice. Coffee?'

'A mugful, please,' Emily said happily with her mouth full of scones. She was in her kingdom again and her appetite had returned.

With Charlotte and Anne away at school the tiny study room had become her own domain. For the first time in her life she had not only a bed but a room of her own where she could sleep solitarily confined within her own space. It was good to close the door and sit down on the edge of the camp-bed with its cover and the view through the window across the front garden to the high church tower.

She had little interest in the graveyard, dripping soon with the first sleet of November, or the church tower pocked with the bullet holes from her father's daily target practice with his pistol. The sky above the church that changed colour and texture with the seasons interested her more. When she looked at the night sky with its powdering of faint stars she felt some inner turmoil, not articulated, resolve itself.

The night sky and the moor had nothing to do with the pew where she sat Sunday after Sunday, letting Papa's sermons drift over her head. Seated beneath the high pulpit and perforce facing the congregation she kept her eyelids lowered to the stone floor, her carriage upright, her mouth compressed.

'Your sisters taught in the Sunday school,' Papa said.

'I will not, Papa.'

Dark blue eyes met pale blue eyes.

'Very well, my dear. As you please.'

'Thank you, Papa.'

116

He enquired no further, perhaps fearing to hear that she had no patience with the doctrines he propounded week after week. Charlotte had been weaned on the Old Testament with its jealous Jahweh and its plagues and prophets; Anne was imbued with the New Testament with its constant emphasis on sacrifice and suffering. Emily sought for a space between the two, somewhere that was her place alone.

Charlotte and Anne came home for Christmas and the study room was no longer her own. But Charlotte no longer cuddled up to whisper in the dark. She reserved her confidences for Branwell and the two of them whispered and chatted together. Catching a sentence or two Emily gleaned that they were deep in Angria again and that both were weaving dreams of being published one day. Meanwhile Charlotte grumbled about the long hours of preparing and marking lessons, the stupidity of her pupils, the lack of time in which to get on with her own writing. Branwell was not going to London after all. Instead he was going to set up as a portrait painter in Bradford where Papa was arranging to rent a studio for him and fix him up in some respectable lodging.

She and Anne played at Gondal, surprised to discover that their ideas still ran in tandem, though Douglas was a stranger in Anne's secret world.

'He sounds rather fierce and wild,' she complained.

'He is,' Emily said serenely.

Anne had actually made a friend. She confessed the fact as they sat in the dining-room one afternoon.

'Her name is Ann Cook – without an "e",' Anne said. 'She is much younger than I am. Not yet twelve. She is a new pupil as I am and most pitifully homesick. I like her very much because she is sweet-natured and has a mind that thinks and doesn't merely absorb information fed into it by others.'

'She will suit you, then.'

'And of course as I have always been the youngest it's nice to have a friend who is younger yet. You don't mind, do you?'

'Mind what?' Emily enquired.

'My having a friend of my own.'

'Good heavens, no!' Emily looked surprised. 'I'm pleased for you, Annie. One day I'll astonish you all and get a friend too. Meanwhile, enjoy Miss Cook. It lifts a worry from my mind to know that you have a companion at Roe Head.'

For her own part she failed to find space for anyone else in her world.

When the others had left, Charlotte and Anne returning to Roe Head, Branwell setting out for Bradford where he planned to astonish the world with his artistic genius, the house was still full. Emily helped Tabby in the kitchen, sat sewing with Aunt who shook her head over the straggly stitches, and played the pianoforte for Papa for half an hour after tea.

She loved music, felt the rhythms of the Scottish ballads she played flow through her veins and into her fingertips.

Though the weather was hard she still contrived to walk out on the moors, more slowly now in deference to the aged Grasper who found walking difficult and panted a great deal. Now and then she glimpsed the tall figure either on horseback or trudging with his spade across his shoulders and once when he nodded and waved she turned her back rapidly and walked away, overcome with something deeper than shyness.

Augusta Geraldine Almeda had betrayed Douglas too and now the savage outlaw sought revenge, waited for the moment to strike. Others lay in wait – the golden-haired Angelica who had once been a loving child and the black-haired boy, sprung from a red hell, who would grow up to be the outlaw Douglas and Quashia. Time was not continuous but folded itself in layers so that at any moment she might unfold a section at her leisure and explore its possibilities. Now and then she took pen and paper and expressed a mood, a situation in a few lines of verse that petered out into nothingness when Tabby, in her guise as the old witch who gathered elflocks in the fairy cave under Ponden Crag, demanded help with the vegetables. Emily Jane, living in two worlds at once, was perfectly content.

Eight

'A slinky girl'

Haworth Resident

Emily bent over the back kitchen table, her long fingers deftly untying the splint. Under her hands the young hawk lay quiescent, feathers unruffled, beak unthreatening. Its wing was healed. She stood back, cooing softly beneath her breath as the bird righted itself, hopped a step and experimentally fluttered its wings.

'Come, Nero! Time you went into the wild again!'

The hawk gathered itself together and flew unsteadily to her shoulder.

'Emily, have you got rid of that bird yet?' Aunt Branwell's voice sounded as she clacked along the stone-flagged passage.

'I am taking him out to the moor, Aunt. His wing seems quite healed now though it will take time to strengthen completely.'

'Put your gloves on, dear! You don't want your hands pecked.'

'Nero only pecked me because he was hurt and frightened, Aunt,' Emily said cheerfully.

'You should've left him where you found him,' her aunt muttered.

'Would you have had me leave Black Tom where I found him?' Emily demanded truculently. 'In a sack weighted with a stone about to be drowned?'

'Kittens are different. A cat is always a comfortable addition to any household. Birds are not. Certainly not birds of prey!'

'What about Anne's canary?'

'Little Dick sings most sweetly and remains in his cage most of the time. Emily, are you arguing with me again?

119

'Of course not, Aunt.' Emily opened the back door and went out into the crisp winter day.

Miss Branwell heaved a small sigh of relief. Her tall niece had, in the two years since her return from Roe Head School, become quite formidable in her manner, she thought. There had been that distressing episode during the Christmas holidays of the previous year when Tabby had slipped on the ice in the village street, breaking her leg severely in two places and calling fruitlessly for help for nearly an hour with nobody hearing because the shops were closed.

'We cannot possibly give her the care she needs here,' Aunt Branwell had decided. 'We can have her conveyed to her sister's house in the village where we can visit her daily and pay her medical expenses.'

'It seems rather harsh, Miss Branwell,' Patrick had frowned. 'Tabby is like one of the family.'

'Tabby is one of the family!' Emily had backed up her father. 'You would not pack Charlotte or Anne off to another house if they break a leg, will you?'

'Charlotte and Anne return to school next month, dear. That means that there will be nobody to assist you with the housework, which takes you a long time anyway, or to help with any nursing at which you are all quite unqualified. Mr Brontë, when I left my pleasant home in Cornwall and all my friends there in order to care for my poor sister's children I was assured that I would be in complete charge of the household. Does that still hold good?'

'Naturally, Miss Branwell. Certainly. Do as your aunt bids, girls.'

She had thought the argument ended there, but she had been wrong. When she had come out from her room in order to take dinner as a mark of her approval she had found her three nieces seated mutely before untouched plates of food.

'W-we cannot eat if Tabby is going to b-be sent away,' Anne said.

'My dear child, she will be at the bottom of the main street, five minutes walk away. I shall make a point of visiting her every day twice and seeing she has everything she requires. Now eat your dinner.'

Three plates remained untouched.

At teatime she faced the same scene. Her nieces sat mute and unfed. When Charlotte's gaze strayed to the teapot Emily said sharply, 'No liquids either!'

Breakfast was worse. Mr Brontë barely touched his own meal and the three ate and drank nothing, their eyes downcast, their lips compressed.

'You are being,' she exploded irritably, 'completely ridiculous! Mr Brontë speak to them.'

'I have urgent business over at Mr Brown's,' her brother-in-law said, making good his escape.

'Let us hope you have come to your senses by teatime,' Aunt Branwell said.

By teatime it was obvious they hadn't come to their senses. They had prepared sandwiches and baked cakes and she had been careful to remain in the kitchen eagle-eyed for any perceived weakening of will.

'This is helping nobody! Emily, I suspect that you are the instigator behind this nonsense. How can it help Tabby if you go without food? Anne, at least drink some tea. Your mouth must be quite parched.'

Silence! Three blanched faces were obdurate.

'Very well! Very well, Tabby may stay to be nursed here,' she said at last, throwing up her hands. 'I never knew such obstinate – you will have a great deal of work to do, Emily! Now will you please eat?'

'The cakes look very good,' Emily said. 'Charlotte, will you pour the tea?' Her mouth had curved into a triumphant little smile.

At least the hawk was gone. Emily was not a person to keep animals captive. Aunt Branwell sighed and went back along the passage to the kitchen where Tabby, still lame despite the months of care she had received, limped slowly from the fire to her chair and sat down with her knitting.

It was still possible to walk a long way over the moors, Emily thought, striding across the fields towards Ponden Crag, Nero still on her shoulder. The first snows had covered the crags and the faint sunshine gilded the white, shading it with other colours borrowed from the sky and the limpid water of the pools and streams where a few sprays of heather still lingered. Beneath the snowline frost rimed the trees and bushes and gave the pebbled paths a hard white gleam.

'Fly free now! Shoo!' Clambering on a rock Emily clapped her hands loudly. Nero fluttered away, cautiously at first and then climbing higher, circling about her and then arrowing upwards.

'Fly free and find your mate!' Emily stood for a moment, feeling the bitter air settle around her.

In a day or two Charlotte and Anne would be at home. The previous day Papa had received a panic-stricken letter from Charlotte.

'It seems that Anne is not well at all,' he had informed her at the breakfast table. 'Miss Wooller was of the opinion that it was merely a heavy cold but Charlotte became so anxious that she insisted a doctor be consulted and it appears that Anne is suffering from a severe bout of gastric fever. I fear that Charlotte lost her temper and spoke most disrespectfully to Miss Wooller. One cannot blame the poor child. Naturally she worries about Anne's condition. I have sent word that as soon as dear little Anne is fit enough to be moved she must come home immediately. Your aunt is in complete agreement. Anne has spent two years at Roe Head and acquired considerable knowledge so she has earned a rest. Whether Charlotte will return there to teach she doesn't say.'

Anne had endured two years, Emily reflected. She herself had endured less than three months. There was a quiet strength in little Annie.

They would play at Gondal together again. Augusta Geraldine Almeda had escaped from the prison caves and been crowned – a fortunate coincidence since the Princess Victoria had ascended the throne of England and would be crowned in the same period. There was however a republican movement growing which needed to be crushed before new colonies could be established on the newly discovered island of Gaaldine.

Someone had hailed her. She swung round and stood motionless, only her cloak fluttering in the chill breeze.

'G'day, Miss Emily!'

Heaton had paused on the slope below her.

Emily nodded.

'I heard as how thy dog died,' he said.

'Grasper, yes. He was very old.'

'I've a dog seeking a home. Ten months old, Miss. I took him from a gypsy who were beating him wi' a stick. He'm a fierce dog – a mastiff – and cannot abide t'be struck wi' stick or fist, but there's good stock in him. Would tha like him mebbee?'

'My father misses having a dog. He would be grateful.'

'Cans'tha wait five minutes?'

He had turned and was running back down the hill.

'Douglas has brought the gift of a savage wolfhound to his queen,' Emily said softly.

'Lord knows that I've done my best for my sister's boy!' Thus Mr Heaton, calling upon Papa as she had lingered in the hall. 'I gave him a home, tried to educate him, to impart to him the advantages my own lads have, but he has a wild streak broader than your arm. Always off over the moors when he's supposed to be helping out on the farm! It's his father coming out in him, of course, but my patience is wearing thin.'

'I never see him in church, Mr Heaton,' Papa had said.

'He hasn't a Christian bone in his body. Past twenty and he sneers at religion and calls kindness weakness and charity stupid.'

The wild boy was growing into a dark and vengeful man, without pity. The girl who had loved him had never ceased to do so, but the world they inhabited was dividing into two. Somewhere on the moor the two children ran freely, hands and hearts clasped, their world secure but in their adult selves they were being pulled apart.

'Miss Emily?'

He stood before her, taller and broader than she was, his black hair uncombed, his garments rough and patched as if he took pleasure in looking like a labourer. His dark eyes were feeding from her with peculiar intensity. In one hand he held a leash on which a half-grown dog whose paws already outstretched the rest of him was leaping and barking.

'Good dog.' Emily crouched, holding out her hand palm upwards. 'Good boy. Easy now. Easy now.'

The dog displayed sharp white teeth, then unexpectedly licked her hand.

'Tha's got a way wi' dogs, Miss Emily,' Heaton said approvingly.

'I shall call him Keeper. Long ago my grandfather in Ireland had a dog named Keeper. Papa told us about him.'

'Thy dad's t'parson.'

'Yes, yes he is.'

'Minds his business and leaves us to mind ours.'

'Is that what folk say?' Rising to her feet, taking the leash from his hand she laughed. 'Small praise indeed!'

'Better than some folks get.'

'It probably is. Thank you for the dog. Papa will be delighted.'

'It were for thee, Miss Emily,' Heaton said. His dark eyes lingered for a moment on her face. Then he stepped back, clearing his throat. 'Mebbee when winter's done,' he said awkwardly, 'we may . . . tha might well walk on't moors again?'

'With my sister. She is leaving school and coming home again.'

'With thy sister. Aye, that reckons.'

Somehow she had said the wrong thing but she didn't know why. The eager look had faded and he dropped his hand to his side, shuffled his feet and said abruptly, 'Aye weel, tis better so. G'day, Miss Emily!'

She felt as warm as if she had just received a declaration of love. She opened her mouth to call to him to walk back with her to the parsonage and receive her father's thanks for himself but he was already striding away from her down the hill and the words died into a whisper.

'Come, Keeper! Let's introduce you to your new master!' She held the leash more tightly and walked back across the frostbitten grass.

'Emily, they are come! I have ordered Anne to bed immediately. She looks very weak and worn, poor child. And Charlotte is overstrained though she has made up the quarrel with Miss Wooler and agreed to return next half-year. Apparently the school is to be moved to Dewsbury because the building at Mirfield costs too much to run but she will tell you – who's this?'

'Keeper. Your new guard dog, Papa. Heaton says he has been badly treated and will not tolerate punishment with fist or stick, but he's loyal.'

'He's going to be a large dog. Here, boy! Aye, he's a fine fellow. We shall have to get a brass collar and a licence for him.

Lord knows what your aunt will say! Put him in the kennel Emily, and I'll break the news by degrees. And go and see Charlotte. She will be glad of a comforting word.'

'Yes, Papa.'

She put the dog in the kennel, found fresh straw and an old shawl of her own, settled him with a bowl of water and some scraps. When she went into the dining-room Charlotte sprang up.

'Have you seen Anne yet? She is really poorly, Emily! Miss Wooller would not listen to me. She actually said that I was making a fuss about nothing and finally I lost my temper completely and said some very sharp things. She actually burst into tears. I'd've respected her more if she'd turned me out of doors immediately, but she begged me to stay on. In the end I said that I would. You look well!' Her voice was suddenly accusing.

'You look worn out,' Emily said frankly.

'Teaching is not the most congenial of occupations,' Charlotte said bitterly. 'I was so happy there as a pupil, Emily, and I never realized how hard the staff worked in order to instruct us and care for us. Oh, Miss Wooller is no harsh taskmistress but there is scarcely an instant when every thought isn't taken up with preparation and testing and marking and those dreadful crocodile walks. If those boobies knew how I disliked their vapid chatter they would not seek my company as they do. There have been times when the secret world has risen up before me and obliterated what was actually happening in the classroom. I saw the Marquis of Douro, saw him bodily before me, strained to hear him speak, and then someone came up and thrust an exercise into my face and he was gone. I nearly vomited!'

'Gondal seems—'

'I hope that Branny comes home for Christmas. I was sad to hear that his portraits are not more sought after. It was Papa told me that, for Branny seldom bothers to write. Have you been busy? With Tabby still so lame much of the work must fall upon you. Well, one of us must earn a living, and you always said you wanted to be the housekeeper. What have you been doing?'

'Nothing very much,' Emily said. 'I must go up and see Anne now.'

She was met by Aunt Branwell coming out of her bedroom.

'Two minutes, Emily dear. The poor child is exhausted and needs several days' rest and plenty of good food to build her up. I shall watch over her myself!'

Long ago, or had it been yesterday, she had gone into this same room and seen a little skeleton grimace at her in welcome. Feeling cold and sick she went in.

'Don't hover at the door!' Anne said weakly but cheerfully. 'I am not yet on my deathbed. Oh, I am so happy to be home again. It seems a century since we were on holiday here and wrote our diary papers together.'

'You look very well,' Emily said, in faint surprise.

'You would not have recognized me a week ago.' Anne sat up alertly. 'I could keep no food down and I wanted to cry all the time! I felt so hopeless, so certain that I was damned.'

'You? Damned?' Emily stared at her.

'Sin.' Anne whispered the word. 'We are all of us so weak, so inherently wicked. I was quite in despair sometimes when I examined my conscience, added up all the times I had put my feet on the rungs of my chair, been rude to Aunt, let my mind wander during one of Papa's sermons. The burden on my soul was terrible and there was nobody to whom I could open my heart. My one friend in school, Ann Cook, is a dear girl but too young to understand. And poor Charlotte was herself over-worked and depressed.'

'Annie, you're one of the best people I know. You can't possibly—'

'I asked that a minister be sent to bring me some consolation. A Mr Trobe from the Moravian Community came and was so very kind. He made me see that there is hope for everybody.'

'Of course there is! Anne, you've allowed your conscience to dictate to you and harm your health.'

'That was what Mr Trobe said. I shall be cheerful again now that I'm at home. Here comes Aunt. She has been so good since Charlotte and I came. We haven't appreciated her kindness half enough.'

'Probably not,' Emily said. 'Give your conscience a holiday, Annie, and I'll go down and help make the tea.'

'Emily, my dear, have you a moment?' Mr Brontë was holding open the parlour door.

'Of course, Papa.'

'How do you think Anne looks?' he said anxiously, closing the door behind them. 'She appears to me to be very weak and pale.'

'She will pick up her strength soon enough,' Emily said.

'Of all of you she is most like your dearest mother,' he said restlessly. 'I could not endure losing her.'

'You will not, Papa. She is stronger than we any of us realize.'

'About the dog?'

'We may keep him, may we not? You have missed Grasper so much.'

'Of course. Of course we shall keep him, introducing him to your aunt by degrees. The Heaton boy gave him to you, you say?'

'For you, Papa. He wanted no payment.'

'You did not permit any familiarity I hope? In speech I mean. Though we are not rich we occupy a certain position in society and sometimes the lower orders may try to take advantage of our natural courtesy. Now that you are a young woman it becomes necessary to guard your conduct so as not to . . . give the wrong impression.'

'Yes, Papa.'

'And in the coming months you will have your hands full with Tabby still so lame and dear little Anne to be cherished.'

'Yes, Papa.'

'Now run across to the pharmacy for me, my dear. Charlotte mentioned that she has been somewhat troubled with toothache. Cloves will relieve the pain. Here is the money.'

'Thank you, Papa.'

In the street she wrapped her cloak around herself and pulled her hood over her hair, fixing her eyes on the cobbles.

'Miss Emily, I hear your sisters are come home!' Mr Heaton, coming out of the Black Boy, stopped her.

'Yes, sir. My sister Charlotte will return to teach in the New Year but Anne will stay at home now.'

'Tell your father I'll call upon him shortly. At the moment I'm seeking my nephew. You recall Heaton?'

'Yes, sir.'

'He left the stable door open, took one of my best mares and galloped away as if the devil was chasing him. Well, bad blood will out, I suppose. My regards to your sisters.'

'Yes, sir. Thank you.'

Walking on, entering the crowded pharmacy with its myriad
bottles and spicy, varied scents, asking for the cloves, she stood
in a cold field. In her mind's eye a broken tree bled upon the
ground and a figure hung limply, turning slowly in the chill
breeze.

'If the bird returns then Heaton never will.'

'Your change, Miss Emily.'

'Thank you.'

Judas coins heavy in the palm of her hand. The newly
crowned queen wept, invisible knives piercing her heart.

'If the bird returns then Heaton never will.'

Walking on, turning into the lane where the stones sparkled
with frost, the garden gate swung gently on its hinges.

She paused, her hand on the latch and felt the dark boy slip
away, running, running, becoming shadow not substance. A fluttering of wings, claws digging gently into her shoulder. Nero
lowered his head and rubbed it very gently against Emily's
cheek.

*'If the bird returns then Heaton will never come again. Never.
Never.'*

Nine

I cry as the grim walls enfold me
I have bloomed in my last summer's sun
                                Emily Jane Brontë

'Would this be Mr Brontë's house?'

Emily straightened up from her desultory weeding to stare at the immensely tall man who stood at the gate, his greying red hair springing up in a crest that reminded her of Branwell.

She nodded slowly.

'Then you'll be one of my nieces then. You've a look of Pat.'

'I am Emily Jane.'

'And I'm Hugh Brontë. Now will you be opening this gate or leaving me to stand here like a beggar?'

She hastened to open the gate, stood aside to let him pass her, and closed it again as if to repel invaders.

That marked the beginning of her uncle's visit. Papa came from his parlour to greet his younger brother with a hearty handshake and a sudden burst of Gaelic as if he had been transported back to his youth, and other members of the family were summoned to meet the first of their Irish relatives they had ever seen.

'My son, Branwell, is in Bradford carving out a career for himself as a portrait painter. He joins us often at the weekend. Charlotte was a teacher until recently but has given up her post since the air of Dewsbury did not suit her. She is away at present paying a visit to her great friend Miss Ellen Nussey – a very fine family, by the bye. One of her brothers was surgeon to the late king. Anne completed her schooling almost a year ago and is presently at home, her health being somewhat delicate. Emily you have met. Miss Branwell, there you are! Come and meet my brother Hugh. Emily, bring up a bottle of whisky from the cellar! We'll toast old times while you tell me how things fadge at home.'

She had seldom seen her father so animated. Taking in the whisky and the glasses she found them seated at each side of the parlour fire, both talking in the strange liquid tongue that fascinated her by its very unfamiliarity.

'Leave the bottle. If I remember rightly Hugh is not averse to a couple of drams. You'll stay, brother? Emily, can you prepare Branwell's room for your uncle?'

'I'm over here to find work,' Hugh said bluntly, 'so I'll not be staying more than a few days. They'll be hiring for the harvest soon, won't they?'

'Conditions in Ireland are not good?'

'Wet weather, absent landlords, high taxes – we've a harsh winter ahead. Willie does well enough for he's opened a shebeen and when there's no food men drink to cheer themselves up a bit. *Slainte!*'

Emily, closing the parlour door behind her, leaned against the wall, delighted mirth rippling through her. So one of her Irish uncles had an illegal drinking tavern! Charlotte would be mortified if she ever got to know about it. Poor Charlotte was always so particular about the society with which they were connected.

'Why is he come?' Anne whispered when the two of them were laying clean sheets on Branwell's bed.

'To look for farm work but if it's not forthcoming he'll likely dun Papa for a handout,' Emily said.

'Emily, dear! he looks like a respectable man.'

'Even respectable men are sometimes hard up for cash – not to mention respectable women,' Emily said dryly.

'Charlotte asked Papa if he would grant her a small allowance,' Anne confided. 'She could save nothing at Roe Head because once she had clothed herself and me there was nothing over, and she so dislikes having to ask for every single penny from Papa, though he always gives her what he can.'

'But not to the extent of an allowance.' Emily smoothed down the coverlet and raised an eyebrow.

'He asked her what a woman would do with money of her own.'

'Aye, for most men power resides in their pockets! Anne, did you know there is hardship in Gondal? The harvest has failed and the revolutionary forces are gaining strength from the disaffection of the peasants.'

'Will Julius Brenzaida escape from prison and ascend the throne?' Anne enquired.

'Or Gerald Exina will seize the crown and set up a rival royal house. I haven't made it out yet.'

From below Aunt Branwell called, 'Hurry up, girls! We must prepare extra scones for our visitor.'

By the time the scones were baked only a third of the whisky remained in the bottle and Mr Brontë's mellow mood was observed with quiet disapproval by Aunt and Anne and secret amusement by Emily.

Before the next week was out Uncle Hugh Brontë had departed, carrying silver pencils for his sisters and ten pounds in cash to distribute as he thought fit.

'I wish it were more, brother, but Branwell is not yet self-supporting and there are the girls, of course. Poor Charlotte has been greatly overstrained during her teaching and Anne is too young to think of leaving our protection.'

'And Emily?' Hugh asked.

'Emily is an invaluable help in the house. Tabby has never been able to resume her full duties since the accident I told you about. Indeed she agrees with my sister-in-law that the time has come for her to retire to her sister's house. My sexton has a quiverful of daughters who will come in daily to help with the rough work and Emily, of course, has been trained for housekeeping.'

Papa, thought Emily, walking out with Keeper at her heels and Nero on her shoulder, has written our parts in his private play. But I want something for myself, some proof that I can exist away from Haworth, some money of my own.

'Teaching? Emily, what on earth has put that idea in your head?' Charlotte, home from Ellen Nussey's, stared at her sister.

'You had your nose to the grindstone for two years and you deserve a rest,' Emily said stolidly. 'Anne is not yet strong enough to go out among strangers and Branny cannot yet support himself entirely so one of us must lift the financial burden on Papa. I have answered an advertisement and been accepted as a teacher at a school called Law Hill on the outskirts of Halifax. Miss Patchett, the headmistress, requires a junior assistant to replace her sister who is leaving to be married. I will have charge of the younger children.'

'You'll have to teach them how to read and write,' Charlotte said.

'I didn't spend all my time in peeling vegetables and walking the dog while you and Anne were away,' Emily said with a smile. 'I set my own timetable and contrived to stick to it in large measure. You would be surprised to find out how much my spelling has improved.'

'You will have to ask Papa's permission.'

'I have already told him. He agrees that one of us should earn something and to be honest I look forward to testing myself. I cannot droop and pine every time I leave Haworth, Charlotte. I'm not a hothouse flower but a healthy twenty-year-old.'

Time, she told herself silently, to grow up. Time to face the real world and leave Gondal to rest for a while.

Miss Elizabeth Patchett, her hair elaborately ringleted, her skirts trimmed with black-ribbon bows, greeted the tall young woman who alighted from the gig with genuine kindliness.

'Miss Emily Brontë? Did you have a pleasant journey, my dear? Come along in!'

The newcomer bowed stiffly, ignoring the proffered hand, and said in an unexpectedly sweet and musical voice, 'It is only eight miles from Haworth, ma'am. I had not time to become weary of the view.'

'This is your first post, you said?'

'Yes, ma'am.'

'And educated at . . . Cowan Bridge?'

'Yes, ma'am, for less than a year when I was a young child. I also spent nearly three months at Roe Head School at Mirfield but my sister took my place and since then I have continued my studies and helped keep house for my father.'

Miss Patchett smiled, leading the way through the portals of the bleak grey house set high on the moors above the town.

'This is a working farm as well as a school,' she said, ushering Emily up a handsome flight of stairs into a pleasantly furnished drawing-room. 'I myself keep horses and give riding lessons. Do you like animals, Miss Brontë?'

'Oh yes, ma'am!'

The blue eyes had darkened suddenly to violet and the pale, pasty face with its distressingly high-bridged nose and too-full mouth lit into a joy that transformed the uneven features.

'Your own work will be with the younger pupils. We have twenty boarders and a further forty day pupils. The school proper is in the former warehouse across the yard. Classrooms on the ground floor and bedchambers above. There is a small room at the end of the large dormitory where you will sleep in some privacy. Now drink your coffee and I'll show you round.'

So far so good, Emily insisted to herself. Miss Patchett seemed genuinely well disposed and the high hills among which the building was set pleased her. From the windows she could look down at the hollow basin from which the mills and factories of Halifax sent up clouds of misty grey smoke.

The headmistress was outlining the daily routine.

'We rise at half past six and prayers are at seven, breakfast at eight before the day pupils arrive. Lessons are from nine to two and after dinner we like our girls to take a healthful walk before lessons resume until five. Then there is tea and afterwards you will be expected to supervise the children until their bedrooms are opened up again for them at seven. You do sew?'

'Sew? Yes, ma'am.'

'As you will have very little marking to do since your pupils are all under the age of eleven then you may profitably employ the evenings in sewing. Now let me show you your room and leave you to unpack. School proper begins tomorrow so that gives you a few hours to settle in.'

She was introduced to two other teachers who bowed cordially and then Miss Patchett, still talking brightly, was ushering her down the stairs and across the yard to a large stone building with steps leading up to the main door. Her eyes registered tables, benches, blackboards, shelves with exercise books piled on them, and on the floor above narrow bunk beds and a row of washstands.

'Earnshaw will bring up your bag,' Miss Patchett said. 'Take a little time to find your way around. The bell will summon you to supper over in the main house, or would you prefer a tray up here in peace and quiet?'

'Up here,' Emily said gratefully.

She was finding it hard to concentrate on all the information being flung at her and the prevailing greyness depressed her spirits. Irritated, she gave herself a mental shake and turned to look out of the window. At least she had a private space where she could escape when the day's work was done, and through the glass she could see the moors that stretched away towards Haworth.

The next morning she found herself after a few confused hours of sleep standing before a class of children, all brightly scrubbed with their hair neatly plaited or tied in bunches. Fourteen pairs of eyes were fixed on her in polite expectation.

'Good morning, children.' She held herself upright, her eyes moving from face to face.

'Good morning, Miss Brontë!' A chorus of voices answered her.

'We will begin,' Emily said, 'with a reading test. As we read you will, when your turn comes, give me your name, so that I can get to know which of you is which.' Her career, she thought wryly, frantically jotting down names, had begun.

The children were not exactly naughty but they giggled and fidgeted and mispronounced words in a way that set her teeth on edge. Once or twice during the endless morning Miss Patchett put her curled head in at the door, murmured, 'Splendid, Miss Brontë!' and withdrew, leaving Emily to find her place in the textbook while the small girls seated before her yawned and whispered.

The afternoon was much, much better. The day being fine and crisp, Miss Patchett sallied forth to join Emily and her class as they walked on the moor.

'You seem to have made a good beginning, Miss Brontë.' The headmistress smiled at her encouragingly. 'The children always take a few days to settle into our routine. Of course this is an interesting district in itself. Law Hill, for instance, was originally built by a man named Jack Sharp. You haven't heard of him?'

'No, ma'am.' Emily turned her attention from the long sweeps of autumn grass, over which she longed to run, to her employer.

'He was an orphan, Miss Brontë, adopted into the Walker family who live still at Waterclough Hall very close by. He was treated as a member of the family, indeed favoured above some of them for he had great charm of manner, but that charm hid a wild and wicked heart.'

'What did he do?' Emily's interest was caught.

'When the father of the family died Jack Sharp made it his business to corrupt the heir, himself scarcely more than a boy at the time. He led him into evil habits, Miss Brontë – drinking, gambling, other things one hesitates to mention! Eventually the true heir was reinstated but before he was forced to leave Waterclough Hall he denuded it of furniture and hangings and used the money he had swindled from the family to build Law Hill.'

'The school?' Emily said in surprise.

'In the end he accumulated so many debts that he was forced to sell the place. He went to London and died there – of drink some said. The odd thing is that the boy he had cheated and brutalized never lost his old affection for him and even gave him money later on when he was in trouble. That casts a curious light upon human behaviour, don't you think so?'

'When did this happen?' Emily enquired.

'Not more than twenty-odd years ago. I was a very young girl at the time. Miss Caroline Walker, who is a daughter of the original heir, still lives there and is a great friend of mine. Shall we turn back? The wind grows somewhat cold.'

Jack Sharp. Casson. Welsh Brontë. All cuckoos, cheating and robbing the people who had been kind to them. Families torn by conflicting emotions. Property stolen and laid waste. Dark boys growing into men of flint.

'Miss Brontë?'

'I beg your pardon, ma'am.' Emily jumped slightly. 'I was just thinking that history often repeats itself in various settings.'

'Indeed it may but one hopes there will be no more Jack Sharps!'

Miss Patchett spoke lightly, signalling the crocodile of small girls to retrace their steps.

Her employee had fallen silent again. The wind had brought a touch of colour into her cheeks and her face, while she had listened to the story, had been vivid with interest and enthusiasm. Now she looked remote and faintly sulky again.

It was past eleven before Emily left the small sewing-room on the ground floor of the main school building and, leaving a half-finished petticoat to be completed the next evening, crossed the yard to the schoolhouse which still looked rather like a warehouse despite the alterations made.

The lean yellow housedog growled warningly from his sentinel post near the gate.

'Here, boy! Good boy!' Emily stooped, palm outstretched as the dog padded towards her, licking her hand with a rough wet tongue.

'Good boy!' Caressing the rough fur she saw again the lively Keeper, felt the swift contact of flesh on flesh as he had strained at the leash that Heaton had transferred to her grasp. He had spoken to her – commonplace words but in his eyes something deeper had spoken. Or had that been merely in her own mind? No, she hadn't imagined the interest, the liking, the spark that had leapt between them at the instant she had made some stupid remark and crushed the spark for ever.

She gave the dog a last pat and went up the steps, let herself in and went silently, a shadow flitting between shadows, into her own small space where a full moon shone as brightly as a chandelier.

Augusta Geraldine Almeda was in captivity again. She stared at the bars of her cell and willed them to burst asunder, but she knew that her lover, the dark boy, had gone beyond her reach, hung on a scarred and broken tree turning softly in the breeze that blew from a far country. Before dying he had cursed her, prayed that the hell in which he burned would consume her spirit too.

There were writing materials on the broad window-sill. She knelt on the floor and lifted the pen, dipped it into the ink, wrote beneath the cold light of a hunter's moon, the walls that enclosed her dissolving.

'Miss Brontë, it is my custom to take some of my older pupils to musical soirées or occasional visits to the museum. Would you like to come on Friday evening?'

Miss Patchett paused in the sewing-room on her way to her own quarters, feeling a pang of conscience as she noticed the younger woman toiling away still though it was past ten at night.

'Thank you, ma'am.' Emily looked up, her eyes brightening. 'If you wish it.'

'Oh, these occasions are entirely voluntary, Miss Brontë. I would be glad of your company if you have a mind to come.'

'Thank you, Miss Patchett! I would indeed like to come.'

'You have not finished the mending yet?' Miss Patchett lingered a moment.

'I am slow at the work,' Emily said, flushing dully.

'Well, never mind! Leave it until tomorrow. You are having no trouble with your class?'

'None, ma'am.'

How could she tell her headmistress that it was a constant, soul-searching task to keep her small pupils in any kind of order at all. They were neither rude nor disobedient but they seemed incapable of sitting still for more than five minutes; they fidgeted, giggled, flicked pellets of paper at one another, seemed unable to follow what she tried desperately to teach.

More than once her temper had bubbled to the surface and she had gripped her left hand with her right to prevent it from striking out. When that happened she saw Maria again, her neck bruised by the birch. To strike a child would place her beyond redemption.

The pupils, stealing glances at her burning eyes and the dark hair that refused to stay tidy but frizzed around her face, told one another that Miss Brontë wasn't unkind but she was peculiar, often going off into a kind of dream in the middle of a sentence, her eyes glowing when she looked through the window as one of the horses was being led by or the dog ran into the classroom and jumped up to her.

'My friend Miss Anne Lister of Shibden Hall gives the occasional musical soirée at her home. Invitations there are highly prized,' Miss Patchett said, ushering Emily and three of the older pupils into the gig.

She herself, it transpired, was accompanying them on horseback. In her dark-green riding-habit with a feathered tricorne on her long ringlets she was a striking figure. Emily, who had heard one of the other teachers, a thin, fluffy creature, whisper that Miss Patchett was near forty, hoped she herself would acquire during the next twenty years something of the older woman's elegance and grace.

The gig bowled down the steep hills, rounded the corners and along an avenue bordered by trees whose last leaves fluttered in the November wind and drew up before the façade of a splendid manor house with mullioned windows and double doors which, hospitably open, revealed a panelled hall with a fire blazing and many portraits hanging on the walls.

A young man stood on the steps to welcome them. No, not a young man, Emily realized, as she stepped down. The person was a young woman, pale faced, androgynous with black hair drawn severely back, her black clothes cut in a masculine style with a divided skirt which gave the illusion of wide trousers, and a high white cravat.

'Miss Patchett, you know where to stable your mount. Young ladies, good evening! Come along in and warm yourselves by the fire. And this is. . . ?' She was favouring Emily with a frank, forthright stare.

'My new assistant teacher – Miss Emily Brontë from Haworth,' Miss Patchett said, dismounting.

'Welcome to Shibden Hall, Miss Brontë. Shall we go in?'

It was the beginning of an enchanted evening. There were glasses of hot punch and sandwiches filled with spiced meat and a variety of fruits dipped in sugar sauce and a large cake cut into thick slices and heavy with cherries. There was no formality. They sat as they pleased at a long table or in high-backed chairs with strange dragonlike creatures carved on them, and two manservants moved noiselessly about the room, refilling glasses, proffering food.

Then they moved into a large room with one part cleared save for a grand pianoforte, several violins and a guitar on which Miss Lister began to strum, her long fingers plucking the melody out of the strings with a passion that hinted at fires banked down. Other guests were arriving, all ladies, and cups of coffee were being distributed as a quartet of people were settling themselves at the instruments.

These musicians had obviously been engaged to provide the entertainment. Emily had attended an occasional recital in Haworth with her father and aunt but these performers played like angels. She was lost in the music, her eyes wide open, something within her newly released and expanding.

'You are still inside the music, Miss Brontë.' Anne Lister had taken a seat next to her and was leaning forward slightly, her deep husky voice seeming part of the melody.

'Yes, ma'am. You express it exactly,' Emily said.

'Music has always been my escape from the workaday world. Do you play?'

'A little, ma'am.'

'I play myself and would spend more time at my pianoforte had I leisure enough, but since my uncle who brought me up died I have had an estate to run. I breed horses and flatter myself I can choose a good strain of wheat which will resist most diseases. What do you do when you are not teaching children?'

'I help in my father's house. He is perpetual incumbent of Haworth.'

'So you ran away in order to teach?'

'Not at all!' Emily found herself laughing. 'I have two sisters and a brother who is an artist and we appreciate one another's company but it was, I felt, my turn to earn some money.'

'And to sample independence?'

'That too.'

'Shake hands with me, Miss Brontë! It pleases me when I meet a young woman ready to make her way in the world as she thinks best.'

Her hand was gripped and warmly shaken. Dark, slightly slanting eyes seemed to read the secrets of her face.

Then Anne Lister rose and sat down at the pianoforte and launched into a Beethoven sonata, her fingers caressing the keys as if the ivory was flesh.

Outside the darkness was shot with starlight. People were leaving, their outer garments brought in by the two servants. Emily put on her cloak over her dark grey dress and adjusted the hood, conscious suddenly of an aching regret. She would have loved to linger, to draw the walls of this manor house about her like an extra cloak.

'Adieu to you, Miss Patchett! You will come again after Christmas, will you not? In the spring I start for foreign parts again so I must see my friends as often as I can. Bring Miss Brontë with you! She strikes me as a kindred spirit!'

'With pleasure, Miss Lister. Come along, girls.'

In the gig, oblivious to the icy wind and a spattering of snow, Emily sat shrouded in the warmth of recent experience. Had she found a friend who would be her special friend as Ellen Nussey was for Charlotte or Ann Cook for Anne? Ellen and Charlotte paid each other visits, wrote long letters to each other; Ann Cook had not yet visited or invited Anne to stay but affectionate notes were exchanged from time to time.

'You look very well!' Charlotte exclaimed almost accusingly when she beheld her sister at the start of the holidays.

'I am very well,' Emily said placidly. 'You were right, Charlotte. Not all schools are like Cowan Bridge. Oh, the hours are long and the work is hard but Miss Patchett could not be more kind or considerate! There are horses there too and a splendid dog and some interesting local legends. No, I am so far satisfied with my position.'

She moved through the festival in a contented frame of mind. Anne was clearly stronger, eager to share the latest events in Gondal; Branwell came home from Bradford looking vaguely discontented.

'The studio is given up!' he announced abruptly. 'People are ready enough to order their portraits be taken but less eager to pay for them. I may look about for a tutoring post. I need time in which to polish my verse. Charlotte, why the devil did you bring Mary Percy alive again after I killed her off?'

'Because I could not bear to have her die alone and friendless of a broken heart,' Charlotte said.

People didn't really die of broken hearts, Emily thought impatiently. They picked themselves up and carried on regardless. Even after a loss that bruised the heart compensation came.

'Did you have a pleasant Christmas Miss Brontë?' Miss Patchett asked the question as if she genuinely wanted to know.

'Yes, ma'am. My whole family was together,' Emily said.

'Let us hope for a pleasant term,' Miss Patchett said, smiling.

But the term began badly. Emily's class, having lost their slight awe of an unfamiliar teacher, had begun to pay less attention, their whispering became louder, their giggling shriller.

'Do try to pay attention,' Emily said wearily.

'Why cannot we go out?' one of the girls demanded. 'Tomorrow it may be snowing again and we shall be penned up like cattle!'

Someone at the back of the class mooed loudly and there were little shrieks of laughter.

'We shall begin the exercise again,' Emily said.

'Miss Brontë, you can't mean it!' One of her older pupils looked at her in horror. 'Why, you cannot feel any affection for us if you make us drone through all that again!'

'Care for you?' Emily's patience snapped. 'I care for the yard-dog more than for any of you!'

It was wrong to lose her patience with them. Charlotte would have brought them to heel, hiding her feelings beneath a poker face and a slightly sharper voice. No wonder Charlotte suffered from headaches and stomach upsets!

Miss Patchett took them all to Shibden Hall again and this time as well as music there was a talk given by Miss Lister, full of vivacious accounts of her travels in Europe which should have held Emily's attention but somehow did not, for why learn about foreign marvels when she was unlikely ever to leave Yorkshire? Miss Lister had greeted her cordially again but she had a friend staying with her, a pretty young woman in a frilled dress whom Miss Lister seemed anxious to propitiate by seating her in the most comfortable chair and plying her with first choice of the dainties on offer.

It was a beautiful house, refined, luxurious. Emily wanted to wander through the rooms and up the carved staircase that seemed part of the great hall. She thought suddenly of Heaton, seeing him in her mind as a younger child, peering through the windows with a companion at his side, both envying and mocking the delightful scene within.

There was a letter from Anne. Charlotte had received a letter from Henry, Ellen Nussey's brother, proposing marriage. She had rejected it politely on the grounds they were not suited. Papa had approved her refusal but Anne and Charlotte both feared that Ellen could be disappointed.

'Miss Brontë, you are greatly behind with the mending.' Miss Patchett paused to speak to her. 'Linen will not mend itself, you know!'

'No, Miss Patchett. I do try to hurry.'

'Well, try a little harder, dear, and do endeavour to keep your class a little quieter. It disturbs the other girls.'

'I will try, Miss Patchett.'

141

Her employer was right. She was falling behind in the work. It was her fault. She was slow and stupid. Her sewing was painstakingly done but still unevenly stitched; her pupils were not progressing as they should; her own time for writing was limited to those hours after midnight when, by the light of her candle, she poured out poems about a female spirit, white-gowned and ethereal, who rode the white horse through the white snow under the white sky where the moon hung like a great ball.

The winter wore away and Miss Lister left for a protracted tour of the Continent with her frilly little friend.

'Will you take a walk with me today, Miss Brontë?'

Miss Patchett had come into her room and was smiling at her.

'Thank you, yes. The snow is melting!'

At least she had invited her to go for a walk, Emily thought, hastening to put on her cloak. That must mean that Miss Patchett was not angry with her for her slowness and inefficiency.

Outside the snow was indeed melting and the first wild snow-drops were thrusting their way up through the borders that ran beneath the windows of Law Hill.

'Miss Brontë, are you sleeping properly?' Miss Patchett looked at her.

'Yes, ma'am.' Had her candle been seen shining long after midnight in her tiny room?

'Your eyes look heavy, and one of my staff noticed that you are not eating as well as you did. If there is anything wrong . . . you may, I hope, confide in me.'

'Nothing is wrong, Miss Patchett,' Emily said uncertainly. 'It is only that when I have time alone my imagination carries me away and sleep is not of very great importance.'

'Which does not benefit your classroom work, my dear. Ah! here is High Sunderland Hall! This is a building I have always had ambivalent thoughts about. So grand in one aspect but so forbidding!'

They had paused to look across the snow-wet turf to the house that reared its turrets before them, its windows set deeply in the stone cladding that covered the original medieval wattle and daub, its main door carved above its portal with the figures of naked men and goblins and the Latin mottoes that sent a little shiver through Emily when, with difficulty, she had deciphered them.

'*Nunquam hanc pulset portam qui violat aequum*', she said now. 'Let no one who violates justice knock at those portals'.

'You have studied Latin, Miss Brontë?' Miss Patchett had turned, the early evening breeze ruffling her long ringlets.

'My father taught my brother both Latin and Greek, ma'am, and at various times my sisters and I have shared his lessons. My youngest sister Anne is the real Latin scholar among us.'

'You have intelligence, Miss Brontë.' Miss Patchett inclined her head.

'Thank you, ma'am.'

A warm glow suffused her features. She felt suddenly free to express herself as a young woman with ideas of her own, not a mere employee who sewed badly and couldn't keep a class of small girls in order.

'I, intend,' she said breathlessly, 'to do my utmost to improve in every possible way. You cannot know how much it means to have the approval of a woman such as yourself whose thoughts I dare to believe march to the same tune as my thoughts, my imaginings – to speak frankly I did not expect to be contented here, for my home is very dear to me but your friendship – it means a great deal to me!'

She stopped, bewilderment in her face as Miss Patchett turned a stony face towards her.

'Miss Brontë, I employ you as assistant teacher. I pay you a salary of fourteen pounds a year with full board and lodging,' Miss Patchett said. 'That does not give you the right to ignore the respect due to my position, my social superiority—'

'But I thought – you invited me to accompany me to Miss Lister's—'

'I also invited a few of the senior pupils, Miss Brontë. It was not an invitation to any intimate friendship.'

'I would not presume – Miss Patchett, I never would presume – I know that I could never stand in the same relation as Miss Lister to—'

'Miss Lister and I are social acquaintances,' Miss Patchett said icily. 'Surely you are not equating her desires and needs with my own! Miss Brontë, do you imagine that respectable parents would trust their daughters to me if I led the same life as Miss Lister? Her nature is – different from most females. Surely you are not so stupid as to imagine – Miss Brontë, I am betrothed to be married to a most worthy clergyman. He has had family responsibilities that have caused our union to be delayed.'

Emily stood, fighting for breath, feeling her stomach lurching. She had said something wrong, done something wrong but she didn't know how it had begun.

'I will acquit you of deliberate malice,' Miss Patchett said at last. 'Your knowledge of Latin may elicit praise but your knowledge of real life leaves a great deal to be desired! We will not speak of this again. In future you will learn to constrain your feelings according to the demands of society. I shall expect you to exert yourself a little more and to try to gain some mastery over your class. Good evening, Miss Brontë!'

She turned abruptly and walked off. Emily stood motionless, feeling the shaking within her rise to a tempest and then subside.

She had been stupid after all. The dim outline of Anne Lister rose before her. The mannish costume, the boyish figure, the deep voice – they were clear now. She had not known that such beings existed.

She had wanted a friend but friendship was to be denied her. By some cruel quirk she had been denied what other women accepted as part of their human condition.

She had betrayed Sarah, left Sarah to take the blame for the broken tree. She had betrayed Maria and Ellis. They had suffered and she had stood mutely by. She had betrayed Heaton, spurned his offer of friendship with a light, inconsequential remark. And they had all left her.

She stared at the rearing carved stone of the great house. The grotesque and naked figures writhed before her. Who lived in such a place? A giant, with raw meat hanging from the rafters. An iron-hearted man who had once been a little lad harboured by a good man to his bane.

She imprinted the façade of the house upon her mind like a drawing to be taken out and examined later. Then she turned and walked slowly back over the bleak moor towards Law Hill.

'You are late for supper, Miss Brontë!' The servant Earnshaw greeted her as she came through the gate.

'I am not hungry,' Emily said and went slowly with dragging

gait to her small sanctuary at the top of the old warehouse.

Here there was at least a measure of peace. She knelt down and leaned her forehead against the cold glass of the window. Her whole being ached with longing for home.

Ten

Yes, I could swear that glorious wind
Has swept the world aside
Has dashed its memory from thy mind
Like foam bells from the tide.

Emily Jane Brontë

'Here are your stockings, Emily. Do you think six pairs will be sufficient for you?'

'A pair for each day of the week and I shall go barelegged on Sunday!' Emily sat down on the edge of her bed and laughed up at her sister.

'Don't say that when Aunt's around or she will swear you're planning to lead a life of dissipation,' Anne said, smiling in return.

'Oh, Anne, I wish you were going with us!' Emily's expression sobered.

'Or instead of you?' Anne ventured.

'No. No, I've been nearly three years at home and it's time I exerted myself again and completed my education,' Emily said.

'And now that I am settled at Thorp Green and earning fifty pounds a year it makes better economic sense.'

'Are you really settled there? You were so unhappy when you taught at Blake Hall.'

'At Blake Hall I was useless and incompetent,' Anne said stoically. 'I allowed the children to bully me; when I tried to speak to Mrs Ingham my stammer returned with a vengeance; they were right to dismiss me.'

'And the Robinsons?'

'Mr Robinson is irritable sometimes and Mrs Robinson seldom unbends sufficiently to notice me, but the children are

147

not bad-hearted. They are growing up fast and I think that I'm making headway with them. Little Edmund is a dreadful dunce but fortunately I've a large stock of patience. And the house is very fine, Emily, with some splendid walks all about it. There are many compensations.'

'Well, I shall endeavour to be as philosophical about studying in Belgium as you are about teaching at Thorp Green! And Aunt has been generous. To offer to pay for our instruction at a good foreign school so that we shall be fully competent to teach French and German when we start our own school was very good of her.'

'Our own school!' Anne breathed the words like a litany.

'Not that I like teaching.' Emily frowned slightly. 'However you and Charlotte can divide the teaching between you and I shall be matron and give music lessons. And the three of us will be together in some pleasant house with cash in our pockets!'

'When Miss Wooller retired she offered Dewsbury to Charlotte. It was unselfish of her to refuse the offer.'

'Very, but Charlotte didn't like Dewsbury anyway. She calls it a poisoned place, and Miss Wooller didn't offer anything to you or me.'

'And it is so much better to be together,' Anne said.

'With Branwell,' Emily said.

'Yes, of course.' Anne hesitated, then said slowly, 'Sometimes Branwell's future prospects trouble me a little. He has so many talents and yet he never seems to stick at anything very long.'

'He has had ill luck,' Emily said. 'The proposed London trip came to nothing; he receives no replies to the letters he sends out offering his work to *Blackwood's Magazine*; he could not find clients enough in Bradford for his portrait studies and he was dismissed from his tutor's post.'

'It is more than ill luck,' Anne said. 'Emily, Branny drinks too much. He cannot hold his liquor and afterwards he is sick and sorry. I think it wrong that boys should be given so much more freedom than girls as if in their natures they were inherently superior!'

'You think that you and Charlotte and I should spend our evenings in the Black Bull or the White Lion supping ale and making brilliant conversation?' Emily said, amused. 'Branny will find his feet! This post on the railway is a good opportunity for him to make something of himself. The railways are the coming thing you know. If I had any money I would invest in railway stocks.'

'Girls, why are you chattering up there when half the packing's to be done?'

Aunt Branwell's voice echoed up the stairs.

'Just coming, Aunt.' Anne rose.

'Perhaps there will be compensations for you while we're abroad,' Emily said playfully. 'Willie Weightman was gazing at you in church in a most soulful manner last Sunday.'

'Willie Weightman gazes soulfully at every single lady who crosses his path,' Anne said. 'As a curate he is incurably flirtatious. Remember how he tried to tempt Ellen Nussey to walk out alone with him on the moors when she stayed here?'

'And I went leaping out to chaperone them? Miss Nussey is a dear girl but rather romantical. Anne, go down and pacify Aunt while I check that I've everything from here that I need.'

'I'll tell Aunt that you'll be down later.'

The younger girl went out.

Not girl! Emily thought. Woman! We are young women now even though Papa and Aunt insist on referring to us collectively as 'girls'. Time rushes past and the child in us is buried beneath the years.

Those years were flashing by so quickly. Charlotte had spent two unhappy periods as a private governess, confessing that she found small children almost impossible to handle and life in a strange household insupportable. She had sent some of her stories to Southey and Wordsworth and received civil but discouraging replies; she had turned down two offers of marriage, the one from Henry Nussey and an unexpected one from a handsome young curate who had visited Haworth and been so taken with her that he'd asked her to marry him in a letter the very next day. They had made a great joke of it but Charlotte had been upset when word came a few months later of the young curate's sudden death. Then William Weightman had been appointed as assistant to Mr Brontë and she and Ellen Nussey had teased each other and flirted with him and nicknamed him Celia Amelia to prevent themselves from becoming too emotionally involved.

Emily had joined in the general merriment, finding it balm for a sore heart. Willie was like a younger brother, she mused. One who was always kind and lighthearted and did his work conscientiously and took a great deal of strain from Papa's shoulders.

What Branwell needed was a wife to steady him. They had hoped that Mary Taylor might be the one. She and her sister had visited them and with Branwell home at the time and William Weightman to add his share of any amusement that was on offer it had been a happy time. Branny and Mary had gone walking with the rest over the moors and Branny had leaned over her shoulder when she and Willie had played chess.

A happy time but with undercurrents. Branwell had been very attentive to Mary but when she began to sparkle in his company, to look up eagerly when he came into the room, he had unaccountably begun to back off, to absent himself from the circle.

'I wish she didn't show her feelings so plainly,' Charlotte whispered to Emily. 'Men are frightened off by women who show their feelings too clearly. They like to be the pursuers.'

'You being the expert on men?' Emily raised an eyebrow.

'Of course not, but I know that if I ever meet a man who likes me I shall conceal my feelings until he has declared himself.'

'When such a man comes along I shall remind you of that,' Emily said.

Charlotte was right though, she supposed. Girls should wear masks of polite indifference, never offer their hearts freely. That way one avoided hurt even though one remained only half alive.

Mary's younger sister was one who showed her feelings plainly but she was so childlike, so impertinent in her saucy answers that nobody minded.

Martha wasn't in the least pretty but with her impetuous laughter and sparkling eyes one forgot her turned-up nose and big mouth. Papa had been charmed by her and praised her liveliness.

Emily had found herself watching the Taylor girls, deciding that while she could never feel real esteem for them as she did for quiet Ellen Nussey she could admire Mary's quick intelligence and independence of mind.

There had been one particular afternoon when she had lain on the hearthrug reading a book with her arm round Keeper and caught stray phrases from the others who were chatting.

'I told him,' Mary was saying, 'that my religion was between God and myself.'

'That's right.' Emily had spoken decidedly, her approving tone drawing a quick glance from Mary Taylor who had continued with the conversation without seeking to draw her further into it.

Yes, Mary was a young woman who called forth admiration, Martha a girl whose joyous spirit woke echoes in the mind. Ellen was neither brilliant nor particularly amusing but she had a quiet constancy.

'Emily, are you coming down?' Aunt was nagging again. Emily sighed and went downstairs to find her aunt hovering in the hallway.

'Anne is finishing the tea for us,' she said. 'We appear to have run out of sal volatile and the train journey is sure to give Charlotte a megrim. Can you fetch some?'

'Right!' Emily grabbed her cloak and took the money.

It was ungrateful of her when Aunt Branwell had so generously offered to finance their six months in Brussels but she would be glad when that fussy voice was an ocean away!

'Good day to you, Major!' William Weightman coming up the lane paused to salute her by the nickname he had bestowed upon her.

'Good day, Mr Weightman.'

'I am on my way to see if there is any service I can perform for the intending travellers.'

'Against all the odds I think we will be ready by tomorrow. Papa is escorting us to Brussels so he will rely on your diligence during his absence. I think he intends to make a little holiday of it and visit some of the sites of the great battles fought during the wars with Napoleon.'

'That will be a great pleasure for him,' Weightman said. 'You stay over in London for a couple of days?'

'We are meeting Miss Mary and Miss Martha Taylor there. Their brother Joe is escorting them to their own finishing academy, so we shall be quite a merry party.'

'Haworth will seem very empty,' he said. 'With Branwell gone to start his clerkship on the railway and Miss Anne returning to Thorp Green. She seems to have settled there.'

'Once we have our language qualifications then she will share in our school project. Mr Weightman, I have to buy sal volatile at the pharmacy so I must hurry.'

'Let me get it for you, Miss Emily. You have other last minute tasks to perform, I'm sure.'

'Thank you, Mr Weightman.' She relinquished the money to him gladly and turned back, hurrying past the parsonage gate towards the stile that gave on to the moors.

She had resolved that there would be no sentimental mooning over the landscape she loved but the temptation to have one last swift walk across the turf where the half-melted snow still lingered, swelling the soil beneath, was not to be withstood. She climbed the stile, hugged her cloak about her and strode on, her thick-soled boots sinking into the wet grass as she traversed the lower fields and mounted up on to the common land.

'Miss Emily?'

A voice she could imagine that she remembered, a tall figure with dark hair that had gone away and never returned.

She stopped dead, shading her eyes against the last of the sun.

'My father has sent over some books for the long journey, Miss Emily. He begs that Mr Brontë should keep them and not trouble to return them.'

One of the five Heaton sons whom she scarcely knew apart. They were all musical, it was said, and not accustomed to mingling in company.

'Thank you. You are very good,' she said haltingly. 'Please convey our gratitude for the books. Papa will be delighted.'

'He looks forward to the trip no doubt.'

'Yes. He and my sister Charlotte both—'

'But you, I think, will miss the moors,' he said shyly.

Emily stared at him.

'I see you walking with Keeper and with your bird on your shoulder,' he was continuing. 'I like walking myself and have often – forgive me. I am Robert Heaton.'

The eldest son. He would be eighteen or nineteen now, four years younger than herself. He seemed older and graver than most young men, she thought. Not that she knew many! But Branwell and Willie Weightman were fresh faced and took nothing seriously. This boy was dark, though not with his vanished cousin's darkness. His eyes were blue and not brown and his dark hair had glints of chestnut in it.

'Mr Heaton, I see you now and then in church,' she said stiffly. 'Please forgive me if I hurry on.'

'Of course, Miss Emily. I'll take the books to Mr Brontë. I wish you a safe journey and a pleasant stay. My father tells me that you are going to study.'

'With the intention of opening a school of our own. We shall be away for six months.'

'Perhaps when you return,' he said, 'we could take a walk together. It is sometimes nice to have company.'

Time had run backward and was repeating itself in a slightly different way. For an instant she felt sheer panic and then she smiled.

'In six months. I shall look forward to it, Mr Heaton,' she said.

He nodded and walked on past her, the books under his arm. A Heaton but not the Heaton who would never come again. She gazed after him for a moment and then went on rapidly, scrambling over the rough ground that bordered the inchcape grass now stiff with the remains of winter.

The wind was rising, clearing away cobwebs of memory. It swept aside the doubts and fears she had hidden so carefully from Charlotte.

'Mary and Martha are studying on the Continent! Of course we cannot hope to attend such an expensive finishing school but if we could find something at a more modest fee and if Aunt could be persuaded to help out financially – you would come with me, wouldn't you, Emily?'

'What about Anne? She deserves—'

'Anne is earning money with the Robinsons and seems fairly content with her position. Perhaps later on Anne could take her turn. And when we have a thorough knowledge of French and German then we can open a school and Anne naturally will be part of that. You will come, Emily? You can't spend your life helping in the kitchen!'

'But the Brown girls are young and inexperienced,' Emily had argued.

'Then let Aunt supervise them. She is as capable of cooking a decent meal as you are and less likely to fall dreaming in the middle of it. Emily, I want us all to get on! I want to extend our horizons beyond what is familiar. You will come?'

'If Aunt agrees that she can do without me then – yes.'

It was next to impossible to withstand Charlotte when she got an idea in her head. Besides it would have been selfish to refuse and condemn her sister to another governess post where she would be miserable and badly paid and not valued at her true worth.

Aunt had agreed to finance the six month visit and a cheaper school had been found through the good offices of the Taylors. They would be only two miles from Mary and Martha.

'We can meet up and do some sightseeing on Sundays,' Charlotte had said happily. 'Monsieur and Madame Héger have written a most civil letter to Papa. His French is somewhat rusty but I was able to translate for him. He plans to come with us and see us settled there.'

At least Charlotte looked happy and well. Her eyes glowed and her soft brown hair had a sheen on it. When Charlotte was happy she sparkled and one somehow didn't notice the too broad forehead, the big nose and the mouth that was crammed with misshapen teeth. It was no wonder that poor Mr Bryce had been so taken by her vivacity when her shyness was forgotten!

Emily lingered, letting her hood slip back and her long hair stream out behind her in the wind. It sang in her ears, set the sodden grasses dancing, twisted the bushes with their red berry drops into goblin shapes.

The wind was clean and clear with no memory of betrayal and rejection. In Gondal it blew through the deep forests where the outlaw Douglas hid; it roared down the wide chimney of the banqueting hall and the more modest chimney of the cottage. Across the threshhold the housedog stirred and growled and shifted aside as the tall dark stranger entered, his cloak wrapped about him, melted snow dripping from his black hair. He moved silently to the high mantelshelf and stood there, his head bowed. Then as the others gazed fearfully he raised his head and lifted his eyes. Basilisk eyes, deep as caverns, bitter with unshed tears. Not human eyes. The iron man in whom feeling was dead. Where had he come from this little dark thing harboured by a good man to his bane?

Turning at last she ran down the slopes and across the fields, climbed the stile and went down the lane.

'Young Mr Heaton called with some books for the journey.' Papa came out of the parlour.

'I suspect we shall all be too seasick to read,' Emily said.

'I found that I am quite a good sailor,' he said. 'The Irish Sea can be as rough as the Channel you know! And first we have the train journey to anticipate. We shall be whirled down to London in less than twelve hours, only think of that!'

'Then we shall be dizzy *and* seasick, Papa!'

'Best chain up Keeper and cage Nero before we set off in the morning,' he advised. 'Otherwise they will try to follow.'

'Yes, Papa.'

Keeper would understand that she was returning but Nero would not. He was still part wild but he was not wild enough to survive alone out on the moors. She hoped Aunt would take good care of them both. Miss Branwell was never unkind but she preferred animals to be kept in their place. She saw them as somehow alien and not part of the great cycle of life.

'Emily, have you nothing better to do than stand staring into space?' Aunt Branwell enquired.

'I'm sorry, Aunt Branwell. Did Mr Weightman bring the sal volatile?'

'He did. I asked—'

'I'll go up and help Charlotte,' Emily said.

'She's in the dining-room. I shall go upstairs and rest for half an hour.'

'It is very good of you,' Emily said impulsively, 'to pay our expenses in Brussels!'

'Your mother would've wished all of you to get on in life. She herself was an intelligent woman. If she had not – well, never mind! Do as you have done, my dear, and she will look down with pride. I know how hard it can be for you.'

Aunt Branwell patted her arm and mounted the stairs.

'Emily?' Charlotte opened the dining-room door and beckoned her within. 'I have a gift for you! It is to mark our going abroad together for the first time.'

It was a Bible. Emily looked at it silently.

'I want us both to draw closer tomorrow,' Charlotte said breathlessly. 'After Papa leaves us in Belgium we shall be the only English pupils in the school – in a Roman Catholic school, Emily! We must stand out against any possible attempt to convert us.'

'I don't suppose anyone will trouble,' Emily said. 'Thank you for the gift. It was a kind thought. However I daresay I shall resist the blandishments of Rome for six little months.'

'I intend that we shall stay longer,' Charlotte said, lowering her voice. 'We shall require a year at least to perfect our languages. We may obtain part-time employment in order to support ourselves.'

'Anne will be lonely.'

'Anne has great inner resources. When we heard her school friend, Ann Cook, had died then she was quite calm and resigned. Anne does not expect much out of life. She is a realist.'

Emily nodded vaguely, flipping up the lid of her younger sister's writing-desk. There were Gondal verses there and a page covered with sketches. The heads of babies, plump and idealized, smiled out in the lamplit room.

Emily frowned slightly and closed the lid. Anne, it seemed, had her unacknowledged dreams too.

'I'll go and get the tea,' was all she said.

Eleven

'I wish to be as God made me'
Emily Jane Brontë

Monsieur and Madame Héger sat at their ease in the pleasant sitting-room to which they invariably retired for an hour or two at the end of a long day, she having overseen the smooth routine of the pensionnat and he having divided his time between the boys'school next door where he taught and the lessons he gave in his wife's establishment.

It was an opportunity for them to compare notes, to enjoy a little private conversation before the four children were brought from the nursery to indulge in a little rough and tumble before Constantin Héger gave his usual *lecture pieuse* to the older pupils.

They were a handsome couple, well matched despite the fact that Zélie was six years older than her husband. She looked younger than thirty-seven with her clear complexion, her light auburn hair and slightly plump figure. Her husband whom she loved with a watchful passion was the same height as his wife, dark haired and sallow with a harsh countenance which could, when he chose, light into beaming handsomeness.

They spoke in French though Monsieur Héger was of German descent, their voices rapid, their expressions reflecting mutual interest in each other's affairs.

'We shall have to make a decision fairly soon, *ma petite*. The English demoiselles are due to return to England next month.'

'To that father of theirs!' Madame made a small face. 'You were fortunate not to meet him, my dear. He talked with such pomposity about his family and his parsonage and how he intended to visit the site of the Battle of Waterloo – to me, a

157

Frenchwoman! Mademoiselle Charlotte had the grace to look embarrassed at least.'

'And Mademoiselle Emily stared into space with a look of complete boredom on her face I've no doubt!'

'I have never seen her with any other expression on her face,' his wife said.

'You should slip into the classroom when she is arguing with me,' Monsieur said wryly. 'When I suggested that instead of formal grammar they could learn best through a kind of osmosis by studying the works of great writers in French and German and then writing essays in the same style Mademoiselle Emily had plenty to say for herself. She declared it would stunt their own individual styles. This from someone who has not yet mastered the subjunctive!'

'And Mademoiselle Charlotte?'

'Is the more yielding. She is eager to please. Yet her sister strikes me as having the more powerful intellect and they both work so very hard!'

'And make no friends.'

'Charlotte would make friends,' Monsieur said consideringly. 'She would mingle with the other girls but Emily clings to her all day, hardly ever letting her stray more than a few yards from her side! You have seen them yourself in the garden, walking round and round with Emily leaning on her sister's shoulder as if she were ready to fall down without support, and making it impossible for her to talk to anybody else.'

'Perhaps they are livelier than we see when they meet their English friends? The Taylors, are they not?'

'One hopes so. However, whatever their unsociable habits the fact remains that both of them have made extraordinary progress in both French and in German, and Emily has taken both drawing and music lessons with very great advantage to herself. One would like to encourage them further. What do you suggest my dear?' Knowing her good sense he looked at her enquiringly.

'We could offer to continue the present arrangement without charge if Miss Charlotte agrees to give English lessons to some of the older pupils and Miss Emily instructs the younger pupils in music. What do you think?'

'That I may join the English classes myself. My command of

that tongue is sadly deficient.'

'One only wishes,' Madame said feelingly, 'that they would learn a little elegance in their dress. Charlotte is, at least, always neat and dainty but what in the world induces her sister to wear those dreadful dresses with perfectly straight skirts and huge ballooning sleeves?'

In the garden outside where Emily had slipped out to read another chapter of a German novel which had excited her imagination, three or four girls recently arrived at the school surrounded her. The Wheelwright sisters had been pleased to find two compatriots already settled at the pensionnat, but rather less delighted to find that Charlotte, who looked pleasant, was commandeered by her sullen faced sister and never managed to snatch more than a few words with them.

'Miss Emily!' Letitia, more forward than the rest, challenged Emily with a teasing smile. 'Where is Miss Charlotte? Have you lost her?'

Emily shook her head and read on.

'What are you reading?' Letitia dropped herself down on the bench. '*The Entail*. What is that?'

'A book by Hoffmann.'

'In German! You must be very clever.'

'I work hard,' Emily said.

'Perhaps that is why you have no time to devote to fashion,' Letitia persisted.

'Nor time for impertinent girls.' Emily stood up abruptly and stalked off.

'I think you have hurt her feelings,' eleven-year-old Frances said.

'So?' Letitia tossed her fair curls.

Frances hesitated and then broke away from her sisters to follow Emily.

'My sister was only joking, Miss Emily.' She caught up with the other and skipped round in front of her. 'If you like I can dress your hair for you. It's beautifully thick but like mine it must be hard to keep it tidy. I have some extra long hairpins we could—'

'Thank you,' said Emily icily, 'but I prefer to be as God made me.'

She sidestepped the other and walked on without looking

back. How dare other people draw attention to her appearance! How dare a mere child try to persuade her to wear her hair in a different style! How dare they try to interrupt her when she was immersed in a fascinating ghost story about a stranger who arrives after nightfall at a haunted castle high on a bleak moor? Though she could as yet follow only the general gist of the plot she could see the castle clearly, with its grotesque carvings lavished over the door, the Latin motto. She could see the bent figure of the old servant admitting the stranger.

'Emily, here you are! Such good news!'

'Branwell has received another promotion?'

'Not as far as I know.' Momentarily sidetracked, Charlotte frowned. 'He is still at Luddenden Foot, I believe. A railway clerk!'

'It looks to me as if he's getting on at any rate,' Emily said. 'So what is your good news?'

'Madame and Monsieur have just intimated that they are willing for us to remain a further six months and very likely six months after that as students here for no fees. Madame suggests that I might teach English to some of the older pupils – and you might teach music to some of the littler ones. It's what I hoped for you know!'

'Yes. Yes, I know.'

Another endless six months, perhaps twelve, shut up in a pleasant, well conducted school whose large and beautiful garden was hemmed in by high walls. Another six or twelve months living among girls who were either Belgian, Catholic or stupid and English and Protestant.

'What will you, bonnie love?' Charlotte slipped an arm coaxingly through hers.

Emily was silent, gathering her thoughts together.

She would have Charlotte's company and the weekly visit to Mary and Martha Taylor when the four of them walked out into the countryside; she would progress further with her languages for though she had summed up Monsieur as a flirt and a poseur, she had recognized his talents for teaching. It stimulated her to argue with him, and then to produce a piece of work that caused him to exclaim at its subtlety.

'Madame particularly mentioned your music,' Charlotte said. 'Both she and Monsieur admire your playing immensely and your drawing lessons – you gain pleasure from those, do you not?'

Poor Charlotte! So eager to stay on in this foreign place. Never missing the moors or longing to run down the slopes of a hill with her hair flying out.

'Would I be teaching music to the Wheelwright girls?' Emily asked abruptly.

'Yes, and they are practically from home for their papa is very well acquainted with the Taylors and the Nusseys, you know.'

'I won't give up my own study periods in order to teach silly little girls,' Emily said, 'but they can come for instruction to me during their play hour. Tell Madame so.'

'Thank you, Emily! I'll write at once to Papa and Aunt.'

'And to Anne and Branwell!'

'Yes. Yes, of course! I'm sure we've reached the right decision.'

Charlotte was off like a bird, skimming across the grass. Emily resumed her walk, the book tucked beneath her arm.

Somewhere within the school a bell rang. The daily *lecture*, when Monsieur read from some religious work and then explained it, was predominantly Catholic. The Brontës might attend or not as they pleased. Generally they absented themselves but this evening Charlotte would be there, Emily surmised, beaming her gratitude for the Hégers' kindness.

She herself went towards the studio behind the two large classrooms where the eighty pupils, forty of them boarders, practised reproducing various still lifes and one another's heads and profiles. She liked best the hours when she was free to draw in her big sketch-book. Nobody disturbed her then. Charlotte whose sight, even with her spectacles, was too weak to permit her to draw or paint or play an instrument never ventured here.

To her annoyance there was someone there already: a slim, fair-haired girl of sixteen or seventeen, her dress neat and pretty as were the dresses of all the foreign students. A silk dress of green and white check with a small lace collar. In some dwelling of Emily's mind a girl with dark hair wore the same kind of dress in a kitchen where raw meat hung on hooks from the raftered ceiling.

The girl had Emily's sketch paper in her hand and was looking at it with an intense, thoughtful gaze. Then she looked up, saying in French,

'This tree is wounded, mademoiselle. It writhes and weeps in sorrow. Is it your drawing?'

'Yes. How did you know?' Annoyance swallowed up in curiosity, Emily approached her questioner.

'I saw you earlier when I arrived. I am a new pupil here. Madame Héger gave me leave to explore and when I saw this I wondered – it was not my business to look. *Pardon!*'

'You may look at it,' Emily said, surprising herself. 'I copied it from a book.'

'And put more there than the book had, I think.' The girl put down the sketch and held out her hand. 'My name is Louise de Bassompierre.'

'Emily Brontë.'

Two hands clasped.

'I must go and unpack,' Louise said. '*Adieu*, mademoiselle.'

She smiled and went out briskly. Emily remained where she was, looking down at her sketch. The tree was split at the roots, its bark whorled into the suggestion of a face in agony, its stump dark with what might have been blood. Was there, she wondered, healing in a new friendship?

With Monsieur Héger there could be no rapport. Invited to write an essay on the Battle of Hastings she had amused herself by telling the story from the point of view of King Harold, musing on the futility of ambition as Norman hordes prepared to invade. When he ordered her to write about an animal she had produced a piece about a cat – not a cosy domestic cat, but a savage one, preying on birds, a rat's tail hanging out of its mouth. If Héger had cast her as sentimental then she would quickly disillusion him!

'For your next exercise, Miss Emily, compose for me a letter written to your *maman*,' he said.

He knew very well her mother had died when she was a small child. Did he hope to surprise her into some cry of pain so that she joined the ranks of those who regarded him as their father-figure? Emily took her pen and wrote a bland letter, remarking that she hadn't seen her mother for a long time, and that she lived in an uncongenial place where she found no kindred spirits.

'Very few errors, Miss Emily.' His brows drawn together, he handed back her paper. 'A little chilly perhaps in its phrasing? Write me a short piece on family affection.'

He wanted to tear off the mask and probe into her feelings.

She gave a grim little smile and produced an essay arguing that there was no merit in parents loving their children since that was Nature's way of propogating the species!

The piece was not long, so she added a coda. A brother writing to a brother who has been abroad for ten years and whose natural affections have dried up might convince him that her feelings were not for display.

'She thinks like a man!' Monsieur complained to his wife. 'When I lose my temper, as, my love, happens now and then, the other pupils cry and protest they will try harder. Miss Emily stares at me with those odd shifting eyes and a sneer on her mouth. Look at this! I told her to write me a little exercise about a butterfly. Does she do that? No! she uses the life cycle of a butterfly in order to show me that Nature is pitiless with one species feeding on another! Well, I shall set her a piece in which she will be forced to reveal herself! I shall invite her to describe a palace. She has a fondness for sketching ruins, I am told. Let her show me a palace that is not ruined.'

Emily wrote a long essay, detailing the splendour of a great palace where Death ruled supreme and chose as his chief servant Intemperance.

'Miss Charlotte would never dare produce such a composition,' Monsieur fumed. 'The piece mocks all religious belief! It is . . . I would not allow any impressionable young person to read it. Such ideas are . . . iconoclastic!'

'Is the piece well written?' Madame enquired.

'Very well written,' he admitted. 'She has acquired a wide vocabulary in French and she makes rapid progress in German. But as for anything else! I cannot teach unless I have a certain rapport with my pupils.'

'Miss Emily has no liking for anyone except her sister,' Madame said. 'The children complain that she gives them their music lessons during their recreation time and has no patience with their mistakes at all. Miss Charlotte, on the other hand, is liked by her pupils. You yourself enjoy them, do you not?'

'Miss Charlotte corrects errors without biting one's head off,' Héger said.

'You look sad today, Miss Emily.' Louise de Bassompierre lingered after the others in the drawing-class had gone.

'My sister and I are both sad,' Emily said. 'A friend of ours, a Mr William Weightman who was our father's curate, has died suddenly of cholera in Haworth. He enlivened many an afternoon for us. Charlotte is writing home to condole with Papa who regarded him in the light of a second son.'

'And you yourself . . . liked him?'

'Yes. Yes, I liked him very much. He found out that we none of us had ever received a Valentine so he bought some and walked all the way to Bradford to post them so that Papa wouldn't guess! Yes, we all liked him very much.'

Her heart ached a little when she remembered the drawings of babies in Anne's portable desk.

October came, with the roses in the borders cut back, a fire lit in the dining-room. Everything in this country was so neat, so constrained, Emily thought. At home the last of the heather and gorse would have faded but there would still be whinberries on the low bushes and the early lambs would be bleating in the fields below Ponden Kirk.

'Emily, there is a note come from Mary Taylor.'

The tone of her sister's voice alerted Emily. Rising from her seat she said, 'Something has happened.'

'It's Martha.' Charlotte began to cry. 'She's dead, Emily. She died very suddenly last night!'

'Little Martha! Tallii, what happened? Has there been an accident?'

'Mary's note makes nothing clear,' Charlotte said, fumbling for a handkerchief. 'She says it was very sudden, under heartbreaking circumstances, and that we are not bidden to the funeral, Mary has been taken to stay with her uncle on the other side of the city. We are to give out that she died of cholera.'

'To give out? I've heard there was cholera in the city but the Taylors have only now returned from their vacation in England. Does she say nothing more?'

'Only that she will be glad to see us in about a fortnight. I feel I ought to go to her at once.'

'Better wait,' Emily advised.

Little Martha who had possessed such artless charm, who had wheedled her way into every heart, was dead. It seemed incredible. She had been only twenty-three and seemed much younger. When they finally met Mary they found her as calm and practical as ever, no less lovely in her black dress than in the dark red she usually favoured.

'We can walk out to Martha's grave,' she said when they had finished the light luncheon prepared for them. 'We can talk privately there, but don't expect me to give a full account of what occurred. I knew nothing until word came—'

'She wasn't with you?' Charlotte looked at her.

'No.' Mary shook her head and looked fixedly at the carpet. 'Come, let's walk. It's two miles off but the exercise will do us good.'

Not until they reached the bare grave with its one wreath and temporary wooden headstone did she speak again, her voice tight with pain.

'She lies here. My family would not have her body taken home. In a few weeks I will write to Ellen Nussey and tell her the full story in as far as I know it. Well, her fault is buried with her and I don't wish her back. She was always too trusting.'

'Mary, do you mean. . . ?' Charlotte had paused, hand to her mouth.

'She died of cholera,' Mary said flatly. 'I have resolved to leave Belgium and go to Germany. I shall study there and teach. I'll not come here again. Shall we go back now?'

Emily, staring at the frosted soil, saw the slight figure of the girl beneath, saw other things only hinted at by the dry-eyed, unnaturally calm Mary. Her own pain was too deep to be felt yet. Later, she thought, she might find the time to grieve.

'Goodbye, Martha,' Charlotte said softly.

The three of them walked back, Mary and Emily silent, Charlotte still crying softly. There was still the evening with Mary's relatives to endure before they could leave.

In the few days that followed Charlotte threw herself into her studies again, so eager to please Monsieur that Emily felt slightly ashamed for her sister. Charlotte was too transparent in her likes and dislikes, too apt to sentimentalize commonplace events. She was in raptures over the fact that Héger had given her a printed copy of a lecture he had delivered at the Academy. Emily, putting in her small trunk the two German novels he had presented to herself quietly after the class had been dismissed, said nothing. If Charlotte couldn't see that he was a man given to quick and impulsive gestures of kindness and that his flattering words to some favoured pupil meant little then Charlotte must learn the hard way. And everybody was entitled to be a little silly from time to time, Emily allowed, remembering her own pleasure when she had opened the Valentine from Willie Weightman.

'Emily, there is news from home,' Charlotte said.

'More bad news?' Looking up from her work Emily spoke almost indifferently to hide the fear leaping up in her.

'Papa writes that Aunt Branwell is very ill. Some kind of intestinal disorder. Anne has been sent for from Thorp Green and Branwell is at home.'

'Has he leave from the railway?'

'It seems that he was . . . dismissed back in the spring.' Charlotte swallowed convulsively. 'He was frequently absent from duty – drinking with his friends, I daresay, though Papa doesn't say so – and some money went missing. The theft was traced to the porter but Branwell had neglected his post. Papa thought it advisable to keep the news from us so as not to upset us.'

'So Branwell still has no work, I suppose?'

'He has suffered greatly from depression, Papa says. Poor Weightman befriended him and was proving a good influence but then Weightman died and now Aunt . . . Papa says that Branny has been a great comfort and spends all his time tending Aunt but . . . do you think we ought to offer to go home?'

'No, I think we should pack our bags and leave for home immediately,' Emily said. 'Charlotte, we cannot waste time sending letters when Aunt lies gravely ill and expect Branwell and Anne to cope with everything. We must inform Madame Héger at once.'

'Yes. Yes, of course you're right. I'll do that at once.'

Charlotte went out, reluctance in the dragging of her steps.

Emily put down her pen and went in search of Louise de Bassompierre. Now was not the time to regret that their friendship hadn't progressed beyond a few civil words exchanged at the beginning or the end of a drawing lesson, or an occasional smiling nod as they passed each other on their way to or from a lesson.

'Miss Louise, I wished to tell you that my sister and I are returning to England at once. Our aunt is dangerously ill,' she said abruptly.

'Oh, I am sorry!' Louise looked genuinely distressed. 'I have enjoyed our friendship so much. The other girls here are well enough in their way but they seem to me shallow in so many respects! You will be coming back?'

'No.' Emily shook her head. 'No, I will stay at home from now on. Even if my aunt recovers my father will require my help with the housekeeping.'

'And Brussels has nothing more to teach you?' Louise looked at her.

'It has shown me that I can study perseveringly and that I can formulate my own philosophy of life without fear or favour. I shall continue my studies at home under my own direction.'

'And walk on the moors. You told me once that every leaf and every blade of grass had a separate and distinct identity of its own.'

'And walk on the moors!' Emily repeated the phrase dreamily. 'With my pets! Papa writes so seldom and never mentions how they're getting on. I wonder if Keeper and Nero have forgotten me.'

'I think that would be impossible,' Louise said.

'So! I hate farewells.' Emily spoke briskly. 'I wished to give you a small memento of me. You were good enough to admire the sketch of a tree I made, so I have signed it for you. Will you accept it?'

'Thank you.' Louise took the signed drawing with a look of quiet pleasure on her face. 'I shall always keep it.'

'We will, I feel, not meet again,' Emily said.

'Nor write.'

There passed between them a glance of perfect understanding and then Emily turned and went out, mounted the stairs to the long dormitory and found Charlotte in the curtained space allotted to them at the far end of the room, struggling with a pile of books that had somehow to be fitted into the trunks.

'We seem to have acquired a great many extra possessions since we came to Brussels,' she complained.

'Roll up the nightcaps and stockings and put them inside the shoes at the bottom,' Emily advised. 'You've told the Hégers?'

'They were both so sorry to learn of the troubles at home,' Charlotte said.

'You didn't tell them about Branwell?'

167

'Of course not. About Aunt I meant. Monsieur was kind enough to say that he would write to Papa urging our return in the New Year. That was very kind of him, don't you think? Yes, what is it?' She broke off as a maidservant entered.

'It's another letter. You'd better open it,' Emily said.

'From Haworth and hard upon the heels of the first.' Charlotte broke the seal. 'Aunt is dead,' she said, rapidly scanning the few lines the sheet contained. 'We cannot hope to reach home in time for the funeral. Do you think that perhaps—?'

'I think it more important than ever that we go home now,' Emily said firmly. 'Only think, Charlotte, Anne and Branwell will have had to do everything themselves! They will be so glad to see us and know that we shall have Christmas together! And Papa relied so greatly upon Aunt to keep the house running smoothly and to provide company for him after tea. Of course we must go!'

Shaking hands with Madame and Monsieur with unwonted cordiality she felt herself buoyed up as if on wings. The journey by diligence to the nearest railway station passed like a dream and the motion of the ship beneath her feet as it ploughed through the November Channel sent her up on deck, her eyes straining over the heaving grey water towards the first sight of England, leaving Charlotte vomiting weakly into a bucket in the small cabin which was all they had been able to obtain at such short notice.

'Is it really only ten months since we were making this journey in reverse?' Charlotte marvelled as they sat in the train heading to Yorkshire. 'So much has happened since then! Papa was with us and we met Mary and poor Martha in London and saw all the sights.'

'You dragged us round all the sights you mean,' Emily said. 'My heavens, but I never beheld so many buildings, pictures and statues in such a short space of time before!'

'I could hardly believe that I was really and truly on my way to Brussels to study in a large school. And so much of it has been valuable.'

'I'll grant you that,' Emily allowed.

'And it has benefited us both in so many directions! Our command of French and German has improved out of all recognition; your musical ability has been recognized; you have made great strides forward in your art. And while we both are agreed that Catholicism is one of the most repressive doctrines on earth—'

'Most doctrines are repressive.'

'And the Belgians rather a cold-blooded kind of people, we have endeavoured to retain our own integrity of spirit. If only everything had stayed the same! I cannot help thinking how two of our gayest spirits have been taken from us – Willie Weightman and poor Martha. Both of cholera.'

'Yes,' said Emily. 'Of course. Both of cholera.'

'And now Aunt is gone. Everything seems such a dreary waste.'

'Until you return to Brussels perhaps?'

'Oh, I am determined upon that,' Charlotte said, setting her mouth very firmly.

And then at last they came to the outskirts of Bradford, then to the small station at Keighley and the hired cab that brought them the four winding, jolting miles to Haworth's steep main street.

Anne came running out to greet them, traces of tears still on her face, as she hugged them fiercely, crying, 'I knew you would come! Oh, it is so good to see you both! Branny and I have taken it in turns to watch the road ever since we reckoned that Papa's letter had reached its destination! Aunt suffered so terribly before she died, and Branny was so good in sitting with her day and night. Papa, Charlotte and Emily are here!'

'And here is Keeper!' Emily stood still and allowed the dog, now fully grown, to come to her, black muzzle quivering, tail wagging frantically. From his throat came deep groans of delight.

'You see Keeper is in fine fettle!' Charlotte said.

'And you look worn out,' Emily said, putting her arm about Anne's shoulders. 'Papa, how are you? This is a melancholy homecoming in many ways.'

'Aye, we are three less in our happy band,' Branwell exclaimed, running down the stairs. 'Poor Weightman, the best fellow in the world! And then Aunt who was always so generous to us! And little Martha Taylor too! She provided amusing distraction when we were on holiday.'

'It is a comfort to have you both home again,' Mr Brontë said.

169

'Your aunt had her odd little ways which we must expect in a spinster, but she was invariably good-hearted. She divided her money between you three girls and her niece in Cornwall, and left instructions regarding the disposal of her personal property. You are to have her China sewing box and her ivory fan. She often recalled how you admired it when you were a child.'

'Where's Nero?' Emily had stopped dead, staring at the empty cage.

'I don't k-know,' Anne stammered. 'Papa?'

'I expect he went for a flight across the moors, dear.'

'Alone?' Emily stared at him. 'He was accustomed to his long leash. Even when I loosed it he never flew far from my shoulder! Surely Aunt did not – when did you last see him?'

'Some weeks past,' Mr Brontë said. 'My dear, we have been much occupied with other concerns recently.'

'Did Aunt let him fly free?' Emily's face had whitened, her blue eyes paled to ice.

'I don't know, my dear. If so he will surely fly back in his own good time.'

It was not yet dark. Turning, pushing past Charlotte, her face resolute and set, Emily went out, striding in her long narrow skirt along the path and into the lane.

When she reached the moor she broke into a scrambling run, pausing now and then, putting two fingers in her mouth and whistling shrilly. It was the special call she always used for Nero, the one that brought him winging home.

No swoop of glossy black wings rewarded her. She stood at last at the foot of Ponden Kirk and looked up at the bare sky. There was the scent of snow on the wind.

'Miss Emily? I thought I recognized you.' Robert Heaton swerved aside as his mount galloped towards the still, tall figure.

'Have you seen Nero? Have you seen my hawk?' she demanded without preamble.

'No. Is the bird lost?'

'My aunt let him go,' she said bitterly. 'He was tame and would not survive in the wild.'

'Perhaps some local farmer found him and sheltered him?'

'Perhaps. I'll make further enquiries tomorrow. We are just returned from Brussels.'

'Because of your recent bereavement. We were all sorry to

hear of it. Your late aunt was not well known in the district—'

'She preferred to stay within doors as much as possible.'

'And now you are home again.'

He sounded pleased. Emily looked up at him. He must be fully of age now, she thought vaguely, and no longer resembled his cousin so startlingly. He was of lighter build, his hair lightened slightly by the sun, his features more refined.

'Yes,' she said, her rare smile transforming her own features. 'Yes, I am come home again.'

Twelve

'It was always understood in the family that there was something between Emily and Robert.'

Edith Heaton

Summer sunlight arching through the windows burnished the wainscoting to rich burgundy and flashed off the fire-irons at each end of the huge hearth. On the long table Yorkshire parkin and curd cakes flanked the teapot and substantial mugs from which they were drinking their tea.

'And what happened then?' Emily enquired.

'There was a lawsuit and Casson was declared officially dead.'

'Without a body ever being found!'

'As it happened more than a century ago he is certainly dead by now,' Robert said.

Emily laughed, completely at her ease as she sat, both hands round the mug, sipping the sweet, black tea.

'Strange,' she observed a moment later, 'how the same themes recur again and again. My own grandfather, Hugh Prunty, was taken from his home by an adopted uncle when he was a child and mistreated. My great grandfather had taken in the uncle – Welsh was his name – years before, out of charity it was said, and favoured him over his own children, and I have sometimes wondered if Welsh was a by-blow of his own. That would explain his partiality and Welsh's determination to get his hands on the family property.'

'What do your sisters say?'

'Good Lord, I wouldn't dream of talking about such ideas with the family, not even Papa!' Emily said, laughing again. 'Charlotte doesn't like to talk about our Irish connections at all

173

and Anne would fret over the eventual destination of Welsh's soul, so I keep such cogitating to myself.'

'And share it with me,' Robert said.

'It is always good to share with a friend.' She put down the mug and smiled at him.

'You must have left friends in Brussels?'

'No. I am very slow to make friends. Like you and your brothers we were a close-knit family group in childhood and the habit persisted. Only Branwell has the gift of making friends and of being at his ease in polite society.'

'Aye, Branny sometimes came out with us on a shooting expedition when Weightman was alive,' Robert said. 'We had some good times.'

'Charlotte nicknamed Willie Weightman Celia Amelia.'

'Did she so? She has a shrewd intelligence your sister.'

'Oh, it was only to convince herself that she wasn't a little in love with him,' Emily said. 'He was a great flirt but so kind-hearted and merry. We were all fond of him.'

'And now he has gone and your aunt has gone and your sister is back in Brussels. Is she glad of it?'

'She was at first.' Emily took a curd cake and bit into it thoughtfully. 'The Hégers wished her to return as a teacher with a small salary and free board and lodging. She was very happy at first but of late her spirits seem a little depressed. She has confessed to feeling homesick. She rushed back early in the New Year and perhaps now she wishes she had thought more carefully about it. Being a student is very different from being an assistant teacher you know.'

'And Miss Anne is still at Thorp Green. She must be pleased that Branwell is with her.'

'She is relieved to be rid of the burden of teaching Edmund Robinson,' Emily said. 'He is the most frightful little dunce, Anne says, but when she recommended that they engage Branwell as tutor her suggestion was eagerly adopted. Branny likes children though he has less patience than Charlotte! What's that?'

She spoke in sudden alarm as a strange yowling noise issued from beneath the table.

'Juno? Oh, no!'

Both had dived to their knees and were looking beneath the table where a yellow-coated pointer lay on the rug, the same odd sounds rising to a crescendo and diminishing into a series of grunts.

'What's wrong with her? Is she poisoned?' Emily demanded.

'No.' Robert's face had flushed fiery red. 'No, she's not poisoned. I'm very much afraid that she's . . . whelping! Miss Emily, this is no place for a lady!'

'Oh, stuff and nonsense! It's a perfectly natural process,' Emily said. 'Come along, girl! There's a girl! Oh look!'

She watched, enchanted, as the puppies wriggled and Juno lazily licked at the afterbirth.

'Four. At least we'll not have to drown any,' Robert said. 'I am sorry! I really didn't know she was there or so near her time!'

'It was one of the best things I've ever seen!' Emily withdrew her head and stood up. 'I would not have missed it for anything!'

'Would you like one of the pups?'

'I'd say yes at once,' Emily said regretfully, 'but Anne has written to say that the Robinsons are giving her a spaniel puppy to bring home with her at Christmas. Otherwise I'd take one the instant it was weaned.'

'I'll have one of the lads take her and her litter to the kennels. Excuse me for a moment.' He went out, still slightly flushed.

Emily looked after him. Heaton, she thought suddenly, would not have been embarrassed. He would have laughed with her, have carried Juno and her pups to their kennel without help. But Robert was a gentleman, eldest son of a squire. One day he would inherit Ponden Hall and its surrounding land. They were a large family – the sons who lived at Ponden Hall and their cousins who lived at Royd House further out of Haworth. Nobody ever mentioned that other cousin who had stolen a horse and ridden away.

'I'll walk you home,' Robert said, returning. 'Your father will become anxious if you're too late.'

'I forgot to tell you! Papa is away this week. Did your father not say? He has been invited to Thorp Green, so naturally he will be happy to bring back report of Anne and Branwell.'

'You're surely not alone at the parsonage!'

'Tabby is back with us. She was bored at her sister's house and very glad to be home with us. She'd never have retired at all but Aunt Branwell insisted on it.'

'An old woman in her seventies with a lame leg can hardly protect you against intruders,' he objected.

'Possibly not but Keeper can. And if the intruders, as you term them, shoot Keeper, why then, I will return the compliment!'

She dug into the deep pocket of her skirt and produced a pistol.

'Miss Emily! do be careful!' Robert took a step backwards. 'You must be very careful when handling firearms you know. The safety catch—'

'Must always be kept on save when cocking and aiming.' Emily laughed at the expression on his face. 'Papa lent me one of his own pistols! He is teaching me how to shoot. With so much unrest in the district these days, so many out of work, then a woman should go protected when she walks on the moor. Anyway Papa's sight is troubling him greatly. He can no longer see clearly enough to hit the target, so it pleases him that our house has a defender. I practise daily.'

'And hit the target every time I'll be bound!'

'In between baking scones,' Emily said wryly. 'Tabby and Papa have a passion for them. I must cook some parkin soon as a change. Papa will groan that his digestion is being ruined but he'll make short work of a batch. I'll tease the recipe out of your cook! Shall we go? I left Keeper to go a-hunting over the moors. Do you think he can have sired Juno's litter?'

'Miss Emily!'

'Probably not. He is far too respectable.'

She went out ahead of him, her eyes glinting with mischief. Robert was a dear and she flourished in the warmth of his friendship but he could be amazingly conventional at times.

In the garden she paused as she always did to look back towards the orchard with its fruiting trees and tiny wild roses twining over the wall.

'Your aunt and your grandmother,' she said abruptly. 'Do they still walk?'

'The servants mutter that they do,' he said still uncomfortable. 'My father refuses to have the subject discussed. He regards it as morbid and superstitious. He prefers to regard them as beyond earthly ties.'

'In a cold heaven with no kin to welcome them? Surely they are more at ease walking together in the garden they loved!'

'Don't you think that heaven is where we shall all be happi-est?' he said.

Emily wrinkled her nose and considered the matter. 'I think I would be homesick there,' she said at last. 'I would make such a dreadful fuss that the angels would fling me down on to Ponden Kirk and leave me there, sobbing for joy! Keeper, here!' She put two fingers in her mouth and whistled loudly.

'When I'm with you,' Robert said, holding the gate for her, 'I feel more alive than with any other person. There's a joy in you that's infectious.'

'Joy?' She looked at him, suddenly sober. 'There have been times in my life when joy was far distant. But these past months have been good ones, even with all the sorrows of last year to remember. Charlotte had her wish and returned to Brussels; Anne and Branwell are in steady employment; Tabby is back in her rightful kingdom; Mary Taylor writes from Germany to say she is well and happy; Miss Nussey is content and well as far as I know – she is Charlotte's special friend you know.'

'And you. . . ?'

'I am mistress of the parsonage with my dog and my books and my pistol and the three hundred and fifty pounds Aunt left me safely invested in railway bonds. I study the financial markets and make myself quite an expert I can tell you. I may be an old maid of twenty-five but I am happy I promise you.'

'You left something out,' he said.

'What?' Emily looked at him.

'That I am also your friend,' he said. 'I have hoped. . . .'

Not the Dark Lover who had never articulated his feelings. He had gone away, repelled by her coldness, betrayed by a casual little phrase. This was the Fair Lover, young and malleable, handsome and romantic if she cared to let him be.

'Your friendship,' she said breathlessly, 'gives me the greatest joy. Truly, Robert.'

'Truly?'

He would have taken her hand but she was whistling again, running ahead of him with her dark hair tumbling from its pins.

'Keeper! Here, Keeper! Bad dog! Where have you been?'

'Emily—'

'Race you!' She fled before him, her laughter echoing back. She took the winding path that led to the highest of the three

Withins farms. This land too had once belonged to the Heaton family. Now Top Withins was unoccupied, its windows boarded up, planks nailed across its door, the thorn-trees alone bearing their bright berries every year against the crumbling walls.

Having outrun Robert she sat down, panting, on the step that led down into the yard of the old farm and watched Keeper sniff his way round the walls. From here she could look down to the two lower farms, modest enough dwellings but in their greyness perfectly married to the moors.

She leaned against the wall and thought of High Sunderland Hall which somehow insisted on superimposing its grotesque image on the simple house here, just as when she approached Ponden House its long low façade took on the lineaments of the black and white timbers and mullioned windows of Shibden Hall where once – it seemed now almost like a dream! – she had sat in the music room and listened to Anne Lister play the pianoforte.

The moors were never empty. Apart from their full complement of birds and animals and local farmers going about their business they teemed with other shapes. That old rogue Casson who, like Jack Sharp in Halifax and Welsh Prunty in far off Drumballyroney, had risen from nowhere to cheat his benefactors walked here. Heaton who had stolen a horse and galloped away from a home where, though kindly treated, he had never been regarded as quite one of the family! She was sure in her own mind that he was dead. Perhaps by now Nero had found him and they roamed the moors together. There was the little shepherd boy who had been lost in a snowstorm and wandered now seeking entrance at any window where a candle burned.

She thought of Robert Heaton who was handsome and kind and would one day inherit Ponden Hall. Words flowed into her mind.

> *I well may mourn that only one*
> *Can light my future sky*
> *Even though by such a radiant sun*
> *My moon of life must die*

She needed to write it down before the words disintegrated like cobwebs when the fly is sucked dry and the spider sleeps.

Rising, whistling to Keeper, she took the track to Haworth in
time to see Mr Greenwood emerging with his wife from the
parsonage gate. Mrs Greenwood merely nodded and smiled and
scurried away, as if, Emily thought with amusement, she feared
I might turn savage and bite her.

'Miss Emily.' The little man removed his top-hat and bowed.

'Mr Greenwood, have you been visiting my father? I'm sorry
I was not at home.' She always made a point of greeting Mr
Greenwood because she knew that he was unhappily conscious
of his small stature and his limp.

'I fear it was not exactly a social visit, Miss Emily,' he said.

'Not bad news, I hope?'

'It is only that my wife and myself, having Mr Brontë's best
interests at heart, wished to acquaint him with certain rumours
gaining credence among his congregation,' Mr Greenwood said
awkwardly.

'What rumours?' Emily asked sharply.

'I dislike troubling you, ma'am.' He twisted his hat round in
his hands.

'Pray get to the point, Mr Greenwood!'

'There is talk of your father's drinking,' he said. 'Several
people have intimated to me that Mr Brontë has about him, on
occasion, a certain odour of . . . strong liquor, Miss Emily. And
the long hours he spends closeted in his parlour. You must know
that his curate Mr Smith has an unfortunate habit of imbibing
rather too freely on occasion. We took it upon ourselves to
inform him of the gossip.'

'I hope he was not too uncivil to you,' Emily said.

'No indeed, Miss Emily. Your father is always the soul of civil-
ity,' Mr Greenwood hastened to assure her. 'He promised to
think about our warning but, of course, he utterly repudiated the
suspicion of his . . . indulging.'

'Papa has been advised by his doctor to take a glass or two of
wine before his evening meal and a small whisky on retiring,'
Emily said. 'In moderation they are aids to digestion.'

'As St Paul so aptly reminds us! Good day, Miss Emily.'

She went in and tapped on the parlour door.

'Come!'

'What have you and Mr Smith been up to, Papa?' Emily took
off her cloak and laid the pistol on his desk. 'Apparently there

are rumours of all kinds of disreputable goings-on.'

'You've been talking to Greenwood.'

'He means well, Papa.'

'Aye, so he does! There's nothing to it, Emily. I'm an Irishman and not a canting Methodist, and I enjoy my whisky the same as the next man. Can you think of one occasion when my speech has been slurred or my duties neglected?'

'No, of course not, Papa! But a stronger mouthwash—?'

'The eyedrops I am prescribed have an alcohol base. That is what people occasionally smell and, having nought better to do than slander their parson, ascribe it to another cause. I have a good mind to sue for slander!'

'Much wiser to deny it once and for all with dignity and let the matter rest,' Emily advised.

'I'm sure you're right, my dear.'

'Meanwhile why are you home? I thought you at Thorp Green! There's nothing wrong?'

'Nothing in the world, but a coach was returning this way today instead of tomorrow so I took the opportunity of travelling by it. No, the news is excellent! Both Branwell and Anne are wondrously valued in their situations. Thorp Green is a handsome estate with beautifully landscaped grounds and though Mr Robinson is something of an invalid his lady wife is most hospitable and charming. They entertained me most graciously and both Branwell and Anne look very well indeed.'

'And I was out when you came! I'll see about your tea at once.'

'You've been walking on the moors?'

'I took some borrowed books to Ponden Hall and Mr Robert insisted I stay for a cup of tea.'

'Young Robert, eh? A very pleasant young man. Musical like his brothers.'

'You have no objections to a . . . friendship?'

'None in the world, my dear. As a member of the clergy with a certain position in society to maintain there are unfortunately few families of the same standing in our neighbourhood but the Heatons are worthy people and who knows but – well, well, get along and make the tea, dear!'

As she left the room he enquired,

'Young Mr Robert is the sole heir to the Heaton property, is he not?'

'Yes, Papa, though he will make ample provision for his younger brothers when the due time comes, I'm sure.'

Closing the door, she stood for a moment, her mouth grimacing with a mixture of amusement and chagrin before she went through to the kitchen where Tabby was scolding fourteen-year-old Martha Brown for not giving the tea sufficient time to stew.

There were letters from both Charlotte and Anne to be savoured as the year chilled into its later quarter. Anne wrote briefly, being occupied with her pupils – though she had only the two younger girls to instruct, the oldest having come out that spring and the boy being in Branwell's care. She had sent copies of two poems she had written on the particular portion of Gondal history they were exploring together but mentioned also she was trying her hand at a 'real' story. Why real? Did she no longer regard Gondal as real? The tone of her brief letters was flat. Was she homesick or still thinking about poor Weightman, building up a Valentine and a few amorous glances into a grand love-affair, or was she merely labouring under one of her periodic fits of depression when her smallest fault loomed in her eyes as a heinous sin? The Robinsons had been very kind to her, giving her the spaniel, taking her with them on holiday to Scarborough.

Charlotte's letter from Brussels gave more cause for concern. The Hégers had begun to withdraw their friendship by small but definite degrees, with even Monsieur withdrawing the light of his countenance. They had left her alone in the empty echoing school with only a couple of maidservants during the six-week vacation and she had found the days dragged, had even taken it into her head to go into a Catholic church and make a real confession.

'You had better not tell Papa or he may think I am going to turn Catholic, whereas it was but the whim of a moment,' Charlotte had written.

Better not tell Papa indeed! Emily folded up the letter and frowned. It was not her right to pry into another's heart but Charlotte was clearly lonely and unhappy. She hesitated and then reached for her own writing materials.

She would write to kind, calm Ellen Nussey who might be urged to write to Charlotte and insist she come home for a spell. Perhaps Ellen herself might be persuaded to go over to Belgium and bring Charlotte back with her. That possibility was unlikely. Ellen was too useful at home, with an invalid sister who spent most of her days in a wheelchair, a brother who had given the family endless grief with his drinking and gambling, another brother who had suffered a severe mental breakdown. And Ellen was no independent Mary Taylor to take her life in her own hands and travel alone on the Continent.

Winter came but no Charlotte. Emily chopped wood for the fires, laid in supplies, helped young Martha with the washing and ironing, took the broom from her hands on several occasions and packed her off to play in the clean, crisp air, rolled out dough and experimented with curd cake and, finding time to study so limited, propped up her German grammar on the table, and chanted verbs aloud as she kneaded the pastry.

Once or twice a week, usually with a book to return beneath her arm, she put on her thickest boots and tramped through the snowdrifts with Keeper at her side.

The library at Ponden Hall with its thousand volumes was on the first floor. Slipping in through the side door she could come and go whether or not any of the Heatons were at home. It was an all male household now, Mrs Heaton having died some years before. All the Heaton lads were growing up, into quiet, studious young men, though eight-year-old Michael was still at the age when he loved pranks and jests. However in the library she was usually left undisturbed, to browse contentedly among the various volumes or leaf through the piles of illustrated periodicals that lay on the table.

Robert was frequently absent, seeing to estate matters or in town. Men, Emily knew, lived lives that were kept secret from women, were free to travel to places where females were barred. When he was there he invariably walked back to Haworth with her, their walks punctuated by lively talk about the old legends passed down through the centuries. Mr Greenwood, meeting Emily one day as she hurried down the lane, marked her sparkling eyes and joyous air and hurried home to note in his diary that Miss Emily looked as if she had been conversing with angels.

Anne and Branwell came home for Christmas but the occasion wasn't as happy as she'd hoped. Branwell stayed only a few days before taking himself off to Bradford to have a reunion with his friends there and Anne seemed troubled and quiet. Emily, seeing her so withdrawn, held her peace, knowing her sister would speak when she was ready but the brief holiday closed and she returned to Thorp Hall still silent.

Then a brief scribbled note arrived from Charlotte, announcing that she would be returning home in the New Year, and that though her health was good her mind was a trifle shaken for want of comfort.

Emily put the letter away and spent the rest of the day cleaning out Aunt Branwell's old room and laying clean linen on the double bed there. She herself had appropriated the tiny study room. Once she and Charlotte had cuddled there together, making Maria and Elizabeth alive again, but they were adults now and she needed her own private space.

'Miss Emily, cans't tha coom?' Young Martha burst into the kitchen, her face indicative of some dreadful calamity. 'Keeper's got another dog by t'throat and no one can stop it!'

Keeper, Emily thought, must be taught that the lane outside the parsonage was not his own private preserve. She wiped her hands, seized the pepper pot and dashed into the snow-covered lane where both dogs, being of almost equal size, were locked in a combat that had already drawn blood, while a group of local millhands hovered round, vainly trying to call off the fight without themselves getting physically involved.

'Idiots!' She strode up to the snarling animals, emptied the contents of the pepper pot over their heads and seizing both collars yanked them apart.

'Miss Emily, tha'll get bitten!' one of the men exclaimed.

'Not if you get hold of the other one's collar and pull, William Wood! And the rest of you can go about your business if you've no help to give. Have you no work to do that you can stand round watching a couple of dogs scrap as if you were at a prize fight! Keeper, inside! Now! Why are you lot still here?'

A violently sneezing Keeper had fled into the back yard. The men, grinning and muttering, touched their forelocks and moved off.

'Tha was a mite hard on them, child,' Tabby complained as Emily went round to the back door which Martha had left wide open, the better to hear the altercation.

'Nonsense, Tabby! There's nothing men like better than a

sound rating now and then,' Emily said, plunging her hands into a bowl of water and shaking back her hair. 'What's that?'

'It's the gig.' Martha, who had hurried out came slithering back up the icy step.

'Charlotte is come! Now we shall have some good long talks!'

Emily, towel in her hands, ran round to the gate.

The tiny figure of her sister, bundled in cloak and extra shawl, was climbing down stiffly.

'Take the luggage to the back. There's hay for your horse and a hot drink for yourself before you return to Keighley. Tallii! it's wonderful to see you! Did you have a smooth crossing? The Hégers must've been sorry to let you go after your useful labour.'

'He has given me leave to write to him,' Charlotte said exhaustedly. 'Our parting – I will not soon forget what it cost me. I'd best go in and see Papa.'

With her coming the winter suddenly seemed colder.

Thirteen

Come, the wind may never again
Blow as now it blows for us
And the stars may never again, shine as
    now they shine;

                    Emily Jane Brontë

'It was Madame Héger. She could not endure the fact that her husband showed kindness and – yes, friendship to a teacher. She invented excuses to stop the English lessons I was giving him. Extra work at the boys' school, the children missing his company, anything to prevent his talking to me!'

'Surely not!' Emily said mildly.

'Yes, Emily. Yes!' Charlotte paused in their walk, her voice low but passionate. 'At first I couldn't understand what was happening. Then they ceased to invite me to spend time with them in their private sitting-room in the evenings, though when I returned to Brussels they said I must join them whenever I chose. I seldom did. I always waited for an invitation. They dribbled away to nothing. And Monsieur was suddenly so occupied with other matters. He had no leisure in which to correct the essays I still wrote for him. When they went off on their vacation and left me alone I – it was like being buried alive in a great shiny well-furnished tomb full of white graves with the other beds all shrouded. When they returned I gave Madame my notice. Had it been left to her I'd've been back in England last October but Monsieur came to me, begged me to stay, told me how valued I was. So I withdrew my notice and remained but nothing changed. I saw less of him than before.'

'But wasn't Madame pregnant? You mentioned—'

'Oh yes, exceedingly pregnant! Full of fads and fancies! She had been been through it four times before so why should this time demand almost constant attention from her husband? You know it actually occurred to me that sometimes she suspected us of . . . well, flirting! I didn't know whether to laugh or cry! Can you imagine any man with a pretty wife like Zélie Héger becoming besotted with someone who looks like me?'

'He admired your mind,' Emily said uncertainly.

'Yes, of course. Our mutual minds struck fire one from the other! I took nothing from Madame! A little conversation, a book lent or given, a glance exchanged – what difference could it make?'

'Perhaps she feared talk – some scandal?'

'Oh, that is one of her greatest fears,' Charlotte said bitterly. 'She is obsessed with the appearance of things. Yet she might have been present at any meeting we had and heard nothing out of place.'

'But she was not there.'

'There were few enough meetings towards the end. I taught my pupils; walked in the garden; accepted an occasional invitation from the Wheelwrights – they are back in Brussels, by the bye. The girls are quite amiable though I know you didn't care much for them. When I finally decided to come home and offered my notice a second time Monsieur did not protest. He accepted my decision. The child was born – Madame named it Victor. That was a crow of triumph if you like.'

Emily said nothing. Charlotte was in no mood to be told that the name was popular in Belgium.

'Mary Taylor advised me to leave the pensionnat. She plans to go to New Zealand with her brother Waring and set up in business. Can you imagine it! A young woman going into trade in a far-off savage land! I walked over to visit poor Martha's grave. It looks so lonely, so untended now.'

'You were right to come home,' Emily said.

'Madame certainly thought so! She would not even allow me a private goodbye with Monsieur. Can you imagine that? She even escorted me in the diligence to the railway station – lest we snatch a sentence or two, I daresay. But he has promised to write to me. That is something to look forward to. Now tell me something to cheer me up. Branwell and Anne are doing well, Papa tells me, and young Martha Brown is shaping well as a maidservant?'

'He was most hospitably entertained at Thorp Green. Of course his sight is very bad now. He can no longer see to read or write, and once out of the parsonage he becomes disorientated.'

'Well, we are both educated to the required standard,' Charlotte said.

'Required standard for what?'

'To realize our great ambition, of course! Our own school.'

'We can't leave Papa with only Tabby and Martha.'

'I realize that,' Charlotte said impatiently. 'I have thought long and hard and come up with the perfect solution! I have Papa's leave to start a school at the parsonage.'

'Where?' Emily stared at her blankly. 'We have no room.'

'I wasn't suggesting a school on the scale of the pensionnat or even Miss Wooller's establishment,' Charlotte said. 'Papa agrees with me that we could use Branwell's studio as a bedroom for three or four girls and the dining-room could double as class-room. Later on we could build a couple of rooms at the rear and make room for more.'

'They would be dreadfully squashed!'

'There is the loft over the back kitchen. That could be made into another bedroom. It's the perfect solution for us, Emily! I shall design a leaflet to be sent out as advertisement. Ellen will help to distribute them. Anne will be able to come home and share the teaching with us.'

'With you,' Emily said flatly.

'But your command of French and German—'

'Is for my own satisfaction. Charlotte, I liked the idea of our having our own school, of our being together, but I cannot teach! At Law Hill I couldn't keep order and at the pensionnat I found teaching music to the Wheelwright girls absolute misery for them and myself! I have no gift for teaching. Anyway if I am teaching and you and Anne are teaching who is going to cook the pupils their meals or wash their clothes? Tabby is too old and Martha is too young.'

'You propose to do that, do you?'

'Yes. I flatter myself that I'm a decent housekeeper.'

'Emily, I've said nothing since I came home but I cannot help noticing that the kitchen is never tidy since you took charge of it.' Charlotte's suppressed fury burst out against the one nearest to her. 'There's waste there, Emily! I've seen you throwing out

187

scraps for the birds that would have provided a second meal. The animals are in and out of the place and Flossy is not yet fully house-trained yet, though you always laugh when an accident happens. And you're not neat with your own possessions either. How can we inculcate habits of order and tidiness when you come home with the hem of your skirt trailing in the wet, lie on the floor reading and leave the book open anywhere you choose to drop it?'

'You know,' said Emily, standing stock still, 'you sound exactly like Aunt!'

Charlotte burst into tears.

'Oh don't cry,' Emily said wearily. 'I didn't mean to be unkind. You're right of course. I'm very careless and untidy and not in the least ladylike and your idea is a good one, honestly! But I won't teach whatever you say. Lord above, but if I'm to be cooking, washing and clearing up my muddles there won't be time for anything else!'

Certainly not much time for Gondal, she thought, watching a comforted Charlotte scrub at her wet face with a handkerchief. Yet though she still immersed herself in the secret world, playing and replaying variants of the epic tale she and Anne shared, other images persisted in rising to the surface of her mind. A large building decorated with grotesque carvings where the abandoned little farmhouse now stood, a manor-house handsome and surrounded by a landscaped park where Ponden House stretched its walls.

A dark boy growing into an iron man, a runaway wife called Isabella, a gentler lover with money and social position, and the passionate figure of Augusta Geraldine Almeda who in the Gondal saga was now being killed off but might rise again in more familiar surroundings. A girl who had met her counterpart and betrayed him for the sake of a milder love but who might in the end bring forth a girl child with compassion in her soul.

'Tell me about the Gytrash,' she begged Robert when she next saw him.

Charlotte had gone to visit Ellen Nussey and bid farewell to Mary Taylor and for a few days the kitchen could be delightfully and defiantly untidy again.

'Oh, that's an old legend,' Robert said, laughing. 'You've heard it dozens of times already.'

188

'Tell me again!' Hands tucked beneath her knees she sat on a grass mound and looked at him expectantly.

'It appears sometimes as an old man with a long grey beard and sometimes as a fierce black hound and sometimes as a flaming barrel – though that's only when someone's been drinking too deep over at the Black Bull!'

Emily laughed. 'There must have been a time,' she said growing serious again, 'when strange misshapen creatures roamed the earth. A time when the Creator was experimenting with various forms of life and made a few mistakes.'

'God cannot make mistakes.'

'Then we ought to be perfect. I don't know anyone who's perfect, do you?'

'That's the result of original sin.'

'Which God put in us in the first place? I don't believe that! I wonder sometimes if God just made our souls which are pure and the rest of us evolved as well as it could. Or God made our souls and the Devil made our bodies. What do you think?'

'I think your father would be very shocked if he heard you express such sentiments.'

'Oh, Papa is more tolerant in action than in thought,' Emily said easily. 'What does your father think?'

'We never discuss such matters. Anyway he is not well,' Robert said.

'Papa mentioned something of that.'

'He frets about his family,' Robert said sombrely. 'Five unwedded sons and only one to inherit an estate which has suffered business losses this last year. My uncle Michael at Royd House is one of the shareholders and is constantly complaining about the loss of dividends.'

'Your uncle should look to his own affairs,' Emily said.

'The family is his affair.' Robert moved restlessly, plucking at a tuft of grass.

Emily bit her lip. Michael Heaton of Royd House had a reputation for what her father called 'leading the ladies on'. She knew him only by sight and had found herself wondering how two brothers could look alike and yet be so dissimilar in character.

'Your father gave me a pear-tree once,' she said. 'I have always remembered his kindness.'

189

'He becomes more reclusive as his health fails,' Robert said moodily.

His father was now an elderly man – no, not elderly but aged beyond his years, shutting himself away in his library to grieve for a dead wife and a runaway sister.

A young girl with dark eyes and flaxen hair, product of two families, came trippingly into the library. In the corner Emily, an apron about her waist, listened to the conversation, her face as calm and sensible as Ellen Nussey's.

'Miss Emily?' Robert's face swam into view.

'I'm sorry,' Emily said. 'What were you saying?'

'That I ought to be getting back. I don't like to leave my father for too long.'

'Please give him my regards. If Papa's sight didn't trouble him so much he would come to see him.'

'Yes, I'll tell him. You'll take care of yourself, Miss Emily?'

'I always do,' she said vaguely.

Poetry didn't often spring easily into the mind. Prose was more accommodating. She would write the life story of King Julius of Gondal, whose daughter/lover glinted in and out of his stormy existence, describe how a soul made for gentleness could grow hard and unforgiving. She would begin it at the end. Despite her resolve lines flowed into her head.

> *Cold in the earth and the deep snow piled above thee.*
> *Far far removed in the dreary grave*

No, that didn't scan!

> *Far far removed, cold in the dreary wave*

'Grave, grave,' she muttered, fingers itching for a pen.

> *Cold in the earth and the deep snow piled above thee,*
> *Far far removed, cold in the dreary grave.*
> *Have I forgot, my only love, to love thee,*
> *Severed at last by Time's all severing wave?*

And next? What followed?

> *Fifteen wild Decembers*

190

Fifteen? Why fifteen? What had she lost when she had been eleven years old? Eleven, twelve? The cellar steps yawned before her. The little knife glittered on the kitchen floor and her hair was soaking wet from the pump. She had lost something then but she could never remember what it was because the dark boy had risen in her and hidden it from view.

She stood up, shivering a little in the cool spring breeze, and whistled Keeper to her side.

Tonight she would lie wakeful, waiting for the dark boy to come in that tiny study room which was her own cherished private space. Before that she had the tea to get and little Dick to feed.

Summer came but with the rest of the family at home there was less time in which to wander along the ancient tracks that joined the far-flung farmsteads. Anne was always willing to help out in the kitchen but she deserved a holiday, Emily decided, after the long months of being constantly with two lively young girls.

'The eldest is "out" of course but she is self-willed and difficult,' Anne confided. 'Mrs Robinson has little sympathy with her.'

'And with you? Has she sympathy with you?'

'Since when did any employer sympathize with a governess?' Anne said, her lip curling. 'Governesses are there to be used and exploited, didn't you know?'

'Anne?' Surprised at the unusual bitterness in her sister's voice Emily stared at her.

'Don't take any notice of me,' Anne said. 'The Robinsons have, for the most part, been kind to me. Certainly far better than the Inghams! But back then I had no experience and very little self-confidence. Now, to be fair, I manage better. Young Lydia is in competition with her mother as to who looks the most charming and flirts the more outrageously, but my own charges are good-hearted and affectionate enough. Bessy is rather too fond of hanging about the stables but Mary is more biddable.'

'And you have Branwell's company.'

'Not very often. He and his pupil are lodged in a separate house in the grounds – it was the keeper's lodge at one time I believe. He comes up to the main house in the evenings but I am not often invited down into the family quarters. Oh, don't look so solemn! I get along very well in the best way I can and my story is coming along nicely.'

'The governess tale?'

'I've titled it Passages In The Life Of An Individual.'

'Dull!'

'Oh, the story itself is terribly dull,' Anne agreed placidly. 'It makes no matter. We are the only ones who will ever read it. What of you?'

'I'm making slow progress with the life of King Julius. I shall read you the beginning when we've a few spare moments but it strikes me as somewhat feeble and artificial.'

'Is Charlotte writing anything?' Anne had lowered her voice slightly. 'She seems so quiet and withdrawn that I hardly like to ask.'

'She is a little depressed because the school plan isn't going as well as she hoped. So far nobody has displayed any interest in sending a small daughter to us.'

'I hope we get a couple of pupils,' Anne said sighingly. 'It would mean so much to me to be able to live at home and earn a living at the same time.'

'Well, we shall have to see.' Let the subject drop. It wasn't her place to tell Anne about the hours that Charlotte spent writing letters to which she had clearly had only a few replies. Nowadays she was always the first to hurry to the door when old Feather, the postman, came. Emily, coming downstairs once, had seen her sister standing, empty-handed, eyes closed, seeming to hold her tiny frame together through sheer pressure of will under an almost insupportable burden of anguish.

What was wrong with them that they all three appeared to have a skin too few? Why had her sisters dreamed themselves into relationships that were no more real than the languishing beauties and handsome heroes they drew? Anne had almost certainly permitted herself to regard Willie Weightman in a sentimental way, but he had been jolly and flirtatious with them all and in the end he had died young as good people did. As for Monsieur! Couldn't Charlotte understand that Madame had had good reason to worry when her husband found a plain, shy employee so mentally stimulating?

Even Branwell seemed irritable and restless now he was on holiday, though his services were obviously valued at Thorp

Green! It was time Branny exerted himself to more than coaching a stupid boy. He was twenty-seven and apart from a few poems published in a local newspaper under the grand pseudonym of Northangerland and some portraits he hadn't bothered to varnish his gifts lay idle.

'Take a walk?' He looked at her when she tapped on the door of his bedroom studio to make the request. 'Why?'

'It's a fine afternoon and I've a mind to stretch my legs,' she said.

'Why bother? They're long enough already!'

'If the mood took you,' she said testily, 'you'd walk all the way to Halifax or Bradford to meet your friends!'

'Grundy and Leyland are splendid companions.'

'And both of them are pursuing their chosen careers and beginning to settle down.'

'I'm in no position to take a wife.'

'I cannot think of anyone who would have you!' she retorted.

'Ah, that's where you're wrong, sister dear!' He looked at her, his eyes glinting mischievously. 'When I was up in the Lake District there was a pretty little creature came fluttering round.'

'A Miss Varens. There was gossip in the village about that. Charlotte refused to credit it.'

'More important when I was in those hallowed hills, Hartley Taylor Coleridge was good enough to praise the Latin translations I had sent him and invite me over for the day. That was an occasion to be written up in letters of scarlet and gold.'

'But nothing came of it. Branny—'

'Do spare me the nagging!' he said peevishly. 'Charlotte and Anne have appointed themselves the conscience-keepers in this family.'

'Do you still write about Angria?' she asked.

'Sometimes. I dream about it more often. I dream that the infernal world surrounds me and crushes me to death as the characters that have burnt themselves into my brain close in on me. Go away, Em! I want to think.'

She closed the door quietly, went down the stairs and put on her cloak. Outside the moor was dancing with sunshine. Climbing the stile, crossing the lower fields, she took the track to Ponden House.

The long low building was bathed in sunlight, every flower in the garden etched with gold, the scents of the season bathing the air.

She let herself in at the side door, conscious as usual of the peaceful atmosphere that pervaded the house. More and more recently she had pictured how it might be if she married Robert. He was only twenty-two to her twenty-six but he met her easily on most intellectual grounds and she fancied that in time she could tease him out of his conventionality. He was tall and handsome and she sensed that his affection for her was growing stronger. Married to Robert she would be comparatively rich, able to help Charlotte and Anne in whatever way they eventually went. Robert set great store by family ties.

Her hand was on the latch of the partly open library door when she heard the voice.

'It won't do, brother! Be they Prunty, Brunty or Brontë the fact remains they're shanty Irish at the core.'

'Their mother was a lady.' That was Mr Heaton's voice, tired and weaker than it once had been.

'She was a merchant's daughter. And apart from the aunt has any member of the Branwell family ever lifted a hand to help those girls? You know they have not!'

'Robert has a great liking for Miss Emily.'

'Which you should have nipped in the bud!' Michael Heaton of Royd House was the younger and more forceful man. 'I've nought against the lass save that she's a gangling creature with nothing to say to me on the rare occasions we meet, but if she was the prettiest little darling alive she is not the mate for our Rob! She has no money, no breeding, no social graces. It won't do, Robert! Surely you've the sense to see that!'

'My son's of age.'

'And has good sense and the welfare of the family at heart. Let me talk to him, Robert. He'll not stand out against the family. I take it there's no understanding – no promises—'

'Merely a friendship.'

'Which will grow into something too strong to stop unless Rob is made to see his duty.'

One of the books she had borrowed from the library here had been a life of Byron. She had read it twice, her sympathies going out to the club-footed youth who, deeply in love for the first time, had stood behind a door and heard his sweetheart say, lightly mocking, 'You don't really think that I'd dream of marrying that lame boy, do you?'

In real life events duplicated themselves. Robert would heed his uncle and his father because he wished more than anything to please. Heaton would have defied the world if she had said the right thing at the right time to him.

She turned and went softly down the stairs and through the door again. In the garden the sunlit beauty of the flowers and their perfume hurt her heart.

In the deep cleft that ran beneath Ponden Kirk there was a cool, green gloom. She crawled into it and sat there, holding herself together as she had seen Charlotte do. In Gondal there had always been betrayal but at this moment she could no longer summon Gondal. It hovered out of reach, its characters cardboard, its events impossibly melodramatic. It was a world where inexperienced children had played.

The Fair Lover had evaporated like mist at morning. Of course Robert would heed his family's advice. There had never been any real question of his ever doing anything else. And the Dark Lover – gone too. Dead almost certainly since nothing had been heard of him for so long.

It didn't matter. It didn't matter because she could call the Dark One into herself. Perhaps he'd always been there, hidden in her heart and tapping at the edges of her mind. He came when she was alone, uniting the many facets of her nature. Like the heath that crept over the granite of the cliff. And when the two were one then her soul could reach out beyond mere personalities to something other. She had no name for that other but she knew it to be there. Sometimes at night when she sat on her bed in her tiny room and watched the sky above the rooftops beyond the glass she felt her outward senses whirl upwards, seeking to touch the something more that would absorb her spirit into itself. She had no name for it, though she had scribbled on a piece of paper: *My darling Pain, that wounds and sears*, but then the experience had fled and left her, locked in the prison of brain and blood, flesh and bone.

'The new curate has arrived,' Anne greeted her.

'What?' Emily looked at her.

'Mr Smith's replacement. A Mr Arthur Bell Nicholls from Northern Ireland. Of Scottish extraction, Papa says.'

'Let's pray he's an improvement on Mr Smith. Where's Charlotte?'

'Showing him the church. He's rather large and stolid-looking but quite young. Did you have a nice walk?'

'Very nice,' said Emily.

Fourteen

I'll walk where my own nature would be leading:
It vexes me to choose another guide.

Emily Jane Brontë

'At least our shares have paid out handsome dividends,' Anne said. 'Ten per cent, only fancy! And we receive the bonus every year do we not?'

'Unless the value of the shares fall,' Charlotte reminded her. 'I have tried my hardest to persuade Emily that it would be safer to buy life annuities which don't fluctuate in their market value.'

'But stay at a measly four per cent,' Emily said. 'That's about fourteen pounds a year which is scarcely more than we pay Martha. I'm inclined to take the risk.'

'Well, you've managed handsomely for me so far,' Charlotte admitted, 'so I'll leave it in your hands. Oh, I wish we had contrived to get pupils and start a school! Ellen Nussey tried so hard to interest her friends in our scheme.'

'It was no go!' Emily said slangily. 'For myself I have no desire to have workmen tramping in and out extending the house followed by noisy little girls to disturb everybody – and you never did like teaching, Charlotte.'

'Sooner or later I must look about for a post though,' Charlotte said. 'There was one advertised in Manchester but the lady wanted music and I never learned an instrument. If I'd known then you were going to leave Thorp Green, Anne, I could have recommended you for the situation.'

'Anne has been slaving away in the House of Bondage for nearly five years, and deserves a good long rest,' Emily said.

'I have a plan in mind.' Anne sat up a little straighter. 'Emily

197

and I would like to go on a trip together.'

'Where to?' Charlotte looked at them blankly.

'We thought we might travel to York and stay there overnight,' Anne said. 'The Minster is sublime and I long for Emily to see it. Then we shall do some shopping in Bradford and come home again.'

'By yourselves? Don't you think it rather risky for two girls to—'

'Tallii, I'm twenty-seven at the end of the month and Anne is already twenty-five-and-a-half,' Emily said, laughing. 'We're hardly young girls.'

'But to go jaunting off alone?'

'You and Ellen Nussey went off to Bridlington for a fortnight together when you were younger than we are now,' Anne pointed out. 'And I always went alone to Thorp Green as Emily did to Law Hill.'

'Governessing made that a necessity. Aunt would—'

'Aunt has been dead for nearly three years. Do stop trying to be like her!'

'I'm not. It's only that. . . .'

Charlotte's voice trailed away uncertainly. The truth was that she never had accustomed herself to the notion that her sisters were grown-up women. Neither could she ever look at them without feeling a pang of jealousy. Once they had been four – Branny and herself, Emily and Anne, sharing a secret world. Life had parted them for long intervals but she had never managed to get as close to Emily as Anne had always been even in Belgium. And since Anne's return from Thorp Green the two of them had been thick as thieves again, even planning a trip together without inviting her to join them. Branwell had gone his own way, the old tie between them weakening rather than strengthening. He would be returning to his post at Thorp Green after the summer holidays. She had to admit that there were certain habits of his that distressed her. He spent too much time over at the Black Bull, drinking with his cronies, or legging it over to Halifax and Bradford to drink there. Sometimes when he came home he was unsteady on his feet, prone to sudden gales of laughter or bursts of irritable temper. He had grown away from her.

'You are going to Ellen Nussey's soon, are you not?' Anne

---

said. 'We shall only be away for a couple of days. You'll manage, will you not?'

'Yes, of course I will!' Charlotte forced a cheerful note into her voice. 'I was merely being selfish! But won't it be expensive?'

'It will cost us four shillings each to take the train to York via Leeds and back and we can walk to and from Keighley in this fine weather,' Emily said in her decided way. 'The hotel in York will set us back – three and sixpence each – and a further three and sixpence if we stay over at Keighley to avoid walking home in the dark. That makes fifteen shillings. Add a further pound for food and coffees and something for souvenirs – three pounds will fit us out handsomely for such a brief jaunt.'

'Well, you seem to have it all worked out,' Charlotte said reluctantly.

They left early on the Monday morning, each carrying a small overnight bag, alike and yet unalike in their cloaks and straw bonnets. Emily, with her slim frame emphasized by the long narrow-skirted dress, towered over the smaller Anne whose fair ringlets contrasted with her elder's frizzy dark mane.

The postman was coming up the path. Charlotte lingered at the door, her heart leaping into her throat as it always did.

' 'Morning, Miss Brontë! Lovely day! There's one for thy feyther. Nowt for thee.'

'Thank you, Mr Feather. Yes, it is another day of bright summer, indeed it is!'

She held herself against the pain of no word from Brussels until she was able with a composed face and voice to go into the parlour and read her father's letter to him.

The travellers returned on Wednesday morning, both looking uncommonly pleased with themselves, Charlotte thought enviously.

'It was a splendid trip!' Emily dumped down her bag and took off her bonnet. 'We played at Gondal the whole time, Tallii! It was great fun for we were members of the Royalist Party escaping from the victorious Republicans!'

'You went all the way to York and played at Gondal? You could've stayed at home and done that,' Charlotte said, amused.

'Well, the rascals still delight us,' Emily affirmed.

'Emily greatly admired the Minster too,' Anne said hurriedly.

'I did indeed. It was sublime. The hotel at York was very

comfortable and the Keighley inn so-so though we enjoyed a tasty supper, and we made a few useful purchases in Bradford so we are well satisfied.'

'We saw Mr Heaton the younger in Bradford,' Anne said. 'He looked straight at us, didn't he, Emily? But I daresay he didn't realize properly who we were being out of our usual setting as it were. Anyway he turned and mounted up before we could cross the road to greet him. And Emily was not well.'

'The motion of the train had made me feel slightly sick so don't start fussing,' Emily said. 'After a glass of wine and a rest I felt fine again. You are right, Charlotte. Excitement is better anticipated than enjoyed. I'll get these bags upstairs. You leave for Derbyshire in a day or two, don't you?'

'I shall nerve myself up to applying for another teaching-post while I'm there,' Charlotte said. 'We will do well in future to allow the bonuses to accumulate in readiness for our old age. Papa is not far short of seventy and cannot live for ever!'

'He's not been unwell?' Anne enquired anxiously.

'No, but his eyesight is failing very rapidly. Fortunately Mr Nicholls is proving a responsible curate and reads well. Narrow-minded and slightly pompous as are all his kind but steady and respectable.'

'William Weightman was not pompous or narrow minded.'

'No, Anne. Of course not! You know if he had lived I like to think that he might have married Ellen Nussey. She would've settled him nice—'

'Anne, give me a hand with the bags,' Emily broke in. 'Charlotte, we're both dying for a cup of tea!'

'I'll get it!' Charlotte dived into the kitchen.

'She seems so restless,' Anne remarked a few days later when they had seen Charlotte depart in the gig for her visit to Ellen.

'Because her talents are not being employed to their fullest advantage,' Emily said. 'She is wasted as a teacher but what else can she do? Mary Taylor has broken free and sailed to New Zealand. I admire her but I don't envy her! Ellen is content to remain with her family who impose on her to a degree a less unselfish nature would bitterly resent. Well, she and Charlotte may natter to their hearts' content while they're curling their hair before the fire. Ellen is sure to want her to stay an extra

week and I'm fully determined that she shall get as much pleasure as possible before she goes on the governessing grind again.'

'Shall we walk over and borrow some books from Ponden
House?' Anne suggested.

'No! No, I think not. With Mr Heaton so feeble in health they'll
not want too many neighbours popping in and out,' Emily said.
'Are you going to make a start on your new dress?'

'If I can find one of Aunt's pattern books. Grey figured silk! It
looks difficult to work with. But the current fashions are very
becoming. Neat little waists and full skirts held out over stiff-
ened petticoats and narrow sleeves.'

'Try wearing one of those when you're climbing up to Ponden
Kirk,' Emily said, 'and you'll float away like a balloon.'

It was useless to try to persuade Emily to dress more fashionably, Anne thought. She was so utterly free from normal
feminine vanity that she went around with her lank skirts cling-
ing to her uncorseted frame, her sleeves puffed out like wings,
her hair slipping from its combs, and her boots innocent of
polish. Or was such behaviour a sign of vanity carried to its
utmost extreme?

The blow fell on the morning of the day that Charlotte, after
staying on an extra week in Derbyshire, was expected home.
There was a letter for Branwell in the post. A few minutes later
the sounds of passionate wailing filled the house and sent Emily
and Anne up the stairs to meet Branwell, hair and clothes disor-
dered as he struggled with some unseen assailant at the top of
the stairs.

'Branny! what on earth is it?' Emily had reached him first but
he thrust her aside and rushed down the stairs, throwing the
crumpled letter at Anne as he pushed past her.

'What is it? Is it bad news?'

Emily ran down to join her.

'It's from Mr Robinson,' Anne said tremblingly, scanning its
contents. 'Branwell is dismissed. Mr Robinson threatens to make
public his conduct, to . . . ex-expose it, unless he breaks off all
communication at once and for ever with the whole Robinson
family and n-never goes to the neighbourhood of Thorp Green
again.'

'But he was highly valued there!' Emily snatched the letter and
read it for herself. 'What has he been supposed to have done?'

'I don't know. I can't say for certain.'

'You were there! You must have some idea—'

'His wife and I,' Branwell shouted, banging back through the door. 'My dearest Lydia, though she is seventeen years my senior, bestowed her undying affections upon me! Her husband is a cold, heartless man who gives her no affection, no consideration. I read poetry to her – Byron! Shelley! she praised my delivery, invited me to call her Lydia! Oh, the exquisite danger of those stolen moments!'

'Where's Papa?' Emily demanded.

'John Brown offered to escort him for a walk. Branny, you must be calm.'

'Calm? Calm? My love is discovered, much that you care! My life is ruined, much that you care! My existence is wrecked – and hers! Oh, God! it is unutterable! I cannot live without her. I cannot!'

He turned and dashed through the door again.

'Did you know about this? This love-affair?' Emily asked.

Anne shook her head mutely.

'Is it true?' Emily ran her eye down the page again. 'Mr Robinson says he will expose Branwell unless – but that would mean exposing his own wife as well! Is he the kind of man who might do that?'

'I only know,' said Anne, trembling violently, 'that while I was at Thorp Green I had undreamt of views of human nature. Please! I must find Papa.' She took the letter and ran through the front door.

Branwell and Lydia Robinson? Emily sat down on the lowest step, glad that young Martha had walked with Tabby down to the latter's sister's house for an hour. She had the place to herself for a little while.

Rising, she mounted the stairs again and went into her brother's room. As usual the bed was a tangle of blankets and sheets, the pillows tossed hither and thither, half-finished drawings and pieces of writing scattered over the lot and sliding to the floor. The chamber smelt of burnt candle-wax, whisky and the pipe that Branwell sometimes smoked. She went over to the window and threw the sash up.

When Branwell came home, she reflected, he'd want nothing more than to fall into a clean, neatly made bed. She began to pick up the stray papers, to shuffle them into a pile. Why hadn't he persevered at his art? He had lacked technical expertise but he had the gift, even now, of catching a likeness. These sketches were vivid and lively and – her well marked eyebrows flew up as she looked at the top sketch on the pile she had gathered. A group of young gentlemen sat at their ease, left hands holding smoking churchwarden pipes, right hands – well, Charlotte and Anne had best not see that!!

By the evening Branwell had staggered home from the Black Bull, been sick, been dosed with the blackest coffee that Emily could brew, and lay on the sofa, still drunk, still moaning about his lost love.

Mr Brontë, his expression set and cold, had held family prayers at which only herself, Anne and old Tabby had been present, young Martha having been packed off home down the lane.

The prayers completed, Mr Brontë closed his Bible and addressed them.

'As you know Branwell has been dismissed. He says that he entered into an adulterous relationship with his employer's wife. Anne tells me that she was aware Mrs Robinson flattered Branwell but she knew nothing further. It is not necessary for any of us to know anything further. It is clear to me that Branwell has been entrapped by the wiles of a sophisticated and amoral woman whose name will not be mentioned in this house again. Branwell has done wrong. However the artistic temperament can sometimes waver on the edges of sin. John Brown has offered to take him to Liverpool for a few days. The change of scene may be beneficial. Meanwhile any gossip occasioned by Branwell's frantic reaction to this unfortunate affair will, I hope, have died down by the time he returns. You will tell Charlotte what has happened. Now I bid you good night.'

'If I know Haworth the gossip will grow and grow and gain in the telling', Emily thought, and felt a stab of impatience when she glanced at the distress on Tabby's and Anne's faces.

Didn't any of them yet know that there was a dangerous imbalance in Branwell? They had all seen the fits of temper he had suffered from in childhood when his will was thwarted; they all knew the nerve storms that occasionally struck him down twitching and foaming at the mouth; they had all succumbed to his wayward charm, believed in his extravagant protestations of future greatness and made excuses for his frequent failures.

'Charlotte will be here soon,' she said aloud. 'I'll wait for her in the garden. The night's very mild. Anne, can you give Tabby a hand to bed?'

'Yes, of course,' Anne said quietly.

Outside the sky was littered with stars. Emily wrapped her shawl around her and stood near the pear-tree, which needed pruning badly just as the flower beds were greatly in need of weeding.

They were, she mused, a sorry crew, Anne imagining that she had given more than a passing thought to light-hearted, feckless Weightman, Charlotte eating her heart out for a man who had lost all interest in her once she had left Brussels, herself mourning for two loves who had never really existed at all save in her own romantic imagination.

She had killed off Augusta Geraldine Almeda and then broken her own rule and tried to bring her to life again, but Gondal no longer satisfied her deepest instincts. It was no more than a left-over childhood pastime. She was rooting her story now in the places that had haunted her, and King Julius was no longer a monarch but a gypsy brat taken in by a kindly farmer whose natural son he might be. She had to work out the dates and the family trees accurately in order to make the tale more believable. The ingredients were there. Now she needed to craft her art. She needed to find out who she truly was.

'Emily, dear, can you deal with Branwell? He is losing his temper because I asked him to go to bed.' Anne's quiet distress was more powerful than a shout.

'I'll see about it. Here's the gig. Tell Charlotte what's occurred while I deal with Branwell.' Emily went indoors again, banishing stars and gypsy brats from her mind.

Branwell was raging round the kitchen, clattering pots and pans, sending a batch of dough rising by the red ashes of the fire off its board and onto the stone floor where it rapidly diminished in size.

'Thank you, Branwell!' Hands on hips she surveyed the damage. 'Now I shall have to throw that away and start again first thing in the morning. Not to mention picking up the utensils you're busily dislodging! If you've been dismissed then I'm sorry for it and sorrier still for the cause – if you've told us the truth. Have you?'

'Told you the truth!' Branwell swung round, his face distorted. 'What does that mean, pray?'

'Exactly what I said. I generally say what I mean. Is it the truth?'

'You think no woman of consequence would fall in love with me? Lydia – my Lydia – is a lady of the finest sensibilities, the most delicate—'

'Oh, fudge!' Emily said impatiently. 'Ladies with fine sensibilities don't take their son's tutor to bed! You're still drunk, Branwell, and you're talking complete rubbish. The woman is seventeen years older than you are, with growing children, for heaven's sake! She led you on a little with her flattery and—'

'Not one word more! You know nothing of such emotions!'

'Indulge them in your own room then. Charlotte is just returned.'

Branwell flung down a pan and made his unsteady way towards the stairs.

Emily scraped up the spoilt dough, righted the pans and stirred up the ashes. She was measuring spoonfuls of tea into the pot when Charlotte came in, her face pinched with fatigue and shock.

'Anne has been telling me – where's Branwell?'

'Gone up to bed. Wait until tomorrow when he's sober for you'll get no sense out of him tonight!'

'How could he?' Charlotte sank on to the nearest chair and moaned. 'To allow himself to be seduced by a married woman! Emily, what possessed him?'

'Mr Robinson's letter wasn't specific as to the exact nature of the offence,' Emily said. 'What matters is that he is dismissed and tearing every passion to shreds. Papa is greatly discomposed. Drink your tea and tell me how Miss Nussey does. Is she well?'

'Very well, but she has her troubles too.' Charlotte sipped the tea tremblingly. 'Her brother Joseph is very ill due to his own excesses and poor George is no better mentally. It is a great burden to them all.'

'Well, burdens are to be endured I suppose. I'll take Anne her tea.'

She carried the cup through into the dining-room where Anne sat by the dying fire, the lamp turned low, her attitude one of the most extreme dejection.

'Don't take on so, Annie! Branwell isn't the first young man to be led astray by a stupid woman,' Emily said.

'I never should have suggested he come with me to Thorp Green. Oh, I did it for the best but the road to hell is paved with good intentions, isn't it?' Anne said on a sob.

'It wasn't your fault, Anne! Don't go piling up imaginary sins at your own door! Drink your tea and go to bed. Charlotte is shocked and angry and tired after her journey. Tomorrow John Brown is to accompany Branwell on a visit to Liverpool. Papa is arranging it. Tomorrow everything will look brighter.'

'You don't know, Emily,' Anne said, finishing the tea and dragging herself up as if her will to move had gone. 'I am so sick of it all. So tired of mankind and its disgusting ways!'

'Anne. . . ?'

'You don't know,' Anne repeated drearily. 'You simply don't know.'

Something else had happened at Thorp Green then, something that Anne had suspected and would never confide. And she herself would never ask, she privately decreed. Whatever unmentionable behaviour had caused Branwell to be dismissed in such harsh terms, let the family go on believing that an adulterous affair was the reason. It might, Emily thought, bending to extinguish the lamp, even be true.

If they had hoped for a season of recovery after Branwell's frantic conduct the hope faltered and died in the weeks following his return from Liverpool.

'It served only to remind me of my loss,' he complained. 'We went on up the North Wales coast you know. Brown thought the sea air would revive me, but I saw her face in the waves, in the clouds, in the hills! God knows but the only faint hope that remains to me is that her husband – the man to whom she is legally bound – will die soon. It would be a blessed release for her, her one chance of happiness.'

'How can you stand there and say such wicked things?' Charlotte burst out. 'To fall in love with someone who is married and allow yourself to wish for the death of a partner! You disgust me!'

'I might have hoped for some sympathy and understanding from my own family.' Branwell grabbed his hat. 'Happily there are others who understand the agonies of love.'

'Where are you going?'

Charlotte had half risen. Branwell turned to fling his reply.

'To hell by the quickest route!'

'Not a bad way of describing the snuggery in the Black Bull,' Emily said.

'Where he will pour the whole story into the ears of anyone who cares to listen! How could he have allowed himself to feel as he does for someone who is already married?'

She had picked up her little writing-desk and left the room, not waiting for an answer.

'Going to write to Monsieur again?' Emily said under her breath. Branwell, she fancied, was living in his own invented world, playing out in his own person the frustrations of thwarted romantic love. He was Lord Byron and North-angerland and the Duke of Zamorna – all the men he had read about and written about. Perhaps even Branwell didn't know exactly how much was true.

For one thing she was grateful to him. With Branwell in his present state there was no possibility of the school scheme being revived. No impertinent little girls would troop into the parsonage or workmen bring their mortar and stones and hods of bricks to enlarge the building.

Life, she thought, glancing round the dining-room which needed tidying up but could wait until later, held its compensations. Summer was sliding into a mellow autumn and at least Anne was at home where she could be roused from the depression into which her too sensitive spirits fell. The two of them had written joint diary papers which they planned to open and read in three years' time. It was always interesting to find out how close their descriptions of events had been.

She summoned Keeper and Flossy, the latter the only other dog that Keeper would allow within a few yards of him, put on her shawl and went out.

It was a relief to get out into the clear fresh air, away from walls and human voices and tasks waiting to be done. She walked out, humming under her breath. Her new tale was progressing well. Somehow all the strands of the themes mingling in her mind were coming together into a coherent whole.

For once nobody from the village stepped out to greet her or loomed on the horizon and forced her to take a roundabout way. She walked on, leaving the cares of the moment behind, her mind empty of all save the crisp beauty of the day.

The striking of the church clock reminded her that the tidying-up still needed to be done and the scones baked for tea. She swung about, whistled to the dogs and headed home. Branwell, she suspected, would linger in the conviviality of the Black Bull until someone persuaded him home. With any luck they would have a peaceful tea by the fire and she'd get in some writing before his stumbling footsteps disturbed the gravel.

She went round to the back and through the kitchen into the dining-room. Charlotte stood by the table, a book held close to her shortsighted eyes, shoulders hunched and expression rapt as often happened when she was caught up in her studies. For an instant Emily paused, the smile on her lips freezing there as Charlotte, suddenly jolted into awareness of her presence, looked up, saying in an awed tone,

'I never was more stirred in my life before than by these lines. They blaze in my heart like the sound of a trumpet!'

'That's my notebook,' Emily said. She spoke almost flatly as if her mouth refused to shape what her eyes were seeing.

'I was tidying the room up. Your desk was open. Listen! These lines are – listen!

> But first a hush of peace, a soundless calm descends,
> The struggle of distress and fierce impatience ends,
> Mute music soothes my breast – unuttered harmony.
> That I could never dream till earth was lost to me.
> Then dawns the Invisible, the Unseen its truth reveals. . . .'

'Be quiet! Be quiet!!' Emily's voice was raised into a shriek. 'Not one word more! How dare you read my work without leave? How dare you poke and pry into my mind?'

'I glanced over the page and began to read, Emily! The book was there, open! You have never said—'

'Because it never occurred to me that you would read what was never meant for any eyes but my own! Must I lock up all my belongings and throw away the keys for fear you'll come sneaking round?'

'That's not fair!' Charlotte stood her ground, clutching the book to her flat chest protectively. 'I found them by accident and once I'd scanned a line I couldn't stop myself from reading! These are real poems, not just verses such as I write myself. The experiences you write about—'

'Are private!' Emily interrupted. 'Not for you, not for anyone! For myself alone! You have no right to dabble your fingers in my thoughts. You have no right—'

'What's wrong? Is it Branwell?' Anne, clutching a piece of sewing, had pattered down the stairs.

'Charlotte has been reading my poems,' Emily said.

'Anne, they're truly wonderful! Have you read them?' Charlotte began.

'I've never even showed them to Anne,' Emily said chokingly. 'Why the devil would I show them to you then? Give them here! In future keep your nose out of my affairs!'

'Girls! what is all the noise about?' Mr Brontë's voice sounded from across the hall. 'Is someone hurt?'

'It's nothing, Papa. Merely a lively discussion!' Anne said, going out.

'Try to be a little less lively, my dear!'

'Your tea will be ready very soon,' Anne said soothingly.

The parlour door closed again. Anne came back into the room.

'I don't blame you for being angry.' Charlotte's voice was low and shaking. 'I ought not to have read them, but you ought not to keep such work to yourself. They should be published.'

'Now you are out of your mind! They're rhymes – rubbish! Published!'

'Read them, Annie!' Charlotte thrust the book towards her. 'The one here – *Listen! tis just the hour, the*—'

'Oh, read them by all means, Anne,' Emily said. 'Since when did I keep anything from you that I allowed Charlotte to see? Go stand in the graveyard and declaim them aloud for all I care! I take no further interest in them!'

She flung out of the room and up the stairs and into her tiny bedchamber, where she hunched on the bed, careless of her dusty boots, drumming her long fingers on the window pane.

'Are you very angry?' Anne had come in and stood with her back against the door.

'You didn't knock!' Emily said harshly.

'Charlotte is crying,' Anne said. 'She didn't mean to pry, Emmii. She saw them by accident and read them before she could help herself. Her soul was stirred by them. She never guessed that you wrote such pieces. Neither did I. Emily, Charlotte's right. You ought to get them published. Other people should have the opportunity—'

'To invade me? No.'

'I've offered to let Charlotte read some of my poems,' Anne said. 'They cannot compare with yours but if they give her some pleasure—'

'So Annii turns traitor too?' Emily scrambled off the bed and sat on the edge of it to yank off her boots.

'When we were small we used to pretend that we were published writers. Branwell and Charlotte in Angria and you and me in Gondal. We used to share in those days, Emily.'

'And then Charlotte decided that I needed educating and dragged me off to Roe Head and later on dragged me off to Brussels. Always interfering!'

'If she hadn't then you would still be forming your letters backwards.'

'Aye, that's true! But she had no right to . . . try to shape me and mould me into something I'm not!'

'We were all shaped a long time ago, I think,' Anne said thoughtfully. 'Charlotte recognized our talents. She always has you know. And she's so hurt by Branwell's constant failures, Em! They were always so close and now he casts her off and goes his own way and she's sick at heart about it. Emily, we could try to get our work published – the three of us—'

'And betray the existence of Gondal? Reveal our identities? Can you hear the gossip in the village? "T'lad's a drunkard and tha knaws them three lasses mek up tales like childer." I'd rather die!'

'All the references to Gondal or Angria could be edited out, and we could use pen names. Nobody need ever know – not Papa or Branwell or the neighbours, nobody! It would be our secret, Emily. Just the three of us. Well, think about it.' Anne moved to open the door. Over her shoulder as she went out she said quietly, 'After so many disappointments it would mean so very much to achieve something.'

Damn Charlotte with her curiosity and Anne with her pleading! Emily scuffed her long feet into a pair of slippers and scowled. On the other hand who would ever guess that a girl designated as housekeeper in an obscure parsonage, a member of a family sprung from shanty Irish, had ever penned a line? To hold that knowledge under her habitual mask would grant her a secret pleasure, afford her some delight.

She'd wait a day or two lest Charlotte think the victory too lightly won and then, by degrees, she'd yield. Her name, she mused, would be Ellis. Ellis Bell.

Fifteen

*'Nelly, I am Heathcliff – he's always, always in my mind –
not as a pleasure, any more than I am always a pleasure to
myself – but as my own being—'*
Emily Jane Brontë

'I like your Agnes Grey,' Charlotte said, folding her shawl neatly
over her narrow shoulders as the three began their usual nightly
walk round the dining-room table. 'She has realism and a certain
dry humour. She reminds me in some respects of my own
Frances. Both see life as it is.'

'Calm irony is not the only touchstone of reality,' Emily said.

'Your notions of reality are quite horrifying,' Charlotte said
with a shiver. 'Some scenes in your story give me uneasy
thoughts by day and very bad dreams at night!'

'Oh, don't be so silly!' Emily said, laughing. 'They are no
worse than the stories Papa and Tabby used to tell us when we
were children.'

'Which frightened Ellen Nussey so,' Charlotte remembered.

'You have not told her anything about our publishing
venture?' Emily said sharply.

'I gave my word and I'll not break it. Besides I think it only
right that we should remain completely anonymous. How could
we write truthfully if others knew we were writing? We'd be
forever looking over our shoulders for fears of what the neighbours might think!'

'Branwell is writing a novel,' Emily said. 'He has called it
"The Thurstons Of Darkwell". Fifty pages of it are done. He
showed it to me—'

'You didn't—?'

'I've already told you. No, Branwell knows nothing of our

writing or our publishing ventures. From me nobody ever will.'

'Branwell may guess,' Anne said uneasily. 'All those letters you wrote and the replies we received when we were arranging for the publication of our poems – he must've noticed.'

'Branwell is only wrapped up in his own fantasies!' Charlotte said. 'He ought to be looking round for work but he does nothing except drink.'

'That's not fair!' Emily said. 'He has applied for work but with the current rate of unemployment—'

'Not to mention the fall in the value of railway shares. Emily, don't you think—?'

'No, I don't. The value of the shares will recover so we'll leave our legacy where it is. You did leave it in my hands, Charlotte.'

'Emily has managed for us very capably so far,' Anne, the peacemaker, intervened.

'As you say, but we laid out nearly forty pounds on the printing of our poems.'

'Perhaps someone will pay us for our books,' Anne said brightly.

'They make up a good three-volume package at any rate,' Charlotte agreed. 'I wish that yours didn't end so abruptly, Em. Catherine dead and her two lovers left forsaken. It leaves such an unpleasant impression on the mind.'

'I long to know what happened to the little girl Catherine bore and the little lad whom Heathcliff has cheated out of his inheritance,' Anne said.

'Would you really, Annie?' Emily had paused, half turning in the dim, firelit room.

'Yes.'

'Then I'll continue the tale if that's your wish. Meanwhile we can still send out the three books as they are.'

'I obtained a list of publishers who deal with fiction the last time I went to the Mechanics Institute Library,' Charlotte said.

'I leave all that business to you,' Emily said. 'It would be rather good if we actually made some money out of our stories, wouldn't it?'

'Currer, Ellis and Acton Bell,' Charlotte said dreamily.

'It's past eleven. Is Branwell in yet?' Anne asked.

'He'll be at the Black Bull. I'll slip over and remind him that he's a home to come to. You go up!'

Emily bent to light the lamp, wound her shawl round her and went softly to the front door.

She went down the lane and turned into the narrow street in which the schoolhouse and the sexton's house stood side by side. The curate, Arthur Bell Nicholls, lodged with the Browns. By now he would be peacefully asleep, she thought with an inward chuckle. How shocked he would be to find out that they had appropriated his surname for their pseudonyms! The joke had amused them all.

When she reached the uncurtained back window of the Black Bull she looked in, seeing, as she expected, her brother lounging in the chair that was always kept for him, glass in hand.

She tapped on the glass, wondering what reception she would get. There were times when Branwell refused point-blank to notice her or respond to her signals. Tonight however he looked up, grinned at her and downed the rest of his drink before rising and coming round via the main entrance to join her.

'Come to collect the black sheep, Em?'

He was only slightly unsteady on his feet.

'I've nowt better to do!' she retorted.

'Charlotte and Anne having scuttled off to bed? Home then!'

'You're in a good mood,' she ventured.

'A fellow cannot waste his whole life in tears. Anyway the book's going well!'

'Had you not thought of reapplying to the railway for a situation?'

'Oh, I see! I must write in my spare time but spend my days in tedious labour while you three plot and plan your little volumes of poetry!'

'What?' Emily stopped dead and stared at him in consternation.

'I'm not always drunk,' Branwell said. 'D'ye think I don't notice the furtive rushings to meet the postman, the reams of paper you buy from Greenwood, the conversations that cease when I come into the room? Three slim volumes titled in gold—'

'Charlotte said the parcel had been opened! Branny, you had no right!'

'It was addressed to the Messrs Brontë. I thought it was for

215

Papa and me. When I realized I stuck the books back in the parcel and left them on the dining-room table – and you need not trouble your head about my telling Charlotte or Anne or anyone else about it! If you girls want to waste your money on some little enterprise of your own then that's entirely your own affair. I know nothing and care less!'

There had been a time not very long before when he would have been the moving spirit in the enterprise. Emily felt his hurt as keenly as if it had been her own. She said nothing but silently handed him the lamp and went on soberly into the parsonage.

'I'll lock up,' said Branwell. 'You've heard the news I suppose?'

'What news?'

'Mr Heaton died late this afternoon. His brother called into the Black Bull to inform them. Robert is master of Ponden House now, though I suspect his uncle will keep a firm fist in the pie! I used to go with the guns with the Heatons when Weightman was alive. Do you—?'

'I don't visit Ponden House these days,' she said shortly. 'I'm too busy.'

'Ah well! life whirls on,' Branwell said, yawning.

'Good night, Branny.'

Going up the stairs, closing the door of her room behind her, she sat down on the edge of the bed, pulling her shawl more tightly round her.

She recalled herself as a small girl watching as Heaton came out with Grasper on his leash; Mr Heaton bringing the pear-tree over and planting it for her himself; the times she had slipped through the side door to borrow or return books; the few snatches of conversation she had had with Heaton; his bringing Keeper as a replacement when Grasper had died; her lively talks with Robert Heaton; Dark Lover and Fair Lover but in her mind alone.

Her story ought to be continued, retold through the second generation as it might have been with lover finding lover and old enmities set free to roam the moors in satanic harmony. What had been was completed, but the might-have-been rose in her like a promise.

A few days later she was peeling vegetables in the kitchen when young Martha came flying in.

'Miss Emily, Master Branwell's fallen in't Black Bull! In a fit! Maister Sugden says tha mun get theer quick,' she gasped out.

'I'll go at once. Where's your father, Martha?'

'Wi' Master Branwell, Miss Emily.'

'Right!' Emily whipped off her apron and flew through the churchyard.

'There's nae need t'fret, Miss Emily! Branwell's coming out of it.' The heavily handsome John Brown came to meet her.

'Surely he is not in his cups so soon in the day, John?' Emily leaned against the wall and looked at him.

'Nay, he were sent for to meet someone earlier,' John Brown said. 'A fellow frae Thorp Green. Seems the Robinson gentleman died and theer's a will left seemingly that forbids the widow frae seeing Branwell on threat of losing her fine house and the younger childer. If tha leaves it wi'me, Miss Emily, I'll talk some sense in't lad and get him back to t'parsonage when he's in better fettle.'

'I'll see for myself first.' She stepped decidedly into the inn where her brother was slumped in a chair, face ashen and hair falling about his face, a series of incoherent mutterings issuing from his lips.

'Branwell? Branwell, what happened?' Emily demanded.

'Lydia! My Lydia! My lost and only love! Torn from me . . . forbidden to see me . . . her coachman brought the news. My life . . . ruined!'

'It isn't necessary to inform the entire world of your private affairs,' Emily said coldly. 'Keep him with you, John, until he's fit to be seen at home.'

'He talks about t'lady all of th'time,' the landlord informed her. 'If bar's empty he'll rattle on to t'dog!'

'You ought not to encourage him to come here, Mr Sugden.'

'Bless yah, Miss Emily, he doan't need no encouragement,' Mr Sugden said energetically. 'He comes hisself quick enough!'

'Do what you can, John. Branwell, try to pull yourself together! We all have to suffer disappointments but we have to learn to live with them. I'll alert Papa.'

'How is Maister Brontë?' Sugden enquired.

'He can hardly see anything at all but we have hopes of getting him to a surgeon who can deal with the cataracts. Excuse me but I must speak to my sisters.'

Leaving Branwell, who was writhing in a fresh outburst of hysterical grief, she hurried back to the house.

'Emily, there's an item in the newspaper for last week announcing the death of Mr Robinson.' Charlotte met her in the hall. 'Will Branwell go there now?'

'It seems not.' Briefly Emily related the information she had just had.

'Mr Robinson left a will which debars his widow from ever seeing Branwell again.'

'Apparently someone, a coachman from Thorp Green, did come to see Branwell at the Black Bull,' Emily said carefully.

'William Allison. He is a most respectable man,' Anne said, coming down the stairs. 'Is he still here?'

'He left apparently. He brought Branwell word of Mr Robinson's orders. Branwell has taken it very badly.'

'Did you see the will? Was Branwell telling the truth?' Charlotte asked.

'I didn't see it and as for Branny. . . !' Emily shrugged and went into the kitchen.

'What's up wi'Master Branny now?' Tabby demanded from the chair where she spent most of her time these days.

Emily told her.

'Yon lad allus did laike his play-acting,' Tabby said. 'Happen tha has a worrisome time ahead, child.'

'Happen!' Emily said.

Branwell, she thought as she punished a carrot by chopping it into little pieces, no longer seemed to know which was real and which imagined in his world. He trailed along strings that pulled pieces of Angria into his life, and the tragedy was that he found it difficult to tell the difference between them.

'If tha asks me,' Martha said, 'Maister Branwell in't half as bad as some folks mek out.'

'Hold your tongue and get on with the cleaning!' Emily said sharply. As the girl passed her she gave her a quick, hard hug.

Tabby proved more accurate than many prophets. Whatever the truth of the Thorp Green affair Branwell had cast himself in the role of tormented lover and Mrs Robinson as the bullied and imprisoned widow. He spent half the day in his room, lying on his bed and endlessly turning over poems and the beginnings of novels and stories that he had laboured over and never completed. By early evening he had dressed himself and gone across to the Black Bull where, using the small sums of money he cadged from his father, he drank away the hours, talking, talking, talking. When he could summon the energy he borrowed a horse and rode over to Halifax to run up debts there.

'If his friends refused to indulge him then he might be forced to pull himself together,' Charlotte said, tight-lipped, reading the latest short note from the latest publisher to reject the three novels. 'His latest story is that Mrs Robinson is thinking of going into a nunnery, that her mind is totally wrecked by her sufferings. I don't know what to believe. His friends should stop pandering to his moods!'

'They are fond of him,' Anne said. 'Branny always had the gift of making friends. And he has great charm, Charlotte.'

'Integrity is better,' Charlotte said curtly. 'Well, I have friends too and though Mary Taylor is in New Zealand Ellen Nussey is still in this country and we cannot risk asking her to stay for a few days lest Branwell make a fool of himself before her.'

'She is accustomed to difficult brothers,' Anne said.

'And I've no intention of inflicting mine upon her. If we don't get our books accepted soon I've a mind to go to Paris and teach there! They advertise in the French newspapers often for English governesses.'

'You know that you wouldn't leave Papa in his present condition,' Anne said.

'His general health is very sound so Dr Wheelhouse says,' Charlotte said. 'Emily, you and I must go to Manchester soon and find a reputable eye-surgeon who can advise us as to the best action to take.'

'Better if you take Anne with you and leave me to deal with Branwell,' Emily said.

'Anne has not that air of authority which is required in at least one of us if we are to obtain the best treatment at a reasonable price for Papa. John Brown will hold himself in readiness for any emergency.'

When, Emily thought, would Charlotte stop dragging her around to places where she didn't want to go? It was too bad of her to contemplate going to the city when on the heights the heather would be in bloom and the cry of the curlew would fill the world with music.

She said nothing, her eyes straying to the window. She had completed the second part of the book now, writing at white-hot speed. Charlotte, hearing portions read aloud, had exclaimed in warm praise.

'I like Catherine Linton better than Catherine Earnshaw,' she said. 'There's a gentleness in the daughter that is appealing, and Hareton has the instincts of a gentleman despite the brutality to which he has been subjected. But Heathcliff stands unredeemed. Emily, can it be right to create such monsters? What we create in fiction may be regarded by those who read our work as aspects of ourselves?'

'Since nobody knows who we are it won't matter,' Emily pointed out.

'But our books will influence people,' Anne said anxiously. 'Is it right to make savagery and violence so attractive? I agree with Charlotte that whether we are known or not we must always bear in mind the moral effect our books may have.'

'Let's fret about that once someone has accepted them for publication,' Emily said briskly. 'Since only two copies of the poems have been sold I refuse to worry about our effect on the general conscience. Now what?'

'Someone coming?' Charlotte hurried to her side, raising her eyeglass.

'Probably someone dunning Branwell for some pressing debt,' Emily said. 'I'll deal with him.' She went out, fumbling in her pocket for the few coins she carried there.

'You'll be Emily Jane.' The elderly man who stood below the steps, calmly ignoring Keeper's ferocious growl, took off his cap to reveal thick, grey hair with a tinge of red.

Emily nodded briefly.

'Emily, who is – oh, it must be one of our Brontë uncles!' Anne had flitted past her down the steps, her face alive with delight. 'Cannot you see the family resemblance?'

'I'm your Uncle James.' He stepped forward and shook hands with her.

'I am Anne and this, as you surmised, is Emily Jane and Charlotte is within. Are you come to visit? Oh, Papa will be so happy to see you! His sight is so very bad that he cannot distinguish features unless they are placed against a strongly lit background. Is this your bag? Come in! See who has come to see us, Papa!'

Emily followed more soberly.

'James?' Mr Brontë was groping for his brother's hand. 'You come at an opportune time! Can you stay?'

'No more than a few days. I'm looking for seasonal work. You'll be wanting news of the family back home, I daresay.'

'I'll get the whisky from the cellar,' Emily said, smiling faintly.

'Is it one of the uncles?' Charlotte drew her into the dining-room.

'Uncle James. We've not met him before.'

'He looks respectable from the little that I could make out.'

'Don't be such a snob, Tallii!' Emily shook her head at her sister.

'You know that in their youth the uncles were very wild.'

'And certainly not fit company into which to introduce your friend Ellen Nussey! He's come to work during the harvest here, and his coming is a blessing because now you and I can visit Manchester and not fret about Anne dealing with Branwell.'

'That's so!' Charlotte had brightened. 'I must go in and introduce myself while you get the tea. It will be interesting to hear about the Irish connection.'

She spoke as if the Irish half of the family was no more than the vaguest link. Emily mentally shrugged and went to unlock the cellar door and bring up the whisky.

Two days later, having packed up the three novels yet again, she and Charlotte seated themselves in a corner of the train and prepared to rattle towards Manchester.

'I have a list of surgeons and a list of respectable hotels,' Charlotte said. 'It may take a day or two before we can secure an appointment. At least we can be certain that Anne is all right at home. I did rather dread leaving the poor child with Papa but Uncle James seems very competent and Branwell appears to have taken to him. Just look at those slums! Did you ever see anything so dismal?'

'I don't suppose the people who live there admire them either,' Emily said dryly.

'I pity the poor but I cannot help feeling that with the right education they could better their lot,' Charlotte said thoughtfully. 'And there must be something in the maxim that we are born for some particular reason. What do you think?'

Emily shook her head slightly and stared out of the window. She could see her reflection in the glass as the train steamed into a tunnel. Her face looked white, disembodied above the collar of her dark cloak. It was, she mused, an Irish face – high cheekbones, jutting high-bridged nose, wide full lipped mouth with a long upperlip. Not a pretty face like Anne's or Ellen's. With her long dark hair cut off and her skirt exchanged for breeches she would make a handsome boy.

Then the train screeched into daylight again and Charlotte began fussing about getting their bags down.

Two days later they made the return journey, Charlotte well satisfied with the results.

'In a fortnight I shall bring Papa here and leave you and Anne to deal with Branwell. Of course if Uncle James is willing to stay on for a while – but that would be taking advantage of his generosity, don't you think? And I know how well you can deal with Branwell. I wonder where you get your patience from, I really do! Perhaps we will have good news about the books before very long. *Wuthering Heights*, is rather long now for a three-volume set but *Agnes Grey* and *The Professor* are rather short novels so it might not prove a disadvantage.'

'We must wait and see,' Emily said.

'With sufficient money we could travel to the Continent – see Paris and Venice and Rome, admire great paintings and sublime buildings, meet talented and famous people! Does that prospect appeal to you at all, love?'

Poor little Charlotte, with her mottled complexion and crooked teeth, her beautiful hazel eyes and soft brown hair, her pathetically manicured and polished nails and tightly laced corsets!

'No,' said Emily and turned her head to stare out of the carriage window again.

Anne met them, her expression one of anxious reassurance.

'All's well!' she said. 'Uncle James had to carry Branwell home last night from the Black Bull, but nothing dreadful has occurred. Papa is eager to hear if you found a surgeon or whether an operation will be possible in the near future. You must both be so weary!'

'I'll go in and speak to Papa directly.' Charlotte hurried indoors.

'Is all well?' Emily took Anne's arm.

'As well as it can ever be. Branwell has been making a fool of himself as usual, but Uncle James told me that he drinks less than we think. It is merely that he cannot hold his liquor.'

'He still drinks more than he should,' Emily said.

'And takes laudanum – but don't tell Charlotte.'

'Laudanum's only a pain killer,' Emily said.

'A derivative of opium, only to be used under prescription. Branny has been buying it at the pharmacy.' He's getting money from somewhere. He says that the Robinsons' doctor, Dr Crosby, acts as go-between and sends him varying sums from . . . her. I don't know what to think.'

'That Mrs Robinson is anxious to keep Branny at a distance while she goes husband-hunting. You know there was no such will as Branwell described, don't you?'

Anne nodded unhappily. 'It was published in the newspaper,' she said. 'Branwell read it but declares the published version is a forgery. There's no reasoning with him!'

'Then don't try!' Emily said. 'As for the laudanum it's cheaper than gin, so let him alone. We all need our consolations.'

Their uncle left the next morning, promising to send word of his efforts to find work.

'For I'll not trespass on your kindness, Pat. Your eye operation will cost a goodly amount. To tell you the truth I doubt if I'll manage to get more than a few days' labouring as it is, so I'll probably be back in Ireland and home before you're in Manchester.'

'I wish I could go to Ireland with you,' Anne said, suddenly and softly.

'Why, Annie, if you've a mind to pay a visit. . . .' He looked at her.

'Anne has romantic notions,' Charlotte said, laughing. 'You know the damp climate would get on your chest and bring on your asthma, Annie! It's one reason why I considered it unwise to take you to Manchester. My sister has ideas that outrun her stock of energy sometimes, Uncle.'

Emily shook hands silently, aware that by her side Anne was trembling with indignation.

'Two weeks to go before we are in Manchester again.' Charlotte shut the door rather as if she were banishing Ireland out of her consciousness and walked back into the dining-room. 'I wish someone would accept our books before Papa and I leave!'

'What will you do in Manchester while Papa is confined to his bed?' Emily enquired.

'Probably begin a new novel.'

'Even before the other books are accepted?' Anne said.

'Why not? It does no good to bury one's talents. I shall write something with more excitement and action in it than *The Professor*.'

'Then my novel has had an influence after all,' Emily said mischievously.

'Only in as far as I admit the Gothic element might be more attractive to the general public! My heroine will be no Catherine Earnshaw though. She will be as plain and small as myself and work her own way through life.'

'And nobody will want to read about her!' Emily said.

'Heroines are always beautiful, Charlotte,' Anne agreed.

'Mine won't be,' Charlotte said obstinately.

'Perhaps the next publisher will accept the novels,' Anne said hopefully.

'I don't intend to wait for a small success before aiming for a bigger one. Not that I shall have much free time in Manchester! I'm resolved to manage our own catering but there will be the nurse to think about. She will expect to be well fed. Never mind!'

By the end of the week she and Mr Brontë were gone to Manchester. Emily turned back into the parsonage with a feeling of relief of which she was immediately ashamed. She loved Charlotte dearly but poor Charlotte was always so full of busyness!

'Emily, I've been thinking over what Charlotte said about starting a new novel,' Anne said. 'I have a plot in my head that is unwinding slowly.'

'Another Agnes Grey?'

'No, something quite different. I've been thinking about Branwell.'

'You can't put him into a novel!'

'Not the real Branwell, of course not, but aspects of his

224

upbringing, of his character. Em, if Aunt and Papa had been stricter with him when he was young, don't you think it might have made a difference? He might have gone to school, to University. . . .'

'And then what? His height precludes him from a military career; his nerve storms debar him from ordination if he had ever displayed the least interest in it; he has as little gift for instructing children as the rest of us. We are what we are, Annie!'

'Upbringing counts for much too,' Anne argued. 'And are there not aspects of Branwell in Hindley Earnshaw?'

'Perhaps a touch here and there,' Emily admitted. 'What will you call your new tale?'

'*The Tenant Of Wildfell Hall*,' Anne said. 'It will have an element of mystery and be narrated by two people, mainly in the form of letters and diaries.'

'It sounds a bit like my book,' Emily said.

'Not in the least! In your book violence is made to seem exciting. In my novel I want to depict violence as it really is, realistically.'

'With a plain heroine?'

'Well, no,' Anne admitted. 'My heroine will be beautiful and very moral.'

'Yes, I see her now,' Emily said. 'As dull as ditchwater!'

'But realistic,' Anne said firmly, beginning to mount the stairs.

'Charlotty!' Emily said under her breath and went into the dining-room.

If Anne was going to side with Charlotte and seek to point a moral in her books then she would keep her own new project to herself. Already the threads of the plot were taking shape in the interior landscape of Gondal. The story would have to be distilled first in poetic form and then transcribed into a real setting. She recalled the dirty, soot-laden air of the city she and Charlotte had recently visited, the white, joyless faces of its citizens pouring into the mills and factories. There was the muttering of discontent in the atmosphere which had flared into open revolt across the Channel. The general embodied the particular. In every life there was conflict, sometimes resolved, sometimes festering. What made people the way they were? What caused them to be good or bad, male or female?

'Emily! Emily!!'

Anne's voice shrilled from the landing.

'What is it?' Emily strode into the hall, her train of thought broken.

'Branwell's bed is on fire and I can't rouse him!' Anne shrilled.

Emily dashed into the kitchen, grabbed the bucket of water that always stood ready in the corner against the possibility of fire and lugged it up the stairs.

The studio room was filling with smoke and fingers of flame were crackling up the bed curtains. Anne, sobbing with effort, was trying desperately to wake Branwell who lay in a stupor.

'Get out of the way!' Pushing her aside Emily tugged an incoherently mumbling Branwell off the bed and drenched it with water.

'Oh, Branny! How could you be so careless?' Anne had started to weep helplessly.

Emily surveyed the wreckage with a dismay that turned suddenly to humour.

'Better not tell Papa!' she ordered, choking back laughter. 'This really is the end of enough!'

Sixteen

Fall leaves fall die flowers away
Lengthen night and shorten day
Every leaf speaks bliss to me
Fluttering from the autumn trees.

Emily Jane Brontë

It was difficult to realize that she had been a girl of sixteen when she had first visited her schoolfellow, Charlotte, at the parsonage. Now she was thirty, though she knew she looked much younger, still able to wear white muslins and pink-ribboned bonnets. She couldn't avoid a slight pang of apprehension as the gig turned into the lane. In her last letter Charlotte had warned her that they must pray for fine weather so that they could spend most of each day out on the moors since Branwell was now the complete rake in appearance, lying on the sofa or on his bed most of the day, sometimes not even appearing to hear when he was addressed. At least there were no more reports of his being violent and threatening suicide and murder. Ellen knew that she would not have been invited had that been the case.

'Here you are at last! We have been anxiously waiting for hours.'

Charlotte had opened the gate and was helping Ellen from her seat.

'I am on time I think.' Ellen returned her friend's kiss, glad to see that the other looked well and had lost the strained look she had borne when she had last seen her in Derbyshire. 'Emily! Anne!'

The younger women came down the steps, Anne to embrace her, Emily to give her a smiling nod and pick up the luggage.

'Come along in! Papa's sight is quite restored now since his

227

operation last year and he looks forward to greeting you properly.'

'Miss Nussey!' Mr Brontë, his white cravat higher than ever,
his grey hair powdered snow-white, emerged from his parlour
to offer his hand. 'It is always a pleasure when old friends visit
though you, Miss Ellen, look younger every year. I may say so
without fear of contradiction because in my youth I had an eye
for a pretty woman and in those days—'

'Ellen wants her tea, Papa. Do excuse us,' Charlotte said, her
cheeks flushing as she steered Ellen into the dining-room.

'Of course, of course!' He bowed courteously as he withdrew.

'Papa has developed a most irritating habit of talking about
his youthful conquests,' Charlotte said, shutting the door. 'It's
not seemly in a man of seventy. Let me take your cloak and
bonnet. Now give me your news!'

'Shall we just take in tea for the two of them and join them
later?' Anne said to Emily. 'Charlotte likes to have her friend to
herself for a little while.'

'We can take our tea in the kitchen,' Emily agreed.

'So have you read the latest from Mary Taylor? She is settling
down in New Zealand like a true pioneer. And your own family?
Your mother must appreciate your company. What of Joe Taylor?
Is he still sniffing around or has he flown on to the next blossom
in the garden?'

'Joe Taylor is a dreadful flirt. One cannot take him seriously!'

'I learnt that lesson when Weightman was alive for he
convinced almost every girl he met that he was fathoms deep in
love with her. Have you heard anything of Mr Vincent since you
refused him?'

'Nothing.' A fleeting expression of regret crossed Ellen's
smooth, bland countenance. Mr Vincent had been kind and
young and attractive but Charlotte, in her letters, had mocked
his devotion so unmercifully that the little flame of romance he'd
ignited in Ellen's heart had quickly been blown out.

In the kitchen where Tabby dozed over her knitting the
younger sisters talked quietly.

'I am glad Miss Nussey is come. Poor Charlotte needs some
pleasure,' Anne said thoughtfully. 'It was such a cruel disappointment when our books were accepted and her *Professor* turned
down. Do you think that we did right in accepting Newby's offer?'

'Had the shoe been on the other foot,' Emily said, 'Charlotte would not have hesitated, and to do her justice she insisted that we take the chance anyway.'

'Not much of a chance,' Anne said with a grimace. 'We have to lay out fifty pounds for publication, and it's doubtful we'll see any of our money back!'

'The tea's brewed.' Emily slipped from the table where she'd been perched, swinging her legs. 'Remember! Not a word about writing while Miss Nussey is here!'

'We shall take a little vacation and enjoy ourselves,' Anne said.

Carrying the tea through, Emily wondered how Anne could speak so lightly of taking a holiday. Could she shrug off the epic of Gondal and lay her half-written second novel aside so easily? It seemed that she could even welcome the idea. They hadn't played at Gondal since their expedition to York and when Anne read portions of her new novel aloud Emily heard many disturbing echoes of her own book as if Anne was reproducing the themes of *Wuthering Heights* through a distorting mirror.

'Ellen is determined that we shall take a little trip to Bradford while she's here,' Charlotte said as Emily took in the tea. 'We do need new summer dresses, Emily! What do you think?'

'I think Miss Ellen's smallest wish shall be granted,' Emily allowed.

'That's settled then!' Charlotte looked pleased.

The trip to Bradford having been arranged and approved by Mr Brontë, the four set off, Charlotte having vetoed the hire of the gig as too dear, and walked the four miles to Keighley. Charlotte and Ellen went ahead while Emily accommodated her long stride to Anne's shorter steps. The few people they met on the way glanced at them incuriously or offered a brusque salutation.

'I certainly am not!' Charlotte's voice was raised suddenly. 'Emily, you had better disabuse Ellen at once of the latest idea she is cherishing.'

'I merely wished to know if Mr Nicholls was a likely candidate for a romance,' Ellen said.

'For Charlotte? I shouldn't think so for a moment,' Emily said, smiling. 'Her opinion of the whole race of curates is frightfully low, and Mr Nicholls strikes me as dreadfully dull.'

'And he regards me as an old maid,' Charlotte said tartly.

But everybody regarded them as old maids, Emily reflected as they walked on, Charlotte still bristling slightly. It wasn't merely their ages. She was scarcely twenty-nine and Anne not yet twenty-eight. Perhaps it had something to do with the clothes they wore. Charlotte and Anne wore the sombre greens and browns that Aunt Branwell had dressed them in since childhood and she herself wore drab greys and blues that muddied her complexion.

By the time they reached the drapers in Bradford she had made up her mind and, ignoring Anne who was choosing another figured grey silk, and Charlotte who was hesitating between brown with a pattern of green leaves or navy blue, Emily pounced on a length of brilliant purple silk patterned with flashes of white lightning.

'Em, you can't! That's far too bright!' Charlotte exclaimed.

'Isn't it though!' Emily held the material against herself. 'It's not expensive either. I shall make it with a fuller skirt than usual.'

'Emily, dear, what will Papa say?' Anne asked timidly. 'We are the daughters of a clergyman after all.'

'There's no church law that confines us to dull patterns and muddy colours as far as I know!' Emily argued. 'Charlotte is right. Of course people regard us as dull old maids when we go round looking like watchers at a funeral. I shall make a more cheerful dress for a change.'

'But Em—'

'Not another word, Charlotte, or I will buy a white bonnet with purple feathers on it! Yes, thank you. I'll take this.'

'I can't think what's got into her,' Charlotte whispered.

I can't think what's got into me either, Emily thought. Yes I can! The sun is shining and my railway shares have recovered their value; Ellen Nussey whom I like is here; Branny hasn't been violent for a month; Papa has completely regained his sight and I've a book of poems – part of a book of poems published and my first novel accepted even if I do have to contribute to the cost of publishing it; the revolution in Gondal is fast gaining momentum and my second novel is gestating in my mind.'

'I have an idea,' she said aloud. 'When we get, back to Keighley let's all take tea together at the Devonshire Arms before we walk home in the cool of the early evening. Wouldn't that be jolly?'

'Oh, do let us, Charlotte!' Anne pleaded.

'It would be rather pleasant,' Charlotte agreed.

Coming out of the shop, their purchases rolled under their arms, Anne clutched at Emily's hand.

'This is becoming quite a red-letter day, isn't it?' she said.

It was, when they looked back on it, a red-letter visit. The weather stayed bright and Branwell had the decency to absent himself in Halifax for much of the time. Every day the four of them rambled on the moors, reaching the shallow valley where the waterfall splashed over the cool brown stones.

Emily, springing ahead as was her habit, paused on a hillock to wait for the others to catch up.

'Look there!' Ellen was pointing skywards. 'Two suns! There are two suns in the sky! Surely that's a good omen?'

'I believe it's an optical illusion caused by the refraction of the rays of the sun, like a mirage,' Anne said, squinting through her fingers.

'I shall take it as a sign of good fortune!' Charlotte cried. 'We are all of us destined for fame and wealth and—'

'Handsome husbands!' Ellen said.

'Oh, there must be a husband to complete the happiness,' Charlotte said laughingly.

Emily smiled, saying nothing. They dreamed still of husbands, real men who would protect and cherish and stifle them. They didn't know, perhaps never would know, that the husband one carried within oneself was far more satisfying.

Ellen had been gone only a day or two when Charlotte came into the dining-room, her returned novel yet again in her hand, but her face bright.

'Another rejection? Oh, Charlotte, I'm so sorry!' Anne breathed.

'A rejection yes, but couched in such civil, gentlemanly terms! Mr Smith of Smith and Elder in Paternoster Row declines *The Professor* on the grounds it is too short and deficient in incident, but he praises the quality of much of the writing and asks me to try again with a longer novel.'

'And you will send him *Jane Eyre*, will you not?' Anne said.

'I've started the fair copy of it.' Charlotte's eyes were shining.

'I can complete it within a month. Do you think he will like it?'

'He will love it and so will the public,' Emily said warmly. 'It's a wonderful tale, Charlotte.'

'I shall answer his letter at once.' Charlotte scuttled to her writing desk.

'Oh, I hope the book is accepted,' Anne said softly, clasping her hands tightly together. 'It will make up for so much to her.'

Emily nodded soberly, thinking with painful sympathy of the heartbreak of Branwell's failures, the endless waiting for letters from Brussels that came so seldom and had dried up completely months before, the disappointment of not getting her school project into operation, the bitterness of knowing that her younger sisters had written books that were evidently worth the publishing while her own book was not ... Charlotte, she decided, was long due for a treat!

'They have accepted it.'

A month later as the rich browns and reds of September spread over the surrounding hills Charlotte came out into the garden where Emily and Anne were doing some half-hearted weeding and tying back of plants.

'Will you have to contribute much to the cost?' Anne asked.

'I don't have to contribute anything.' Charlotte's voice was a breathless whisper. 'They are paying me five hundred pounds. Five hundred pounds! Can you imagine that?'

'If you invest it at ten per cent it will yield you fifty pounds a year which together with the thirty-five from Aunt's legacy will make you free of any necessity to go governessing again!' Emily said.

'Oh, the money will be useful,' Charlotte said, beaming, 'but the really important thing is that now, at last, I shall be a published author. It's my passport to the society of clever and amusing people who count for something in the wider world!'

'It's nothing of the kind!' Emily had paled slightly. 'Currer Bell must remain unknown, Tallii, completely unknown! If Branwell ever found out – or Papa – could you answer for the consequences? And some of the incidents in the book might yet be traced to you unless we are all very careful. Do you really want people to equate Lowood School with Cowan Bridge? For they will you know. You would be pointed out by the neighbours as the one who writes novels.'

'And then be judged as a woman writer and not an author.' Charlotte bit her lip. 'You're right, Emily. We must retain the secret at all costs for as long as we can.'

'For ever,' Emily said flatly.

'I go to stay with Ellen in a few days.'

'Certainly not Ellen. I like her very well and I believe that she would keep the secret but one never can be sure. If you want to tell anybody then tell Mary Taylor, swearing her to secrecy. She is like a clam when she wishes to be and will say nothing to anyone even to Ellen.'

'I'll send Mary a copy of *Jane Eyre* when it comes out. You're right, Emily. She is the one friend whose intellect matches with my own and she will tell nobody.'

Charlotte whisked into the dining-room.

'I wonder when our books will come out,' Anne said, looking after her.

'When Newby decides that it's worth his while to bring them out,' Emily said. 'Having taken our money he'll delay publication as long as he can. If you ask me Mr Newby is a somewhat tricky customer!'

Though she refused to admit it she felt a real longing to see her book in print, to read some reviews of it, to find out if her story touched a chord in any other heart. She had put her whole self into the tale of two generations of Earnshaws and Lintons torn apart by the scheming of the adopted gypsy brat who grew up into the iron man. All the tales of the Heatons with which Robert Heaton had regaled her in the months of their friendship, the legends her father had recounted, names that had stayed all her days just beneath the surface of her mind – Isabella which was Spanish for Elizabeth, Catherine who had been Geraldine in Gondal, Hareton who might be a blend of Robert Heaton and his vanished cousin, Edgar Linton who was certainly a more faithful Robert, Hindley who reflected the worst bits of Branwell, and the boy from nowhere who had come to life when she was six years old and provided her with the whip that Catherine craved – all melded together and told by a light-hearted young man who resembled poor Weightman in some aspects, and Ellen Dean, who was as calm as Ellen Nussey and yet represented a part of herself, kneading dough while the epic of Gondal took shape in her brain and unrolled before her eyes.

'Emily?' Anne was looking at her.

Emily shook her head, her eyes clearing. 'Time to prune the pear-tree,' she said. 'The fruit is small and hard and the trunk diseased. I'll ask John Brown to lend a hand.'

Charlotte's absence on her visit to Ellen Nussey gave her the chance to work at her second novel. This one, emerging slowly and painfully from the night terrors she had suffered in her early years, was herself alone, entirely herself, not to be discussed or argued over by the three of them as they took their nightly exercise round and round the table, in and out of the firelight. Not even Anne must see this book. She had disliked *Wuthering Heights*. Disliked it so much, Emily thought, tugging off some dried leaves from a misshapen branch, that she had sought to undermine it by writing a kind of parody in her almost completed *Tenant Of Wildfell Hall*.

Anne, she thought sadly, had in some measure gone over to the enemy.

Charlotte returned weighed down with presents for the family provided by the always generous Ellen.

Emily, seated on the floor, looked thoughtfully at the basket of rosy apples and the pointed lace collar that comprised her share of the largesse. The collar would look well on the purple dress now nearing completion and the apples had a cheerful rosy glow and a delicious scent.

'Crabapple cheese!' Anne was exclaiming over her present. 'Oh, they say it's very good for asthma! Ellen is so kind!'

'Too kind.' Charlotte was frowning. 'She has a very small allowance, yet she hides these in my trunk for me to discover. Well, perhaps *Jane Eyre* will make some money and then I can give her a handsome present.'

'Making some other excuse for your sudden wealth,' Emily said warningly.

'I've said and will say nothing,' Charlotte said. 'Oh, now that *Jane Eyre* will soon be in the bookshops surely Newby will bring your novels out! I long to read the reviews!'

'We had two very good reviews for the poems,' Anne said. 'And a gentleman in Warwick did ask for our autographs.'

'Then he purchased one copy. I wonder who bought the other one,' Emily said.

'Hush! I hear Papa coming.' Charlotte raised her voice slightly as she went to the door. 'Here I am, Papa! Home safe and sound. Ellen has sent you a little firescreen as a gift. Isn't that kind of her?'

'Very kind, my dear. Emily, is there any chance of my having tea fifteen minutes early? Mr Nicholls is calling round later about the church rates and I wish to be able to concentrate fully on the problem.'

'I'll get it for you at once,' Emily said.

Now she lived three lives: the housekeeper who made the tea and peeled the vegetables and chopped up the meat, the author who waited for the printed copy of her novel to appear and astound the critics, the woman who walked in Gondal where revolutionary fires blazed. One man, she mused, and two women – all three aspects of the same, a captive six-year-old child who washed herself in a bloodied fountain while the male counterpart of herself was stabbed and stabbed again as he sat on his father's knee. She felt the cold damp chill of the dungeon floor where the soul was imprisoned, red everywhere flooding the world, the straining upward into the brilliance of the light as the soul broke the fetters and the body blended into the earth.

'Emily, tea?' Charlotte was looking at her.

'I'm going,' Emily said.

In the hall she paused to watch Branwell coming slowly down the stairs. He gazed at her with dull eyes before brushing past her.

'Where's he going now?' Charlotte demanded.

'Need you ask?' Emily said.

'If one of us could talk to him. If you—'

'He's a hopeless being,' Emily said shortly. If Charlotte wanted her to pry into the secrets of someone else's soul she had chosen the wrong person. Emily shrugged at Charlotte's worried face and went into the kitchen, relaxing into its cosy untidiness, brewing tea while all around the fires of revolution blazed.

October was half-way through when Charlotte came into the dining-room after prayers and put a parcel on the table.

'I opened this after the post came,' she said tremulously. 'Branwell was up and about and Papa not settled in the parlour so I have had to hold it back until we are more private. What do you think of the lady?'

'*Jane Eyre* is published! Oh, Charlotte, how happy you must be!' Anne embraced her sister, laughing.

'She's a handsome lady!' Emily looked approvingly at the volumes. 'I am very pleased for you, Charlotte.'

'I was lucky to get to Mr Feather before anyone else did,' Charlotte said. 'As it was I almost dropped it. Six copies free and now we must wait and see if anyone is willing to pay one pound and eleven shillings for three slender volumes.'

'Of course they will,' Emily assured her. 'They will be caught by the very first paragraph.'

'One copy is for you and one for you, Annie. I shall send a copy to Mary Taylor with strict instructions to show it to nobody. One copy for myself and two ... I shall hide those away. I wish. ...'

The sentence wasn't completed but they all knew that in Charlotte's mind her lost partnership with Branwell loomed heavily.

'Currer Bell, will you graciously sign my copy?' Emily asked.

'Mine too! Oh, do you think Newby will bring our books out soon?' Anne said longingly.

'We must wait and see. Charlotte, we'd best hide these away,' Emily said briskly.

If only Branwell could have shared in the excitement! As it was their pleasure had to be muted and great care taken to ensure that one of them reached the postman first every day, for Charlotte's mail had suddenly increased. She was in regular correspondence with Mr George Smith, her publisher, and with Mr Williams, chief reader in the firm.

'A most sagacious and interesting man!' Charlotte said. 'He was a personal friend of Keats. He knows Thackeray and Dickens and so many important writers and yet his letters are so modest, so friendly. And Mr Smith himself seems to be an excellent man of business. He tells me the second edition is being rushed into the bookshops. People are beginning to talk about Currer Bell.'

'Let's pray that Mr Newby hears the talking and brings out Ellis and Acton too,' Emily said.

It wasn't until December that free copies of the Ellis and Acton books arrived at the parsonage, to be hastily hidden away until evening came.

'They're not as well got up as mine was,' Charlotte said critically.

'And there are printing errors. We corrected them when we read the proofs but evidently nobody took any notice,' Anne said.

'Let's hope we get some good reviews and that they sell,' Emily said practically.

Mr Smith was sending copies of all the reviews to Charlotte who read them over and over, her face glowing when they praised her book but paling with anger when an occasional overcritical opinion fell into her hands.

'You cannot expect every critic to approve of a plain and poor governess who falls in love with a man and makes her feelings clear to him before he has declared himself,' Anne consoled.

'And him married and contemplating bigamy!'

'At least Mr Rochester doesn't go round digging up graves and consigning the woman he adores to the devil!' Charlotte flashed.

'At least your stories are causing a stir,' Anne put in. '*Agnes Grey* pales in comparison.'

'You're wrong, Anne!' Charlotte rounded on her. 'Your novel perfectly reflects your mind – low key, patient, realistic, with a touch of sly humour here and there. Those who appreciate excellent writing and don't strain after sensationalism will like it enormously.'

'Meaning I do?' Emily glanced up.

'I think your book has passages of lyric beauty to which I cannot attain,' Charlotte said. 'But you disfigure it, Emily, with scenes of such cruelty, such brutality, such . . . it cannot be right to create characters like Heathcliff and Catherine. I told Mr Williams—'

'You what?' Emily had risen from the window seat.

'He wrote to me, enquiring if I was connected with Ellis or Acton Bell. I could hardly lie to him. I could not ignore the question.'

'You didn't tell him that we were sisters? You didn't give him our real names?'

'I told him that we were brothers,' Charlotte admitted. 'As far as my publishers are concerned we are three brothers living in the north of England. Neither he nor anybody else has the least idea of our real identities.'

'We shall let it lie then.' Emily resumed her place. 'May I ask what you told Mr Williams about my novel?'

'That your writing has a strange sombre power but that sometimes you break forth in scenes that attract and shock in equal measure. I have to be honest, Emily.'

'And I must write as I must write.' Emily laughed suddenly. 'Your opinion is at least gentler than the few critics who have deigned to notice my efforts. Savage, brutal, disgusting – those are the milder words I've had the pleasure of reading.'

'It must be very disappointing for you,' Charlotte said.

'I really don't care much what the critics say,' Emily said. 'The books are beginning to sell and we may yet derive some monetary profit.'

'What troubles me,' Charlotte frowned, 'is that some of the critics have noted the similarity of names and are starting to hint that the three Bells might be one Bell. Don't laugh, Emily! It could be very awkward.'

'You mean that someone might believe that it was Currer Bell who actually wrote that shocking book *Wuthering Heights*, don't you?' Emily said.

More awkwardness was in store. Mr Brontë, coming in from his afternoon walk round the village, greeted Charlotte who came to relieve him of his overcoat and hat with a puzzled, 'Do you know of a Mr Currer Bell, who has just moved into the neighbourhood? Apparently he's having his mail delivered to the parsonage. I told Feather I'd never heard of him. I'll have my tea now, dear. This must be my last walk for the season. The cobbles are frosty and treacherous.'

'I'll bring you your tea,' Charlotte said, escaping to the kitchen.

'Papa must be told,' Emily said when Charlotte had hurriedly related Mr Brontë's words.

'About all the books?'

'Of course not! Since he never reads popular fiction he is not likely to hear about them. But we cannot risk him mentioning the mysterious Currer Bell to anyone in the parish. Take him a

Child of Earth

copy of *Jane Eyre* with his tea, and make him understand that it is a great secret. Branwell in particular must never be told. It would be too hurtful.'

'But should not Papa be told about you and me?' Anne ventured.

'Papa will be shocked enough to learn that Charlotte has actually had a book published. He'd as soon believe that Keeper had entered the literary world as believe that you and I have printed works to our credit,' Emily said. 'Hush now! Here's Tabby coming down!'

'Them stairs get higher every blessed day!' Tabby limped in slowly and sat down with a groan.

'I shall get some embrocation from the pharmacy for your leg as soon as the tea is brewed,' Emily said. 'Where's Martha?'

'Gone to her mam's. Mrs Brown is none too grand this weather.'

'I'll call in and make sure she has whatever she needs. Now drink your tea.'

'I mind the time when I were t'one giving th'orders,' Tabby said.

'So you still do, Tabby! I cannot imagine this kitchen without you in it.'

'Well, I'll not be in't kitchen nor anywhere else,' Tabby said, 'for much longer. This cauld'll finish me afore long. I'm getting on, child.'

'On my nerves!' Emily said with a grin. 'Good lord, Tabby, you're not much past seventy-five yet. Now drink your tea!'

She took her cloak from the back of the door and went out, sure-footed on the frost-slippery cobbles.

'Miss Emily!' John Brown hurried towards her. 'Would theer be owt tha wants? Martha's tekking care of th'missus. She's laid up wi'ague.'

'Thank you, John, but we need nothing. Will you get Mrs Brown a bottle of wine?' She pressed some coins into his hand. 'Branwell went over to Halifax to visit his friends.'

'Aye.' His tone was noncommittal. 'Thank thee kindly, Miss Emily. Th'missus will bless thee too. She thinks a powerful deal o'tha kindness.'

'You're a good man but you talk too much!' Emily said, scowling as she turned away.

In the pharmacy she bought embrocation, agreed that a chilly New Year always meant a warm spring, and made her way back to the parsonage. The parlour door was closed and in the dining-room silence reigned save for the nervous tapping of Charlotte's fingers on the edge of the table.

'Have you. . . ?' Emily slipped off her cloak.

'I took in some reviews and read him a couple,' Charlotte said. 'He seemed quite stunned by the information that I had written a book and had it published. He kept on saying that I would lose money by it. I left the book with him.'

'He's coming,' Anne said.

Heavy footsteps crossed the hall and Mr Brontë opened the dining-room door.

'What d'ye think, girls?' he said genially. 'Our Charlotte has been writing a book and it's better than likely!'

Emily, watching, saw with painful clarity that, proud as he might be of Charlotte's achievement, his main feeling was one of regret because it was a daughter and not his son to whom congratulations were due.

Seventeen

He comes with western winds, with evening's wandering airs,
With that clear dusk of heaven that brings the thickest stars;
Winds take a pensive tone, and stars a tender fire
And visions rise and change which kill me with desire.
                                                Emily Jane Brontë

Emily reached the summit of Ponden Kirk and subsided, panting slightly, on the grass that still bore the tiny, star white flowers of summer though the heather had faded to a dull brown lit by gleams of gold from the long prickled stems of gorse that still flamed in the valleys.

It had been, she considered, a good year so far. Though neither she nor Anne had seen back a penny of the money they had laid out for publication their books were selling in increasing numbers and, though the critics had been rough, here and there a phrase that praised the power and beauty of parts of *Wuthering Heights* had gladdened her.

And Anne's second novel, published back in April, was by way of being a bestseller, with Anne herself earning fifty pounds so far. When Emily thought of her sister's book she was gripped by conflicting emotions.

The Tenant Of Wildfell Hall was powerfully written, with scenes in it that had caused Charlotte to exclaim in pain, but it mocked so much that she herself held dear. Gondal had been belittled, with Anne turning resolutely away from the romantic epic in which Emily lived and moved and had her being in order to fling a morality tale in the face of the public.

'She ought not to have written it! She ought not! The debauchery, the immorality! What possessed her to depict such things in detail?' Charlotte had mourned to Emily.

'She says in her preface to the second edition that she wished to point a moral,' Emily said mildly.

'She made a mistake then! The entire novel offends public decency. And now Newby is putting out advertisements claiming that the book is a new work by Currer Bell. Mr Smith has written to me to ask for an explanation since I promised him my next book!'

'Write and tell him so then!'

'Letters are no proof of straight dealing,' Charlotte said impatiently. 'No, I have decided we must go to London and show ourselves to our publishers.'

'No!'

'Emily, see sense! We must make it plain—'

'You and Anne may make yourselves plain if you wish but you'll not bring me into it!' Emily flashed. 'Not under any circumstances! Leave me out. In your time you've dragged me all over the place, for God's sake! Not any longer! Not any longer, Charlotte.'

'Then Anne and I will go,' Charlotte said. 'We can walk to Keighley and catch the night train to London. First thing in the morning we shall seek an interview with both Mr Smith and Mr Newby. We shall insist that our identities continue to be kept secret and we won't mention you, but go we must!'

'At least Anne will see London for the first time,' Emily said. 'Very well, go. It's starting to rain and you'll both be soaked but I don't suppose that will stop you!'

She had hoped that Anne might protest but Anne had seemed rather pleased than otherwise at the prospect of the trip, and Emily had held her peace, trying not to fret at the thought of her sisters trudging through the heavy rain to the station.

Papa, raising his eyebrows when she informed him that Charlotte and Anne had gone to London, settled the matter to his own satisfaction by saying, 'Ah, yes, dear Charlotte will have some business to transact there no doubt and Anne will keep her company. We must give way to her whims now and then, eh?'

'Yes, Papa.'

They were away for three days, returning on the fourth with excited accounts of the rapid round of visits they had paid.

'We registered at the Chapter Coffee House – where we stayed before we went to Brussels, you remember? – we were rather tired and bedraggled but we tidied ourselves and had some breakfast and then set out to find the business premises of Smith and Elder.'

'The traffic was so thick,' Anne took up the account, 'that we were scared to cross the road. However we found the offices and went in and Charlotte asked to speak to Mr Smith. After a few minutes we were shown into his office and then—'

'I put one of the letters he had sent to Currer Bell in his hand,' Charlotte continued. 'He is a young man, in his twenties, rather handsome with bright eyes, and he fixed them on me and demanded where I'd got the letter from. Then I explained we were three sisters—'

'You what!' Emily was on her feet.

'It just slipped out,' Charlotte said hastily. 'I immediately corrected myself and explained that we were desirous of retaining our anonymity.'

'No you're not!' Emily held down her temper with difficulty. 'You are positively panting at the leash to fling yourself into society and to be recognized as an author of a book that's still in the bestseller lists! It's written all over your face!'

'Mr Smith and Mr Williams will say nothing, Emily. They gave me their solemn word.'

'And you will say nothing further about me!' Emily blazed. 'If you ever refer to me at all then it will be as Ellis Bell, nothing more. You didn't tell Newby my real name?'

'We didn't even see him until after the weekend and we were very guarded in our conversation,' Anne said placatingly. 'Mr Newby has promised us much fairer terms for our next novels—'

'Mr Smith has offered more,' Charlotte said.

'You stick to your publisher and Anne and I will stick to ours. So what else?'

'We went to the opera.' Anne's voice was hushed. 'Oh, Emily, it was splendid, really splendid. Mr Smith insisted and we didn't like to refuse so off we went in a carriage and—'

'And looked rather provincial in our travelling dresses and boots,' Charlotte said.

'But you enjoyed yourself, Anne?' Emily looked at her.

'Yes. Yes, I did! It was very tiring but I'm glad we went.'

'How has Branwell been behaving over the weekend?' Charlotte asked.

'Very badly.' Emily grimaced. 'He screwed a shilling out of Papa by threatening to kill himself and went and spent it on gin and laudanum. John Brown helped him home. His language wasn't particularly pleasant but there you are!'

'I have been receiving some letters,' Anne confided. 'From the Robinson girls – Bessy and Mary. I don't know why they suddenly began writing to me but they say their mother is very happy and well and only concerned about Lydia.'

'The daughter who eloped with that actor?' Emily asked.

'At least they are married now, though it was a most imprudent match,' Anne said with a sigh.

'And the mother is obviously not pining for Branwell,' Charlotte said cynically.

'Branwell must never find out that your former pupils are writing to you,' Emily said urgently. 'They don't mention him?'

'Not a word.'

'Sometimes I wonder if Branwell and she ever had any kind of. . . .'

'Charlotte, Branwell said that they did. It isn't for us to doubt his word,' Anne broke in.

'I find Branwell's histrionics exceedingly tedious anyway,' Charlotte said. 'I hope this drinking bout isn't the harbinger of worse excesses. At least when he stuck to laudanum he was merely stupefied and not violent. Papa is right to insist that he moves into his room. At least he can keep an eye open at night.'

'Poor Papa! he must be so desperately disappointed about him,' Anne said softly.

'At least he has a daughter who he knows has published a successful book,' Emily said.

'He has never mentioned it to me since he first read it,' Charlotte said with a touch of bitterness.

'Have you decided on your next theme yet, Charlotte?' Anne asked.

'Something less dramatic, more true to life,' Charlotte said. 'I may call it "Hollow's Mill" but I'm not sure yet. I have set it in the time of the Luddite riots. Miss Wooller told us such interesting stories about that time, and then I'd like to say something about the position of women in society.'

'It sounds like a formidable project,' Anne said. 'I can't get started on anything at the moment. The excitement of having two novels to my credit is turning my head slightly! I may grow very grand and wear my Sunday dress every day!'

'Emily?' Charlotte looked at her.

'I'm writing some poetry,' Emily evaded. 'If you and Anne are going to rush up and down to London regularly then someone has to get the meals on the table and the beds made. Anyway I always preferred housekeeping to any other occupation!'

It was not, of course, true, she thought now, drawing up her knees and wrapping her arms about them. They none of them were being entirely honest with one another. Charlotte still rifled through her mail with a look on her face that spoke of stifled longings for the Brussels letter that never came, and Anne still sighed sentimentally whenever Weightman's name was mentioned. And she herself wore the thickest mask of all even though in her novel she had delineated all the facets of herself.

'Is Heathcliff supposed to be an illegitimate son of old Mr Earnshaw's?' Charlotte had enquired during its writing. 'If so should you not make it more clear? We never learn where Heathcliff comes from or where he goes when he's absent three years.'

'He was gaining an education,' Emily said. The period of Heathcliff's absence roughly corresponded to Emily's eight months in the hell of Cowan Bridge, the almost three months in the stifling gentility of Roe Head, the six months of pleasure-pain at Law Hill and the ten months in Brussels. During those periods the dark boy had seldom intruded into her consciousness.

'And Ellen Dean,' Anne said. 'You speak of her as foster sister and she seems very close to Hindley but where are her parents? Why does she behave sometimes like a servant and sometimes like Catherine's older sister?'

'I like mystifying my readers,' Emily said.

Even Anne didn't understand that nearly all the main characters were herself, that Hareton was Heaton had he never run away, and Edgar Linton a more faithful Robert.

Someone was riding slowly across the lower slopes. She felt her heart beat rapidly and then subside as he looked up the long swathes of grass and she recognized the features of Michael Heaton from Royd House, on his way no doubt to give his nephew more than was needed of his good advice.

Something in his expression made her scramble down, to stand in her vivid purple dress with its ballooning sleeves, her dark hair escaping from its Spanish combs to cascade over her shoulders.

For an instant he stared at her before curling his lip slightly and spurring his mount away.

She knew as surely as if he had spat the words at her that *Wuthering Heights* had found its way into the hands of the Heatons. They were all great readers of fiction and would not have failed to trace their own family records in the tale. She stood looking after him and then, a fierce glow of satisfaction warming her, whistled Keeper and Flossy to her side and walked back to the parsonage across the sunlit moor.

As she went she thought of the new novel now completed in first draft and lying in her tin box. It needed polishing and extending in places, her style, save when inspiration descended and her pen took wing, being too abrupt and unvarnished. A man loved by and loving two women, one of the women a dark boy stabbed as he sat on his father's knee, the other washing herself in the bloodied water of a fountain as she shrank into a corner of her own mind and felt the dark boy stride forth.

She hadn't fathomed all the memories yet but they lay on the surface of her mind. When she was strong enough to bear the truth of them they would wake into the light and the dark shadow that had stalked her would diminish into nothingness, leaving her soul to strain upwards and know again that first innocence before the dark boy came.

Tabby was dozing by the fire. Emily blew her a kiss and went out again to pick some of the blackcurrants in the ill-tended garden. Ellen had once sent her a gift of sweet pea and poppy seeds and she'd planted them carefully and watered them assiduously but the winter had killed them.

When she looked over the wall she saw a dog slinking along, clearly lamed and thirsty for it stumbled as it came, tongue hanging.

There was fresh water in the back kitchen. She hurried to fill a bowl, shut the door on Keeper and Flossy and came out into the lane, kneeling to put down the bowl.

As she did so the dog, lean, yellow and slavering sprang.

Emily threw up her arm to protect her face and felt the sharp teeth tear the flesh.

Then the animal suddenly gained strength from somewhere and streaked away.

She rose, picked up the basin out of which water had splashed over her skirt and stood for a moment against the wall, waiting for the pain to subside.

Clogs clattered down the lane. A bunch of farm lads, one with a rifle, pounded towards her.

'Tha'd best lock up Keeper and t'other hound!' one called as they went past. 'One O'Maister Heaton's dogs has run mad and gotten free!'

She nodded silently. When they had turned into the street she looked down at her bleeding arm, then carried the basin inside again.

Tabby, woken by the odour of burning flesh, blinked at the tall, slender figure by the fire.

'Miss Emily, what in't world art tha doing?' she demanded.

A perfectly white face with eyes darkly shadowed was turned towards her.

'I was bitten by a dog I was giving water to in the lane,' she said through gritted teeth. 'Some lads said the animal was mad. Such bites have to be cauterized – burnt out, Tabby, to prevent infection.'

'Eeh, lass, but not wi'my iron and not by thysen!' Tabby cried, struggling up out of her chair. 'Miss Charlotte! Miss Anne! Coom quick!!'

'Tabby, hush!' Emily said sharply.

It was too late. Charlotte and Anne were hurrying in, faces primed for disaster.

'Miss Emily bin and burnt out th'infection!' Tabby was scolding. 'She were bit by a mad dog!'

'Oh my God!' Charlotte sank on to a stool, her eyes dilated.

'I'll get some arnica!' Anne went to the cupboard.

'It's nothing. Tabby makes a song and dance about nothing,' Emily said.

'Nothing!' Charlotte's voice was shrill. 'Emily, only last year a friend of Ellen Nussey's was bitten by a rabid dog. Thank heavens she was not infected but she was very fortunate indeed. I must tell Papa!'

'You'll do no such thing!' Emily hissed. 'Hasn't Papa enough to fret him these days? The poor dog was probably not mad at all. You know how people hereabout exaggerate. You'll say nothing to anybody!'

'If you insist,' Charlotte said doubtfully.

'I do, so there's an end of it. Anne, do stop fumbling around with that bandage! Anyone would imagine that I'd been shot in battle the amount you're wasting! Tabby, why not make yourself useful and make the tea.'

'Yes, Miss Emily, but—'

'And put a drop of brandy in mine,' Emily said with a sudden grin. 'I cannot say that I enjoy being bitten by anything at any time!'

'Is it Branwell? What's all the shouting about?' Mr Brontë's tread sounded beyond the door as Emily hastily pulled down her sleeve.

'Nothing, Papa! We were only talking,' Anne said.

'Do try to keep the noise down, girls. I was hoping to get a little rest before tonight. Branwell finds it so difficult to sleep these days.'

'We will, Papa.' Anne had hurried to placate him.

'Emily, rabies can take up to six months to develop,' Charlotte said nervously.

'Don't fuss!' Emily ignored the throbbing in her arm and began to set out the tea things with her eyes cast down and the sulky, resolute look on her mouth.

Not until much later after Papa had had his tea and Tabby's bad leg had been massaged and John Brown had looked in to mention that a rabid dog had been shot and Branwell had come in, flinging himself on the sofa and complaining that he owed a pressing debt to pay over at the Talbot in Halifax and needed an instant loan – not, in short, until the usual routine of the afternoon had been gone through was Emily free again to take Keeper and Flossy for a run.

'Don't you think you ought to rest?' Charlotte said anxiously.

'Why? I'm not sick.' Emily pulled on her shawl and glowered.

'You did have a shock earlier—'

'Don't be ridiculous!' Emily stalked past her, the dogs scrambling after.

There was a crispness in the early evening air. She lifted her head, smelling the clarity of the breeze. For some days past she'd noticed a recurrent stitch in her side that troubled her when she moved suddenly, catching her breath in her throat. A touch of a cold probably. Laycock's Cough Wafers were the best thing for that. She reminded herself to buy some at the pharmacy and went on along the lane, climbed the stile and took the route to the waterfall. She and Anne had nicknamed it the Meeting of the Waters and thought of it as their own private place, to be shared only with Charlotte and Ellen Nussey, and far in the past a more hopeful Branwell.

When she reached the grassy hollow she sat down, grimacing slightly as the pain stabbed her again. It was not as if she wore corsets, she mused. Poor Charlotte did everything in her power to make the most of her meagre feminine charms, pulling in her waist to a tiny sixteen inches, polishing her beautiful filbert-shaped nails to a rosy glow, scenting her handkerchiefs, taking off her spectacles whenever possible so that the real loveliness of her hazel eyes might be the better seen. And for what? For a married man she hadn't laid eyes on for four and a half years. A copy of *Jane Eyre* had been sent to Belgium but no answer had come. Since then Charlotte had apparently ceased writing though she still started when the postman came. Poor silly Charlotte who wrote endless letters to Miss Nussey, anxiously discussing the possibilities of marriage with this, that and the other! So far the only man who had looked at her in recent years with more than indifference was the solemn Irish curate and Charlotte regarded him with ill-concealed contempt.

She thought of that other curate with his red-gold hair and blue eyes and merry sense of humour. Charlotte had flirted with him and drawn his portrait and teased Anne when he cast long glances at her in church. Would anything have ever come of it? Possible, Emily thought, thinking of her sister's graceful figure, her violet blue eyes and dark blonde ringlets. Of the three of them Anne fitted best the current notions of beauty but she was not really beautiful. Her long nose, too full mouth, her timid, shrinking manner were not attractive.

No, they were a sorry crew! On the other hand their books were in print and selling, their railway shares yielding modest but steady dividends, and in the late evening hours when they walked in file round and round the dining-room table, in and out of the firelight, they recaptured some of the enchanted world of their childhood.

She leaned to the pool, dabbling her fingers in the cold water, the ripples wiping out her reflection, breaking her image into a thousand pieces. Catherine – Heathcliff; Cathy – Hareton; Nelly Dean; Edgar Linton and the rest – parts of herself, parts of those she had known or might have known – pinned down on paper as Branwell had pinned her likeness on canvas long before.

It would be dark soon. It was only in darkness and in solitude that the Vision came. She had tried to express the rapture of rising up out of herself towards that Other but it was impossible. It came too rarely and went too soon. It was safer to stay closer to the earth, to lie on the grass and feel herself dissolve into the earth beneath.

> *Well there is rest there*
> *So fast come thy prophecy –*
> *The time when my sunny hair*
> *Shall with grass roots twined be*

Her own words sang in her mind. She had written that for a Gondal character long ago. She had written it for herself.

She was at the door, turning to enter when she saw Branwell at the gate. The light was fading but a last blaze of dying sunlight illuminated his thick red hair so that for an instant, as he stood there, panting, he was Little King again, Branny who ruled Angria and whom they had all adored.

The instant fled. William Brown, the sexton's brother, appeared at her brother's side, an arm about him, his voice rough with concern,

'Pat, lad, tha shoud-na be out in't wind! Miss Emily, he's noan fit – aye, that's it! Tek tha breath naow!'

'We can manage, William!' She went to open the gate. 'Thank you for your kindness. Come on, Branwell! Are you not well?'

'Not well at all, Miss Emily,' William said. 'Ma brother's missus were joshing him just naow for getting that thin it looks laike he's wearing t'parson's coat!'

'Thank you, William. Oh Papa, Branwell is none too well. If you take the other arm—'

'Anne, run for Dr Wheelhouse!' Mr Brontë said. 'Looks like a dose of influenza, my son! We'll soon have you right.'

Of course they would. Of course! Emily helped her father drag him up the stairs.

'Is he drunk again?' Charlotte stood in the doorway of the dining-room.

'A bad cold Papa thinks. Anne is fetching Dr Wheelhouse.'

It was, of course, only a bad cold. Emily went into the dining-room and sat down, her arm throbbing. There were voices and footsteps beyond the room. Dr Wheelhouse came down the stairs again.

'A few days in bed won't hurt him. A touch of bronchitis.'

'At least Papa will have a peaceful night,' Charlotte said.

'I'll help Martha get supper.' Emily pushed her into the hall.

That night the Vision eluded her. She lay wakeful, yearning.

'Branwell seems quite like his old self!' Charlotte said at breakfast time. 'So much more sensible and affectionate than he usually is. John Brown is coming to sit with him for a bit of company while we're in church. How is. . . ?'

'I'm fine,' Emily said curtly.

She was putting on her bonnet when John Brown's voice sounded loudly from above.

'Maister Brontë! Miss Emily! Tha'd best coom! Branny's took bad!'

They were all filing in to watch Mama die. No, not Mama but Ellis who was making haste to follow Maria. Papa was praying in his deep musical voice from which the years had not quite stripped the brogue; the room was full of praying and the harsh rasping breaths of the figure who arched and strained in the bed.

'Amen!' Branwell gasped and started up in a last convulsion.

'My son! My poor son!' Papa's voice was harsh and ragged. Charlotte had sagged against Anne, her face colourless. In the corner Martha put her apron over her head and sobbed loudly.

Emily turned swiftly and walked out of the room, down the stairs, and into the kitchen. 'He's gone,' she said flatly.

Tabby nodded, putting her hands over her face.

Emily came out into the hall and opened the front door. Why had she never noticed before how close the graveyard was to the garden, tombs crowding round, headstones rearing up? John Brown was standing there, hat in his hand. She wound her way towards him.

'Ask Mr Nicholls to take the service and do toll the bell for us, will you, John?'

'Just afore he went,' John said, 'he took ma hand, he did. "John," he says to me, "I'm thirty-one years old and in my whole life I've done nothing great or guid." Eeh, he were a guid 'un he was!'

'He thought much of you,' Emily said.

'Aye, weel! we had some reet guid nichts together mony a time,' John said.

'Aye,' she agreed.

He turned and went clumsily away, wiping the back of his hand across his eyes. At the windows Anne was drawing the shutters close.

Soon there would be the black-bordered cards to send out, the black gloves and veils to buy, the undertaker to contact, the doctor to inform. There would be the funeral and the memorial service and the letters of condolence to answer and the black-ribboned wreath to hang on the front door. All the disguises of death when what Branwell in his heart would have wanted was a wake with the drink flowing and local poets bewailing his passing in the ancient tongue his father still remembered.

Overhead there was a dull rumble of thunder and a streak of brightness across the sky.

Branwell would think that fitting, Emily thought. It would appeal to his sense of humour.

'Making a grand exit, Emmii!'

' 'Bye, Brannii!'

Mama, Maria, Ellis, Aunt, and now Branwell. All tapping on the other side of the dank cellar wall. Was he there already in spirit or hovering somewhere near?

'Emily, dearest, do come indoors out of the rain!' Anne plucked at her sleeve. 'I cannot comfort Papa and Charlotte has utterly collapsed and poor Tabby and Martha are crying their eyes out. I can't deal with it all by myself!'

'Go and settle Charlotte comfortably. Where is Papa?'

'In the parlour.'

'Then leave him some time in which to grieve. We all need our solitude. I'll get some tea brewing and a bit of sense into Tabby and Martha.'

'Someone must inform the doctor,' Anne said falteringly.

'Dr Wheelhouse who said he had a touch of bronchitis? He probably poisoned him with his wretched concoctions quicker than anything else,' Emily said bitterly.

'And the undertaker?'

'I'll slip down and get him. Listen!'

From the church tower came the dull, regular tolling of the bell.

There was little time to mourn with the preparations for the funeral and the memorial service that would follow the next week. The quiet house was suddenly full of people. William Wood came to take the measurements for the coffin.

'He were no more than five feet four inches, Miss Emily! I allus fancied 'im taller laike!'

'He walked tall for much of his life,' Emily said.

'I mind 'im when 'ee were a lad. Allus full o'speerit. 'Ee allus 'ad a smile and a bit of a jest did Pat!'

Pat to the villagers who had called out the Irishness in him and Branwell to his family, Northangerland in his secret world and the few poems he had had printed locally.

'Tabby will help you lay him out,' she said. 'She considers it her right.'

'Aye, Auntie's a reet good soart,' William Wood agreed. 'She'm gitting on though. Happen she won't be laying out ony more on ye.'

'Well, if I should get knocked down by a runaway horse,' Emily said briskly, 'just remember that I'm five feet seven inches high.'

'And thin wi'it,' he said critically. 'Tha looks reet clemmed, Miss Emily. Art tha eating proper?'

'Get on with your task, William! You're an undertaker not a nursemaid.' She patted his arm and went into the front bedroom where Charlotte lay, propped on pillows, weeping quietly.

'Was that Wood? Oh, how is it to be endured?' she said feebly. 'Such a waste of a life, such squandering of high promise! I feel such a bitterness of spirit when I think of the high hopes we had!'

No use in trying to tell her their hopes had perhaps been too high. To have been the favourite child with all the ambitions of the family centred in him must have been a terrible burden for a boy whose talents never quite matched the aspirations of others.

'We must remember his good points,' she said aloud. 'And you must stay in bed for a week or two. You are quite worn out.'

'I ought to be helping. . . .'

'Much good you'd do in your present state! No, Anne and I are coping very well and Martha is a tower of strength. You stay where you are!'

'If you're sure?' Charlotte began to cry again.

The short interval between death and burial wore away. There was scarcely time in which to snatch a cup of tea let alone sit down to a meal. In any case the smell of the food she cooked sickened her. Visitors came. They hadn't realized how many people locally regarded themselves as Branwell's friend, had an anecdote to share. Mr Brontë, now composed and solemn, held court in the parlour. Emily went once into the studio bedroom and drew back the winding sheet. There was nothing there but the outer semblance of the brother she had loved and envied in equal measure.

The church was full, every villager having apparently decided to come and give Patrick Branwell Brontë a good send off. Only Charlotte remained still in bed, curled under the bedcovers, constantly weeping.

'I cannot stop,' she said pathetically. 'I cannot stop.'

'Then weep away. A good cry cleanses the heart they say,' Emily soothed.

Inside she felt indignant anger rising . Charlotte wasn't crying for the real Branwell who had been a faulty human being, with much weakness of will and a boastful streak as well as a great deal of charm and a nature that was genuinely kind but for the brother she had created in her mind, the Little King who had known at the very end that his life's path had led nowhere.

She sat upright in the pew, lips compressed, hearing the sudden pattering of rain against the windows. At her side her father sat equally stiffly, enveloped in dignity and his huge cravat.

The Reverend William Morgan, Papa's oldest friend, had come over to conduct the service, his sonorous tones with the singsong Welsh accent interrupted by stifled sobbing from the congregation.

'Dr Wheelhouse is of the opinion that Branwell died of acute bronchitis and general wasting,' Papa had said. 'He suspected that consumption had already attacked the lungs.'

No doubt Papa would make the requisite notes in the margins of the huge medical directory in which down through the years he had chronicled the various illnesses from which he imagined he had suffered and the various treatments he had tried out. Tincture of myrrh mixed with ether and oil of cloves painted on an aching tooth: magnesia and ginger for an upset stomach: nuts of nitre for quinsy; roast onion with dry bread for a cough; cold water sprinkled over the head for headache. And while he made his notes and thought no doubt about poor Mama and Maria and Ellis he hadn't noticed – they none of them had noticed – that Branwell was fading before their eyes.

The flagstones in the aisle were being slid aside, the coffin lowered on ropes into the darkness below. Anne seated on the other side of Papa stifled a sob.

How Branwell would be hating all this if he was anywhere around to see! The dirge-like hymn, the droning sermon, the silent lowering of his remains would have set him mocking viciously all the hypocrisy of the creed in which they had been reared.

'When I go,' Emily thought fiercely', I want to be laid in earth, not enclosed in stone. My body will melt into the soil and meanwhile as it nourishes the flowers and feeds the worms I myself will be free, walking the moors with companions who were created in my own mind but then will exist in reality.'

They were finished at last and the flagstones replaced. She rose, took Anne's gloved hand and walked with her silently behind Mr Brontë, with Tabby and Martha following behind past the massed ranks of the neighbours.

A few had been bidden to the tea and ham sandwiches and little cakes she and Martha had prepared. They stood or sat quietly, talking in hushed voices as if they were still in church! Where were the wailing women, the rounds of whisky, the extravagant praises of the departed that Branny would've loved?

Her head was aching furiously. Headaches were what Charlotte suffered from, not herself! She slipped into the kitchen and leaned her forehead briefly against the cold stone of the wall.

'Miss Emily, I'm that sorry t'bother thee but Keeper's on't clean white bedspread and won't get off,' Martha said.

Emily straightened up. The pain in her head was pounding; her side hurt when she breathed deeply. She turned and went up the stairs, noting with faint surprise that the funeral guests were gone and that Charlotte had bestirred herself to come down-stairs, face swollen with weeping.

'Emily, don't forget Keeper cannot abide to be slapped,' she said nervously as Emily went by.

So Charlotte was up and around and offering advice. Emily's face set into a white mask and her eyes glowed ice blue.

Keeper was stretched on Branwell's bed! Branwell was locked up in the crypt of the church and Keeper was on his bed. She seized the dog by his brass collar and dragged him down to the floor.

From the great hound's muzzle issued a throaty, warning growl. It had never happened before but now the moment was come when two wills met and clashed.

She dragged him step by step down the stone staircase, aware dimly that there was no sign of Anne but that Charlotte and Martha shrank together against the door.

She planted the now snarling dog in the niche by the cellar door and as the ache in her temples increased to screaming pitch she felt rather than saw him spring. There was a red mist before her eyes. She was no longer Emily, no longer Ellis Bell. She was the ironhearted man, the dark shadow that had haunted her and now took possession of her. She punched rhythmically, violently, hearing the high squeals that had replaced the snarling as if they came from a great distance.

The terrible headache had gone and the red mist cleared. Keeper, bloodied and beaten, crept to lick her hand. Cold fear filled every pore of her being. Outside the rain still fell softly.

Eighteen

When I am not and none beside
Nor earth nor sea nor cloudless sky
But only spirit wandering wide
Through infinite immensity.

Emily Jane Brontë

'Miss Emily, may I beg a favour?'

Arthur Bell Nicholls, emerging from the parlour, detained her as she was about to slip into the kitchen.

She had paused, caught in mid flight, her face chalk-white above the high collar of her black dress, luxuriously thick dark hair framing sharp cheekbones and burning blue eyes.

'In this weather,' he said carefully, taking her silence for leave to continue speaking, 'it is too rough for you and your sisters to get out much and I've wondered if the dogs miss their walk. As they are yours—'

'Keeper officially belongs to Papa and Flossy is Anne's dog,' she said.

'I was going to offer to take them with me when I myself go further afield than the village,' he said, 'but I'd not presume.'

Emily studied him more closely for a moment. He was a large, clumsy-looking man with heavy sidewhiskers and the air of having chosen to be middle-aged before his time. Not interesting or attractive but having about him something solid and kindly.

'The dogs would enjoy a regular walk with you, Mr Nicholls, while the weather remains so bad,' she said. 'Papa would concur, I know. He cannot get much farther than the church in this wind and since his health is delicate any easing of a worry is to be accepted.'

'He suffered a grave blow. You have all suffered a great

sorrow. Your sisters seem – fragile. If there is anything Miss
Charlotte or – if they need anything—'

And heigh-ho, so that's the way the wind is blowing!

'If we do,' she said pleasantly, 'then someone will inform you.
Thank you, Mr Nicholls.'

Not a man to be mocked or disliked, she thought, watching
him leave. Papa had come to rely on him a great deal since he'd
come as curate.

She looked in at the kitchen door and saw Tabby and Martha
knitting, one at each side of the fireplace. The old witch and the
young witch, gathering elfbolts beneath Ponden Kirk.

When she went into the dining-room Charlotte looked up
from the book she was reading.

'What did Mr Nicholls want?' she enquired.

'He offered to walk Keeper and Flossy while this bad weather
continues and I told him Papa would be glad of it.'

'That was kind,' Charlotte said indifferently. 'Emily, why
don't you sit down?'

'I was looking for Anne.'

'She's sewing in Branny's room. Emily—'

'Why are you reading *Wuthering Heights* again?' Emily said.
'You have not told Papa?'

'Of course not. It would be too cruel to let him know that three
of us are published authors so soon after Branwell – I have been
rereading your book because parts of it strike me as more powerful, more lyrical than anything I've ever read. Those critics who
complain there are no normal human emotions depicted in it
forget how Edgar Linton's constancy and love are almost female
in their—'

'Are you saying that men cannot love as deeply as women
love?'

'No, of course not, but I'd venture to suggest that women are
more apt to love longer, hope longer—'

'Fudge! both sexes have equally strong emotions. Edgar
Linton loves Cathy as a husband should. You do make me cross
when you produce your schoolgirl theories!'

'And Heathcliff? How would you describe his feelings?'

'Heathcliff loves his own soul,' Emily said. 'Put the book
away, Charlotte. It irritates me to see you trying to find a moral
in it! You had a letter from London?'

'From Mr Williams.' Charlotte closed the book and covered it with a plain wrapper. 'He has been kind enough to send his booklet about homoeopathy to me.'

'That new fangled craze! You haven't told him—'

'You may read any of my London letters whenever you choose. Nowhere are you referred to as anything but Ellis Bell. I've glanced through the booklet but I cannot reach any firm opinion about it. Glance through it and tell me what you think.'

'What I think,' Emily said, taking the booklet, 'is that all doctors are poisoning fools and this is probably merely another form of quackery. You're so transparent, Tallii!'

She went out and up the stairs into the tiny space she had made her own for so many years. Two months since Branwell's death and the sharp edge of grief was blunted a little. But the strain had told on her sisters. Poor Charlotte suffered from attacks of indigestion and faintness and Anne had a dreadful cough and cold. When spring came they must all make an effort and go somewhere for a little holiday. A couple of days in York or in Bridlington perhaps? She could do without the moors for that long!

It would be Christmas soon and after that Anne's twenty-ninth birthday.

Little Annie twenty-nine! And herself halfway to thirty-one! The years went so fast. She sat down, rubbing her temples where the vicious headache had gripped again. Her pulse, as usual, was racing and her throat felt dry and sore. She went to the washstand and dipped a glass into the water there, letting it trickle down her throat. Would the day come when she would be terrified by the mere presence of water in her vicinity? It was not here yet.

'Ellen Nussey has offered to come for a few days,' Charlotte said. 'She is most concerned about your illness and—'

'You can write and tell her to stay away!' Emily rose from the tea table, her pupils dilating. 'I won't have visitors until this bad weather is done, And I'm not ill! Stop saying that I'm ill! I never in my life knew of such an almighty fuss being made about one little headcold.'

She broke off, coughing, clutching the edge of the table.

'I'll tell her that she must wait until spring,' Charlotte said hastily.

'I must see to the dogs!' Pulling herself upright, wiping her hand across the back of the chair as she took it from her mouth she stared dully at the little scarlet stain.

'She's eaten nothing,' Anne said.

'She says that she has begun to have diarrhoea,' Charlotte said shakily. 'She thinks it will rid her body of the cold infection, cleanse her. I keep on thinking of the day she was bitten – it haunts me like a threat. I have told Papa—'

'Charlotte, you promised!' Anne's expression was aghast.

'Anne, I had to tell him. She may have been infected by the brute in which case – Papa took the news with his usual courage. He has little hope as it is.'

'But we must have hope,' Anne said tremblingly. 'She insists that she feels better and she has not spent an hour in bed! As for the bite, I'd reckon it was harmless.'

'She has lost her temper in the most violent manner. . .'

'Emily always had a temper. It's her way of dealing with grief,' Anne said. 'Papa must try to be more hopeful.'

Charlotte was silent. In her mind the last interview with him still hovered.

'A rabid dog? And she cauterized it herself?'

'Yes, Papa.'

'When I look at her,' he said slowly, 'I see Maria and Elizabeth at the back of her eyes. They sickened and died. I hoped then against all hope but they still died. I hold out no hope now.'

'Papa, we cannot permit ourselves to lose hope!' Charlotte had said. 'She has always been the most agile and energetic among us. She never ails.'

But she was ailing now though she refused to admit it, refused to do anything to stem the hacking cough except suck Laycock's Wafers, refused to spend an extra half-hour in bed or put her feet up for a spell after the midday meal.

'I have written to a specialist in London – Mr Williams recommended him very highly – giving as minute an account of her pulmonary symptoms as possible,' Charlotte confided to Anne. 'She refuses to see any doctor. Perhaps this specialist – a Mr Epps – will send some good advice.'

'She doesn't want to worry us by making a fuss,' Anne said loyally.

'But she must see that it's far worse for us when she refuses to

Child of Earth

speak about her condition. If we could get her to discuss the matter, to sit down together and decide what's best to be done ... I try to continue with my new novel but I find it so difficult to concentrate!'

Whisper, whisper! Mutter, mutter! Did they imagine she didn't know how they talked about her?

All my life, Emily thought, gripping the banister as she slowly climbed the stairs, I have been controlled by others. First Papa sent me to Cowan Bridge and then Charlotte insisted that I go to Roe Head and to Brussels. The only move I ever made on my own account was to Law Hill and that ended badly!

She sat down on the edge of her bed fighting for breath. The little room was icy but she no longer noticed. Her brain flamed with images. The shepherd boy lost on the moor all those years ago melded with the figure of the ghost child who was both Catherine Earnshaw and herself when at the age of six she had entered a bedroom in a house within sound of the sea. In her story the visitor had seized the childish wrist and rubbed it to and fro on the broken window pane until the blood ran down and soaked the bedclothes. At the end the dead Heathcliff, snarling his triumph silently, had a graze on his wrist.

Somewhere deep inside herself she had wanted Charlotte to put a comforting arm about her and tell her that she understood. But Charlotte had declared the scene was shocking and unrealistic. Only Anne had looked at her thoughtfully as if she were beginning to understand something, but then she had written her own second novel, diminishing Heathcliff into a stock figure of Byronic romance and now she conspired with Charlotte to make Emily go in the road they wanted her to travel.

She had eaten nothing since the day before and her body felt light and insubstantial. That was one thing over which she had control. They could not make her eat. They could not force her to talk. In those two areas she had complete control. And fasting was an excellent way of driving out infection.

Evening came early now. It was one of the great blessings of winter. The bright sun revealed too much. The moon was gentler, bringing with it the quiet time when the talking was done, when she could wait for the Comforter to come. Sometimes it might be Byron, who had fled England after an incestuous affair with his sister, or Shelley whose revolutionary

261

aetheism had excited her imagination, or Chatterton who had killed himself in his lovely youth. And then they had merged into the state of silence when nothing breathed and the universe expanded, lifting her and carrying her to some place where she once had been long before in early childhood before the lies and betrayal had sickened her soul. Before the dark boy came.

She had tried to write about it, to capture it on paper.

> *I'm happy now and would you tear away*
> *My blissful dream that never comes with day*
> *A vision dear though false for well my mind*
> *Knows what a bitter waking waits behind.*

She had doodled round the edges of the page – a winged serpent that reminded her of the curious carvings at High Sunderland Hall and the carved chairs at Shibden Hall – a feather twisting this way and that, the double circle that was a sign for infinity, for old griefs played out again over and over. Her pen had rewritten at the foot of the page over and over the word 'regive' but she no longer remembered why.

A few days later Uncle Hugh arrived from Ireland. She stayed in her room, ignoring Anne's tapping and gentle entreaties. He had heard from Papa, of course, about Branwell's death and come to pay his respects to the memory of an only son. She stayed where she was, hearing the faint murmur of voices from the parlour – what was Papa saying to his brother?

Keeper came in from his walk with Mr Nicholls and bounded up into her room, taking his favourite position at her feet. In one of the diary papers she and Anne had last written three years before and opened on her birthday she had sketched herself twice – from the back as she stared through the window and from the back again with her heavy coils of hair waving at each side of her face and her long shawl almost reaching the hem of her gown. Now she took out a Gondal poem begun and abandoned long before and began to tinker with the metre. In the icy tiny space that was her kingdom her breath rasped white spears into the air.

When the footsteps sounded on the stairs and the knock came on the door she braced herself to meet her uncle's searching gaze. Papa, she was quite certain, would have told him everything, unburdened his deepest fears.

'Niece!' She flinched from his touch. 'I'm told you are not well?'

When he had gone she sat for a few moments with her eyes closed. Relief flooded her whole being. The worst wouldn't happen. He had given his word. There would be no period of agonizing insanity, no smothering mattress pressing the life out of her.

Her uncle was sleeping in Branwell's old room. No matter! Branny wouldn't mind. Hugh had arrived quietly and now kept to the house, spending hours with Papa as they talked about their shared boyhoods, about the pranks and jests they had played on the neighbours and the five sisters with red-gold hair who had blown a buffalo horn to call them home from the fields.

On Sunday 17 December the rain turned finally to ice. Papa remained by the parlour fire sipping a hot toddy with his brother. Charlotte and Anne sat in the dining-room, Anne sewing, Charlotte writing one of her interminable letters. Poor Tallii! She no longer sent any to Brussels but she seemed to be in almost daily touch with her publishers. Emily choked down a few mouthfuls of the meal she had helped Martha to prepare, aware of Charlotte's pleased expression when she swallowed. It hurt to swallow. Her throat and the inside of her mouth were badly ulcerated but when the ulcers burst and expelled the poisons she would feel better.

In a day or two she would go through her papers and tidy up her writing desk and her tin boxes. The new novel needed to be fair-copied and then sent to her publishers. Mr Newby might be a rogue but he had written to her in very civil terms, telling her to take her time over her second novel and not mar it by hurrying. He had said nothing about owing her any money for the increasing sales of *Wuthering Heights*, but in the New Year he might bestir himself.

'Mr Smith is very anxious to have your second novel, Emily. He would give you such good terms,' Charlotte said that evening as they walked round the table.

'I'll stay with Newby,' Emily said curtly.

'I have promised to give my next book to Mr Smith,' Anne said timidly.

'You do as you please!'

So Charlotte had persuaded Anne to change allegiance. Emily

swallowed the thick, bloody phlegm collecting in her mouth and moved on silently, one foot in front of the other.

'Shall we sit down for a little,' Anne said pleadingly.

'There are a clutch of new reviews come!' Charlotte went to her writing desk. 'The critics are beginning to see the power in your book, Emily.'

They also continued to call the story savage, brutal and disgusting.

'As if you had described in actual words the intimate bodily contact between Catherine and Heathcliff!' Charlotte said.

But there had been none! How could there be when both were the same person, torn apart by Catherine's betrayal? Drawing her breath as gently as she could Emily wondered how Charlotte could be so unknowing.

The next day began with sunshine gilding the thin layer of snow that had fallen during the night. Emily, rising at her usual hour of seven, felt a little current of delight run through her. She had slept for a few hours and her mouth wasn't so painful.

The day wore on, only the rising wind providing any variety as it tore through the churchyard and whistled round the eaves, shaping the fallen snow into grotesque shapes like tiny, deformed children dancing.

Scarborough perhaps in the spring? Anne had loved Scarborough when she had holidayed there with the Robinsons. Anne herself looked pale and thin. It would do them all good to get away for a time.

By evening the wind had increased in its ferocity. She went into the kitchen to put out dinner for Keeper and Flossy, irritated with herself because her hands shook when she measured the meat into the bowls. When she opened the door that led to the flagged passage the wind, roaring through an open window in the back kitchen, threw her against the wall.

'Emily! are you all right? Are you hurt?'

They must have been following her, spying on her. What were they hoping to see? Her surrender to their united sisterly wills? She dragged herself up, retrieved the fallen dishes and went on into the back kitchen where the dogs waited for their meal.

The next day, she told herself, she would try to eat more. The problem was that if she ate a lot the iron man within her grew stronger, blotting out the woman who loved her sisters and wanted to walk again on the moors. She had the odd sensation that if she ate a good meal and then looked in the glass she would see him looking out of her.

Towards morning she woke, hearing in her sleep the sound of moaning. Someone close by was moaning in pain. She sat up and listened and heard the sounds again, issuing from her own lips. This would never do. It would disturb the rest of the household. She pulled up a corner of blanket and stuffed it into her mouth to stifle the cries.

Dressing took a very long time once the firing of Papa's pistol gave the signal that the new day had begun. She dragged on the black mourning dress and grimaced as she buckled the belt. Unless she gained a little weight soon she would have to take in all her dresses. She thought of the purple gown that had so shocked Ellen Nussey. Dear Ellen! It would be good to see her again.

Martha, going upstairs to see if Miss Emily needed anything, found her in Charlotte's bedroom, her long thick hair tangling round her face. She sat in the low chair near the fire, leaning her head on the knuckles of her hand.

'Miss Emily?' Martha stood uncertainly within the door.

'I was combing my hair and the comb fell into the grate,' Emily said gaspingly. 'I can't pick it up.'

'I'll get it!' Martha took the tongs and gingerly rescued the half-burnt comb.

'Thank you, Martha.'

Her voice sounded almost normal as she pulled herself up and began to make her slow way to the door and down the stairs.

In the hallway Mr Brontë stood straight and stiff against the wall and watched his daughter come down. When she reached the ground floor she paused for a moment, seeming to steady herself by an effort of will. Then she came on, her long fingers trailing along the walls.

'Papa.' Her voice sounded faint and far away. 'I have to tell you that I was the one who climbed down the tree and broke it.'

She had said it at last, had wiped her conscience clear. She looked at him for some sign of forgiveness but he stared back at her blankly before turning and going abruptly into his study.

'Her mind is reverting to childhood,' he said harshly. 'I regard that as a bad omen, brother.'

In the dining-room Charlotte sat frantically writing a swift note to Ellen Nussey:

'Emily seems the nearest thing to my heart in the world'.

The morning wore on. The wind had blown itself out and the sun was shining, making roses out of the snow. Emily sat with her sewing in her lap, but the stitches she tried to make straggled like jagged teeth, and in any case the dark boy didn't do women's work.

'Look!' Charlotte's voice and Charlotte herself in a wet cloak, her boots treading slush across the carpet. That would have to be swept up later.

'I found a sprig of heather in a hollow,' Charlotte's voice said.

Heather? What did heather matter now? Soon she would be in the cool, dark earth waiting for her brother and sisters to join her.

Anne's voice, calm and low. 'Wouldn't you be more comfortable if you rested on the sofa?'

Why not indeed? Poor Anne needed some comfort.

She levered herself out of the chair and began the slow miles to the sofa, holding on to various pieces of furniture as she passed. The room was so quiet, warmed by sunlight. She had been wrong to refuse medical attention. The bubbling of blood in her chest was not to be mistaken. Fortunately it was not too late. She gathered her breath and spoke.

'If you send for a doctor I'll see him now.'

Her uncle stood by the door. He had a bottle in his hand. But she hadn't meant – there was still so much life to be lived! She struggled upright, saying desperately, 'No! Oh, no!'

Afterwards

An interpreter ought always to have stood between her and the world.

Charlotte Brontë

Emily had been lowered into the crypt, her coffin the narrowest for an adult that William Wood had ever made. The flagstones had slid into place, leaving her coffined in wood and stone. For the next five months Charlotte had devoted herself to Anne who sickened rapidly, though it was comforting now to recall that she had been willing to try every remedy. In May she had gone to Scarborough with Charlotte and Ellen and died there peacefully and with the delicate tact she had always shown, making no fuss but seated in an armchair and looking out over the sunlit bay. Charlotte had buried her there, high on the cliffs overlooking the sea she had always loved.

Then she had returned to the parsonage and continued work on her novel, retitling it *Shirley,* and seeking desperately to bring Emily alive again in the person of the spirited and independent young woman who strode across her estate with her great dog at her side and whose fear that she had caught hydrophobia proved unjustified.

Only then had she carried Anne's two published novels and Emily's book into Papa and left him with them. It had been almost a month before he referred to them at all and then, inviting her to drink a cup of tea with him in the parlour, he had looked at her over the tops of his round spectacles and said,

'I was not entirely surprised to learn that you had all been publishing. Dear little Anne! Her work does not compare with your *Jane Eyre* but it has the value of sincerity.'

'And Emily's book?' She had looked at him questioningly.

'Emily had more genius than you and Anne combined,' he had said.

She had been glad for Emily's sake that the novel hadn't angered him. Of course she had been glad! So why did she, in the midst of her grief, feel such shafts of blazing anger?

Shirley had received good notices; she had ventured again to London to be thrilled and appalled to find her identity becoming increasingly known. She had agreed to Mr Smith's request that her sisters' books should be reprinted – but not *The Tenant Of Wildfell Hall*. Anyone reading that again would imagine the gentle, retiring author to have had experience of drunken debauchery. *Agnes Grey* with its simple plot and touches of dry humour reflected more clearly the little sister she wanted to remember.

As for *Wuthering Heights*! She had agreed to its reprinting but she had written a biographical notice of her sisters, setting them before the public as she wished them to have been. So Emily became a secluded and unlearned woman with no practical gifts or worldly sense who, visited by inspiration, had been driven to write a novel whose characters she herself did not understand. She herself had to believe that, because it would have been unbearable to have been forced to confront the possibility that all through their lives Emily had lived a secret life of her own.

She had been through the poems, altering, editing and softening. She had put away the sketches and portraits of her sisters, describing them as plain and ill-featured.

Now she finished reading the manuscript she had left until daylight to peruse and rubbed her eyes tiredly. Her whole being was consumed with anguish and revulsion. This must never be seen. This ripped away the mask for all time. But what ought she to do? Should she consign the whole thing to the flames or wrap it carefully and hide it securely, bury it perhaps in the earth?

She put the manuscript carefully back into the tin box and sat for a long time, her mind seething. It was very still save for the ticking of the clock but she was almost certain she could hear Emily laughing somewhere out of sight.

Author's Note

The foregoing characters all existed in reality and the incidents and dialogues in the book are based upon proven fact and what I hope is intelligent speculation drawn from the clues that have survived.

Charlotte wrote a final novel, *Villette* in which she detailed her relationships with her publisher George Smith and rewrote her relationship with Monsieur Héger. In June 1854 she married her father's curate, Arthur Bell Nicholls, after long and vigorous opposition from her father. The following spring, just before her thirty-ninth birthday, she died of exhaustion following excessive vomiting in early pregnancy. Old Tabby had died of typhus fever a few days before. Mr Brontë outlived all his children by six years, taking great pride in Charlotte's posthumous fame.

None of the Heaton sons from Ponden House married and for reasons not yet made entirely clear Mr Brontë refused to bury Michael Heaton of Royd House in the Heaton tomb. Neither would Elizabeth Patchett ever allow the name of Emily Brontë to be mentioned in her presence. Neither Ellen Nussey nor Mary Taylor ever married though both survived into old age. Martha Brown worked at the parsonage until Mr Brontë's death and then returned with Mr Nicholls to Ireland where she stayed until his remarriage whereupon she returned to Haworth (though remaining on friendly terms with him) and herself died unmarried of consumption in her early fifties. Sarah Garrs emigrated to America, married and bore children. Nancy Garrs died in Bradford Workhouse.

References to the Irish side of the family were cut out or toned down in all surviving letters and manuscripts, leading to the growth of some rather suspect traditions. It seems certain however that Hugh Brontë did stay at the parsonage in the late winter of 1848 and equally certain that for the rest of his long life he refused to discuss that visit or his reasons for being there.

After the death of Mr Brontë and his burial in the family vault the vault was sealed and later encased in concrete. Only Anne lies near the sea she loved. Whether Emily who longed to meld with the earth sleeps sound in her concrete tomb is a question for the reader to ponder.

Acknowledgements

In this book I have tried to present Emily Brontë, not as a writer who happened to be a woman but as a woman who explored her own personality through her writing. Many of the ideas here presented are, as far as I know, new and as yet probable rather than certain.

I am indebted to many who have taken this journey of discovery with me though the conclusions I have reached are entirely my own. So, in no particular order, my grateful thanks to Mrs Woolridge of the Brontë Museum Shop who keeps me supplied with books – over two hundred during the past three years; to Dr Edward Chitham for his advice and his own books which have shed new light on Emily Brontë; to Sarah Fermi and Audrey Hall for their encouragement; to Oliver Stone who patiently answered my enquiry regarding certain psychological conditions, to Dr Ednyfed Wyn Parry, MB, F.R.C.Path., who gave me great help with medical matters pertaining to the nineteenth century; to Mr Butterfield who made his late wife's work on the Brontë–Heaton connection available, to the staff of the Brontë Parsonage Museum and Shop who are invariably helpful, and the staff of Shibden Hall, Halifax who were also most helpful in answering numerous questions.

Finally my thanks to Emily Peters, Irene and David West and Carol Williams who accompanied me on my visits to Brontë country, discussed all my ideas often until the early hours of the morning and contributed interesting insights of their own which often caused me to think afresh about some particular aspect of an enigmatic woman.